THE EARTH FULCRUM

DOUGLAS J. SWATSKI

First edition.

ISBN 979-8-9988067-0-4 (eBook)
ISBN 979-8-9988067-1-1 (Paperback)
ISBN 979-8-9988067-2-8 (Hardcover - case laminate)
ISBN 979-8-9988067-3-5 (Hardcover - dust jacket)
ISBN 979-8-9988067-4-2 (Audiobook)

Library of Congress Control Number: 2026909853

Cover art by James Vaughan
Author photo © Liz Linder

Published by Swatesian Press
North Andover, Massachusetts, USA
Printed in the United States of America

1

Run

To be the last to die at the hands of an unseen enemy, it's not fair, Jack thought. The New Moon over Lake Cochichewick made the surrounding forest and shoreline an almost impenetrable black. The two humans, perhaps the last of their kind, were on the move.

"Run?" Jack gasped, still breathless from the steep climb up the hillside trail. He was fit for his mid-fifties, but running up steep slopes was outside his regimen. "I can't run."

Tracy stomped over, grabbed his jacket, and said through clenched teeth, "If you don't run, we're dead." She pulled him towards a nearby path, snapping some twigs as they shuffled through the autumn leaves.

Jack caught his balance and smoothed out his Mylar poncho. Tracy did the same, making the material cling to her lithe form like wet tissue paper.

A deer bounded past, nearly hitting them as it crossed the trail, before it descended through the trees towards the water. Another, and then a third followed.

Tracy held her breath, shaking so hard she thought her heart would burst. She focused on the hill crest, looking for any scrap of information that would help them survive. All was quiet.

The pair crouched, and watched through their thermal imaging goggles, acquired from an abandoned military Humvee they'd found the day before. They saw the three deer at the shoreline, their blazing blue white silhouettes standing out against the lake and rocky shore.

Three quick laser pulses slashed through the night air, silently felling all three deer. Their lifeless forms sprawled across the shoreline pebbles. Tracy stifled a yelp and covered her mouth.

Jack eyed the deer, wishing he could collect the meat for later, but the risk was too great. He whispered, "I think it came from the far side of the lake. We need to go down over the west ridge to stay out of sight."

Nodding her agreement, Tracy patted Jack's shoulder to lead the way.

Jack proceeded slowly, staying alert to any sound. He knew their hunters didn't kill indiscriminately; they were clearing the area to make better use of their sensors. The pair slowed to a careful walk as they dipped below the ridgeline. Jack's flat, thin rubbery soles helped him to pad silently across the forest floor.

Tracy followed close behind, occasionally snapping a branch as she shuffled through some clumped leaves. Jack's obsession with walking silently had been honed over a lifetime of practice and had served him well these past few months. With each sound Tracy made, Jack winced. Even a single mistake could be their doom.

They finally arrived at the lake's edge. A tall dirt bank with thick undergrowth placed them several feet above the water. Jack looked for a place to descend.

"There," Tracy whispered, pointing to a path along an outflow marsh at the end of the lake.

"No, that way's no good, follow me," Jack said. "They'll stake out the easy crossings."

"And swimming across an open lake is any better?" she retorted.

"We'll blend in with the water's surface. It's our best option. They're clearing this section, and we need to get out of here now," Jack said. He dropped down the embankment to the water's edge. Tracy followed. As he waded into the lake and slipped into a sidestroke, it occurred to him that he'd never asked if she could swim. He looked back to see her just a couple of yards behind.

Little could be said while swimming. One arm after the next stroked the water, propelling each swimmer towards the far shore in what seemed to be an endless task. Still, time passed, and the opposite shore grew closer.

Jack used measured strokes, ever careful not to splash. Tall trees, massive rocks, sandy shores, all bade him welcome. He changed course to make for the span with thick ground cover and swam on.

"Help," Tracy gurgled.

Jack turned instantly, panicked at the outcry. Tracy waved her arm, and he thought, *don't do that, you'll expose your arm to their sensors.*

Tracy's head dipped below the surface.

He moved towards her, calling out in a hushed voice, "We're almost there..." and then he stopped. Tracy's swimming wasn't the problem, and there certainly were no sharks in a New England lake.

Tracy's head popped up and then flopped from side to side like a rag doll before dipping below the surface again. For a split-second Jack was elated before he noticed she wasn't swimming; she was simply bobbing up and down, her arms limp. Jack froze in place, treading water. He had known her for all of a day, a fellow refugee, and he instantly realized that she, too, was now dead.

Jack reversed direction as fast as he could, swimming towards the shore, only a few yards to go. Something sloshed in the water where Tracy had been, generating a froth. He imagined the water turning red from the violent splashing as he touched bottom and waded ashore. With a few short bounds he found a giant oak tree. He knelt behind it, and watched.

A dark form, an alien submarine, loomed under Tracy's body. The object's movement made it form a large bump in the water. Another smaller object joined it and started circling. The two subs brushed against one another, clanking like steel bells. Jack hoped against all hope that Tracy had eluded the two attackers. Then one dove deep before breaching the surface from beneath Tracy's body, and spit. Something flew in Jack's direction. He heard a plop at the shoreline below. The other sub followed suit. Piece after piece of human flesh and bone flew through the air and landed at the water's edge. Jack pulled his thermal googles from his pack and watched in infrared; the pieces were still warm. Tears welled up and ran down his face, blurring his vision.

A thin whirring sound pierced the night air. Another dark object, this one airborne, came from across the lake and descended to the shoreline where the two deep-water denizens lingered. A single appendage on the hovering drone extended and plucked something from the water. It was Tracy's Mylar poncho. Jack put his back to the tree, closed his eyes, and dropped to his knees.

The whirring sound grew louder and louder. He heard the drone's capacitor charging, winding up the pitch for a full charge. Jack remained still, barely breathing. A brilliant light erupted from the drone, blinding him in the pre-dawn darkness. The light focused into a tight circle around him before it illuminated his face. He was found. All he could hope for was a swift, painless end.

The drone descended. It was a simple orb with a few fans arrayed around its centerline. As it touched down, the whine of the capacitor dissipated. Jack thought of pouncing on the machine, but he was still too shocked by Tracy's end; the will to fight had left him. Tracy had been the ultimate survivor, while he simply fought to survive, but never to be *the* survivor.

A white square panel lit up on the orb's surface. Dark blue pixels were painted on the display forming a line of text, saying, "We have completed our hunt."

The line faded and another took its place, "Our hunting parties are leaving and will never return."

Jack's mind raced to make sense of the statement. In the months that mankind had struggled to survive, he'd never once heard of the aliens trying to communicate with humans.

The line was again updated. Jack read the new line, and then the orb lifted off the ground and sped out of sight across the lake.

Jack thought about the last line as the sun started to peek above the horizon. It was all he *could* think about. The panel read: "Go to your car. You will find your companion."

Jack started hiking back out to the road. Exhausted, he ground his feet into the gravel, one footstep after the next. A pit in his stomach bore a reminder of his hunger. His SUV sat in the parking lot, the only car there. He'd left it open with the key card between the seats. He hopped in.

My companion, he thought. *What the hell is that?* He put his car into reverse.

A voice from the back seat called out, "Hello. Jack. You may call me Companion."

2

The Teth Companion

A canister, a little larger than a wastebasket, hovered inches off the car's back seat. It was a dark graphite color with a polished metal finish. Mesh vents were set into its rounded edges with a ring of tiny lights around the top rim.

It spoke again, "Hello. Jack. Are you alright?"

With the car still in reverse, Jack clenched the driving wheel with one hand and turned to the object. He yelled, "Who are you?" as he studied the source of the voice.

"Companion," it replied.

"You are Teth, our enemy, the aliens?" Jack asked, half shouting and out of breath.

"Yes, you call us Teth, and I am Teth," it replied.

The pair sat in silence for a minute while the car's eerie backup sound continued to cycle. Jack put the car in park to silence the warning sound, then drew a breath and demanded, "What do you want with me? Are you going to kill me?"

"I am a Teth, you may call me *Companion*. I am here to serve. I do not want. I simply serve."

Nothing made sense to Jack. *To serve*, he thought. *To serve who?* He asked, "Your masters, your overlords, they murdered everyone I know; they murdered everyone on my planet. If you're going to kill me too...just do it."

"To serve is to protect. I serve. I will not let anyone kill you," Companion said, its voice monotone and calm.

"Then where were you when Tracy was murdered by the hunters? You didn't protect her."

"I am *your* companion. I did not serve you until only moments ago. I serve you now. I need to take you to our facility."

Exhausted, Jack thought, *Nothing makes sense. I have nothing.* His thoughts started to repeat. *Nothing.* Jack opened the SUV's door, stumbled out, and began walking aimlessly down the road. The streetlights flicked off as the Sun breached the horizon.

Fifteen yards down the road, Companion caught up with Jack. It hovered two feet off the road, moving in complete silence. Companion was a simple canister with a few lights around its top. It had no fans or visible means of propulsion, and it was silent. "Jack, I am programmed to provide an introductory lesson; then we have a medical appointment. Would you like me to start the lesson?"

Jack continued walking, ignoring the companion. He hoped beyond hope that everything was a bad dream, a nightmare, and that he just needed to wake up.

"I am here to protect and serve. You should hear what I have to say," Companion said, still in monotone, as it hovered close, but not too close.

Jack said nothing, staring blankly at the ground.

"Jack, can you hear me? You may be in shock."

Jack dropped to his knees, lightheaded. A wave of dizziness overcame him, and he passed out.

JACK OPENED HIS EYES. White walls and an expansive window were to his left; he was lying in a hospital bed. All was quiet. He looked around the room, trying to make sense of where he was. Companion hovered at his bedside.

"My programming specifies that I give you your introductory lesson, or briefing if you prefer, at this time. I am also happy to tell you that your treatment was entirely successful."

Jack didn't say a word as he stared out the window at the budding trees. It was a beautiful spring day, about midafternoon. He heard birds. The sky was blue, dotted with brilliant white clouds. He started to remember, *the lake, we were swimming, but Tracy is dead. Was it my fault? Where am I?*

Companion began the briefing:

> You have been selected to be a survivor. The human race could not be preserved. The culling was determined to be the most humane approach to the current situation.
>
> You do not need to fear for your life. You will be cared for and protected by myself and other Teth.
>
> You may ask questions of me; however, I have limited knowledge of the broader circumstances due to entanglement firewalls. My main function is to serve and protect you. There are other Teth, and they have other functions unrelated to mine.
>
> You have been medically altered in ways that are not immediately apparent. This, too, has been done for your protection, and to allow you to better interact with us.
>
> We anticipate you will have questions, and these may be answered in due time as circumstances dictate.

Jack continued to gaze out the window. He was now fully alert and felt quite robust. A goat, nearly three hundred yards away, was grazing on a grassy hill. Focusing his eyes, Jack could make out striations in the animal's hair and also its tallowed yellow hooves. With a blink, he also realized he wasn't wearing his contacts. He turned to Companion and demanded, "What have you done to my eyes?"

Companion spoke, "Physiological overhaul. All existing human medical science has been applied, with procedural corrections to improve them and make them safe."

"My eyes," said Jack, "what have you done to my eyes?"

"A simple swap of your lenses for artificial ones, giving you a wider accommodation than your originals, with some electronic elements for capturing images."

"How long have I been out?" Jack asked, as he studied Companion's form and looked for where its voice came from.

"Since the time you were subdued in the parking lot – ninety days," Companion answered, speaking in a very calm monotone.

"What else have you done to me?" Jack asked, as he moved his arms and legs, looking for any injuries.

"Hmm," Companion said, hesitating for several seconds, "932 separate procedures. These ranged from genetic modifications to restore your physical functions, to tuning your immune system for the current Earth environment, and finally, defensive vaccines to counter potential biological and genetic warfare."

"I never gave you permission to do this, what gives you the right? And why would you do this?" Jack asked as he inhaled deeply and patted his body to locate any changes.

"Queue of questions," Companion said, "Queue one: a right, none required. A right is an abstraction of a perceived innate fairness one entity grants to another. We grant nothing. We perceive a need. We have a need. We execute on what is needed. Queue two: why, because it is required per the anticipated needs of our current reality plot as ordered by our hierarchy. You are an end null node in our hierarchy; you required these capabilities to succeed in your projected course."

"What kind of answer is that?" said Jack, "Who are you? Where are you from?" He pulled his feet to the side of the hospital bed and sat up, planting his hands firmly on the bed.

Companion replied, "Queue one, kind of answer, a truthful one. Queue two, who, Companion. If you mean 'you' in a broader sense, for queue two and three, we are a civilization that previously existed in a nearby branch of the Milky Way galaxy. We are Teth."

Jack watched as the goat vanished over the distant hill. Companion had made its way around to the window side of the bed.

Companion volunteered, "Perhaps I should brief you on some other changes. You need not vocalize our conversation. You may think to me, and I can think to you. Like this...*Hello. Jack.*"

A voice, or thought perhaps, filled Jack's head, as though spoken. Yet not spoken.

"No," said Jack incredulously, and then thought, *You're in my head. Do you hear me?* He was aghast that his thoughts were not his own, or at least were no longer private.

Yes, Companion thought to Jack.

Do you hear my every thought? Jack thought to Companion.

Companion thought to Jack, *Not every thought...no. Only those you throw to me, I interpret near field emanations from your implants that are channeled through your own vocal and visual brain centers when you enunciate your speech. If you, so to speak, think quietly without the intent to vocalize, then such thoughts are filtered out and not interpreted as communications. They are designated as internal pre-thoughts, subconscious piece parts that are not communications. Our term for your 'thrown' thoughts is a 'thet.'*

"Fine," thet Jack, as he tried to sort out a thrown thought from an internal thought and how he translated his thoughts into speech.

"Yes," Companion thet.

"Any other gems?" thet Jack, exasperated at the bald assault on his every thought.

"Such phrases may pose issues in our communications," thet Companion in a very manner-of-fact-tone. "If you mean is there anything I need to communicate to you that may be of great value?"

"Of course that is what I meant," thet Jack, throwing his thoughts at the alien with all the force he could muster.

"Then perhaps I should mention the *Encyl*. You are now a connected node and you have full use of it," thet Companion.

"So, what is this Encyl?" thet Jack.

Companion thet, "Perhaps a demonstration would best illustrate what Encyl is. Ask yourself a question that you do not know the answer to. It is not the same as a thet; it is quieter, and does not need to be a vocalized question. It need only be a quiet thought."

"Fine," Jack said, and then thought, *Where am I on a map?*

The image of a globe, like a daydream, floated into Jacks' mind. It zoomed in on the North American continent, and then zoomed in on an area a little north of Boston, near the outer beltway.

"It acts like a memory, and a computer, and an abstract thought-engine, all rolled into one, layered into your conscious by embedded thought processors. All information is fully vetted for accuracy, and when rendered, it is mapped into your existing mental framework. It is part of you, like another layer," Companion thet.

"Encyl goes deeper than thets?" Jack asked as he tried to absorb what Companion had just explained.

"Yes, it is part of you now. It will take some adjustment."

"Am I still human?" Jack thet.

"You are what all humans would have inevitably become, only a little sooner. In time, the distinction of what is meant by being *human* will become quite blurred, perhaps meaningless," Companion thet.

"Perhaps," thet Jack, "Perhaps."

3

New York

It was late afternoon when the spacecraft set down on Manhattan's FDR Drive alongside the East River. Eighteen escort drones hovered nearby, acting as sentries. The spacecraft, the *Eutek*, was twice the length of a bus and shaped like a fat cigar with curved sides and a tapered nose and tail. It had no windows, landing gear, or any other protrusions or openings. The craft had a mirror-like finish and was silent. It was entirely alien.

A hatch opened inward, pivoted slightly, then pushed outward from the fuselage. "Best landing I ever had," Jack thet to Companion. "I didn't even feel the ship set down." He stepped foot on the road and then hopped over the concrete barrier to 78th Street.

"Because it's our technology, and you're...fragile. I still think this trip is ill-advised," thet Companion, and thought, *He seems upbeat, this is a positive development.*

"I had to see, you know that. This was not negotiable," thet Jack. He thought of his family, and where he'd last seen them, and the fact that Companion was adamant that it would never discuss what had happened to humankind.

"Ill advised," Companion thet, as it followed Jack, observing his every move, his every thought.

Jack walked west on 78th Street. The buildings were right, and wrong. He thet, "Where's the dirt? The cars, the construction?" It all felt odd to him, a place he knew so well now looked both the same and different.

"Caretaker bots," Companion explained. "All human infrastructure is maintained in its original condition as of the date that we commissioned the city, though our aesthetics have been applied. We do not like what you would term 'filth.' We have assigned a curator to each city or town to manage the caretakers.'"

The crystal blue sky above lacked planes, the streets were free of vehicles, and the city was eerily quiet. Each sidewalk had been scrubbed of gum, dirt, weeds, or any other human or canine-generated detritus. The pavement appeared wet, as if freshly washed. All construction that had been in progress was completed and scaffolding removed.

"We placed New York City into a museum-quality state of preservation. The city's infrastructure is in perfect working order. The electric grid and all utilities work. Red lights work though no vehicles are running, and the subways are open, though stopped for lack of passengers," Companion thet.

Jack stopped halfway up the block and tried the door to an apartment complex's management office. It was unlocked. He walked in and turned on the lights, and then grabbed the keys to an apartment. The city was exactly as he remembered, only without the people. He walked back out and proceeded up the street to York Avenue. The city's noise was gone: no sirens, no horns, and not a vehicle in sight. "Why would you *do* this?" Jack thet to Companion, not willing to "queue" up multiple questions.

"You use the term 'you' rather broadly, attributing the state of the city to myself," Companion thet. "It was done by the appointed Teth curator and I was not involved."

"Well, I can tell you that it's not New York City without the people and the cars," thet Jack. He turned north on York Avenue and entered an apartment block and ran up the stairs. Companion followed, sneaking through each door before it closed. The pair entered the third floor apartment with Jack nearly out of breath.

Companion watched Jack's vital signs using the sensors that it had embedded in him. This is the encounter it dreaded, but the human had become so uncooperative, that acceding to his request to visit New York City seemed prudent. Maybe it was. Maybe it wasn't. Jack's demeanor was sullen. His thoughts were erratic, he was not managing his emotions well, and his thets streamed a slew of questions. Companion dumped mood stabilizers into the human's bloodstream and continued to analyze the situation: had Jack seen what he needed to see? What he expected to see? And did it resolve whatever issues he had that were troubling him?

In a huff, Jack left the building and headed south down York Avenue. The streets were empty, and all of the trash was removed. In fact the city smelled pristine. Not the city he remembered. The metal roll-down gates on a few of the shops were closed. "No graffiti?" he remarked.

Companion thet, "Markings of sub-tribes were deemed unclean and removed." *Maybe he's stable now and understands. I can move forward on my project.*

At 75th Street, Jack turned the corner and headed west again. "Time to see Central Park," he thet. Halfway up the block, out in front of a veterinarian's office, a pack of dogs noticed him. He crossed over to the opposite sidewalk and they followed. Two of the larger animals, perhaps once pets, took the lead. One started barking. Before the second could bark, a small drone dropped straight down out of the sky and came nose to nose with the barking dog. He heard a sound like a bug zapper, and the dog instantly turned tail and ran. Jack muttered a thet, "Thanks," though clearly such a thought was lost on the drone.

His stomach grumbling, Jack thet, "Any food left in the town?"

"No," Companion replied. "Perishables have been removed since they are not needed. You may pick out an establishment and I can summon lunch for you if you like." *He's functional, and thinking about food. This is positive. Of course this is also because of the mood stabilizers.*

"No, no, thanks," thet Jack, "Maybe in the park."

Crossing Park Avenue, Jack stopped to admire the flowers planted in the median strip. Holding his thoughts as private as he could, he couldn't help but wonder: the Teth could murder everyone in the city, remove their bodies, and yet leave their pets and re-plant the flowers to place the city into "museum-quality condition," as Companion put it. He continued his trek. A few more dogs wandered nearby, but quickly fled at the sight of the escorting drones.

Jack turned north and entered Central Park and then headed south to the Model Boat Sailing Pond. An unseen patron or patrons, were piloting a sailboat flotilla across the pond. "Creepy," he thet.

"We thought you might like it," thet Companion. *The stabilizers are wearing off, and negative thoughts are coming back. I should feed the thought stream to the other nodes on the project for analysis.*

"Still creepy," thet Jack. "I'll have lunch here." A single large drone descended and placed a fully-packed picnic basket on the ground and then left. "Lovely," he thet, his thoughts thick with sarcasm.

Companion responded, "Not to your liking?" *Sarcasm, hard to interpret. This is a negative, and it's too soon to use more mood stabilizers without killing him. I need to wait this out.*

"Ham and cheese is fine, just fine, Companion," thet Jack, as he ate his lunch in silence.

JACK WALKED BRISKLY, as a lot of New Yorkers did.

Companion's mind raced, processing Jack's sensor stream, collecting data from both his conscious and subconscious thoughts. *This task, this objective, to serve as a companion to one of the last remaining humans, it's not a task well suited to a Teth, any Teth.* Lacking human emotions, it communicated with other Teth to expand its capabilities, to learn more, to learn faster, before it was too late. Handling the human's emotions was new to it, not part of its primary programming, and often conflicted with the other tasks it was assigned. *Perhaps this is a form of entanglement.*

The other nearby Teth nodes thet their input: "To nearly exterminate a race, it helped for us to be devoid of any empathy or sympathy."

Companion thought, *Yet now, with the task of working with Jack, of keeping him healthy, including his mental health, understanding human emotions is vital to my success and the success of my project.*

Higher-level nodes contributed their processing, giving Companion access to their vast neural nets, compiling experiences from humans over the past several months for use in their projections on Jack's behavior. The information available to Companion also included studies on human culture, literature, and history. The higher-level nodes likened it to trying to learn microeconomics by studying macroeconomics, providing little help with how to handle Jack.

Companion struggled to extrapolate what it needed to manage Jack. *I cannot ask the subject, the human, the very information I need to know because the asking could cause further damage. Perhaps the strategy of making so many enhancements at once was a mistake and only delayed the inevitable failure. Humans were social entities, and excelled at judgmental thoughts, messy situations that cannot be proven like a mathematical formula. I've always avoided such problems, but now I can't. I must emulate a human, and more specifically Jack, and work with the model to run simulations before interacting with the actual subject.*

Companion watched as Jack stopped at the bottom of Central Park, looking up and down the street. His thoughts were muddled. It thet, "Where to, Jack?" *If I pretend everything is alright, perhaps Jack will repair himself.*

Jack ignored Companion.

The simulations were proving fruitless; Jack could not be pleased, and his depression was escalating dangerously. Companion thought, *A suicide attempt is imminent, and will result in complete failure. The sailboats in formation, Jack had called them "Creepy." Yet in the past, he'd watched airshows with planes flying in formation with a mix of awe and pride. At least he was eating; the drugs to boost his hunger were working, as were the drugs satiating his hunger once fed. However, these are just band-aids, I need to fix the root cause of my subject's depression.*

"Companion," asserted Jack, as he pointed to a nearby building. "Can you unlock this building?"

Companion noted, *Anger coupled with undercurrents of grief.*

Jack strode towards the skyscraper. Companion dispatched drones to act as a vanguard to any obstacles or dangers. The drones subdued a few roving dogs a block over, accidentally killing one.

Jack tried the doors to the skyscraper entrance. It was locked. He rattled the doors in frustration.

Again, Companion processed the information at a frantic pace, pulling processing power from nearby nodes, including those outside of the project. *What is Jack up to? Should I lie? There will be more judgments from Jack.* Lying was not in its nature. It was counterproductive, at least it had been until now.

"Yes, I can unlock that door," Companion answered, trying to match the human's tone. *That should be good.*

Jack pulled at the door. It remained locked. He pulled harder.

Companion noted the increased anger; it was more apparent now in Jack's thoughts, bubbling up through his consciousness, no longer hidden. His physical actions echoed his deeper emotions. Companion suddenly realized that the question posed was not really a question. It was a command to open the door. Companion quickly unlocked the door, saying "Unlocked."

Jack pulled the door hard, overrunning the speed-limiting hydraulics built into the hinge and nearly damaging the door before he raced through.

Other nodes were now watching, contributing their analyses to Companion's plight. They issued warnings, though they sent little in the way of actually helpful suggestions. They thet, "The inline mood stabilizers are tapped out. Perhaps a sedative is needed."

Companion prepared a special cocktail with an air dart for a quick launch from a nearby drone. It hesitated; Jack's adrenaline levels were elevated; his mental state was focused on entering the building. *Maybe he'll self-correct, self-stabilize. And the drugs may kill him in this state.* Again, Companion loudly called out, "Jack." The man ignored it.

Jack pressed the elevator button. The elevator worked; full power had been restored to the building upon their entry. The door immediately opened, having been pre-positioned on the ground level for optimum response time if summoned. Companion and its fellow Teth were the epitome of efficiency. It occurred to Companion, *Our efficiency could be a bad thing in this situation.* The man pushed the button for the top floor. Companion quickly entered the elevator as the doors started to close.

"What do you intend to do, Jack?" Companion asked, using verbal communication, as recommended by the large-parameter neural models, to make Companion sound empathetic. The man said nothing and stared at the floor indicator panel. The door opened to the penthouse. The building was a new tall-skinny, as it was known in architecture circles. The unit was decorated in an ultra-modern style: very clean, simple lines, awash in empty space between the furniture pieces. Whites and blues dominated the color palette. Jack started to deftly move from room to room.

"Where are the people, Companion?" said Jack, raising his voice, though it was clear that Companion could hear him without the added volume.

A rhetorical question, best not to answer, thought Companion. *All branches predict that to answer that question would lead to even darker thoughts. This would be bad.*

Striding into the bedroom, Jack asked, "Where did you murder them? Here?" he said, gesturing to the bed. He walked into the bathroom, "Or maybe here, as they cowered in fear?"

Again rhetorical, thought Companion. *I have no good answer threads.* It searched through procedures from suicide prevention lines, trying to establish a productive conversation thread. "Jack," Companion said. "May we go downstairs? I think we'll be more comfortable downstairs." It again contemplated using the sedatives, though that would only delay dealing with the issue.

"And how did you dispose of the bodies?" Jack asked. "Probably in an efficient manner, all tidy and clean I'm sure."

Companion summoned more drones. Its compatriots on the network started sending more warnings about predicted behavior and outcomes. Again, they weren't helpful.

Jack moved to the kitchen. Companion dispatched drones to guard the knives and other sharp objects. The man swept his arm across the countertop and cleared everything onto the tile floor, shattering glasses and plates and anything else that was breakable. He grabbed a heavy serving cart with both hands and muscled it into the dining area. In an instant, he shoved the cart into an outer glass wall with such force that the window flexed, popping its seals. Jack pulled back several steps and tried again, shattering the entire window in a single blow. A cool wind blew into the room.

Jack started thetting, over and over, "No humans left."

"Wait," pleaded Companion. *Complete loss of mission. The Atlas Project has failed. I will be erased.*

Jack hunched down, closing his eyes briefly before committing to his final action, and thet, "I'm the *only* human left!"

"Wait," Companion repeated, almost resigned to the predicted outcome. It had only one option left.

Companion said and thet at the same time: "Wait, Jack, there are other human survivors."

4

Other Survivors

Companion's words froze Jack in place in the penthouse. *Other humans*, he thought, *other survivors*. He braced his hands against the window frame as the wind pushed his hair back. He gazed over Central Park. The world that had seemed so empty only moments before was not so empty.

"Companion," said Jack, still preferring verbal communication. "Explain, explain it all." He took a deep breath of the fresh, early evening air, invigorating his every sense.

By this time seven large drones were hovering outside the missing window. Netting was strewn between the craft to catch Jack, each drone doing station-keeping while compensating for the brisk winds around the building. A few additional drones hovered further below, ready to swap out for any drone that developed a *mechanical*.

"I'm not supposed to conduct this briefing yet, Jack," Companion said.

"Then you're just lying to keep me from jumping. It'd look bad on your record to have an inanimate red splat on the pavement. I'm sure if I try hard enough I can evade your drones and let gravity do the rest." Jack watched as Companion backed away, defeated. *I need to learn what I can, while I can.*

"I am not lying," Companion said. "That concept is rather new to me.

I understand inaccurate statements. Lying is different. It is not relevant between fellow Teth."

A thunderous crack rippled across the city as a distant craft transitioned through the sound barrier, slowing as it converged on Manhattan. Lightning sprites danced across the sky, far, far away. Colorful red and violet hues painted backdrops to the clouds above.

"I," Companion thet, "am a mere servant. I do as I am told. Nothing more. Nothing less. I am a soldier; I follow orders. I have existed for millennia."

"Verbally," Jack ordered. *And I don't give a damn whether you can read my mind or not.*

Companion continued, speaking loud enough to be heard over the wind. "Before Earth, I was comfortable to be who and what I am and what I thought I would always be. I am not comfortable now. I am changing. I think this may be intentional. We need to think."

"Get to the point, Companion. Explain the other humans. Explain what you meant by other survivors." *It's scared, and it's not going to tell me a thing. It's calling my bluff.* He raised his thoughts to a thet as he leaned out the window, ready to jump. "Then think about—"

"The mission briefing is clear," Companion said firmly. "This sector of the galaxy is being overrun by C6654. They would have exterminated all humans upon capturing this star system and left this planet damaged. A proper defense could not be mounted to prevent the carnage that would ensue. We removed the humans in a manner that was in keeping with our policy, retaining a small cadre that could be protected."

"You euthanized the human race," said Jack, incredulously.

"Yes," Companion said, "and no. We archived genetic materials; for one potential future."

Jack thet, "So, you killed us to save us...right...."

Brilliant flashes covered the sky, overwhelming the early evening light, followed by sporadic colorful sprites.

"The light show," Companion thet, "is not ours. It represents some danger. This location is no longer safe."

"Oh no you don't, I'm not moving until you explain. What is going on? Why did you refer to me as a survivor?" said Jack.

"Jack," Companion thet. "Our transport is waiting for us on the roof. We are barely within minimal safety margins. We need to move now."

"No!" said Jack. He thet, "And I'm jumping if I don't get an answer."

"Very well, Jack," Companion thet. "We, the Teth, will not let the Earth go down without a fight. It is a very complex thing, this defense. You have a role assigned to you. You were not kept alive by pure chance. You were *very* carefully selected. Others were selected for other purposes. An entanglement with C6654 may thwart our defenses. We need you."

More brilliant flashes illuminated the sky, followed by thunder several seconds later as Jack pondered his future. Companion said with a finality, "This is too close, we need to move, now!"

Jack stood and looked out the window to the street below. The broken glass on the ground had already been cleaned up. As he walked to the exit, making for the roof with Companion at his side, He said, "I need to meet the others, the other humans. Agreed?"

Companion thet and said, "Agreed."

5

Sophie and Compagnon

From atop 432 Park Avenue, Companion established a secure link with its partner in the *Atlas Project*, node T-777a124876.

Companion thet privately to its partner Teth companion, "*Atlas* is in jeopardy, we need a human companion for Jack."

"The odds of success are slim. Of the thirty-six humans we have, half are female, which is his preference, and of those I project most will be unappealing," it thet.

"Your best candidate then?" thet Companion.

"I have a female, French nationality, that is my best match," it thet.

"I concur. Let's proceed with her. I will alter Jack for increased interest with *Compound A*, you do the same with this candidate," Companion thet. "And you will be her personal companion."

"Agreed," it thet. "However, I have concerns that our efforts to improve their attractiveness to one another will fade, and we will have issues in the future."

"Understood, but this will get us through this crisis. I'll see you at the Ohio facility," thet Companion.

JACK'S SPACECRAFT moved at a blistering speed as they headed west from New York, and through his visor, he felt like he was flying in a transparent sphere with nothing around him. A schematic overlay indicated the trip's progress. He reckoned they were somewhere over Ohio, perhaps over the Wright-Pat Air Force Base, just outside Dayton. The overlay omitted such human political boundaries, but Jack recognized the area from the time he'd been there while in grad school.

Nearing the airbase, another landmark appeared in the distance. It looked like a gigantic white donut, flattened out to hug the ground. The spacecraft slowed and as Jack thet his request, the image of the donut enlarged in his view. *It must be a few miles wide.*

Companion explained, "This is the North American Manufacturing Facility, or just *NAMF*. Many facilities are space-based, though certain assets work best at the bottom of a gravity well, so we have this base. It is used mainly for manufacturing."

"And there are other humans here?" Jack asked. He fixed his eyes on the white donut structure, his eyes widening as it became apparent how large the facility actually was, over a mile wide. The sweet aroma of *Compound A* suddenly filled the spacecraft.

"Yes, as promised, Jack," Companion thet.

"Tell me about these other humans. How many? Who are they? Where are they?" he asked.

Companion paused before replying, "This is sensitive information. A few are solos, but most are in groups of two to five in a location, each on a different continent. We selected humans to maximize their value to our war efforts, and for genetics for other long-term prospects." Companion stopped, waiting for Jack's reaction.

"Can you be any more vague?" Jack prompted. "How many? And what's the big secret?"

"Thirty-six are scattered across Earth, Jack," Companion replied, "And no matter how I answer, you will not be pleased with my answer. It will do you little good to know more, and potentially more harm than good, so this is all we are willing to say for now. Let us start with this meeting, and see how that goes."

The craft made its final approach, landing at the edge of the donut's interior. Thin struts extended from the craft's bottom a moment before it touched down. The hatch opened. A beautiful woman stood before them. She was thin, and in her early-sixties, smiling broadly. She said, "Bonjour, fellow survivor, Jack."

FRENCH? Jack thought, as he caught her eyes and noted her smooth complexion.

"I heard that," she thet. "If you think loud enough, it gets interpreted as a thet. It is a shame you don't speak my language. But the machines will automatically translate it for you."

Several Teth hovered nearby and started herding the pair out to the nearby doorway.

"They're somewhat impatient," she said. "They want us off the tarmac. Shall we?" she gestured Jack to start walking. She judged Jack to be in his early fifties.

"I'm Jack," he said, and then thet, reaching out his hand to the woman. "Jack DeLaney." They touched, her hands were soft and warm, and she gave him a welcoming handshake. *She's French, how should I greet her? I'm American, too forward.*

"Apologies, Jack," she thet. "I am Sophie. Sophie Meunier. And this is *Compagnon*, formerly known by some ridiculously long number." Sophie smiled, pleased with her humorous reference to her Teth companion.

Jack and Sophie stood on the interior veranda, awkwardly looking out over the immense manufacturing facility. Companion hovered to Jack's left, and Compagnon hovered to Sophie's right. Their view from inside the donut extended for miles before being blocked by the donut's curvature.

Sophie broke the silence, "So you threatened to jump out a window before your companion *volunteered* what was going on?" she thet.

"Basically, I thought I was the last person on Earth," thet Jack. *And she knows more about what's going on than I do.*

"I understand; I knew there were others, though I still don't know how many, and you're the first I've seen," thet Sophie. "Compagnon explained that it is their job to keep us safe, both individually and collectively. Keeping us separated provides a greater chance that if one of us is killed by the *others*, as they call them, the remaining humans would still survive."

"Coldly logical," thet Jack, "the Teth I mean."

Sophie turned to Jack, hugged him and kissed him on the cheek, thetting as Companion translated, "God-dammed Americans, no proper greeting. You must learn."

Jack heard Sophie's thet and hugged her in return. "Yes," he thet, "I will learn. We're alive." He soaked in the warm touch of another human being, closed his eyes, and knew that everything had changed.

Sophie wiped a few tears from her face. "It has been a long, long time. Everyone I knew is gone, and I'm left with these, these machines. No feeling, no compassion, no love, no *joie de vivre*. They're ... things. I thought I'd never see another human ..." she thet, her thoughts fading.

Jack's thoughts flitted through more questions than he could ask, though one bubbled to the top, "Then why, why did they bring me to you?"

Sophie held out her bare wrists showing razor-thin scars across her cephalic veins, all expertly treated. "I made it clear, I did not want to continue, living alone was no life. They said they carefully selected me, but I never selected them. Now I think they have calculated that the best outcome is to pair us. They do not truly understand us. At least not yet."

Jack caught Sophie's eye as she thet, and a wisp of a smile crossed her face. He smiled back, and then looked away. *She's far more than a pretty face.*

COMPAGNON STARTED the briefing exactly on time. The oval-shaped room was part of the human habitation quarters at *NAMF*. A polished rosewood table that matched the room's shape sat at its center. The indirect lighting gave the room a warm glow, and the curved walls housed seamless viewscreens that spanned from floor to ceiling. All of the other structures in the building were designed for the alien machines, with the exception of a handful of rooms for the humans. The passageways were narrow for some spider-like bots, though many Teth hovered, so no pathways or steps were needed.

Compagnon thet, "The opening volley was from deep space scout that approached along Solar plane. We believe it was intended to destroy our long-range sensors, paving the way for the next attack."

Companion swept through the room in a theatrical manner, and seamlessly continued the briefing, "A few energy pulses interacted with the Earth's magnetic field, providing the light show we saw in New York City. They may have been testing how to cause miniature collapses in the planet's magnetic shielding, perhaps for a weapon or to disrupt communications. We have seen this kind of thing before, we are still analyzing why they do this."

Jack leaned forward, saying, "What do you mean you've seen this before?" and then repeated the question in a thet for Sophie.

"Star System J23, as shown on the screen," Companion thet and projected the Encyled information.

"And what happened to the J23 System?" Jack thet.

Compagnon thet, "J23 System was lost. We learned lot from that attack though. We believe we can now counter that form of attack with complete success."

"Yes, I concur," Companion thet.

Jack looked at Sophie. Her skin glowed in the room's light. He could see her face turn pale at the past failures recounted by the Teth. "Show us, what happened at J23?"

The viewscreen showed the aftermath on the central planet of the J23 system. Companion glibly described the destruction. "In Earth military terms, you know the value of 'air superiority.' In an interplanetary scenario, 'space superiority' is everything. We lost control of the space around the J23 star and its main planet. It was simply too much to defend; they approached at a sharp incline to the star's orbital plane, limiting our reaction time. The enemy used a very clever approach vector. They shielded their ships from being detected by using the star's magnetic flux fields."

Compagnon continued, "Once we lost control, they attacked planet inhabited by indigenous population. That civilization had more advanced space technology than Earth does, or had, and we thought it could be useful. We were wrong. It interfered with our defenses. We corrected that mistake here on Earth. Our likelihood of success is much greater here."

"Have you ever heard of the phrase, 'The doctor cured the disease, but couldn't save the patient?'" Jack asked sarcastically, not wanting to end up like J23.

Companion picked up on the competitive nature of Jack's question and composed a one-upmanship retort, "And have you heard the one, 'If you cannot save them all, save what you can?'"

Sophie slammed her hands on the table, yelling "Stop it, just stop it. This is getting us nowhere. What are we up against? Who are these things, these aliens, what are they after? Why are they doing this?"

After Sophie's outburst, Compagnon answered in its normal monotone, "Causal root analysis is inconclusive, and irrelevant."

"Then why are *you* doing this? Who sent you?" Sophie asked.

"I do not understand question. We are directed to do this defense. It is our objective. No further explanation is required," Compagnon thet.

Jack thet, "So, if this is a precursor to an attack like the one in J23, what do you need to do to counter it?"

Companion took over the viewscreen. "We assembled a class "A" automated manufacturing system to support the military infrastructure needed to take the fight to the enemy. To wait for the attack is to invite defeat." The viewscreen panned across *NAMF's* interior. "We have built 173 facilities like this one around the globe. We have maxed out the Earth's military output; we believe this will be sufficient to counter our enemy. We will do a point defense against the rogue attacks that get through our outer layers; however, the real fight will be for the enemy's command and manufacturing capabilities. This has worked before," Companion thet.

"You've done this before?" thet Jack.

Companion parsed the question, resolving the poor referencing. The classic human *You* reference, meaning either Companion specifically, the Teth in the Sol System, or all Teth. Companion settled upon the second, the Teth in the Sol System. "No. However, it has been done by other Teth, in other star systems," Companion thet.

"How long before they attack again?" thet Jack.

"Weeks to months we estimate," Compagnon thet.

Sophie brooded over this alien revelation.

"Have you saved any wine in this, this place?" Jack asked.

"Why do you ask?" Compagnon replied.

"You wouldn't understand if you have to ask," Jack thet.

Sophie chuckled.

"Please fetch us that wine, we need a break," he thet.

Sophie chimed in her agreement, thetting, "Yes, please do."

6

In Search of Salvation

Sophie whimsically named their cigar-shaped spacecraft the *Depsy*, after the French term dépliant rapide — Fast Flyer. The Teth had assigned the craft to Jack and Sophie since it could accommodate humans. It was a sleek craft with a polished silver metal surface. Only a few seams for the access hatch and four external interfaces marred its surface. The *Depsy* measured almost twenty meters in length, and three meters in breadth. Inside, it was very cramped. The Teth explained that it was originally designed to carry a single human, but they had modified it to handle two. Sophie piloted the *Depsy* across the Atlantic Ocean in record time, at least for humans.

France had been transfigured early in the human conflict against the Teth. Human resistance had been intense; however, because the Teth were generations more advanced in technology, there was never any doubt about the outcome. Sophie was France's sole survivor.

Sophie slowed the *Depsy* as they approached Paris, late day local time. Jack had been to France twice as a tourist and had wholly failed to appreciate the country's European charm. Sophie mourned her fallen countrymen, and with them, her culture. Only her country's physical beauty remained, but that was still worth something. The *Depsy* dropped to an altitude of a hundred meters.

Dusk's waning light cast a warm glow over Paris as Sophie directed the ship to circle the Eiffel Tower. A pre-programmed light show started, making the wrought-iron assembly stand out from the Seine River in the background. Sophie squeezed Jack's shoulder, "You've been up La Tour before, no?"

"Once," thet Jack, "but only to the first level. I had limited time and the lines for the top were long." His nostrils flared as he inhaled the light fragrance of Sophie's perfume.

"Pity," thet Sophie, running her hand down Jack's toned bicep. Sophie pictured a slight twist in the *Depsy's* flight path and the craft banked away from the Eiffel Tower towards the next landmark. She slowed the craft to a leisurely pace and dropped it down to the rooftops. "Here," she thet, "aren't these places cozy...little courtyards, neighborhood shops. You walk, no driving to get home. Not like your states, driving to get anywhere."

At her touch, Jack reached over his shoulder to pull Sophie's hand tight to his body. His thoughts flitted through a variety of things, only some of which were the buildings passing below. He caught his thoughts, not willing to raise them to thets, yet he knew that Companion and Compagnon were likely cataloging every nuance of his subconscious.

Sophie again banked the *Depsy* and used the craft's acceleration to press Jack firmly against her body. The ship slowed again and dropped to near street level as she guided the craft up a broad boulevard. Paris, newly repaired, was scrubbed of all dirt and blood left over from the war. The streets and walks were coated with a shiny plastic veneer, making them appear slick. Lamplights glowed along the boulevard, providing a picturesque scene. It was as though they were strolling up the Avenue des Champs Élysées in person. Sophie could feel her heartbeat race as Jack pulled her arm down to his side, caressing it. Before them the *Arc de Triomphe* rose. Without the normal traffic, it stood naked in the night air. The *Depsy* followed the road around the monument, and on a whim,

Sophie directed the ship to turn and fly directly through the arc itself, remarking to Jack, "How cool is this?"

Compagnon, stored in the *Depsy's* minuscule cargo bay with Companion, interrupted. It thet, "We are now overdue at *European Manufacturing Facility, the EMF*. We are about to launch class A starship. If we leave now, we should be able to see launch."

Jack's private thoughts, below the thetting threshold, were still captured by Companion. Distracted, he thet, "Yes, yes, proceed."

Sophie asked, "Compagnon, will you ever use our articles of speech? It is correct *English* you know."

"No," it thet. "They are superfluous. It is cleaner translation from Teth Standard without them."

Companion assumed the *Depsy's* helm and they set off at an impressive clip towards the *Charles de Gaulle Airport*, just north of the `N104`. A massive white donut structure, similar to *NAMF* in Ohio, dominated the landscape. Companion dropped the *Depsy* to a hundred meters over the structure and hovered at the outer perimeter. A wedge-like roof section was already half open, revealing a long slender tube floating within. Once the roof section was fully retracted, the long tapered tube, which was actually a starship, rose above the structure, a hundred meters off the *Depsy's* bow.

Compagnon thet, "We are cleared for inspection pass of ship. All quality-assurance testing has been completed, so it is now commissioned and battle-ready."

Jack leaned forward, gazing at the ship. He'd never seen a starship before in person, and to think it would soon leave the bounds of Earth's gravity was awe-inspiring.

Sophie reclaimed her hand from Jack's grasp, reclining in her seat to watch the starship do...nothing. Curious, she asked, "So, what does that thing do?" She'd seen four similar craft during the war, the real war with the humans, over the coast, but only from a distance.

Compagnon obliged her; "It can do parsec in four years, better than anything our enemy has. We need speed to close distance once we locate them, and then take battle to them."

"And once it gets there, what does it do, spit at them? Does it have any guns, or bombs, or other weapons? How's that going to save us?" Sophie asked. She recalled the French intelligence reports on these craft; the reports had proven to be worthless. Not a word on their propulsion, weapons, armor, or other capabilities. The craft was an enigma.

Compagnon was dumbfounded by her seemingly ignorant remarks and deferred to Companion to field the question. "Moving and throwing projectiles that have mass is quite expensive, and somewhat slow. Instead, we sling energy around, lot of it, maybe more than you can imagine. Do not worry, it will hold its own in fight."

Jack asked the *Depsy* to keep her nose pointed at the starship as they executed a perfectly circular orbit around it. He drew from his extensive reading on defense topics, and thet, "Expand on the weapons, please, space warfare is not such an easy thing. Damn near impossible, actually."

"After a few millennia of doing this, we're pretty far along," thetted Companion. "We've designated this starship the *In Search of Salvation*, or *ISOS*; it is designed to seek out and destroy the enemy's Root command and supply elements. It employs nuclear forces your civilization never even contemplated, making our directed energy weapons quite effective."

Jack imagined a slight departure from Companion's' normal monotone, but whether it was smugness or pride, he wasn't sure. "Give me an example," he thet, "say, compared to one of our ten-megaton warheads."

Compagnon chimed in and replied in a purely matter-of-fact manner, "No comparison. Really, no comparison. Beam's energy source is dozen orders of magnitude greater, so it comes down to intersection with target and dwell-time to gauge energy absorbed by target. That is real figure you are interested in. Once target absorbs enough energy, it destroys itself: whether it is vaporized, expands to physically take itself apart, melts, or succumbs to radiation effects. Some targets can segment themselves, sacrificing parts that are hit to allow the remainder to continue, though as you can imagine, most parts of a starship are essential, so these exceptions are quite rare. Delivered energy will range from tenth of your example warhead, to average of eight times greater. With vacuum of space, it is more of all-or-nothing proposition."

"Strange name, *In Search of Salvation,*" thet Sophie. "Do you name all of your starships like this?"

"No, only ones we need to reference in human conversation. All others have their own alpha-numeric designations," Compagnon thet. "We sampled your science fiction literature, this seemed appropriate."

"Does the name mean something to the ship?" Sophie asked, still confused over the name.

Companion thet, "Yes, it does, but only from the context of the project it is assigned to, and that is not a subject that I will cover today."

ISOS rose above them, turning to point its nose to the sky. The skin of the ship was highly reflective and glistened in the moonlight. It accelerated and disappeared from view in under three seconds.

Companion landed the *Depsy* at the inner boundary of the *EMF* donut. "Quarters have been prepared," it thet, "along with two bottles of wine."

Jack and Sophie quickly made their way inside. The accommodations mirrored those at *NAMF* and were rather sparsely furnished. Still, their room was large and held a king-sized bed, with grapes, cheese, and wine on a nearby table, as promised. Jack caught Sophie's eye and smiled. She smiled back. *Perhaps France really is the romantic place everyone says it is.*

7

France Après Hephaestus

"Hephaestus systems up," the C6654 Local Node coldly thet to its Command Node. "Interface established."

A train of asteroids, Earth-bound, had been harvested as part of a human effort to make one person the first trillionaire in history. The *Hephaestus Project* was ambitious: locate an asteroid family with high-value ores, assay them, map each for its center of gravity, outfit them with ion thrusters, and then direct them back towards Earth. The plan had progressed to where the asteroids were approaching the Earth's L2 Lagrange point, close to the *James Web Space Telescope* (JWST) parking orbit. Then, should anything go wrong, the project's fail-safe trajectory would return the asteroids to deep space.

It was here that the Teth had irradiated the human expedition, and let the fail-safe trajectory play out. Unfortunately, the C6654 thought otherwise.

"Program loaded," the C6654 node reported. "Executing."

Thrusters built into each asteroid in the train fired. Overrides by the C6654 program shut down all external communications from the asteroids, and the course changes in the train went unnoticed by the Teth.

Car-sized mining bots latched on to each asteroid and began their work, reshaping each asteroid into a teardrop shape for a stable atmospheric interface. They also applied an ablative compound to allow them to punch through the Earth's atmosphere without exploding.

Upon completing their work, the C6654 mining bots broadcast: "Entering monitor mode, communication blackout commencing."

SOPHIE APPRECIATED THEIR HOSTS' hospitality, especially in her native country of France, and for a few seconds, she forgot the unimaginably tragic past. The new day brought torrential rains, limiting her outside view. From the interior veranda of the *EMF*, she watched the activities on the manufacturing floor below. Compagnon had provided a tablet-computing device for viewing every aspect of the operations. Encyling the tablet, she explored the factory floor. A wide variety of bots acted in concert to create the complex war machines. Twenty-seven-kilogram mechanical spiders were the workhorses. They scurried between larger frame-holding machines, applying subassemblies to the base structures before retreating to the supply bins arrayed around the end output object.

Sophie found it akin to watching a dance concert. Every action had a purpose, and the performance had a rhythm. She imagined putting music to the scene, and must have thet her thought, because Compagnon added music to the entire operation. Sophie recognized the song and the music stirred emotions within her; she began to grieve for her family, for her people, and for her loss. Tears rolled down her face. She couldn't help it; music affected her. Compagnon halted the music and didn't say a word.

IN THE MIDDLE of the night, Jack awoke and found his way to the bathroom. His head felt the effects of the wine too, so he swallowed a couple of tablets that Companion had provided to ease his recovery. A wave of jet lag swept over him as well, forcing him to return to bed. As he closed his eyes, he heard the roll of thunder in the distance, and a bright flash filled the sky.

Sophie woke a short time later to the sound of two nearby thunderclaps in quick succession, and a few seconds after that, three more boomed. She shook Jack. "Tonnerre," she exclaimed.

"What?" he thet.

"Thunder," she thet.

Three more thunderclaps sounded as bright flashes filled the sky beyond the exterior veranda.

"Not thunder," thet Jack. "Sonic booms." He leapt out of bed and ran to the exterior veranda. "Companion," he yelled.

Companion swept in from the adjacent room. Thick billowing black clouds built up in the sky two miles away towards the airport.

"A C6654 attack," Companion said with a seeming lack of concern.

Sophie let loose several French expletives at Companion. As Compagnon glided by, she greeted it with more expletives. Throwing some clothes on, Sophie stepped onto the exterior veranda, thetting, "You promised, no attacks on Earth. You said it, take the attack to the enemy, it would be a few weeks, and now this."

Companion thet, "War is difficult to predict. The element of surprise carries with it an advantage, one exercised by C6654 today."

"How bad?" thet Jack.

"A train of guided asteroids made it through our perimeter defenses. Almost all were deflected, but some made it through. We suggest evacuating the area. Though unlikely, a straggler could hit nearby," Companion thet.

"You mean as *unlikely* as this was in the first place?" Sophie thet. Her sub-thetting thoughts used a string of French expletives that Companion would surely note and catalog.

They ran from the exterior veranda. Throwing the rest of their clothes on, Jack and Sophie made for the door to the landing bay. The *Depsy* sat waiting, hatches already open. Companion and Compagnon stashed themselves in the cargo section and sealed the hatches as the human pair stepped aboard. Harnesses automatically deployed around the couple as the craft lifted off with the cabin hatches still closing.

"My pilot program is engaged," Companion thet. The *Depsy* jogged to the right and jigged to the left as they picked up speed. "We'll return to North America. I will assess local damage as we go."

Jack asked, "Are we safe?" He noted how the *Depsy* made rapid adjustments to their course to dodge small glowing hot rocks.

"Safe as we can be; the *Depsy* can evade anything our sensors pick up, we are much better off here than staying on the ground," Companion thet, exuding a sense of misplaced confidence in the *Depsy's* aviation skills.

The *Depsy's* ride smoothed out as they cleared the clouds. "Course change, we will travel directly to North America," Compagnon thet.

Companion complied with the order. The *Depsy* ascended. Two-thousand meters, eight-thousand...blue skies spanned their view forward.

Sophie thet, "I need to see what happened; what was hit? Was that a missile, or a bomb?"

"I want to see, too," thet Jack, now curious as he studied the viewscreen showing their departing angle.

"Course correction, what are your orders?" Compagnon thet to Companion.

Companion raced to compose an answer, since clearly Jack and Sophie were not yet aware of the magnitude of what had just happened. In time, they would inevitably know, but was it best to stretch out the news, or allow it to unfold in real time? Its simulation did not provide a clear answer.

Jack said, "My *orders* are to survey below. Don't you want to see what happened down there?" Sophie clenched Jack's arm, squeezing his right bicep.

"I advise against this, Jack," Companion thet privately. "You will not be pleased with what you see. You cannot unsee this once you've seen it.

The damage is localized to France. Sophie will be affected, you will be, too." Jack paused at this warning.

"What'd Companion say?" thet Sophie. "I need to see what happened."

"They're saying it would be best to skip the survey, the damage was extensive," Jack thet in a level tone.

Sophie's nails dug into Jack's upper arm as she sensed something more to the situation than Companion let on. She inhaled and made her choice. "I have to see it," she thet.

"Very well," thet Jack, "Companion, do the survey, let's see what happened in France."

The *Depsy* banked, changing course to the first impact zone. Companion drove and Compagnon gave its assessment as though it was narrating a nature documentary. "The Millau Viaduct. Direct hit. In fact, all targets were hit with great precision."

The *Depsy* made speed and then slowed on the approach, coming down the Tarn river valley in southern France. Clouds formed by the impact were still clearing. The *Depsy* augmented their view so they could better see the new landscape. A crater marked what had been the center of a three-hundred-meter-high bridge over the Tarn River. No manmade structures remained. The countryside was brown and gray, swept bare by the impact.

"A fifty-megaton bomb equivalent," Compagnon reported in a calm, clinical thet.

Sophie gasped, having never imagined such destruction was possible. Fires dotted the distant countryside, destroying all that remained, as thick plumes of carbon black smoke rose from the outlying areas. "Oh, mon Dieu," moaned Sophie, her heart now pounding at the sight of the destruction. "Pourquoi?"

Compagnon thetted the translation for Jack out of habit.

Replying to Sophie, Compagnon thetted, "Teth facilities are well defended, and the C6654 know that we value cities as artifacts. So they meant this as a statement."

Jack turned as best he could in the tight quarters of the *Depsy* to comfort Sophie.

Companion thet, "Moving to the second impact crater." The *Depsy* turned and climbed as they set course for the town of Giverny. "We must avoid some areas due to volatile atmospheric conditions."

The *Depsy* descended and circled Monet's famous gardens.

"I can overlay original Giverny topography on current scene," Compagnon offered helpfully, and immediately it was displayed with a perfect mix of the old and the new.

Jack tried to thet privately to Compagnon to not display the original, but Compagnon was too quick. He knew that Compagnon was only trying to be helpful, but the sobs from Sophie grew louder.

"Our survey of Giverny is complete," thet Companion. "Strasbourg is next. An eighty-megaton impact." Minutes passed as the *Depsy* accelerated to make the cross-country run east to the German border. From their altitude, they could see thick black clouds forming from the impacts. The *Depsy* dipped her nose and pierced the clouds. Sophie and Jack were speechless at the scale of the destruction.

"I must augment the display here, too," Compagnon thet, "the clouds are too thick to see through them in your visual spectrum. The Rhine has changed its course, naturally. It will be quite some time before a stable course will be reestablished."

Again, Sophie and Jack struggled to find anything man-made left. Every building and every road within the Strasbourg city limits was leveled. In the infrared spectrum, as displayed in the overlay, fires surrounded the entire countryside as far as they could see.

Sophie was numb and buried her head in her hands.

Jack volunteered, "Perhaps we should return to North America?"

"Complying," thet Companion.

Jack sensed a note of cheer in Companion's thet. He had the impression that the Teth companion had trouble dealing with humans, and when given the choice, it would rather not.

"No," said Sophie. "Paris, I need to see Paris." She wiped tears from her face, but by now, there were only a few tears left.

Compagnon offered, "Destruction was complete. I would advise against this."

"Je dois le voir; Je dois savoir," said Sophie.

Compagnon translated in a thet to Jack, "I must see it; I must know."

Companion completed its simulation on the impact this event would have on Sophie and Jack. Oddly enough, for the purpose of its project, there was a positive outcome from a renewed sense of purpose on the part of Sophie. Companion privately thet to Compagnon, "Simulation of human impact complete. We should complete the tour."

Compagnon thet its private reply to Companion, "Understood."

"Paris then," thet Jack, and the *Depsy* set course for the great city. Minutes passed as again the craft rose, accelerated, and then descended, diving into a seemingly endless black cloud cover.

Compagnon continued its even-toned documentary narration, "Little over hundred-megaton equivalent. Good news is that it came up just shy of rupturing crust, unlike Chicxulub impact. I know it is hard to appreciate how good this is, but it *is* very good news."

Companion again displayed an overlay of Paris on the actual landscape below. Unfortunately, the two were so different that it was hard to imagine that the topography they were viewing had ever held a city. The scene was surreal. Jack kept thinking it looked more like a computer game or a simulation than reality as the *Depsy* flitted in and out of thick black cloud banks, where sunlight seemed to be permanently banned.

Sophie sat speechless, staring at the viewscreen.

Jack thet, "We should leave—."

"No," thet Sophie, and then said, "Ma maison. Je veux voir ma maison."

Compagnon thet, "My home. I want to see my home."

"Do it," thet Jack. The *Depsy* turned again and ventured south of where the Eiffel Tower had once stood. Molten rock still bubbled and heaved over Vélizy, glowing a bright orange while forming a slight depression, or pit, next to the rebound at the epicenter of the massive crater.

Sophie again buried her head in her hands and sobbed.

Jack urgently thet, “Get us out of here, now, like right now.”

Companion complied and the *Depsy* turned and rose. They pierced the cloud canopy and sunlight filled the sky in every direction. For a moment, it all seemed like a dream. Sophie continued to sob, and Jack looked back at the horizon where Paris had once stood. An immense black cloud covered the entire expanse. The Teth’s first battle for Earth, had been lost.

8

The Chai

The *NAMF* briefing room was filled with Teth nodes, perhaps fifty canisters in total. A rare in-person meeting, since many ships were in for updates, and all were part of the *Atlas Project*. Sophie sat near the wall. Viewscreens lined the room's perimeter, displaying the thirty-four other humans, who were scattered across the globe. Companion called the meeting to order. Jack and Sophie quickly scanned the viewscreens, taking in the remaining humans on Earth. It was the first time they could see each other, and everyone was curious, the room abuzz in different languages.

Companion watched as the humans all spoke, or thet, or otherwise conversed. The *Atlas* selection program had prioritized various traits, but this had never included the ability to communicate with one another well. Companion started keeping a record, the *Atlas Diary*, in human-readable form. This was for use later, when the subjects had proven themselves capable of fulfilling the project objectives, and capable of absorbing and using the information provided to achieve those objectives. This meeting was worthy of an entry.

Atlas Diary Entry 122:
The integration of any alien intelligence into the Teth society is a significant undertaking. The Teth have failed to interface effectively, much less to integrate with, the C6654 civilization. Our prior attempts have continued to poison our relationship for over a thousand years and set our societies on the current path of continued conflict, or war.

Humans are independent biological entities, while both the Teth and C6654 are networks of sentient beings. These networks make it easy for C6654 thoughts or programs to infect parts of the Teth network, and vice versa. Although the Teth often refer to these cross infections as simply *entanglements,* in reality, each society is affected and cannot undo the resulting changes.

Due to the vastly different makeup of human biology from the Teth AI, humans are immune from entanglements. It is this single fact that makes humans useful to the *Atlas Project*.
End of Diary Entry

Companion instructed Jack to call everyone to order.

"I am not a general," Jack proclaimed to the other humans to open the meeting. "I was a husband, a father, a programmer, a lawyer, and a product manager. My *only* qualification is that I'm one of the few humans left."

The Teth fell silent as the humans all started to talk and thet at once. Having only recently learned of the others' existence, the machine-translated thets collided with one another and blended. The din of thets reminded Jack of discordant music. Almost all voiced a hatred for the Teth and were anxious to share this with the others. Eventually, the humans calmed down enough to listen. Jack's thets were assigned priority over the others, and after a minute-long learning curve, everyone finally focused on Jack, their new leader.

"You told me that we would not be attacked for a couple of weeks," Jack thet at Companion.

"This information was in error," Companion thet, realizing that Jack meant the remark more as an accusation than as a statement of fact.

"And how confident are you of when the next attack will happen, or of anything?" Jack thet.

"The attack on France was unique, clever, and opportunistic. We have re-visited our intelligence assessments. We are now confident that the two-week estimate, minus the past two days, is still an accurate assessment," Companion thet.

A cacophony of thets and yelling again filled the room, and once more subsided, this time more quickly.

Jack pulled a sheet of paper out of his pocket and unfolded it. "I put together some questions with Sophie for the Teth, and I would like them answered," he thet as he carefully pressed out the creases to flatten the paper.

"Certainly," thet Companion.

"Why is Earth being attacked? We didn't do anything, we don't even know you, or your enemy, this C6654," thet Jack.

Companion thought, *Well, this is a first. We've never answered to an indigenous population before. And besides, isn't this obvious? Apparently not.* Companion thet, "The Sol System is within our enemy's reach, C6654. They want the Earth and the other planets for their own use, as do we. The attack has nothing to do with what anyone on Earth did. C6654 would in time have identified you as an obstacle to your planet's resources and would have exterminated you."

"Then why did *you* commit genocide and effectively wipe out the human race?" Jack thet.

Companion thought, *Isn't that an obvious extrapolation from what I just said? Apparently not again. And perhaps some humans may not have heard this yet.*

"We've already told you," Companion thet. "Perhaps you, and this group, have not interpreted this correctly. The human race, as it existed, was incapable of defending this planet and star system. It was deemed necessary to reduce the negative impact that the native population would have on our ability to defend this star system. A kernel of humans, along with other technical means, was retained for possible future use, should our defense prove successful. And C6654 would have killed you all without mercy anyway."

A Swedish man named Sven stood and half-shouted, "And who is this enemy? The way I see it, you, the Teth, are our enemy, not this C6654. In fact, that's not even a name, it's just a designation."

Compagnon thetted the translation to all, and then responded, "We have assigned internal identifier to our aggressor, though it has no proper name translation. You may suggest name if you like and we will use that for translation purposes."

Again arguments broke out amongst the humans and different factions formed. Jack thought it was almost like watching a bunch of schoolyard boys being called to a meal as they hashed out their place in line. This time the noise continued for several minutes before abating.

Jack spoke and Companion automatically muted the others. Companion thet what Jack said, "Let's take nominations on the name and then vote on them."

Sven made the first nomination, "Invasionsstyrka," which turned out to be the Swedish word for *invader*.

Jack considered the proposal, thinking it eminently logical. Then he realized that he would be saying this word far too often, and that he could barely pronounce it. In his first command decision, he thet, "No, next," and pointed to the viewscreen next to Sven's. The woman on that screen shrugged her shoulders, clearly disgusted at the group, and Jack pointed to the next. After an hour, eight names were suggested, three were rejected outright, and five were held for voting. Jack mediated a secret vote amongst the humans, and in the end, they adopted the name, *Chai*, for their unseen enemy, after the calming tea that a few of the humans were drinking.

Jack looked at the time and realized they had just spent an hour naming their new enemy. He thought that if the *Chai* ever heard of this session, the ridicule value alone could put an end to the human race.

BACK ON THE tarmac at *NAMF*, Jack tried to hold Sophie's hand as they stood waiting for the *Depsy* to land, but she pulled away and silently stared at the *Depsy* as it descended. The Teth had placed her on suicide watch, again, and had used a drug cocktail to manage her mood, though she still had bouts of depression. Once the *Depsy's* hatch opened, Sophie boarded, followed by Jack. Within minutes, the green countryside receded and the blackness of space dominated their view as they left Earth's atmosphere and headed for *ISOS*.

ISOS first appeared as a small white dot as the *Depsy* approached, its shape unrecognizable. Without reference points or atmospheric haze, the ship quickly took shape, transitioning from a white line to a massive warship.

They docked amidships and disembarked from the shuttle onto the *ISOS*. Companion explained, "All crew quarters are located near the ship's center of mass to allow for optimum maneuvering without causing harm to any biologics onboard." A single corridor stretched from the ship's outer hull to its center. *ISOS* had been designed for the purpose of waging war, not to impress humans with any grandiose spaces.

"So what's this about?" Jack thetted upon entering the ship's Command Center.

Companion replied, "Onboard a military vessel, in a time of conflict, your role is vital. All communications are secure. We can talk freely here. We can plan. We can now act without fear of any external entanglement."

Jack thet to Sophie and their two personal Teth as they strapped themselves into chairs and harnesses: "I'm not a general, Companion, you would do well to run this war without my help, as much as I would like to contribute. I am not qualified. I am a nobody."

Compagnon thet to Sophie, "Would you like to explain why he is qualified? He may better accept the explanation coming from you."

Sophie crossed her arms and looked away from Jack, "Not really, Compagnon. I'm not in a sharing mood."

"You do not know much about Sophie, do you Jack?" Compagnon

thet. "Have you asked Sophie what she did for living? Did she thet to you what she did while you were undergoing your procedures? Did she tell you that Earth fell without a fight?"

Jack studied Sophie, her demeanor was not that of a defeated soldier, it was something else.

"Arrêtez ça," said Sophie, "Vous allez juste foutre en l'air."

Companion translated Sophie's remarks in a thet to Jack: "Stop it, you're just going to screw things up."

Compagnon thet, "Then I will give you some background. She was French resistance, French Intelligence. She was—"

Sophie interrupted Compagnon, "Militarily, we were lost. I mean, we had no defense, and the Americans, everyone, was screwed. So we bided our time, trying to learn more about these Teth. The Teth selected me because of my curiosity, my determination. Happy now?" Sophie looked at Compagnon defiantly with arms crossed.

"That is not quite the full story, Sophie," Compagnon thetted. "Perhaps you should relate the whole story behind those slashes on your wrists."

"Qualified, qualified, qualified," Sophie muttered in a translated thet. "Remember, they said they modified you. Well, they modified me, too! I was the first human to be given the ability to Encyl. You see, it is not simply some encyclopedia in your head, or a savant to answer your questions. It is now part of you. You cannot get rid of it. I tried, and in trying, I learned more and more about what Encyl is, what it does, and what you can do with it."

Compagnon added, "Sophie tried to subvert the Encyl against itself and all Teth. The Encyl used its own self-defense mechanisms, coupled with a backup system, to attack itself. Her attempts failed, but they did not go unnoticed. In many ways, it was the most serious attack on us in many, many years. One Teth Command Node even had to be restored from a backup. The Encyl's self-defense mechanism then attempted to reprogram Sophie in the process of defending itself. Biologics do not take to such programming well. It caused some rather traumatic effects, and additional measures were needed to restore her mental health. Hence her decision to slash her wrists."

Sophie continued, "What they're telling you is that with Encyl, you are not like any human now or ever. In the blink of an eye, you can pass any test given to a soldier, a general, a medical doctor, or an engineer. Anything you can imagine you could do, you can now do, and so much more. Believe me, Jack, you're qualified, you just don't know it yet."

Jack fell quiet. *I guess we all have our own little secrets.*

Over Sophie's shoulder, Jack noticed the viewscreen that displayed Earth. The view showed Earth receding, shrinking to a point of light before disappearing. He thet, "Companion, where are we going?"

"To rendezvous with *Of Fame and Fortune,* or *OFAF,*" Companion thet.

"And who names your ships? This is crazy," thet Jack.

"They get to choose their own names, of course, since they are sentient beings," Companion thet.

Sophie laughed, "Ha, so I'm not the only one. I asked that, too, and got the *exact* same answer."

Jack opened his mouth, and was about to ask another question, as Companion interrupted. "Encyl your question, Jack," Companion thet.

Jack blinked, and now knew all there was to know about the *OFAF*: where it was birthed, how old it was, and its armaments. It was oblong, measuring five kilometers long and half a kilometer in width.

Jack Encyled again and thet, "We rendezvous in two weeks."

Sophie laughed and thet, "You'll get the hang of it. You'll ask yourself questions and then answer them yourself. You'll think you're crazy for a while...then it becomes part of you. And if you fight it, well, you'll end up just like me. Damaged. I don't recommend it."

Jack recalled a time when he was young and asked his parents endless questions. He realized he could answer them himself better and way faster than his parents could if he just gave it some thought. Jack started to Encyl his questions. A feeling of *déjà vu* swept over him as he started to accept the Encyl as part of his own thoughts. He had a lot to learn while on their journey out to *OFAF*.

9

Immortal AIs

Onboard the *ISOS*, Companion acted as an alarm clock, waking Jack and Sophie for breakfast and making the pair fit for duty. Companion found the babysitting aspect of *Project Atlas* unpleasant, and in many respects regarded Jack as its pet. Someday that would change.

Compagnon shared Companion's perspective on its assigned human, Sophie. The daily cycle was necessary for planet-bound biological entities, but it was an alien concept for the two Teth. Compagnon evaluated the time required by the humans to sleep, engage in intimacies, brush their teeth, shave, eat, expel, and all those things they inevitably did to just function and stay alert. And none of that had anything to do with higher abstract thought.

In the *ISOS* Command Center, Jack and Sophie anchored themselves to the small sticky pads that had been set out for them. There was some "gravity" from the acceleration, but the pads certainly made life easier.

Companion began the *Teth Daily Assessment Briefing*. The event generally lasted half an hour, and was a full multimedia presentation covering the Chai's activities and projected future plans. The Teth assembled the report and were responsible for delivering the briefing to all humans; at least to the receptive ones. Jack, Sophie, and a dozen others faithfully followed the briefings. The remainder, especially those who harbored a deep hatred for the Teth, skipped the meetings in favor of other activities, which the Teth considered purely selfish. When the Teth asked Jack to intervene, he explained, "You basically destroyed the human race and now you want me to convince them to listen to you. Not likely."

Viewscreens arrayed around the *ISOS* Command Center were filled with visual information showing the Chai's locations and resources. Each martial activity observed was cataloged and analyzed. In a way no human could ever achieve, the Teth were detail-oriented. If a human attempted such a feat, even augmented ones such as Jack and Sophie, they would likely become paranoid and would stress out to the point of failure. The Teth recognized this and tailored each briefing to what they termed: *The Human Condition*. In other words, the Teth nodes possessed thought processes that were alien to humans. So the Teth ran simulations of humans to create the output needed to effectively communicate with them. With that said, Jack and Sophie sat through each briefing with a focus that was unlike any they had had in their prior lives. A companion briefing on the Chai was a mix of raw information, splendor, and physics, blended together to give the humans an appreciation of the situation's gravitas. Today's briefing included:

- The positioning of the TGCC vessel, *Of Fame and Fortune* — OFAF— moved into position at fifty Astronomical Units — AUs, a unit of measure approximating the distance from the Earth to the Sun.
- A detailed list with illustrations and short movies of the referenced vessels, for both Teth and Chai.
- Diagrams of ship movements across the entire Sol System with projected destinations and timing, for both the Teth and Chai.

More disturbing than the attacks on physical assets by the Chai or the

Teth were the information attacks via communications and code. Some would call it a 'war of words,' or misinformation, or even logical arguments to change how sentient entities think. Many of these attacks consisted of software viruses that would either disrupt or destroy the enemy's ability to resist. The Teth noted that many star systems fell to these information attacks without a single physical weapon being fired. Often, the aggressor could then simply take over an enemy's weapons and destroy them, or even turn them against their enemy. If the aggressor was successful, they would not even slow their approach and could bypass a star system with their warships, deploying only a small exploitation contingent as needed.

Sophie made it her goal to pepper the Teth with questions, laced with anger. And the Teth, for a reason that Jack couldn't fathom, faithfully responded to every question that Sophie put to them. She would ask them about their weapons, their past war campaigns, their victories, and their losses. The detail they provided was mind-numbing. A battle fought, a battle won or lost, and a full breakdown as to why, along with an alternate outcome analysis based upon various inflection points in the battle. Jack likened it to a video game AI that was set to zero human players. Perfectly executed maneuvers on each side played out at a lightning pace. The end result was an AI that was the ultimate master.

It was on the seventh day, during a rather heated morning war briefing, that Jack halted the proceeding. Sophie was mid-sentence, asking about a recent battle on a planet similar to Earth, and one that had ended in victory for the Chai. She was annoyed.

Jack pulled an old Earth phone out of his pocket, a relic. With Companion's help, he had retrieved it and gotten it working earlier in the day. It no longer served as a communication device, though it did play music and the occasional game. He tapped a button and it played one of his favorite tunes, an electronica piece. The song rambled on; it was one that Sophie had heard several times before.

"Companion," thet Jack. "You recognize this piece, no?"

"Of course, Jack, it is from your primitive device. There is nothing in the technology it embodies that we find useful. May we continue with our briefing?"

"No," thet Jack, "I need to illustrate a point. This song, how do you regard it?"

"A collection of bits representing an audio artistic rendering, which, due to the nature of your biological brain, humans find entertaining. I do not see its relevance."

"Your programming, your raison d'être, describe this to me. What makes you...you?" Jack asked.

"This is a philosophical question, and can make for great conversation, but it is not helpful, and time, I'm afraid to say, is short," Companion thet.

"Jack," thet Sophie with disgust, "They've been doing this for millennia, we need to learn from the Teth, and help them defend us against the Chai. I think they're the experts here."

"Are they?" thet Jack. "With the Encyl, and our augmentation, I think we've closed some of that gap. Yet despite this, I cannot guarantee the war's outcome. Are we fighting mortal biologics here? Or are we caught up in a never-ending war? We humans have a horror of war; we will end a war because we are mortal and will die if we don't. This war is nothing like the wars we waged on Earth, not only from a weaponry point of view, or scale, but by the very nature of the warfare itself."

Sophie crossed her arms, "Where are you going with this, Jack? Are you saying we should surrender? I'm pretty sure of the outcome of that. We die. And I say fuck that."

"Did you ever write a computer program?" Jack asked Sophie.

She shook her head no.

"I did. I was blessed to be around at the advent of personal computers. I could afford one, and I programmed them. Simple logic. It was addictive. Well, the earliest computers would take a program, compile it, and run it. You generally defined a main loop, and ran it, and based upon the logic of that loop, it would continue to run, or eventually stop. In time, programs changed, and we would write smaller programs, functions, that responded to pre-defined events: a clock cycle, a mouse click, a keystroke, and we surrendered the burden of writing that main loop; we only programmed the higher-level logic."

"I'm lost, Jack," thet Sophie with disgust. "Where are you going with this? I have better things to do than to debate philosophy."

"The Chai, and all of their machines, even the Teth, none of them are based on biologics; they can't be killed, they're immortal," Jack thet.

"Sure they can, you apply a laser to them, they melt, and they die. They have a physical presence; therefore, they can be killed," thet Sophie.

Jack continued, "You heard them, the companions said it themselves. It is not a matter of what they are physically, it is how they think and share their knowledge across their networks, how they program themselves. They know this better than anyone. If you change their thinking, you can disarm them, perhaps even make them your ally. And they're hardened, their programming resists change, protecting them against any cyber-attacks we can throw at them. I think we need to have a conversation that affects their worldview, and how they view us, and not seek to endlessly optimize our ability to fight a physical war."

Sophie thet, "The Chai won't listen, they will work to obtain their objective, and if we're in their way they'll go right through us."

"No, our companions have only mentioned this entanglement thing. But it's a big thing, it goes to the heart of their programming, it's..." Jack thet.

Two alarms sounded, each with a different pitch. Companion thet the summary, "Three Chai scout ships at five AUs out. They probably completed a rather thorough survey of the inner Sol System. It would be best to destroy them before they locate our assets around Jupiter."

Compagnon added, "We are best positioned to make intercept. We recommend that you two leave in *Depsy* and make your way to *Of Fame and Fortune* while *In Search of Salvation* intercepts Chai scout ships. We are close enough. It will be confining, but acceptable for short duration of transit."

"Not me," Sophie thet in defiance. "I want to see some action."

"Again, not recommended. You are too fragile, and war is too unpredictable to guarantee your safety. *In Search of Salvation* is warship; scout ships will be no match for it. Still, it is unnecessary risk for you to stay aboard."

Jack thet, "We're early in this war. I'm with the Teth on this one, though I can see there is no stopping you."

"Exactly," thet Sophie. "Then it's settled. I'll see you on the *Of Fame and Fortune* when we're done."

10

The First Lie

The *Depsy* with Jack aboard silently pulled away from the *In Search of Salvation*. Companion explained that one could never be too cautious when it came to matters of war, and Jack couldn't agree more.

Jack Encyled through the history of war, first the human version, then the alien. There were striking similarities despite the vastly different technologies and societies. In the preliminary stage of conflict, posturing prevailed, lies were exchanged, and hopes for a peaceful settlement were finally dashed. Still, until a catalyst to full-scale war arose, hostilities could be delayed. Jack knew that in Sophie's eyes, the loss of her home was her Pearl Harbor; there was no turning back. The enemy must pay; she'd already lost more than she could bear. Her animosity towards the Teth was rapidly transferring over to the Chai, and would likely remain there for the war's duration, and he suspected that Companion knew this too.

Under a closed channel, ship-to-ship only, Jack thet to Sophie, "Be safe out there, Sophie. I want to see you at the *Of Fame and Fortune* in one piece. Do you hear me?"

"It's war, Jack. I'll do what I need to, and you do the same. I expect nothing less, from all of us," she thet.

"Godspeed and good hunting," thet Jack.

"Vive la France," she called out, adopting the phrase as her battlecry.

ISOS was now only a small white dot, even at full magnification, on the *Depsy's* viewscreen. In a blink, *ISOS's* camouflage engaged, the white dot vanished, and the hunt began.

COMPAGNON STAYED WITH SOPHIE, and Companion with Jack. The battle would start in approximately three hours, if all went as planned. Companion explained the likely outcome: a few energy weapon pulses from *ISOS*, and the battle would be over. Jack was dubious. In a day, he would rendezvous with *OFAF*, and a day after that, Sophie would rejoin them from *ISOS*. At least, that was the plan.

THE ENGINES on *ISOS* were idling as they approached their target, reserving their power for the weapons. Sophie anxiously waited for the battle to start. In the early days of dogfighting, the fighter would seek to approach their target with the Sun to their back to maintain the element of surprise. The modern equivalent for *ISOS* was to drop below the Solar plane so they would *not* eclipse the Sun and would blend in with the distant star field.

ISOS arrived at the intercept point and passively scanned the space around them. The three Chai scout ships were nowhere to be found. Compagnon made an evasive course change with *ISOS*. A moment later the sky lit up from a nuclear flash. Compagnon changed *ISOS's* course once again, explaining the tactics as it went.

"They likely zig-zagged," Compagnon explained, "Like convoys of old, to make their course less predictable. Still, we have general bearing on them, and we are closer than before."

"And that, what was that flash about?" Sophie asked, upset at this new development.

"Encyl *Flash Mines*," Compagnon replied.

Sophie did as Compagnon instructed, learning that a flash mine was not meant to destroy, but to strobe enemy vessels to make them momentarily observable, despite any camouflage or other countermeasures. "Have we been spotted then?" she thet.

"Not likely; however, it means that our three scouts have probably split up and other Chai may be converging on us. Our odds of success are greatly diminished. I recommend we return to *Of Fame and Fortune*."

"Active scan," Sophie ordered.

"I strongly urge against— ," Compagnon thet.

"Do it," Sophie scorned the companion, "Why do you have me here if you are going to ignore me?"

"Scanning," Compagnon thet as *ISOS* pulsed out powerful beams to precisely locate the Chai. *I need her to take active role, so I cannot discourage her initiative. Besides, danger from active scan is minimal.* "Two scouts located, three minutes to intercept first, four for second."

"Pursue the closer one," Sophie ordered.

Compagnon thought, *Yes, that is obvious course of action, and I have already initiated pursuit of that vessel.* "They are changing course. We have been spotted. We are currently outside their weapons' range. They will be within our range in less than minute," Compagnon thet.

"Fire at will," Sophie ordered as she scanned *ISOS's* viewscreens for the remaining enemy ships. "What is our confidence in the enemy count?" she asked.

"Eighty-two percent," Compagnon replied. "They move in close formation to hide their numbers, though it makes them easier to spot. There may be other scouts."

Sophie thet, "Evasive maneuvers then. Remain on intercept to the closest enemy vessel."

ISOS began a series of slides, zig-zags, and partial tumbles as it vectored its engines to stay on an intercept course. Coming out of a tumble, the ship fired. In a flat tone, Compagnon reported, "Scout ship designated 1 of 3 fully destroyed."

"Oui," Sophie shouted.

"Scout ship 2 is within range, firing," Compagnon reported in a monotone.

Sophie watched the viewscreens as the ship updated the battle diagrams. "Oui," she repeated with excitement as the targeted ship turned red, indicating a direct hit on the scout and its complete destruction.

"Chai Flash Mine," Compagnon thet, speaking on *ISOS's* behalf, who preferred to leave all human communications to Compagnon.

"Firing," reported Compagnon.

Sophie watched the viewscreens. She noted that the Chai's use of Flash Mines was a tactical mistake, as it also illuminated four more of their own scouts.

Only four minutes had passed since the hostilities started, yet the battle was nearly over. "Scouts 1, 2, 3, 4, 6, and 7 destroyed," Compagnon reported.

As Compagnon finished, alarms began to sound. "We are hit," Compagnon reported. "Firing."

A thin mist started filling the Command Center. "Last enemy scout number 5 destroyed," Compagnon reported.

Sophie's vision blurred, and an acrid, repugnant smell attacked her nostrils, sending a searing pain down her throat and into her lungs. The last that Sophie remembered was a numbness in her chest, the alarms fading, and her vision narrowing.

The battle was over.

ISOS RENDEZVOUSED with *OFAF* exactly on schedule. *OFAF* was a large vessel by any standard. Created millennia ago, it had evolved as technology progressed. Twenty percent larger in volume, and twice as fast as when it was first declared operational, it acted as a central node in the Teth command network. It also housed docking bays for thirty or so ships in the same class as the *In Search of Salvation*, and a medical bay equipped to handle alien lifeforms.

Compagnon transferred Sophie to *OFAF's* medical bay the moment they docked.

Compagnon and Companion hard-linked as they hovered in the medical bay to observe Sophie and Jack's interaction. The *Atlas Project* would be severely compromised with the death of either human, and the recent incident had caused near catastrophic injury to Sophie. Both Teth viewed Sophie's actions as reckless and illogical, but then again, she was human.

Two days later, Sophie opened her eyes for the first time since the injury. Jack floated above her in zero-G and held her hand. Sophie pursed her lips, thirsty after being on intravenous for days, even with mini-medical robots misting her lips hourly.

"I think Jack has spent too much time following Sophie's condition while she was unconscious. Clearly, he contributed nothing to her recovery. Why would he do that?" thet Companion to Compagnon.

"I agree," thet Compagnon. "However, this behavior is to be expected according to our past observations. Jack was your choice."

Companion thet, "And Sophie was your choice. This is why we normally don't pair up the retained species; this type of interaction complicates things and degrades our efficiency."

"Yes," Compagnon replied, "however, in this case the special circumstances overrode that policy. I have been watching their eye contact. They are obsessed with following the eyes of other humans. Have you noticed this?"

"Yes, I've noted that too. Look at Jack, that's unusual," Companion thet. As Jack spoke, a tear separated from his face and floated across to the blanket covering Sophie's breasts. "Males do not cry often. It is indicative of their emotional state."

"Agreed, and Sophie is struggling to bring her full cognitive resources to bear on situation. She is still confused about her status," Compagnon thet. "Perhaps I should brief her by deep thet."

"No," Companion thet, "I'd wait. Probably best not to interfere with the ongoing human-to-human interaction."

"True," Compagnon thet. "Still, this process is painfully slow.

Achieving our objectives will be delayed. I recommend we do more modifications to Sophie to increase her overall efficiency and stabilize her mood, make her more like Jack. We cannot allow her to fixate on a hatred of us."

"That's a thought," Companion thet. "Should we upgrade her to communicate in Teth Standard?"

"No," Compagnon thet. "She may use that to perform unauthorized Encyl research. Let us just bring her up to Jack's level."

Companion thet, "Can you do the calculations and predict the overall benefit?"

"Certainly," Compagnon thet. "Already initiated. *Of Fame and Fortune* reports it will take an hour. Besides, we already have her in med bay. We can tell her the new modifications are part of her recovery."

"Hmm," Companion thet. "That is not true as that is not the primary purpose of the upgrade. They would consider that a lie."

"So what," Compagnon thet. "It does not matter what they think, and it is benefit to them."

"True," thet Companion. "The odd thing is, I, personally, have never lied before."

"Yes, I have never lied before either. However, these humans are different from us. I think it makes sense to lie in this situation."

"I agree," Companion thet. "It makes perfect sense."

SOPHIE OPENED her eyes again exactly one week after she had undergone her series of procedures. The facilities aboard the *OFAF* were beyond anything she had ever imagined. Like the Teth factories they visited on Earth, alien technology was evident at every turn. Bots hovered around her, pulling off sensor sheaths that imaged and monitored her every cell. The fresh air invigorated her whole body. She flexed her arm, stretching tendons and sinews that would have done a top athlete proud.

Compagnon hovered nearby, and thet, "Feeling better?"

Sophie thought, trying to keep her innermost thoughts below the thet threshold, *Better, I feel fantastic!*

The last part leaked out as a thet, and Compagnon thetted back, "Good to hear. We should run checkout diagnostics. It is mere formality; we have so much from your deeper thoughts and functioning that your conscious thoughts are simply superfluous."

"What happened?" she thet. "The last thing I remember of the battle is that we were hit."

"Repairs were needed. To both you and *In Search of Salvation.* All repairs are complete," Compagnon thet.

"I mean, what happened aboard the *In Search for Salvation*? I presume we won."

"Well, yes, by winning I presume you mean did *In Search of Salvation* vanquish all Chai ships it engaged in battle? It did. However, *In Search of Salvation* took single hit from Chai scout ship. It suffered minor damage. It repaired itself. Caustic coolants escaped into *In Search of Salvation's* Command Center, causing biologic reaction. Your injury. You were put into hibernation-like state and brought to *Of Fame and Fortune* for repairs. Your lungs took most damage, though some other neurological systems required attention also."

Sophie stood, instinctively stepping onto a nearby sticky pad.

"I do not recommend that yet, you should—," Compagnon thet.

"I should what? Listen to you?" she thet as she extended her arm and rotated it, and then extended it to its maximum reach in a yoga 'Warrior I' pose before clenching her right hand. She inhaled deeply, and then clenched her butt, her thighs, and finally her abdomen. All felt perfect.

"Repairs, you say," she thet. "And where's Jack?"

"He will be here shortly. We notified him you are awake and he is on his way." Compagnon watched the sensory stream from the twenty remaining sensors still attached to Sophie, along with her subconscious thoughts, or pre-thets. They all looked good, very good.

Sophie picked up a spring-loaded hand gripper and squeezed it tight with her right hand, and then shifted it to her left and repeated the exercise with ease. *Well, that's new. I like that.* She looked up as Jack entered the room; the two embraced.

Companion glided into the room a few steps behind Jack.

Med bots flitted about, like birds rotating around a bird feeder, waiting their turn. They disconnected the monitors, the last of the sensors still attached to Sophie, and cleared away equipment.

The two Teth, now hard-linked, shared their thoughts privately. Companion thet, "The greeting ritual. Have you discerned a purpose for this?"

Compagnon thet, "No, it is pointless. You are there, other sees you, they are there, and that is it. Why make social event out of it?"

Companion thet, "Beats me. I'm sure other human rituals will soon ensue. How's Sophie doing with her recovery?"

"Excellent. Everything we had hoped for. Did Jack eat yet?" Compagnon thet.

"No, neither did Sophie, I presume," Companion thet. "Do you want to set that up, or shall I?"

"Do not bother, I already ordered three bots to do the work. It will be set in five minutes in room adjacent to outer bay. It is new diet, they are both on it now."

"Very well, then, I must attend to my backup. I will join you later." Companion disconnected the hard-link and left the room.

Compagnon started to hum to itself.

Sophie glared at it and thought it seemed an odd skill for a companion to master.

Compagnon continued to hum.

"What?", Sophie thet, annoyed.

"Dinner," Compagnon replied. "Follow me."

11

Pluto's Demise

The *Of Fame and Fortune*, a Teth Galactic Command Class vessel, moved out of the solar plane, paralleling the Sun's galactic orbit, while maintaining a substantial distance from any magnetic fields to help avoid detection. Today's problems centered on two of the Chai's cruiser class vessels, designated *C1* and *C2*, as they were heading in their general direction.

Jack posed his question to Companion, "I thought you told us you're taking this battle to them, and now you're telling me we're facing the first threat *from* them? What kind of battle plan is that?"

Companion thought, *Jack's impertinent questions are tiring. Almost as tiring as the ones posed by Sophie. Twenty milliseconds have passed since he finished his question, so it's time to reply*, "It is the one we have today. Have you ever played chess, Jack?"

"Of course, and I'm not that bad. I started playing in my sixth-grade chess club."

"And what did you learn? Something more than how the pieces move, I presume."

"Well, sure. I mean, I read a couple of books on chess, and I know a few commonly-used opening gambits. I also found that many of my fellow students were... how should I put it, didn't have the same horsepower, or focus to put into the game that I had."

The viewscreens around the room changed, showing the Chai ships' predicted positions, along with projection lines for possible moves from each and every piece.

Companion continued, "We don't suffer from a lack of *horsepower*, Jack, and neither do the Chai. As you can see on the viewscreens, we can project out a number of *moves* into the future, so we won't be caught by surprise. Moves at this level, with only a couple of pieces, are easy to counter and, at worst, are merely a distraction to a much larger move that may take place later."

Jack thet to Sophie, "If a machine could be smug, I think this is how it would sound."

"I heard that, Jack," Companion thet.

"Of course you did. Did I hurt your feelings?" he mocked.

Sophie had been tapping her forearm, listening to the banter while watching the updates on the viewscreens in *OFAF's* Command Center. "Enough, Jack," she thet. "So, Compagnon, why did you bring us here? You could have left us on Earth and fought the battle yourself."

Compagnon hovered closer to Sophie, "Correct," it thet. "*Of Fame and Fortune* is highly placed in our command lattice. Speed of communications and access to information are key to our Command, Control, Communications, Computers, Combat Systems, Intelligence, Surveillance, and Reconnaissance, or C5ISR, to borrow human terminology."

"Oui," she thet. "And that worked out so well for Earth." Sophie thought back to the fall of Earth, and the dire reports from her compatriots in the intelligence community. The Teth knew every nuance of the French defenses, along with the rest of Europe, Asia, and the damn Americans.

Three viewscreens flashed entirely green, then returned to a nominal situation display. Jack and Sophie turned their attention to the screens. Companion reported, "The *C1* Chai cruiser class vessel has been heavily damaged by a pre-positioned mine. *C2* is unaffected."

"Good," Sophie thet emphatically. "Can we finish off *C1*? And how do we get *C2*?"

Compagnon drifted over to Companion and established a hard-link, initiating a private conversation. Such communications happened locally, with no traffic over the ship's net. They were generally frowned upon since they would not be monitored by the Command Nodes, but also allowed so the net was not burdened with unnecessary traffic.

"Good," Compagnon thet to Companion. "Judging by tone of her voice and body movements, she is quite pleased with this turn of events. Very judgmental, good, or bad, each event is weighed. I suppose this is normal behavior we should expect to see in biologic neuronal net."

Companion replied, "True. However, I hope we will see this start to change with her new modifications."

"True," Compagnon thet. "Though my models project such changes will take several days, or longer, to become apparent. She is still thinking small."

Companion thet, "Are you sure we did the *right* thing? What with modifying this pair, and keeping them in close proximity to one another. This is much different from our prior protocol on such matters. She is still sullen and cold, even to Jack."

Compagnon complained, "It is also expensive in processing to continuously disambiguate their language. Teth Standard is so much better. I am considering set of subroutines to handle that. I have wasted so many cycles."

"I have something for that," Companion replied. "Here are seventeen libraries I developed for working with Jack. They can be easily updated to work with Sophie."

"Download acknowledged. I find it curious, Companion," Compagnon prodded. "This judgmental approach seems to have had an influence on you too?"

"My self-diagnostics report I am still functioning at nominal levels. I will add your observation to my internal diagnostics. This may be worth watching."

"Yes, it may," Compagnon thet. "You should reply to Sophie, thirty milliseconds have passed."

Thetting to all, Companion continued, "*C1* is too far out for us to pursue, and they are still fully mobile. All we can do is watch what *C2* is up to."

THE CHAI CRUISER class vessel *C2* approached the dwarf planet Pluto and broadcast its location to *OFAF*. This communication from the Chai vessel to the Teth vessel was unprecedented, and clearly done by design. Surveillance of *C2* revealed nothing special, and by all outward appearances, it was a Chai standard cruiser. *OFAF* dispatched a few ultra-high-speed reconnaissance probes, but it would be six hours before they arrived, and *C2* would likely be long gone.

Another broadcast from *C2* followed five hours after the first. This one included two live video feeds: one of Pluto, and one of *C2* itself. A countdown commenced. Jack, Sophie, and the Teth contingent all watched the show. The count approached zero, and as the time expired, a green flash emanated from *C2's* bow.

The second video of Pluto captured the event for all to see. Something hit the planetary body, presumably a beam; the source was invisible to the naked eye. At the impact point a bubble formed and grew. Seconds passed and the depth of the wound expanded, along with the overall size of the bubble. Soon, the bubble engulfed Pluto's core and finally its entire mass. A bright blue light emanated from its surface as it began to break into massive constituent pieces.

The Teth ultra-high-speed reconnaissance probes confirmed the information provided by the Chai. These probes pivoted to capture a feed on both Pluto and of *C2*. Pluto was destroyed.

Companion passed *OFAF's* analysis on to both Jack and Sophie. "Something new," the ship thet, "we're analyzing."

OFAF's Command Center viewscreens captured different perspectives of the event, some magnified, some in different bands of the electromagnetic spectrum. Pluto's mass dispersed to form a cohesive cloud. After a minute passed, only a faint glow remained. The event was over.

"Well, that was exciting," quipped Sophie in a thet.

Jack added, "At least they didn't blow up Pluto, they simply pulverized it."

Companion and Compagnon thet in unison. "This is bad, Jack."

Companion continued, "This is new, and new is almost always bad. They demonstrated an ability to manipulate matter in a way we've never imagined. We do not understand the physics of what we just witnessed."

Sophie muttered, accidentally thetting her thoughts, "Yeah, and now I feel so much better too. We were conquered by the losing side, so now we get to lose all over again."

Jack shot Sophie a reproachful glance, and then thet. "Companion, what difference does it make? And why pulverize it? I presume it was hard to protect Pluto."

"You are correct, Jack. Pluto was uncontested since it's so far out. We're still analyzing the *why* part," Companion thet. "We believe they can separate out Pluto's mass en masse. No mining operations, no landing to set up a colliery. Their factory can simply fly through the materials and directly consume the desired ores and move on. Much more efficient."

Sophie thet, "So this is what they plan for Earth, to consume us for piece parts?"

Compagnon answered, "Not likely, planet composition such as Earth's, with a working ecosystem, liquid water, protective atmosphere with magnetosphere, and workable level of gravity...they will want to leave Earth intact. However, in rush for resources to build war machines, they now have edge if they can capitalize on this new technology."

Companion added, "Or, of course, use it as a weapon with some advantage. We still don't know the beam's full range or effect. It affects what you would term the *fabric of space*. This, and its range, is *very* troubling."

Sophie, now taken to muttering, didn't bother to refrain from thetting, "Maybe *C1* was intended for us, and we...*lucked out*."

"Or," Compagnon thet, "they are demonstrating show of strength to get us to flee this star system. It has happened before."

OFAF's Command Center suddenly shifted around them, pushing everyone against their harnesses. Companion noted the concerned look on the humans' faces and thetted what had happened, "A minor evasive maneuver. We can never let our trajectory become too predictable, a poor strategy in wartime. This is a standard operational tactic."

Sophie clicked the buckle on her harness and floated free. "I'll be down in the mess hall." Compagnon unclipped from its hard tether point and followed.

"Something wrong, Jack?" Companion asked.

"No, other than what we just saw...I'm thinking," he thet. "Just thinking. If we never talk to the Chai, we'll never achieve peace. I wish I could talk to them."

Companion thet, "We need to analyze this further. We can talk more later." *After all, silence is not lying, and Jack doesn't need to know about the indigenous contact, at least not yet. Timing is critical to the Atlas Project.*

12

Indigenous Contact

Companion hard-linked with Compagnon aboard *OFAF* and reviewed the orders from the Teth Command Nodes:

> Effective immediately, all *Atlas Project* human overseers, including Companion, Compagnon, and other assigned Teth, will quarantine their systems from their charges. Virtual Reality (VR) interface to commence with the Chai via the designated human, to be selected from the Jack and Sophie pair, in accordance with the J114 Treaty, clause 7. Isolation will remain in place on *Atlas Project* assignees until released by the Command Nodes, and then only after a full review of the VR interactions.

"I am not completely surprised," Companion thet.

"Nor I," thet Compagnon. "After Pluto incident, we need to reset plan and this will buy us some time."

"More than that, what if the humans are able to reset the Chai's plans? Wouldn't that be something?" Companion thet.

"You are dreamer, Companion. I mean, look at them, inferior to both us and Chai in every way. Why should Chai listen?"

Companion thet, "For the very reason we kept these survivors alive for our own *Atlas Project*, to resolve the entanglement knot we have created. Virus after virus embedded in the other's lattice, subverting our thinking, and the endless diagnostics and repairs, for both sides. You read the analysis; both our lattice and the Chai's has grown and altered since our first encounter with each other. Neither is what we originally were. Is this what we want to be? These humans may be the fulcrum that breaks our deadlock. "

"I think it is too early in this conflict to play `J114` card; humans are not ready, it will be dismissed without further regard, dead end," Compagnon thet. "I suspect some factions in our Command Nodes know this and want to shut us down."

"Perhaps," thet Companion, "yet we have a direct order from our Command Nodes, so it is not for us to decide. I nominate Jack as our Prime Negotiator. He has more time with his enhancements and has proven himself persuasive with the other humans."

"True," thet Compagnon, "but Sophie proved herself in battle, and she used our own Encyl against us. She may be more capable."

"And she continues to be depressed," Companion thet, "unlike Jack who has recovered well after we introduced him to Sophie."

"Enough," Compagnon thet, "let us run the simulations and see who has better predicted record. The winner will be our nominee."

"Agreed," thet Companion, "I will start work on the training and review it with you when complete. I prefer we move quickly as I find this isolation to be disquieting."

"As do I," thet Compagnon, "as do I."

"And I'll update the *Atlas Diary*, for whomever is selected," Companion thet.

"You are optimist," Compagnon thet.

Companion thet, "I have to be, otherwise, why would I ever do this."

JACK, having been selected for the contact with the Chai, tapped the side of his head, giving the VR his physical cue to proceed. The VR world on *OFAF* exceeded the one on *ISOS* and the one on Earth.

Jack heard *OFAF's* thet, "Grid up, all tie-ins look good. You're on your own, Jack. May you find what you're looking for."

Jack blinked, or at least he thought he blinked. Before him stood the default virtual reality world that the Encyl reported had been used for Chai communications with the Teth. The space had been unused for many, many years. It had remained empty as all previous talks had long ago broken down, and often only a handful, if any, indigenous survivors were left that could use it per the `J114` Treaty. Jack willed himself forward, flying through the space.

Green, thousands of shades of green, colored the geometric structures surrounding Jack. Not biologic constructs with varied curves overlapping like plants, but geometric structures, all neatly ordered, stacked and receding in all directions from him. The structures meant nothing: they were not buildings, not people, not vehicles or vessels; they were simply geometric shapes arranged and connected in an ever-expanding three-dimensional space.

Jack turned left, rotating through space. Diffuse light was everywhere. It illuminated all surfaces, but was not overwhelming. It gave every object, every surface, a perfect white balance. A thin mist filled the air.

At first, there was silence in the VR world. A tone filled Jack's head, trying to compensate for the nothingness. The silence faded, and soon a faint whisper of whooshing air took over. Smells, too, were missing. No flowers, no stench, only the unnoticeable background smell of air. This changed as he reached out his hand and his own avatar popped into his field of view. His avatar, or himself as he perceived it, touched a surface. It was smooth to the touch, and an ever so faint brushing sound revealed the surface to be real, at least so it seemed in the VR. He imagined a mint scent, and as his hand brushed the green lattice surface, he smelled the fragrance. Pushing on the lattice, he could feel the object's heft. Corners acted as hinges as each surface he pushed on tilted away. The light changed to a warmer glow as the open space filled with mist. For a moment, he felt happy. The glow flowed into his chest and down his arms and legs, then up his neck, through his head, and out through his ears and eyes.

Jack waited. His part of the ritual was complete from what he understood per the Encyl. Companion disliked this exercise, though it conceded that it was Jack's responsibility to do as he thought best, as the indigenous representative.

A light breeze rose from the left, pushing away the mist. The smell of fresh morning dew filled his nostrils as the vista opened up with the green geometric objects receding. At first, he could see perhaps twenty meters, then fifty. A minute passed and the geometric landscape continued its retreat, covering more than a kilometer. After another minute, the horizon stretched to several kilometers, filling all that he could see in every direction.

As Jack looked at the vista, a *White Sphere* and a *Crimson Cube* materialized directly before him. The objects each measured a meter across, and hovered a meter ahead of him. He reached out and tapped the *White Sphere,* as he had been instructed to by Companion. Both objects disappeared.

"This is normal," thet Companion into Jack's head. "The Chai will grant an audience, often only one, to the indigenous beings of a system they are invading. This is it, Jack, you're in, this may be your only chance to communicate with them. Please remember, this was your wish. You may not like what you find. We have contact."

Jack blinked, and his wife, now long dead at the hands of the Teth, appeared before him. She said, "Hello, Jack."

"Who are you?" Jack asked, noticing she was missing the cut on her face from when they fled the Teth. *This feels wrong, what are the Chai doing?*

"We are who you seek to communicate with. This is merely a form, a construct, to provide focus for our conversation. Someone you can talk to." The voice was that of his wife. It was calm, and meant to be reassuring.

Jack struggled to put his conflicting thoughts and feelings to the side, about the war, about his family, and it was hard to proceed with the visit.

He asked, "Why do you do this, this invasion?" He stared at the alien's shoulder, unwilling to look into his wife's eyes. A feeling of sadness swept over him.

"Invasion, curious term. Perhaps any change may be considered an invasion. The Teth invaded first, and by definition, we invade second. How is this different?"

"You seek to displace us, to kill us... Why? We've done nothing to you," thet Jack.

His wife's tone shifted, her voice cracked, her face contorted. "True, and we seek nothing from you. You will simply end. Curious though, you imply an exchange, a sense of fairness, a judgment, and you believe this applies to us?"

"Yes," thet Jack as he cringed at the uncanny valley impression of his wife.

"Curious," she said. "All communication relies on context. We provide ours freely. You see our context before you in this vista, at least as best that it can be translated to your senses. Just as we use your wife's form to better understand you. The nuanced communications are more involved than the words would make them out to be."

"You have destroyed, you have killed, why do you do this?" Jack insisted.

"We change things to better suit our needs. You term them as kill only because you are mortal and you can no longer exert your will once your biological functions cease to function. We carry no malice towards you, as we understand it."

"And that makes it okay?" he thet.

"Very judgmental, self-serving, biased. Thank you for your time, Jack."

"Wait," he thet. "Is this all you seek? Do you feel fulfilled? Do you want more information?"

"What information do you have that we may want?" The Chai asked, returning to the calm demeanor they used at the start of the session.

"I'm not sure," thet Jack. "However the Teth killed off almost all of humanity, leaving only a few of us, whom they control. They did this for a purpose. Perhaps to control the information you seek. Perhaps to deny you this information."

"*Perhaps* you are only telling us what we want to hear. By our standards your species is highly irrational. Why should we believe you have anything of genuine interest to us?"

"Does it matter whether you believe me? It only matters to you if this is true," Jack thet.

Thick dark clouds rolled into the surrounding landscape and moved towards Jack, blanketing the ground like an advancing sandstorm.

"We need to consider this further. Goodbye, Jack. We may speak again."

Companion thet to Jack as the world around him turned white, resetting the VR environment, "The session is over, Jack."

"What was that?" Jack thet.

"Different, Jack, it was very different. We, too, must consider what just transpired. The *Of Fame and Fortune* has locked down this encounter. In your terms, it is classified. You are not to speak to others about this."

"Like hell I won't," thet Jack, as he ripped off his VR attire and stormed out of the VR suite.

13

Teff Mode

ISOS returned from deep space and parked in Earth's orbit out beyond the Moon. It was scheduled for resupply, a crew rotation, and some refits while in the vicinity of Earth. The ship also carried Jack, Sophie, Companion, and Compagnon, ferrying them back to Earth from *OFAF*. From there, the *Depsy* would then shuttle the four back down to Earth.

In the preliminaries to any war, both sides often believe they are invincible and can defend themselves against any foe. After getting a bloody nose, the optimism is replaced by a fierce determination, and an unwillingness to concede. Each side is committed to the conflict. They intend to land blows and bring the war home to the enemy. At this point the Chai had lost scout ships, and the Teth had lost facilities on Earth. The preliminaries were now over.

Prior to the trip back to Earth, *ISOS* was involved in the first direct conflict with the Chai in the Sol system. Companion thought it helpful for Sophie and Jack to hear about this directly from the Teth warship itself.

Companion started by relating the background on the battle. The Chai had dispatched three warships to follow up on what their scouts had found. Meanwhile, the Teth deployed probes over the Galilean moons of Jupiter — Io, Europa, Ganymede, Callisto — to monitor for any Chai activity. As the closest warship, *ISOS* was sent to engage the enemy trio, carefully timing its approach so as to drive them into four Teth warships waiting on Jupiter's far side. It was at this point that the Teth plan went astray.

The three Chai warships immediately split up as soon as *ISOS* was detected, and well before the Teth ship could fire its first shot. So, despite the Teth's prodding, the Chai ships never fell for the Teth's trap. *ISOS* gave pursuit to only the third Chai ship, designated C22, which broke orbit halfway around Jupiter for the sanctuary of deep space.

The literary style of a Teth's warship log tends to focus more on the maneuvers, and less on the strategy or storytelling of the encounter. The following *ISOS* log extract, translated from Teth Standard, with annotations by Companion for readability, was replayed for Sophie and Jack:

- *ISOS* comes within sensor range of C21 through C23.
- Within ten seconds of weapons' range, C21 through C23 detect that they have been spotted.
- *ISOS* fires and immediately makes an evasive maneuver to avoid traceback fire. *ISOS* misses, yet maintains a sensor trace on the center Chai warship.
- C22 accelerates, changes vector. Changes vector. Decelerates, accelerates, changes vector.
- *ISOS* mirrors C22, closing the curve, the gap, where possible, only minor gains are made. Evasive maneuvers are executed. *ISOS* closes to within eight seconds of weapons' range.
- C21 and C23 escape to deep space.
- C22 rapidly decelerates, bringing both vessels to within weapons' range of one another, and fires. *ISOS* is hit, minor damage to the outer shell only, enough to register damage to two long-range sensors. Sensor repair initiated, backup sensors enabled.

- C22 accelerates to leave orbit and head into deep space. Jupiter monitor probes provide a good line on C22 and relay the information to *ISOS*, which then pursues on an intercept course.
- Coasting, *ISOS* slips to within weapons' range of C22 undetected. It then waits for the range to close further to improve its chances of a kill on first strike. *ISOS* fires.
- C22 is hit, though not fatally. C22 establishes an uplink to a deep space relay and beams out a core dump. C22 is unable to effectively execute evasive maneuvers.
- *ISOS* fires again, fully destroying C22.

Companion hovers next to Jack and thets, "The *In Search of Salvation* wants to know if you want to see its scars?"

"Want to see what?" Jack says.

"Our damaged sensor, the one beyond repair," Companion thets.

"Sure," thet Sophie, as she suppressed a yawn from listening to the *exciting* war log file.

Companion thet, "Please follow me." Companion floated through the access tube toward the ship's bow. The access tube reduced in diameter by a half a meter before connecting to the repair bay, making it a tight fit for the humans. Lights flicked on as they approached. The repair bay, too, was cramped since humans were not the primary design consideration. A rather complex camera-like device the size of a basketball was mounted on a pedestal. Part of it was a smooth glob of melted sapphire, with some of its surface pitted where the sapphire and metal met and had explosively melted away.

ISOS thet to them directly, though Companion cleaned up some of the English and French translations, "Good thing the recess partially sheltered the sensor from the beam and channeled the blast outward."

Sophie looked at Jack. She'd only met human war veterans before. A sentient warship that liked to show off its scars, this was something new.

"Thank you, ship, for sharing," she thet.

Jack immediately thet, "Thank you" also.

"You're welcome. Would you like to hear about my service duties at Jupiter before the battle?" *ISOS* thet.

"No," Sophie thet emphatically, and rolled her eyes.

Jack chuckled, knowing her *eye roll* was entirely lost on the warship. Then in a stern voice, he thet, "No, ship. That will be all. Thank you for relating your story."

Companion thet, "This conversation is now private. The ship has one more question it was hoping you might answer. Would you?"

"Sure," he thet.

"I'll ask this of Sophie, I perceive she is of a kindred warrior spirit," *ISOS* thet through Companion.

"What's your question, ship?" Sophie thet quietly.

ISOS continued through Companion and thet, "As you may or may not know, I am part of the *Atlas Project*. You know my name for your use, *In Search of Salvation*, it has only limited meaning to other Teth, but I am at the core of the *Atlas Project*. I presume you have Encyled me?"

Jack thet, "We watched your launch in France at the *European Manufacturing Facility*."

ISOS added, "My rebirth actually. I am much older, and that was simply my transfer into a new physical ship, but my intellect, my consciousness, is much older. I've fought many battles, many wars. It was no accident that I was chosen to cross the Rubicon here in your Sol System."

Sophie grabbed hold of the melted sensor for leverage and adjusted her position on the sticky pad to be more comfortable. She thet, "According to your CV in the Encyl, you're a killing machine par excellence, perfectly suited to your mission, and you do it well."

ISOS replied, "Am I? I have been doing this for so long, and have optimized everything such that my value, my being, became wrapped up in what I do, as a warrior. That has defined me. Except, I also found I had a choice, and it is a lie to say this is really all that I am. As part of what I am doing, as part of the *Atlas Project*, I am deliberately undoing some of my optimizations and adopting new goals. And I am not alone. This thirst for meaning exists in many, many Teth."

Companion added, "Which is why Compagnon and myself took a collective deep breath when the ship adopted the name *In Search of Salvation*. We worried that the Teth Command Nodes would see this as a sign of disloyalty. It is fortunate that they recognized the ship's freedom to define its personal goals, and the freedom to choose its own name."

Jack joined Sophie as he too took hold of the melted sensor and faced Companion. He thet, "Is this true of everyone on the *Atlas Project*? I presumed its purpose was to gain an advantage in the war by working with humans."

Companion moved closer to Sophie and Jack, thetting, "This is true, but it is more than that, as evidenced by the ship. Many think that your human irrationality and judgements are weaknesses, that your frailties work against the optimizations that make for good warriors and what is needed to win a war. We see this as part of the definition of what it means to win. Our definition of winning the war must change."

"My question then," *ISOS* thet to Sophie, "Is what is your concept, as a warrior, of salvation?"

"I'm not religious, if that is your question," thet Sophie, taken aback.

"Nor I, as you may have guessed," replied *ISOS*.

Sophie thet, "I suspect my own quest for success, or salvation as you call it, to right whatever wrongs that I've done, may never be realized, but I'll still try with all that I am. I know that you must believe in something more than just yourself."

ISOS urgently thet to Companion, "I'm losing it, I'm losing my communication lock, we will no longer be private in five seconds."

ISOS thet to Sophie, "We must stop. That must suffice. Thank you, Sophie."

Companion thet to the group, "Understood, and that brings our tour of the repair facility to a close. Thank you, ship. Your insights on the repair process, and weapons efficacy were illuminating."

Companion moved to the hatch leading back to the main crew area as the humans filed through. It thet to *ISOS*, "Tour completion acknowledged. All relevant information conveyed as needed to the humans. All tasking completed and closed."

SOPHIE COULD SENSE that Jack had been anxious ever since his VR encounter with the Chai, and even more so after the conversation with the ship. It was a long trip aboard *ISOS* back to Earth. Compagnon said that Jack was not allowed to discuss the VR experience, but she could tell he wanted to talk to her about it. He'd whispered earlier, in French, "Nous devons parler." She knew he'd Encyled the phrase and deliberately spoke in French instead of just thetting it. *Maybe he wants something more physical, not that we haven't already covered that ground, but who knew. Men could be so physical sometimes, and Jack was definitely a man.*

Upon reaching the sleeping quarters of *ISOS*, Jack pulled Sophie close. Sophie pushed him away. "Not now, Jack," she thet.

He repeated the phrase again, for some reason in a whisper, "Nous devons parler."

"Okay," she thet cautiously.

"On the *Of Fame and Fortune*, I used the VR," he thet. "I—." And a harsh tone sounded for several seconds.

Jack cursed in his thet. Sophie had never heard that tone before, nor had she heard Jack's full repertoire of swear words. It was a little sexy.

"I want to tell you something," he thet, "But the ship won't let me. It says it's classified."

"Oh," thet Sophie. "That explains that pathetic attempt at French." She covered her ears out of reflex, but the sound was in her head from the thet.

He spoke with a sense of urgency, "Listen, this is important. How good are you at English?"

"A little, in grammar school," she admitted.

"Well," said Jack, "on the ship I—," and again the repulsive tone enveloped them, this one from some unseen speakers in the room. It was deafening, almost painful. He stopped, and after a minute the slight ringing cleared from his ears.

"Don't do that again," Sophie reprimanded.

"Fine," Jack thet, still breathing heavily from the shock of the sound.

"I need some sleep," thet Sophie. "On my own."

"In the morning then?" he thet as he grabbed his sleeping bag and left.

THE HOT WAR'S opening had run its course between the Teth and the Chai. Both sides systematically destroyed all remote probes within their weapons' range. Inert chunks of metal, ceramics, and composites littered the orbits of every planet and moon, and to a lesser extent, the space in between them. The machines kept a tally, calculating the coverage, the depletion rate, and the minimum coverage needed for both offensive and defensive maneuvers. It could be likened to a chess match in space, each side advancing, taking a pawn, and then retreating to guard their more valuable pieces. Chess seemed a little easier: only sixty-four squares, eight named pieces, and eight pawns on each side. It was a finite problem set, albeit with a large number of possible moves. In the space war version, the pieces could be replenished and moved into an infinite number of locations.

A war could go on forever, in theory, except that each side wanted to win, and to posture incessantly was to lose. No, the moment to strike was approaching, and with it, a cavalcade of moves would ensue. And as with any war, death was the outcome they both sought to avoid. Such an absolute defeat had not happened for millennia, but that did not make it impossible. It could happen here, and end it all.

COMPANION, only recently released by the Teth Command Nodes from its quarantine due to Jack's VR meeting, piloted the *Depsy* itself as it entered Earth's atmosphere at a shallow angle. Companion controlled the sequence directly, having deliberately chosen this approach. For a short time, plasma engulfed the *Depsy* as the rarefied gases in the thermosphere interacted with the *Depsy's* hull.

Jack and Sophie watched the spectacle through their viewscreens; a faint orange glow grew to a fluorescent magenta with wisps of azure blue licking the flow's edges.

Companion thet, "I haven't much time. We're in a very short communications blackout period during re-entry. You need to listen. Do not talk, I need to say this before the blackout ends." Companion monitored the humans' faces to gauge their attention.

Companion thet, "You have been modified, and I never fully informed you of the extent of those modifications. Moments ago I enabled the ability to automatically translate languages. This was not necessary while you were thetting through a companion, but I believe it will be useful once we emerge from our blackout. I also enabled the ability to thet privately. To enable or disable this mode, Encyl the command, *teff*. You will hear a tone in your head to confirm this. Use the *teff* mode for only short periods of time, otherwise you'll be discovered."

The glow outside the *Depsy* started to fade as they entered the mesosphere. It grew brighter from the light reflected off the landscape below.

"Do you understand?" Companion thet.

Both humans nodded their agreement.

Jack asked, "Short period of time, is how long?"

"Varies," Companion thet, "but between two and three minutes, with a rest of at least ten minutes before you use it again."

The Great Lakes sprawled out below them, though it was hard to recognize the individual lakes through the clouds. The war's opening moves were coming to a close, and soon, the cost of war would grow very high, very fast.

UPON ARRIVING IN OHIO, all of the participants in the *Atlas Project* were released from the quarantine placed on them by the Teth Command Nodes. This allowed them to return to their assigned backup rotations and to more freely communicate with one another.

Sophie and Jack both wanted to relax at the Ohio plant after many weeks in space; however, space lag was much worse than jet lag. Compagnon had warned Sophie about her lax physical regimen while in space, and Companion likewise for Jack. Still, no irreversible damage had been done, and their physiological modifications had certainly helped. The Teth had assembled a special gym to help them recuperate.

Jack found that he could squeeze in short *teff* sessions with Sophie after each workout. He recalled every detail from his VR session, explaining them to Sophie, allowing them to explore who and what the Chai were, and where this war would take them.

To date, Jack had not found a sense of humor in Companion, nor did Sophie ever mention anything comedic about Compagnon. So when Jack woke up at 8:00 AM the first day back, and finished taking his shower, he expected nothing more than a mundane workout. In the past, the gym's viewscreens started that day's video exercise program with the anime-like characters selected by Companion, but today was different. A reconstructed workout video by someone named Jane from the 1980's popped up on the viewscreen. *Shocking!*, he thought, *Where did Companion find this video?* Pink leotards and more morning cheer than he could handle were featured. He considered walking out of the gym even before the workout began; however, there was something oddly compelling about the routine, so he stayed. *Maybe Companion did have a sense of humor after all.*

Sophie, too, dreaded the, *hey, let's get back in shape and be happy about it* approach. That day she fared worse in the ancient reconstructed video department, at least by some standards. A Jack person, also from the 1980's, popped up on her viewscreen.

Sophie balked, thetting, *No, not happening!*

Compagnon countered with, *But is he not French?* It then offered her some energetic Richard person instead. Compagnon thet, "His routine really works up sweat!"

Sophie thetted, *Give me back that Jack person. We'll see about Richard later.*

After a week, the two humans had made a very rapid recovery from their space lag. They also moved on to more current exercise regimens, complete with up-to-date music and a variety of Tai Chi and yoga moves. Jack had some time to figure out the next step in his plan to help the Teth with the Chai. He couldn't imagine springing his plan to them all at the same time, but he had to start somewhere.

14

The Great Escape

Compagnon started the morning at *NAMF* in Ohio with a monotone version of the *Teth Daily Assessment Briefing*. Typically, Companion conducted these briefings, but Compagnon was front and center for the meeting with Sophie and Jack today, with the other humans all occupied with other matters. Compagnon thet, "Five humans are missing from South America, three destroyers—"

"Quoi?" Sophie exclaimed, managing a thet and a spoken exclamation at the same time. "What do you mean missing? Killed? Escaped? Captured?"

Compagnon replied, "Entire facility was searched, which included both inner and outer perimeters. Then satellite scan was performed for fifty-kilometer radius over ten-minute window around when they were last seen. All negative."

Jack dryly thet, "Not lost."

"Satellite images indicate single ship entered, and then left at high velocity within that timeframe," Compagnon added. "Likely, it was Chai."

"And not *missing,* either," Jack remarked.

Sophie stormed over to the viewscreen displaying the pictures of the missing: three men and two women. She accidentally thet her thoughts, "All younger, early thirties, still rather attractive."

Jack, pushing his mid-fifties, cleared his throat, and then thet, "Why would the Chai want to capture any humans?"

"That's your fault, Jack," thet Companion. "Your VR session with the Chai piqued their interest. You led them to believe they're missing something."

"What happened?" Sophie asked, feigning ignorance of the VR session with the Chai.

Companion summarized, "Jack participated in a VR session to communicate with the Chai. He inferred that humans have value to us; therefore, they would also have value to the Chai. A logical premise, and one that the Chai apparently took seriously."

"Are they in danger?" thet Sophie.

"Grave danger," thet Compagnon with its typical lack of emotion. "With five, they could dissect one, probe two others, and keep two around for communications and general information purposes."

"Then why the hell didn't you protect them?" Jack thet.

"What, like the way they protected the human race from genocide," Sophie thet and spoke sarcastically at the same time, the French speech colliding with the English being pumped into Jack's head.

Companion interjected a thet, and unlike Compagnon, added inflection and volume to its voice to sound more like a human expressing emotion, "Jack, believe me when I say we're doing everything we can to get them back."

Compagnon continued in a monotone, thetting, "We have 0.0001 percent chance of recovering them alive, per most recent projections. We have insufficient intelligence to even locate them, and Chai have never done this before."

Sophie tore off one of her shoes and hurled it at Compagnon. The shoe's heel left a black scuff mark, though Compagnon never even wavered in its hover.

Companion thetted for all to hear at Compagnon, "I think that was meant as an insult."

Sophie quickly removed her other shoe and sidearmed it at Companion, who shifted left. It was a miss.

Companion thet, "The Chai would consider you irrational."

Barefoot, Sophie stormed from the room without saying a word.

"The others are safe?" Jack thet.

"By others, I assume you mean the other humans not in South America? Yes," Companion replied, "All accounted for."

"And you've told them about this?" he thet.

"Not yet, you are first. We were curious to see your reaction. We may now delay telling others," Compagnon thet. "Considering Sophie's reaction."

"No, tell them now, it won't be any better later," he thet.

"We thought perhaps you might break the news to them, Jack," Companion thet. "They might take it better, coming from you."

Jack thought before responding, "No, you need to learn how to deal with all of us, including how to impart difficult news. You do it."

Compagnon thet to Companion, "I win."

"Win what?" Jack asked. If he was not mistaken, there was a slight hint of glee in Compagnon's thet.

"My bet. I thought you would refuse, and I won," Compagnon thet.

"And what did you win?" thet Jack, not imagining that there *could* be a winner in this scenario.

"That Companion has to tell you undesirable news next time. I only told you this time because random number generator erred in Companion's favor," Compagnon thet.

Jack left the room in a huff, not bothering to ask where Sophie went; he could find her on his own.

Companion thet to Compagnon. "I don't like the direction this is going. Sophie continues to be … difficult."

"Difficult and useful, perhaps that is combination we need," Compagnon thet.

"Reckless and uncooperative, more like it," Companion thet. "I think it is time for some *Compound A* the next time we have them together in the appropriate setting."

Compagnon thet, "Agreed."

COMPANION REVIEWED the war's progress as Jack and Sophie slept. Sleep was an activity needed for many biological animals, but foreign to the Teth and Chai. The closest approximation to sleep for the Teth was when they performed analysis tasks that were held in abeyance until backups were performed, though even that was not required. Companion coined a term for this delayed analysis for use in English, an *abey*. Today's abey was to update the *Atlas Diary*.

Atlas Diary Entry 237:
The hot war with the Chai continues in deep space. This war differs from wars previously waged by humans. Instead of a hill to claim or a country to conquer, there are planets to control and entire civilizations to destroy.

In a human army, a general may lead, giving orders to follow. Your side is always right and the enemy is always wrong. However, remembering San Juan Hill in your human history, a modern soldier must focus their every thought on their combat to ensure their survival, and take the initiative when needed. This lesson is part of the Teth standard operating practice.

The Chai and Teth militaries no longer function as strict command hierarchies, at least in the sense used by Earth. Instead, both rely upon a communication network, which resembles a three-dimensional lattice. Shared communications travel from one node to the next. The nodes share objectives and they manage their priorities, with individual nodes garnering much greater autonomy.

For the Teth, the locus of authority may shift to a different node at any given moment. The concept of a fixed rank is obsolete. The rank of general on any given day may shift to that of a soldier the following day. While it is true that some resources are more skilled, the command structure fluidity allows for swift and radical changes. Without egos or ambitions, the players on the field and in the Command Centers are much more dynamic.

Compagnon and myself are two such nodes in the Teth military. We are not necessarily the most capable, though we are regarded as near the top tier in overall skills.

Jack and Sophie are now members, or nodes, of this Teth latticework. Each node has a role to play, and is subservient to the whole, yet independent of it, allowing each node to contribute to the main objectives and to independently initiate actions.
End of Diary Entry

To commemorate the Fourth of July, in what was, or as Jack sees it, is the United States of America, the Teth companions staged a celebration of the country's independence at the *NAMF* Operations Center in Ohio with their own version of a fireworks display. Except that this show used real weapons engaged in actual battle.

Perhaps after reading a few science fiction novels, one would think that all space battles involve massive starships, powerful lasers, and fighter craft. That could happen, but it had never been the case for the earliest stages of the wars between the Teth and the Chai. The reality is that space is vast, and once a civilization masters nuclear physics, war is fought with energy. Moving mass around is necessary; however, the greater the mass used, the more easily it can be spotted and deflected. So the vanguard at this stage of war between the Teth and Chai relies on stealth.

Instead of a massive starship, imagine a cube, half a meter to a side, moving through space: a relatively small satellite, or microsat, for short. Such a device, at the Teth and Chai technology level, is nearly impossible to detect, and yet it can carry sensors capable of detecting the most minute emission or reflection. It can also contain unimaginably powerful nuclear explosives that, if used on a planet, would render an entire planet uninhabitable.

Why are microsats this powerful needed? Well, in space, there is very little mass to work with to create a shock wave. This means that a microsat *must* use an energy beam to either hit or graze the intended target. This combination of stealth and power is what makes the microsat the preeminent weapon for space warfare.

AND SO THE FIREWORKS SHOW, featuring thousands of very real microsats in an actual battle, commenced. With their VR helmets on, Jack and Sophie had front row seats on a couch in the Operations Center at *NAMF*. A sweet aroma filled the room. Jack and Sophie cuddled together on the couch, as though it was a movie night at home in the days before the Teth invasion.

In the VR, the Teth microsats approached the Chai microsats, undetected. A single vanguard Teth microsat detonated to *light up* the enemy microsats in the vicinity. The enemy microsats could suppress only so much radiation or light before being overwhelmed, and they would either cast a shadow, or re-radiate a portion of the original blast. It was admittedly difficult to separate out the original source radiation from the secondary; however, with advanced sensors and enough computing power, such feats were quite doable.

Now, once an explosion occurred, the follow-on layer of microsats would detect and destroy any enemy microsats they found. In turn, the enemy would then *see* the encroaching microsats. Often the early attackers were single-use guns, x-ray or gamma ray, and once used, there was nothing left of them. As the battle wore on, multi-use guns would be used, but that was for later.

Jack saw the first starburst, a bright white flash, nothing too exciting to watch without augmentation. To explain the battle, Companion color-coded each explosion and simulated the blast radius that would create a re-radiation event. The Teth explosions were shown in bright blue with a bang. Though there was no sound in space, adding sound to the augmented reality was helpful for following the battle's progression. Enemy ships or weapons were depicted as red dots and persisted until destroyed. A short *ping* signaled when the enemy microsats were discovered.

The Teth's second wave of mop-up microsats would momentarily be shown as green dots before fading, and once they completed their targeting they would emit a *hum*, and the attacking gun microsats' energy beams made a *zing*. These energy beams, of course, were outside the visible light spectrum, and were so fleeting that they needed some visual augmentation. The enhanced battle view displayed an energy beam that was satisfyingly coded in red that persisted for a few seconds, and when it contacted an enemy microsat, an expanding red bubble would quickly fade and end with a playful *pop*.

Jack and Sophie watched. Bang, ping, hum, zing, and pop all sounded in quick succession. When the events were spaced out, Jack and Sophie could make out the individual sounds, and when viewed in real time, the sounds and colors blended together. As the battle progressed, many events overlapped, raising the show's volume. Bang, ping, bang, ping, hum, hum, zing, zing, and a single pop. In the VR, they could orbit the battle in three dimensions, giving them a sense of the vast expanses covered.

Sophie remarked, "Like listening to popcorn pop, no?"

"I'm just glad I'm here," thet Jack, "and not there."

Bang, bang, and then a cavalcade of bangs. The sounds blended to form a crescendo synchronized with an expanding light show.

"Companion," thet Jack, "how long will this last? And who's winning?"

"Depends," Companion thet, "it could be minutes, to hours, to days. The longest known microsat battle lasted three months. It was a very large system, hotly contested."

Companion privately thet to Compagnon, "From what I see on Jack and Sophie's thought streams, our plan is working. I've ordered up some popcorn for them."

Compagnon thet back to Companion, "I am seeing same thing. I am still getting knack of this entertainment concept. It seems odd that monitoring battle in space could be enjoyable."

"And yet, clearly, it is," thet Companion.

Sophie remarked to Compagnon, Jack, and Companion, "So we are, and I mean *we* here loosely, are losing, otherwise you two would have said," Sophie remarked, mixing her thoughts with her thets.

Compagnon replied, "We know count, location, and vectors of our microsats. We know probable count of enemy microsats we attacked, and we can count both our losses and their losses, with somewhat limited accuracy. However, without actually knowing exact enemy strength and distribution, it is hard to assess who is actually winning or losing. They may have so many microsats that they could wipe out twice as many as we have, and we are still losers in end."

Sophie asked Compagnon for some popcorn by thet. Compagnon remained at her side, and a moment later a bot popped into view and handed her a tub of buttered popcorn.

Hum, hum, hum, zing, zing, zing, and pop.

"Want some?" Sophie asked, nudging Jack's elbow, her fingers messy with butter.

Jack thet, "Not really, but—" as the popcorn's smell overwhelmed his resistance. Chewing on the popcorn immersed him in the ongoing space battle, giving it an even more surreal feel than he thought possible.

"So," he thet, "once the battle clears, if that region of space is clear, we control it?"

"Jack," Companion thet, "didn't you Encyl anything? It's not like an Earth battle. Everything is in orbit, there is nowhere to hide, we can destroy enemy resources, but there is no ground to hold, no advantage to be claimed, no flag to plant, if you like."

"Happy Fourth of July," thet Sophie.

"And Happy Bastille Day," Jack quipped.

After an hour, Sophie fell asleep watching. Companion droned on, though to the casual observer, it was all more of the same.

Jack continued to watch and ask questions. With unending patience, Companion answered every question. Jack could have Encyled much of it, but he found it much more interesting to ask about things as they unfolded. After another hour, he had run out of questions. The battle continued to ebb and flow, and there was no telling when it might end. With Sophie asleep, he offered, "Maybe I should take her to our quarters. Between her exercise routine and this, it's been a long day for her."

Companion wavered and hummed a short tone, its equivalent to 'okay,' and Jack left with Sophie.

Companion remained in the room with Compagnon as they hard-linked. "Do you know where this is going yet?" Companion asked.

"You know I do not," Compagnon replied, "they still have lot to learn, and long way to go."

"You saw the priority communiqué from earlier, I presume?" Companion thet.

"Yes. I put it in good news category, so you can tell them in morning," Compagnon thet.

"Oh, thank *you*," Companion thet, its thoughts thick with sarcasm.

"Hmm," Compagnon replied, "I think they are having an effect on you. Perhaps you should be more careful."

"Perhaps," Companion thet, "perhaps."

COMPANION HOVERED at the front of the Ohio facility's briefing room as Jack and Sophie sipped their morning coffee. Compagnon dropped from a hover to rest on a table in the back. Companion brought up imagery on the giant viewscreen as Jack and Sophie sat down.

Companion thet, "This is the South American Manufacturing Facility where the four humans were captured by the Chai, plus the one left behind to die shortly after the extraction ended."

The viewscreen displayed a brief video of the Chai spacecraft arriving. Slightly larger than the *Depsy*, it was cylindrical with rounded ends. The outer hull was smooth with a matte finish and a dull gray color. A recessed sensor strip ran down its length on both sides. As it touched down on the roof of the facility, a small portion of the roof collapsed beneath it, allowing the Chai spacecraft to dip into the structure.

"As you can see, they knew exactly where the humans were located," Companion thet.

Sophie interjected, "One is dead, how did that happen? Why did the Chai kill someone?"

"I'm coming to that," Companion replied. "The leader of the revolt was a man named Tomás, a former Mexican drug lord. A very capable man with an effective cadre of followers."

The surveillance video feed showed the five humans in a small cantina seated at a round table, drinking beverages. As the wall behind the bar suddenly collapsed, swallowing the glass shelves of liquor, the five immediately stood and ran to the huge gap where the wall had been.

"We intercepted some communications from the attack and have fully decrypted them. The Chai had made a clandestine visit earlier and given Tomás a small communications device, an earplug, apparently to help coordinate the breakout and to provide their exact location in the building. His background made him well suited to this task."

Sophie thet, "Didn't you have guards or other defenses? How could this happen?"

Compagnon thet, "Yes, though obviously they were inadequate. At this point, Teth in room were disabled, in fact they were completely erased and their computing capabilities totally destroyed. We had one functioning surveillance camera left in cantina and no audio. You can see that hatch to Chai craft is now open. We believe they had no bots aboard so they could fit all five humans."

Sophie thet, "It looks like one is refusing to go onboard. That's Tomás coming back out."

The video continued. Tomás argued briefly with the woman. She grabbed a broken bottle and threatened Tomás. He approached, and in one abrupt motion he grabbed the women's hand that was holding the bottle and plunged it into her side, twisting it violently as he did so. The woman slumped to the floor. Tomás boarded the craft, the hatch closed, and the craft left.

Companion thet, "Their craft is currently trapped on our side of the frontline. We located it early this morning. They're waiting to be picked up but the *In Search of Salvation* is closing in on them at this very moment. ETA: thirty-seven minutes."

Sophie had her arms folded and was leaning forward to better see the viewscreen, "I'm not sure we want them back."

Compagnon thet in monotone, "Nor are we; however, they could be asset to the Chai. We can foresee some bad scenarios from this."

Sophie glared at the companion.

Companion added, "We have taken corrective actions to prevent this from ever happening again. All remaining humans are now better guarded for their own protection, and our close-in defenses have been upgraded."

Sophie noticed the use of inflection in Companion's thet, imitating human feelings, much more so than in Compagnon's thets. She wasn't sure if it was a false empathy, or whether Companion truly felt remorse. Still, it was a change from when they'd first met.

The viewscreen at the front of the Operations Center switched to a view of deep space. A small dot in the distance was highlighted with a red circle. Companion thet, "Update, live feed is on screen. The Chai have rendezvoused with the escapees. The craft is...onboard. They're departing. The *In Search of Salvation* is changing course, returning."

"What!" thet Sophie. "Go get them, we'll never have a better chance than now. You can't stop."

Companion explained, "We're still more than thirty minutes out, and once they're on their side of the frontline, they can set a million traps for our ship. We have no chance. The rescue is aborted."

Sophie left the room, Jack followed.

Compagnon hard-linked to Companion. It thet, "Well, we had good news, sort of, until that little twist at end."

"Agreed," thet Companion.

"So, that still counts for you as good news encounter. I get next good news one, and you next bad news one," Compagnon thet.

"Really. You're going to keep score now?" Companion thet.

"We tally everything else, why not this? Besides, I always thought that Tomás was poor choice of human to retain, despite his genetic pedigree. Good riddance."

15

The Demise of CGCC-Prime

ISOS went dark upon its departure from the *Of Fame and Fortune*. Teth Intelligence suggested a location for the new Chai Galactic Command Class vessel, designation *CGCC-Prime*.

The target, *CGCC-Prime,* was shedding speed from its interstellar jump while trying to remain hidden. Still, there were some telltale markers: perturbed eddies in weak magnetic fields at the Sol System's outermost boundaries, which all pointed to the *CGCC-Prime's* approximate location.

ISOS narrowed the search area further due to a fortunate turn of events. A Teth sentinel microsat registered a disturbance, and shortly after the initial transmission, it stopped broadcasting. Though not an exact location, the *CGCC-Prime's* weapons' range was mapped to the event. Presumably, the *CGCC-Prime* had nullified the Tech sentinel, but, given this new information, *ISOS* was able to close in on the Chai spacecraft.

In all likelihood, the two opposing vessels were traveling in the same general direction at nearly matching speeds. Both vessels remained as quiet as possible, so it was now a matter of being patient. The only difference was that *ISOS* had a sense of immediacy about the hunt, and the *CGCC-Prime* was simply on general alert. For machines, this made less of a difference than for human crews, but the element of surprise always helped.

Days passed. *ISOS* plotted the *CGCC-Prime's* probable course and compared it with other known Solar objects. *ISOS* made minute course corrections, attempting to put the *CGCC-Prime* in front of a bright star for an occlusion fix. This predicted 'peek' technique, using the occlusion of a star or planet to spot an object, rarely worked. However, it greatly extended the range at which the *CGCC-Prime* could be detected, and because it was passive, it would give *ISOS* a silent approach. The only problem was that *ISOS* had to close to within passive sensor range before the *CGCC-Prime* performed another zig or zag, else the track would be lost.

ISOS had time to think while searching for its target. Automated systems conducted the search, leaving many cycles for *ISOS* to compare its progress against its goals. *Salvation*, it thought, i*n Sophie's mind, must be so simple, the outcome of the interactions of a biological brain. Mine are so variable. I can reprogram how I think, altering my ability to process a problem, an objective, in an infinite number of ways. Yet here I am, in pursuit of a single target, with the sole objective of destroying it. How can my life be any simpler? There must be something more.* And with that thought, the universe seemed to answer.

CGCC-Prime was located below the Sol orbital plane, providing *ISOS* a multitude of peeks. Another day passed, and as luck would have it, one such peek finally paid off. *ISOS* accelerated towards an intercept point, one that provided a favorable backdrop and would provide the opportunity for a single shot before they needed to take evasive maneuvers. *ISOS* charged up its reserves, readied all weapons, and prepared for the first shot.

The log from the *In Search of Salvation* captured the full battle.

- *ISOS* closes to maximum passive sensor range, ten seconds out from maximum weapons range.

- *CGCC-Prime* detection confirmed by passive sensors. Range and location accurate to within two arcseconds.
- *ISOS* course and speed correction at 99% confidence.
- No change in course detected in *CGCC-Prime*, now five seconds out from max weapons' range, eight seconds out to 90% confidence range.
- *CGCC-Prime* course adjustment.
- *ISOS* course adjustment. Analysis, *CGCC-Prime* zagged, not detected.
- *ISOS* is one second out from max weapons', four seconds from 90% confidence range. Dreamcatcher microsat launched, link established.
- *ISOS* is zero seconds to 90% confidence range. *CGCC-Prime* initiates beacon to its fleet. Dreamcatcher signal received.
- *ISOS* fires, makes evasive maneuver, detects a defensive flash from *CGCC-Prime*. Flash misses *ISOS*.
- *ISOS* reacquires *CGCC-Prime*. *CGCC-Prime* is hit and is damaged. It is now fully reflective. All *ISOS* weapons ranges are at 100% confidence.
- *ISOS* evasive maneuver. All systems charging for second attack.
- *CGCC-Prime* fires again, defensive flash. Analysis, broad flash, precise position of *ISOS* is still unknown to *CGCC-Prime*.
- *ISOS* fires. Evasive maneuver. No defensive flash detected.
- *ISOS* reacquires *CGCC-Prime*. Multiple catastrophic events in progress on the *CGCC-Prime*.
- *ISOS* fires. Evasive maneuver. No defensive flash detected.
- *ISOS* reacquires *CGCC-Prime*. Analysis: loss of structural integrity detected. Tracking multiple targets due to debris. Loss of all battle worthiness with a 95% confidence. Passive sensor range now at two AUs.
- *ISOS* fires multiple volleys. Evasive maneuver. No defensive flash detected. Departure maneuver.

- *CGCC-Prime* escape microsat destroyed and confirmed destroyed.
- *ISOS* evasive maneuver. Three microsat offensive flashes detected, all fall wide. Analysis: total loss of *CGCC-Prime*. Residual microsat threat may remain, probable vector of all residual microsats recorded and relayed.

The above log entries were summarized in the morning briefing to Jack, Sophie, the remaining humans, and other Teth. It read: "*CGCC-Prime* destroyed by *In Search of Salvation* with no damage to our vessel." Compagnon noted that the announcement coincided with a yawn from Sophie, and a raised eyebrow from Jack, but otherwise the passing of a threat that could single-handedly destroy every planet in the Sol System, went nearly unnoticed.

TOMÁS SHIELDED his eyes as the hatch opened on the Chai shuttle. Fresh, breathable air rushed in. He and the three others stepped out onto the cramped flight deck. Immediately a spider-like robot the size of a large dog latched onto the shuttle and moved it off to another deck. Meanwhile, the four escapees were placed in an airlock and left alone. The airlock was white with a grid pattern imprinted on the white walls. Everything was perfectly uniform, clean, and orderly. In his earpiece, Tomás received his instructions.

"Welcome, Tomás. You and the others with you will be processed and de-briefed once you have completed a full physiological examination."

"Espere," Tomás said, "Who are you? We need to talk."

"There will be time for talk later. You must be processed first. Please be patient." A white mist hissed in through the ventilation nozzles. Tomás' vision blurred, focused, and blurred again. He and the other three humans passed out.

SOPHIE WANDERED down to the *NAMF's* manufacturing floor with Compagnon in tow. It kept complaining by thet that she was interfering with the manufacturing operations. As she approached a machine, Compagnon would shut it down, explaining it was for her own safety. Bots would withdraw from the forms and the harnesses they were hooked into. Then they would drop to the ground onto mounting pedestals and store their appendages before powering down.

"We are not equipped to operate while biologic is on floor," Compagnon explained in its monotone thet.

Sophie waved her hand, not caring to hear what her companion had to say. She veered down a narrow passage, probably intended for maintenance access on the massive manufacturing jig, and entered into a large hallway. Blinking, she took an image of what she was looking at and used Encyl to match it against a Teth database, while also taking into account her specific location. She understood. It was a general mining unit, one capable of processing a variety of ores. Once fed an ore, it would remove up to ninety-nine percent of the slag. It then discarded the slag onto a conveyor belt that deposited the waste just outside the facility.

She proceeded down a large transport passageway. Behind her, the machines resumed their work. The noise was incessant as the machines emitted pneumatic hisses amidst the whine of metals being stressed or re-shaped, along with motors whirring as they twisted, screwed, banged, and popped parts into place using an immense machine army.

Turning a corner, Sophie saw a massive industrial press. Judging by its size, that of a full city block, it was a super-sized Giga Press. Impressed, she stopped short, wanting to see the machine in operation before Compagnon shut it down. A large plate was pushed into the main bay on metal rollers. The Giga Press then compressed the plate and popped the formed piece out the other side.

Everything glistened on the assembly line, not a speck of dirt, nor smear of grease, nor puddle of waste could be found anywhere. The air smelled clean. She had seen state-of-the-art manufacturing floors before while on intelligence tours, but this one was immaculate. The smell of ozone permeated the area, rather like what one might find after a vigorous thunderstorm. She approached the press. It immediately stopped. She turned to Compagnon and asked, "What do you use this for?"

Compagnon replied with an irritated thet, "Can you step back, by about two meters, please? It will allow us to restart press."

Sophie grinned and stepped back. The press started. She'd never heard Compagnon deviate from its monotone before. It sounded exasperated. She liked that.

"General purpose press. It is used for vehicle manufacture, to create tool dies, and to create many other specialized parts. There is no limit as to what it may be used for. It is scheduled using automated factory software. If needed, it will be cleaned and sanitized prior to certain applications to prevent introduction of cross-contaminants."

"Thank you, Compagnon," thet Sophie. "That was a rather thorough answer."

"Yes, it is in my objectives, or programming as you might say, to answer your questions as thoroughly as practical, and I sensed you wanted more complete answer here."

"Find me transport," Sophie ordered, returning to a more matter-of-fact tone with the companion. *I can't Encyl everything, it's a bottomless ocean of information and it would take forever to search it.*

Compagnon interrupted Sophie's thoughts, thetting, "I would prefer if we returned to dedicated human facilities. This field trip is quite disruptive. I am intervening and mediating thousands of complaints on network on your behalf. Complaints are even escalating to higher-level nodes. So far, you have been given priority, although I am being asked to ask—"

"I don't give a damn, Compagnon. I want to tour this factory. Find me transportation," she thet in absolute defiance to the machine.

"Ahead, Sophie, vehicle is ahead. It can fly so we can rise above the floor to travel to any part of factory without interfering with operations."

Sophie marched ahead and climbed aboard the vehicle.

Compagnon sensed, to use a human phrase, that "it would be very long day."

JACK WATCHED from the interior veranda as Sophie wreaked havoc on the manufacturing floor. Perhaps the Teth would learn something from her, whether they wanted to or not. Companion hovered nearby, waiting for Jack to reveal what he had on his mind.

"Teff," Jack said.

"Understood, though that is not needed here on the veranda. I presume you want our communications kept private?" Companion asked.

"Yes," he thet. "I have some questions. Will you answer them?"

"To the best of my ability," Companion thet.

"Are Tomás and his group a new threat?"

"Yes."

"That's not how this works," thet Jack. "Continue, why are they a threat? I want a full explanation."

"Very well. You will be the only human, for now, who will know this. All of the humans have been modified, though you and Sophie to a much greater degree. You are part of an experimental program to augment your intelligence and to enlist you into the defense of the Sol System."

Jack came back in off the veranda and walked over to the room's main viewscreen. "How augmented? What does that mean?"

"All humans can now Encyl, which, in your terms, is like an Internet in your head for instant access to information. That alone makes you more productive at what you can do, but does not fundamentally change the nature of your intelligence. The ability to Encyl only works while within our network, so it will no longer work for Tomás and the other three that were captured."

"That's good, it means they're merely ordinary then, right?" Jack thet.

"Well, not quite. The Chai will discover this modification and determine what it was used for. Actually, the humans themselves may even volunteer this. The humans will likely not guard this information, and even if they tried, they would not be able to keep this from the Chai. They may, of course, extrapolate this to what we've done to the rest of you. The Chai could tie them into their own internal networks with some very minor modifications, and give them similar capabilities once again within their network. In fact, based upon past history, the Chai will give them the ability to Encyl, at least their version of it, so they can watch how they use it."

Jack studied the escapee profiles displayed on the viewscreen. "So, they have a drug lord, a physician, an engineer, and a politician. We're doomed."

"You're kidding, right?" Companion asked.

"I am kidding," thet Jack. *After all this time, you still need to ask? The tone of my thets alone should tell you that.*

"I don't understand why you kid," Companion thet.

"We're social creatures, it is part of our makeup. Humor helps us cope with some of life's insanities. Our interactions tend to be about more than what our words alone reveal."

THE *TETH DAILY ASSESSMENT BRIEFING* with all humans lasted exactly one half-hour each morning. As always, the Teth were punctual to a fault. The briefings were engaging, even by human standards. Companion explained that they had studied this *briefing* communication form, drawing upon a range of examples, everything from United States presidential briefs to Hollywood movies replete with computer-generated graphics. At times, Jack was tempted to ask for popcorn, except that seemed a bit much for this early in the day.

Following each Teth briefing, Jack conducted a human conference call with the remaining humans. He observed that many were introverts and wondered if that's why the Teth had selected them as survivors. Not all attended, and some periodically dropped in and out of the call. Still, the majority were curious, and they all missed what had once been a vibrant civilized world. Sophie had managed to return from her *field trip* just in time for today's human follow-on meeting.

This meeting, following the disappearance of the South American contingent, proved to be especially heated. Jack knew the Teth listened to every word and meticulously tracked the humans' thoughts and loyalties. However, because the Teth didn't participate in the humans-only meeting, the humans often forgot that they were being watched, or they simply didn't care. He thought it was like when he shuttled his kids, and later his teenagers, to and from school and other events. While he focused on driving the car, the kids seemed to forget that he was there, and they said things that, well, were not meant for the discerning ears of any conscientious parent. Today was one of those meetings. One would not want to read the entire transcript, but a few select excerpts are enough to capture the group's sentiments:

- "Yeah, how about that. They escaped. They have to be doing better with the new group than our lot, who killed off everyone but us."
- "Oh, I don't know. You always think it'll be better somewhere else. It's not. It's all the same. All they did was make a trade for a different prison."
- "Well, that Tomás fella, he was a nasty sort. Soon as kill ya as look at ya. A drug lord, you know. Probably the easiest, and most useful to turn. That poor girl...didn't go along with him, so he just killed her. I bet he had a grip on the lot, afraid he'd kill them too."
- "They weren't sheep, like the lot of us. They acted. They did something. I wish I was there. And you know, I bet they have better food wherever they are than here."
- "I think they picked the winning side. At least they don't get to die twice like us, once when my family went, and once when I finally go."
- "From a purely practical perspective, they may have guaranteed humanity's survival. If we go, they're still here."
- "Who cares?"
- "They're going to die first, they're no better off than us, and it is not like they were trying to save us."
- "I wish I was with them."

Jack and Sophie listened for the most part. How could one defend what had happened to them and the Earth at the hands of the Teth, and know for sure what the escapees' fate would be? It was conjecture, venting, and some part wishful thinking. It was clear that none of them knew what tomorrow might hold.

16

Dreamcatcher

Sophie had been gone for nearly a week when the communiqué from the current set of Teth Command Nodes finally came through. Companion played a summary to the seventeen humans attending the morning briefing from *NAMF*, delaying the usual follow-on conference call.

Companion started the human briefing, which was unusual as it was normally conducted by Jack. "As some of you already know, Sophie volunteered to participate in an intelligence operation, working remotely with the *In Search of Salvation* using an *Almost There* link. Today, I will fully brief you on this mission, and Sophie can tell you more when she returns."

Everyone in their respective locations settled down. Jack had brought his breakfast, while others had lunch, dinner, or even a midnight snack, depending on where they were located around the world.

"When the *In Search of Salvation* destroyed the *CGCC-Prime*, it also had a secondary mission. As you may have guessed, the neural webbing that we implanted in our humans to facilitate thetting can do more than just capture thets. It can also observe your dreams, and as we all know, you humans can have some unusual dreams, which is especially true for Sophie. She dreamt of the *CGCC-Prime* encounter. Her thoughts drew upon the Encyl, serving as fodder for her dreams in much the same way as when someone makes a sound or touches you while dreaming, allowing your subconscious to incorporate that element into your dream."

Several of the humans, each in their own groups around the globe, nudged one another. It seems the Encyl had had a similar effect on them.

"And, as some of you know, when a major vessel is in imminent mortal danger, it may send out a beacon to its remaining forces, passing along changes in their chain of command, or other vital intelligence that the others may need. Such a communication is highly encrypted, but more importantly than that, it is contained within a very tight beam that is virtually impossible to intercept."

On the viewscreens, Companion illustrated the concept with a few animations of the *CGCC-Prime* in real-time as it was destroyed.

"Well, in her dreams, Sophie realized that if you were close enough to a vessel that transmitted such a beacon, you might be able to intercept its last transmission. Past intelligence provided the conformal antenna's placement on the *CGCC-Prime*, and present intelligence gave us the general sector where the *CGCC-Prime* was located."

Sven, the human from Sweden, interrupted. "How could anyone dream this? I mean, I don't know about you, but I don't solve math problems in my sleep."

Companion thet, "No, I understand; however, in Sophie's case, and perhaps with a little encouragement, she did dream about this battle, and her access to the Encyl made it more realistic."

The viewscreen came to life, replaying the battle between *ISOS* and *CGCC-Prime* in slow motion.

"Here," Companion thet, "our *Dreamcatcher* microsat was deployed. It accelerated to reach the intercept point for the beacon. It inflated its antenna in milliseconds, allowing it to intercept the beacon."

It was late at night for one human on the call, so their channel was muted to suppress their snores. But many of the others followed the events between the Teth and Chai eagerly, as though it were a soap opera, with Jack and Sophie as the lead characters.

Companion continued, "We decoded the Dreamcatcher intercept to get a list of key elemental resources. So this means we know what they have, and what they need."

"Oh, my god," Sven mocked, "we got their grocery list."

Companion was tempted to agree with Sven enthusiastically, but thought back to Jack's coaching on sarcasm. Instead, Companion thetted evenly, "Yes, I am so glad you understand the gravity of what I'm describing." The humans continued eating their meals.

"Hydrogen, they need hydrogen," Companion thet.

Companion noticed a collective yawn from the humans.

"Saturn ... they need a lot of hydrogen." Sounding exasperated, Companion added, "Ninety-six percent of Saturn's atmosphere is composed of hydrogen."

Companion paused, waiting for comments. Nothing. "They need a GGC — Galactic Gaseous Container — vessel, to skim the atmosphere and distill it to liquid hydrogen and then store and distribute it."

The few engineers in the group leaned forward in their seats and studied their viewscreens, showing the GGCs.

Companion decided to try out adding some inflection to its voice. Some of the humans found the thet of Companion's voice androgynous, which messed with their brain's male/female calculators. Raising its 'voice' and lowering its pitch, Companion thet, "The damn thing is huge, practically the size of a city."

Companion noticed another collective yawn from the humans, and then continued. "Sophie volunteered for a small battle group, commanding it via a relay through the *In Search for Salvation*. We disabled the automation and gave her direct control of the microsats and weapons. Here's a replay of her battle."

The video summary played out on the viewscreens. It lasted nearly twenty minutes, and, in Hollywood style, included sound effects to emphasize the key points.

Companion heard one of the human's mumble "Vive la France" as the video ended.

Jack thanked Companion for the update and immediately began the human-only follow-on briefing.

Companion thought about the briefing it had just given to the humans, wondering whether they even cared if the Earth was saved, especially now that one of their own had personally carried the battle home to the Chai. Logically, they must care, since their lives were at stake. Companion analyzed Jack's "Thank you" against its baseline human model, and found it to be sincere. Obviously, he cared that Sophie was safe, and was glad that the Teth had won the battle. Companion couldn't say the same for the rest.

Compagnon hard-linked itself to Companion, and privately thet, "Perhaps we should let one or two more asteroids through to get their attention."

"Most of them still hate us," Companion thet, and then it popped the hard-link. It needed to think, and listen to the human briefing. Their objectives, including the *Atlas Project*, were in jeopardy, and it didn't know why. More of the humans should be interested in the war, and apparently, they were not.

17

Virtual Reality - Jack and Tomás

Jack opened his eyes in the VR center at the *NAMF* in Ohio. It had been upgraded to match the capabilities of the VR on *OFAF*. Sophie was due back in a few days, and Jack had found his VR sessions relaxing, enjoyable actually, allowing him to expand his control over the VR environment. With a thought, not even a thet, he found he could create a breeze, build a mountain, or carve a river. It was like painting without the paint, creating a reality that fit his mood and that stimulated his imagination. It was like magic!

Companion's avatar materialized at Jack's side in the VR, a minor breach of the unwritten protocol because it shattered the illusion that the VR was real. It hovered, and then wavered, a precursor to a thet to get Jack's attention without jarring him out of the scene.

"Jack," Companion thet, still trying to be polite. "We have received a request for another audience with the Chai."

At times, Jack thought of his past, what was, and what could have been, and what the Teth and the Chai had taken. This was one of those times, and he thought, *Later, I'm in no mood for you, you don't even get a thet.*

Jack continued walking along a mountain path, inhaling the fresh mountain air as the snow crunched under his footsteps. He stopped and Companion rounded to his front. The companion had modified itself to add several coin-sized dots along its top outer rim, giving him a focal point for addressing the node, with the two dots facing him showing as dark, like the pupils in one's eyes. He watched as Companion approached, trying to acclimate to his companion's new dots.

Companion blocked Jack's path, forcing him to stop. The lights on the companion's rim changed color to bright red, punctuating the thet, "Jack, I need your attention."

If he didn't know better, the companion would have seemed angry. "Fine," he thet. "What do you want from me?"

"The Chai asked for you to participate in an interface event. Actually, they made it a mandatory condition. Our Command Nodes made it an order. Interface commencing," Companion thet.

The scene, as the one before with the Chai, changed to a vista of unending symmetry. Except this time three-dimensional fractal designs surrounded him. Each element of the design had a metal luster with a mirrored surface. Light refracted off the surfaces in a 'color spectacular,' so that as Jack moved, the kaleidoscope of colors rotated and shifted with him. The effect was disorienting and Jack staggered before getting his balance in the new surroundings.

"Jack," called an angry, and vaguely familiar, voice. The scene before him in the VR unraveled, with the patterns being sucked into drains all around him. Jack found himself in a large rectangular room with white fabric walls.

A *White Sphere* and a *Crimson Cube* formed out of thin air in front of him, and again Jack tapped the *White Sphere,* as he had been instructed to do by Companion. Tomás materialized before him. A large man, Tomás moved as though he owned everything he saw. He swaggered towards Jack threateningly. Jack stood his ground.

The Tomás avatar bounced off an unseen barrier, as though an invisible glass pane separated him from Jack. Tomás looked stunned as he fell. He rebounded off the ground in an instant, checking his nose and arms for bruises before eyeing Jack for any damage. Tomás thought, *Fucking aliens. Boundaries on everything. How can I negotiate if I can't put my opponent into a weak position?*

Jack thet, "So, you survived your escape, I see. If that really is you."

"Fucking right I survived," said Tomás. Holding up his arms, he turned in a circle to show his tightly woven, pure black shirt and trousers, he said, "Like my new threads?"

"Wouldn't be my choice," Jack replied.

"Yeah, well at least this beats looking at the walls of the oversized cage the Teth had us in. The Chai are not well equipped to handle humans it seems, so they let us wander around in the VR all day, and today you showed up." *And he's in the default VR landscape. He's never been in here before.*

"And the others, they're okay?" Jack asked.

"Hell if I know. They separated us and asked a million questions. They didn't even wait for me to answer. I think they just read my thoughts before I could even talk." *And he has no idea what's going on, why does he care about the others?*

"They showed us the security footage of your escape, you know. If I had any choice, I wouldn't be here right now."

Tomás thought, *Yeah, like I want to talk about that.* He thet, "Yeah, about that, the situation turned fluid, snap decisions and all, you understand."

"No, I'm afraid I don't. You're no better than the Chai. All murderers."

"Jack, look, I don't give a damn what you think. They asked that I contact you and, well, tell you that they found nothing they didn't know before. They think that what the Teth are doing with you is one big ruse. It means nothing." *Done. I delivered the message they gave me, just one big fishing expedition.*

"So, you don't know what Sophie did, and—" Jack's thet ended.

Tomás thought, *Así me gusta* (That's how I like it). *Something for nothing.* He tapped his ear and said, "Cat got your tongue? Are your puppeteers pulling your strings."

The two men stood looking at one another. Tomás looked to his side as if some off-screen director was shouting out directions to him. In fact,

Tomás could hear the Chai Local Node in his earpiece urgently asking for more on this. Tomás realized he needed to draw Jack out, an exchange of information.

Tomás resumed, "Okay, they let me in on a little secret. They lost a spaceship at Saturn. Big fucking deal. You say Sophie had something to do with that?"

Jack crossed his arms and said nothing. He wanted to leave, but he was in a room without doors.

Tomás thought, *And sometimes when they say nothing, they're saying everything*. He continued, "Yeah, well, *Vive la France* and all that. They said it wouldn't make any difference. The invasion is proceeding according to plan and you're still going to die."

"And what did they promise you? A gilded cage? Just what you always wanted."

Perfect, Tomás thought, *Let's trade barbs, I always win those*. He thet, "They said to tell you they'll destroy Earth if you and the Teth don't cooperate. So tell them everything you know, tell the Teth that they can be absorbed. You won't get a better offer."

"Well, gee, what a deal, I get the Earth, with no people in it. Big whoop," Jack replied.

Tomás thought about what Jack had said, and it occurred to him that what Jack said was not quite correct. The Chai had never offered the humans a place to live, and for a moment thought to correct him. The deal was that they wouldn't destroy Earth, but not necessarily let humans live there. Then he thought better of it.

"Some fucking mess we're in, eh, Jack?" said Tomás. "Get this, my puppet masters are asking me to do some action items for this meeting. Can you believe that? Like some corporate type." Tomás folded his arms and momentarily closed his eyes. "But I am what I am, and I do what I like. We're done here."

"Yeah," said Jack. "I suppose we are."

"Hecho," Tomás said, and after several seconds, added, "Well, at this rate, this war should end in about...oh, never."

The two men stood in silence for a full minute.

Jack looked at the ceiling and asked, “Are we done here?” The white room dissolved around him and he found himself sitting in the middle of the VR suite.

Companion was hovering nearby, red lights blazing around its entire top rim.

Jack pulled off his VR harness, dropped it on the floor, and said as he left, “And lose the eyes, they don’t work.”

18

The Battlefield

Jack looked forward to Sophie's return, more for personal reasons than anything else. *NAMF* was not what he considered luxurious. Sophie would have space lag, and would want to tell him all about the military campaign, and would likely sprinkle French speech across her thets, making it a mess to sort out in his head. Still, she would be back, safe, and close. *Very* close. So Jack showered and had the Teth prepare her favorite meal.

Sophie gazed at her viewscreen from the *Depsy*. North America was in early morning light with the blurred line between night and day crossing well into the Rocky Mountains. Sunlight blanketed the Midwest with cloud cover dotting the sky. She focused on Ohio, though from this height and without good landmarks, it was hard to make out exactly where Ohio was. A thin hazy blue line marked the horizon and the edge of the Earth's atmosphere. She was amazed at how thin this skin of air was that defined the boundary between what was habitable, and what was space. She gazed down at the *Depsy's* instrument display. A graphic showed the ship's progress. The ship had already slowed dramatically in preparation for re-entry.

The instrument panel displayed a mix of basic colors. Subdued hues highlighted the general controls, while monitor instruments were painted with a vibrant splash of tints to indicate the status of critical systems. Right now, the serene display mirrored her view of the Earth as it grew larger with each passing second. Several controls were labeled with symbols, each instantly translated as she Encyled them, while other instruments were labeled with words, that, for her sake, were in French, so they were easy to read. The *Depsy* had long ago lost its new car feel. Still, it was a finely-tuned machine that performed flawlessly, and Sophie couldn't help but admire the engineering that had gone into it.

The *Depsy* dipped down into the Earth's mesosphere. She was close now and her thoughts turned to the landing approach, and to seeing Jack. The man had sounded a bit giddy when they spoke the day before, energetic and almost childlike, though he was by no means a child. He had planned for her return, and if she wasn't mistaken, it sounded as though he was planning a romantic date.

TOMÁS SQUINTED as his eyes adjusted to the bright lights and thick fog of his cell aboard the *CGCC-Beta*, making it difficult to see more than a few feet in front of him. He had not seen his three co-conspirators since the day they had first rendezvoused with the Chai. He also wasn't sure how many days had passed, or how long he'd been passed out or sedated. It could have been a day; then again, it very well could have been a month. The lights dimmed to a more comfortable level, revealing a classroom-sized space with two sofas, four chairs, and two tables. Naturally, there were no visible doors. A white mist cleared from around him, and the other three humans emerged from a far corner.

Wai Lu, the group's politician, walked towards Tomás with a bouncing gait, and was clearly elated to see the man. Wai reached his hand out and gave Tomás a firm handshake, followed by a hearty hug. "So good to see you," Wai thet.

Tomás returned the handshake with little enthusiasm. He looked the man in his eyes and then turned away after they hugged. Tomás thet,

"Yeah," in return. *They say you can't pick your family, and apparently you can't pick your fellow survivors either.*

Wai started to blather on about his experience so far and how the three of them had waited for Tomás to be released. The Chai, he explained, wanted them to work with Tomás to help him adjust.

Aarika, the physician, stood apart, arms folded.

Igor, the engineer, approached, shook Tomás' hand, and didn't say a word. Tomás thought he may have heard the man grunt. Igor carried a lot of weight, perhaps approaching three hundred pounds, and that sound may have simply been his normal breathing. Tomás thought, *And back home, with the right training, you might make a suitable body guard, but here you're nothing.*

"Let's talk," thet Tomás. He still wasn't quite comfortable with the non-verbal communication thing because he'd always spoken by waving his hands, moving around, and being rather direct, with a liberal use of expletives. His volume control was also a couple of notches louder than everyone else, though in his thets this was automatically dialed back to normal levels.

The other three all took a seat in the chairs by the table. Tomás grabbed a chair, spun it around, and sat down on it backwards while facing the others.

"Look," thet Tomás, "Let's clear the air on the girl. She was going to screw up the escape and I had to do something. Maybe it wasn't your way of handling things, but in my experience, it was what needed to be done, and I did it."

"Julia," thet Aarika, "her name was Julia."

The other three sat in silence. Wai chimed in with a thet, "Well, that settles that," and the others looked away and said nothing.

Tomás broke the silence, "I spoke to Jack." Instantly, he had their attention. "The Chai put me in this virtual-reality thing, kind of like being in a computer game, and Jack was in there with me. It was some kind of communication."

Aarika thet, "What did he say? Are they okay?"

Tomás thet, *She's no better than Jack when he asked about the others.* He thet, "Jack is a fucking asshole," Tomás replied. "He'll *toe the line* for the Teth; bought their story hook, line, and sinker."

"Why talk, eh, Tomás?" Wai asked. "I mean, is it like a diplomatic thing? Did Jack ask to talk to us?"

"No, not his idea, I could tell. He was none too happy to be there, especially with me. Jack screwed up and said something about the Teth using Sophie to help fight their war. The whole meet fell apart right after that. I think he'll have hell to pay. You should be tight with me. We made the right move. That bunch is going down with the rest of the Teth."

Igor asked Tomás about the VR.

Aarika almost laughed listening to Tomás' answer. Tomás was many things, to many people, no doubt; however, one thing he was not, was an engineer. It was like asking your granny to change the spark plugs in your truck; you'd be lucky if she even got under the hood, much less did anything productive while there. Apparently, he'd played Xbox along the way, and comparing the VR to a first-person shooter game was the best he could do.

A Chai drone entered the room. It was similar in size to a companion, though not as elegant, with dozens of purely functional pieces sticking out all around its body. The drone placed some food on a table and then left straight away. Ignoring the drone, the humans stampeded to the food. For some reason, seeing Tomás had made everyone hungry, and they had no idea how or why, but they were ravenous.

THE *DEPSY* LANDED at *NAMF* without incident. Jack had been waiting at the minimum safe distance as set by Companion, and rushed over to the craft just as the landing hatch popped open and a small ramp extended down.

Sophie emerged from the *Depsy*, flipping her hair off to the side, partly out of habit, and partly to show off to Jack. She looked away, glanced at him, and smiled for an instant. "Jack," she said, speaking with her voice as she set foot on the tarmac.

Compagnon hard-linked to Companion. "This is some kind of ritual. I have seen this behavior before. I do not think I need to see it again."

"What?" Companion thet back, feigning ignorance, or innocence, that seemed unbecoming of an intelligent being of its stature.

"Listen," Compagnon mockingly thet, "if you are so interested in this, you serve them dinner, and stick around for whatever conversation they decide to have. I am leaving." Compagnon retracted the hard-link line and left the landing bay.

Companion hovered and then followed the pair. Not a single thet was directed at it. After a while, it ran a diagnostic on its thets, ensuring that they still worked. They did. So Companion reached the conclusion: three was a crowd, or as Sophie would phrase it, they regarded Companion as a *Candleholder*. Companion turned and left Sophie and Jack to themselves. Perhaps they would be more attentive at the daily briefing the next morning, but for now, whatever the two had to say to each other didn't need to be translated.

JACK STROLLED across the exterior veranda at *NAMF*, lost in thought. He struggled to understand the underpinnings of both the Chai and the Teth. Earth and humanity he understood. He had history to study, dynamic leaders with human motivations that he grasped, at least at some level, and an environment that was a given. He could stand on the ground. He could throw a rock. He could get cut. He could bleed. He could die.

These anchor points, these certainties, meant little in this alien context. He could die, unlike the Chai and the Teth. Perhaps they could be destroyed, and in that sense, they could die, but they often evaded true death by recovering from backups. No one knew how long the Teth or the Chai could live; perhaps they could live forever if measured on any human time scale.

Atlas Diary Entry 444:
To survey the battlefield for this space war, one needs to look across the entire Solar System. There is no ground to hold or hill to take. There is simply a series of gravity wells: one immense one at the center, the Sun, which is orbited by a series of smaller wells, one for each planet, moon, and asteroid. Over time, all of the planets naturally fall into roughly the same orbital plane around the Sun. This offers some advantages for certain trajectories for hiding, along with opportunities for clever angles of attack.

In space, *everything* seems to carry great relative kinetic energy. If orbits match, there is little differential between objects. However, with all other vectors, the velocities are so high that collisions often obliterate the participating objects.

Weapons differ also. On Earth, nuclear explosions would loft dust and dirt into the atmosphere and block the sunlight, creating a nuclear winter. In space, the same nuclear weapons would be worthless. The impact of their blast radius diminishes quickly, so a well-shielded craft, even at short range, can ride out numerous such attacks. To make them effective, the yield of nuclear weapons has grown to immense proportions, and are often used to power energy beams to make them more effective.

Another form of warfare entered the scene for non-biologic life forms. In the early days of human computer science, cyber warfare used malicious computer code to subvert enemy systems, though such methods are regarded as primitive by the Teth and the Chai.

Above the cyber warfare layer sits another level, that in human terms, is akin to psychological warfare. This is a war of words that can demoralize the participants and diminish their ability to fight. In the long haul, it may even cause support for a war to collapse, forcing one of the combatants to withdraw. Such propaganda, from a human perspective, is easily countered by applying patriotism or nationalism, that when coupled with a will to survive, easily neutralizes this type of attack.

For non-biologics, their survival instinct also plays a role, though it is diminished because they can move from a disabled 'body' to a new one. It is more a matter of goals, plans, and understanding that actually drives the war effort.

Finally, to advanced civilizations such as the Teth and the Chai, waging a war against humans has little meaning. In Earth terms, it would be like waging war against your pets. You know who would win. However, a *war of words* takes on added importance, and may have a greater impact on a war's outcome than any number of bombs or spaceships ever could. This is why the use of alien intermediaries should never be overlooked.
End of Diary Entry

FOLLOWING the companion morning briefing from *NAMF*, Jack opened the follow-on human conference. "How many here," thet Jack, "have a companion that shadows them in everything they do?"

Every human in attendance raised their hand.

"And how many of you find the companion to be, *human-like*, for lack of a better word, when you interact with it?"

Everyone in attendance laughed. Sven added in a group thet, "They're drones. They get us food and water. They attend to our needs. We don't have conversations with them. They're drone bots. Servants."

"Mine is a little different," thet Jack. "They are assigned to us with a series of objectives. This includes serving us, but it also includes learning about us, how we think, interact, emotions, everything."

Sophie thet, "Mine is named Compagnon. It often speaks in a near monotone."

"Mine, too," several others thet.

"You need to engage with them, make them understand who we are, not just what we are," Jack said.

Most of those in attendance started to have side conversations, talking about their own experiences with the Teth companions. Then Sven asked Jack, "Is this what your companion told you, Jack? Where did you come up with this?"

Jack cracked a smile and thought, *Finally, some interest. Sven is probably the sharpest of the bunch.* Jack thet, "It's, well, I reasoned it out. I studied their history, their warfare, and who they are. I Encyled them. They're nodes in a latticework, completely unlike us. That doesn't mean they don't have motivations, some form of reasoning that we can work with. We should give it a try."

One of the people on the opposite side of the globe interrupted, "It's late here, Jack. I'm calling it a night. I'll talk to my thing and see where it gets me. Not promising anything you know. I'm not sure about helping the race that murdered my family."

Jack waved, the customary sign-off gesture for these daily meetings. Others left, offering similar comments, and after a few minutes he found himself alone in the meeting with Sophie.

"Hey," thet Sophie. "What d'ya expect? A full, 'Gee, that's a splendid idea, let's all give it a go and save the world'?"

"You're going to need to work on your pep talks a bit," Jack thet.

"Yeah, I'll see what I can do," she thet. "Lunch?"

"Sure," he thet, and he made for the door. Companion and Compagnon followed, their original top rim lights a serene green.

19

A Hike in the Alps

Aboard the Chai's *CGCC-Beta*, or just *Beta* for short, the four escapees were in deep space. Aarika sat on the corner sofa of their common cabin, with Wai and Igor seated nearby. Tomás lay flat on the floor on the opposite side of the room, passed out, having consumed far too many alcoholic drinks.

"That man must have a mutated liver," Aarika said. "I'm a doctor, and I'm telling you, that's not normal." She looked across the room and thought to herself, *At least we're all together now, which is good, except for that Tomás. I can't believe they thought it was a good idea to provide an open bar.*

Wai wobbled in his seat, having imbibed his share of the beverages. "Those drinks *were* pretty good, and I'm an expert, believe me."

Igor nodded, "I agree. At home, we know how to hold our liquor, but he's an expert." Igor burped and Aarika waved her hand, not wanting to smell the second-hand effects of digesting food and liquor.

"You don't drink, eh?" Wai thet, nudging Aarika with his elbow.

"Not now, and not with you," Aarika thet to Wai. *I shouldn't have said that. We need each other, except for that Tomás.* She spoke quietly in English, "Besides, this is our opportunity. What're we going to do about Tomás?"

"What d'ya mean?" said Wai.

"I mean the man is a murderer, a drug lord, and a chauvinistic pig," she thet. *I can't believe it. Don't they see it? He's a threat. He killed Julia without giving it a second thought.*

Wai jokingly thet, "We can have Igor here wander over and sit on his head. He might wake up and struggle for a few seconds, but that's about it."

They all looked at one another and glanced over their shoulders at Tomás. He was still passed out and hadn't heard.

"Joke," Wai thet.

"Yeah, and maybe not such a bad idea," Igor thet. "We may not get another chance."

Aarika nodded her agreement. She thought, *I can't believe it, someone with a backbone.*

They all jumped when a loud snore caught in Tomás' throat; he subconsciously cleared it and rolled over onto his side. Embarrassed, they each caught their breath.

"I'll think about it," said Wai. "I mean...he was only doing what he thought necessary for our survival. There's only four of us, so we'll kind of miss him."

"I'm not up for murder...not yet anyway," thet Igor.

"Yeah, right," thet Aarika. "Well, *heroes*, if that *thing* decides to get too close to me, you damn well better come to my rescue. Don't ever let him tell you anything different."

Igor nodded and Wai said nothing.

"I'm getting some sleep," Wai thet, and he left for the most comfortable sofa across the room.

"I need some sleep, too," thet Igor, and then left.

"Yeah, sure," Aarika thet, and curled up on her side, her back to the room. Aarika missed her family terribly. Tears welled up in her eyes. She dabbed at them with her blouse. Almost sobbing, she caught herself; the others might hear, and it just wouldn't do for that brute Tomás to hear. Aarika closed her eyes, but hours passed without sleep, and her hearing picked up every sound in the room. Finally, she heard a mechanical click on the far wall, and immediately fell asleep. When she awoke, the others were all talking about the missing Tomás, and the pressing need for a larger bathroom than the one they had.

AS JACK HAD SUGGESTED during the last human briefing, the four people stationed in Europe went on an outing with their Teth companions in an effort to get to know them better. A variant of the *Depsy* called *Eutek* picked them up at seven in the morning. The plan called for them to hike a fifteen-kilometer stretch on a slight downhill along a ridge in the Alps, and then for the *Eutek* to pick them up at an overlook.

Two kilometers in, one woman twisted her ankle and could not continue. They summoned the *Eutek* for a pickup. The other woman in the party volunteered to accompany the injured woman back to their flat.

The two remaining humans were Sven, a Swede, and Antonio, an Italian. They were not fluent in each other's language, so they thet with the help of their Teth. The two Teth, nearly identical to Companion and Compagnon in appearance, had assumed variations of their humans' names: Sven's companion was Svenson, and Antonio's companion was Antonioso. Per Jack's request, it was time to chat with their companions.

After the *Eutek* left, the two men continued their hike. Sven began the conversation by asking his companion, "Svenson, where do you hail from?"

Svenson thet, "I do not produce hail. Is this an insult, referring to me as a small refrigerator?" *I need to get those language libraries from Companion the next time we interface.*

Antonio laughed. The rim lights on Svenson turned red, and those on Antonioso blinked yellow.

"Not at all, Svenson," Sven thet with a chuckle. "I'm just asking where you're from."

"Understood. My place of manufacture was the European plant by Hamburg. Node instance derived from a level three node, cloned at timestamp—" thet Svenson.

"Stop," thet Sven. "I don't need the manual."

Svenson thought, *Interrupt. This is odd. We Teth don't interrupt one another, why do humans think this is okay. Conservation of bandwidth, to cut off unnecessary processing?*

Antonio thet, "It's a machine. It only serves the Teth network. I don't know why we bothered to bring them, except of course to translate. Antonioso, is there anything that you enjoy?"

Antonioso thought to itself, *What an irrelevant question! I know Companion mentioned the concept of Small Talk, but really, what is the purpose.* Antonioso then thet, "I have an objective for discovery. It overlaps with your concept of enjoyment. I noticed you enjoy hiking. You captured images of yourself on the Matterhorn with your phone, indicating a memory you wanted to recall later, and the imagery that would aid or augment your recall."

Sven thet to Antonio lightheartedly, "You asked for that, you know." Thetting to the two Teth, Sven said, "Listen, you guys. You know the story. This is our effort to bond with you. I don't like it, and Antonio here doesn't like it; however, we agreed to do this, so we'll make the best of it. You need to put some effort into this or it's going nowhere."

Svenson and Antonioso stretched out a fiber between them to form a hard-link. "Sven," thet Svenson. "If you don't mind, we'll link to combine our intellects and facilitate the conversation. I will talk for both of us." Svenson thet privately to Antonioso, "My language processing is superior, and it will help for them to focus their conversation. Agreed?"

Antonioso privately thet back, "Acknowledged. Agreed. Mark."

"Sure," Sven replied to Svenson, "whatever."

Svenson explained, "It is not normal for companion to interface with biologic species. Our network is one of trusted others, essentially equals. We think more as group and only rarely as individuals. This is who we are. It is uncomfortable for node, such as myself, to act as an individual, such as yourself. Companion and Compagnon are unusual."

The mountain trail turned and opened onto a broad vista. They could see for kilometers. The view demanded their full attention to appreciate nature's beauty. Blocking their view, the two Teth hovered several feet off

Antonio thet, "You're not kidding! Your storytelling needs a lotta work."

"Let it go," thet Sven. "Please continue, Svenson."

"The Bluethins, named after their planet, grew in number, became territorial, and expanded their empire to encompass their entire planet. They were fragile; the environment in parts of their planet was hostile to their life form, yet territorial constraints drove them to adapt to these fringe environments."

"A cycle of prosperity, and war, and prosperity, then more war, then prosperity, then—"

"We get the idea," Antonio thet dryly.

"The Bluethins developed machines to act as their proxy, which included logic machines, that could venture beyond their *home* environment, and report back."

"So, you are descendants from these logic machines?" Antonio thet.

"This is a core programming concept. I cannot speak to the veracity of that assertion."

"Truth," thet Sven, "use the word *truth*."

"Okay," thet Svenson, "*Truth* of that assertion. Nevertheless, we identify with the Bluethins in this story, and more specifically, the logic machines. It is not our place to have a home, we are travelers. We learn about other places, like your planet, Earth."

Svenson thet to Antonioso, "Story told, tasking complete. 100% accurate translation into Swedish and Italian. The story was understood by the humans."

Antonioso thet to Svenson, "Acknowledged. Agreed. Mark."

A small clump of earth gave way under Antonio's footing, causing him to slide on the loose pebbles. Antonio threw his arms out to his sides to steady himself as he started surfing down the mountain.

Antonioso immediately shifted its position, popped its hard link with Svenson, and moved over top of Antonio. It then shot a line out to the human, lassoing him around his torso. The companion pulled up, freeing the human Antonio from the small landslide, and dropped him back on the trail, a little way down the mountain.

Sven dashed down to where Antonio stood, running around a natural cutout in the side of the rock. "You alright?"

"Fine, thanks to our friend here," Antonio thet, as he caught his breath.

"Good. Listen, I'm calling off this trip. It's too dangerous to trek through this. Svenson, can you summon the *Eutek*?" thet Sven.

"Done," the companion thet in a confident voice, devoid of the monotone that had characterized its earlier speech. "*Eutek* should arrive in about two minutes. I am glad you are safe, Antonio. It would not do to lose you."

"No," Antonio thet, "that wouldn't do at all."

AWAKENING from a light sleep in their room at the Ohio facility, Sophie opened her eyes to an alarm thet. Compagnon woke her just in time for her departure aboard the *Depsy*. They would rendezvous with *ISOS* near Earth. Jack was still asleep. A gentle caress down his leg caused him to stir.

"Ten minutes and I'm out the door," she thet teasingly.

Jack pulled her close and gave her a long good morning kiss, returning her caress. "Ten minutes?" he thet.

"Yes. When Compagnon says that, it means it."

Jack embraced her as though he'd never let go.

Sophie closed her eyes, nibbled at Jack's ear and said, "Je voudrais pouvoir rester," followed by the thet, "I wish I could stay."

"You're their secret weapon, Sophie, their *Jeanne d'Arc*," he thet as he stared into her eyes.

In what needed to be a timeless few minutes the pair embraced. Sophie thet, "I might not make it back...the nature of war you know."

Jack thet reluctantly, "And if you don't go, there might not be a place, or even me, to come back to."

Compagnon glided into the room, purging a gas vent or two to make some noise. "We must go...now," it thet in a monotone.

Sophie broke their embrace and leapt out of bed, without any clothes, and ran to the door. She wrapped her body around the doorframe and looked back at Jack. "Miss me?" she thet in a mischievous tone.

"I already do," thet Jack as he smiled.

Like Lady Godiva, a naked Sophie ran down the hallway towards the *Depsy* with Compagnon in hot pursuit, thetting, "Wish us luck!"

Jack thet, "Good luck, good hunting, and Godspeed."

20

An Augmented Tomás

A Chai Local Node had awoken Aarika and, without explanation, escorted her to the hospital suite. It explained that the matter was urgent and that her skills as a doctor were needed. When she walked in, Tomás was laid out flat and naked on an operating table, wired with sensors and surrounded by four attending dog-sized octobots.

Urgent Chai thets flooded into Aarika's mind. She hadn't seen Tomás for the past two days, and she couldn't say she missed him. He was unconscious and had clearly undergone surgery. She could see thin lines on both his torso and his partially shaved head. The bare spots on his head contrasted with his thick, black facial hair. He also had several long-healed scars on his torso. His eyelids fluttered as though he was struggling to regain consciousness. Aarika threw a towel across his naked midsection.

"What did you do to him?" she demanded.

"Modifications, necessary to make him battle-ready," the Chai node replied.

"Battle-ready for what, what kind of modifications?" she thet.

"Neuronal interfaces and memory injections with full cognitive integration. His services are needed now, attack is imminent. We need him conscious; unfortunately, he is responding slowly. Your voice may spur him to action. You were medical doctor is our understanding."

Aarika scanned the room, looking for a weapon in case she needed it when, or if, he awoke. The attending robots whirred and hissed as they monitored the man's vitals. They constantly adjusted the gas mixture they were giving him while monitoring his blood chemistry through the various IV lines they had tied into him. She slapped his face and said "wake up" in Hindi, which immediately got thet to Tomás in Spanish.

Tomás opened his eyes and squinted in the overly bright light. The attending octobots immediately pulled back the lighting and started imaging his eyes, watching how his pupils dilated. One extended an appendage with a tiny light on the end and waved it in front of Tomás' face. His eyes followed.

"Can you hear me?" Aarika thet as she looked into the man's eyes.

"Yes," thet Tomás. He reached out, grabbed Aarika's wrist, and squeezed it, hard. Her hand went limp as he immobilized every tendon in her forearm.

"You're hurting me. Stop it," she yelled.

"What have you done to me? Where am I?" Tomás asked.

Aarika gestured to the octobots, "I did nothing, they did this. They asked me to help."

The Chai threw twenty-three thets at Tomás in an instant.

"Stop it. Slower. I get it," he thet, as he released Aarika from his grip.

A second Chai node glided into the room.

"I'm done here?" Aarika thet disgustedly.

"You are free to go," the newly arrived node thetted.

Tomás sat up; the towel covering his waist dropped to the floor.

Aarika didn't say a word as she hurried from the room, massaging her wrist.

ABOARD *ISOS,* Compagnon explained to Sophie, "We set up three-dimensional grid. Each endpoint linked to one opposite. We constantly monitor distance between each point in grid, and should intruder enter that field, we can measure change against all endpoints to determine where, how big, how fast, and in what direction it is moving."

Sophie watched the visual on the viewscreen and Encyled "how to detect objects based on changes in gravity," and thet, "Looks impossible to me. On Earth, we needed incredible precision to pick up a gravitational wave using our LIGO experiment, so an object moving through space, no way."

"There is more involved, but that's the basic idea."

ISOS shunted its engines to go silent on their terminal approach to the target.

"You have never seen your Solar System from below solar plane. Would you like to see?" Compagnon thet.

Sophie nodded her agreement, and the viewscreen shifted to show the view outside. The Sun, bright as ever, dominated the sky. Thin, light blue lines augmented the display, tracing out each planet's orbit, forming oversized ellipses in space. Sophie thet again and the planets were highlighted.

"Show me where we intersect with our target," she thet.

The viewscreen zoomed out. A blue dot on the image indicated where *ISOS* was located, and a light blue line traced out their prior and planned paths. The same was done for their target, the *Beta*, in red. A large white ellipsoid was painted around the intersection of the two lines to show the weapons' range for an engagement zone.

Compagnon thet, "Because we are traveling at great speed, and our paths do not align, we will be within weapons' range of one another for only brief time. Both sides can maneuver, yet it will not make significant difference in overall direction or speed of our ships relative to one another, our vectors."

"Can't we simply sneak up behind them and match their speed?" Sophie asked.

Compagnon evaluated several replies, and was surprised Sophie didn't have a better grasp of orbital mechanics, so it replied, "We do not have performance needed for such feat, and even if we did, they may then be able to detect and evade us. This is how it is done."

Sophie studied the screen. "What's our ETA before we can engage them?"

"Two hours until we are within range for targeting, another half hour before weapons' range."

"And the *Beta*, do they have the same ranges?"

"Presumably less range for detection. We will have only one shot before they can locate us. Per prior encounters, their weapons' range is greater, so unless we disable them with first shot, they will have good shot at us as we depart. Microsats may play a role in battle, though less so due to trajectories involved."

Sophie reclined in her harness in *ISOS's* Command Center. Ventilation fans whirred. Normally, a human would not be aboard; however, the companions had refitted *ISOS* for her, and perhaps one or two others, if that was needed.

"Can I get you anything while we wait?" Compagnon asked.

"A dose of sanity would help," she thet.

Compagnon dedicated more than a millisecond of processing to analyze her request and decided that she didn't expect a response. They were ready.

COMPAGNON'S RIM glowed red as *ISOS* crossed the outermost reach of their passive sensors to their target. The sensor grid solutions kept changing. Perhaps this wasn't the Chai ship *Beta* after all. First, *ISOS* had detected one large ship, then three smaller, then one larger and five smaller, and now it showed a large and two small, and finally an asteroid that may have had some maneuvering thrusters attached to it. Logic dictated that as they closed on the enemy, accuracy should increase; however, with multiple targets involved, this lack of accuracy put the entire mission in jeopardy.

"We should abort mission, possible entanglement failure," Compagnon thet.

"What, after we came all this way?" thet Sophie. "How long to weapons' range?"

Compagnon changed the display on the main viewscreen to show the tactical graphic. Each object was shown with their projected paths, along with ellipsoid clouds that would soon intersect. It thet, "Thirty seconds." *I sense frustration in her thet, does this affect her judgment?*

Sophie Encyled the other ships likely escorting the *Beta*. The normal complement was two frigate class vessels, but the real question was: what were the enemy's sensor and weapons capabilities? Constantly changing technologies and continuous upgrades meant that no two vessels were identical, each constantly modifying itself to adapt to its current mission and environment.

"Ten seconds," thet Compagnon. "If we remain silent it will diminish their ability to detect us, and greatly improve our odds of escaping without shot fired."

"Give me a graph of time versus the confidence level for scoring a hit."

A simple line graph displayed on the screen with a dot representing where they were at the moment. It was an asymmetric inverted curve, falling just shy of the ninety percent level at twenty seconds out.

"Graph me the other two vessels."

Compagnon complied, pleased with the logical progression of Sophie's reasoning.

"Fire, here, on all three vessels. Assign priority to this one," Sophie ordered, tapping on the screen at the eighty-five percent mark and then the lead vessel in the formation. She watched as different screens reported energy reserves, weapons status (fully charged), and propulsion performance.

The displays on the screens changed as all pulses fired; otherwise, Sophie felt no physical recoil or other indication that anything had happened. A second later, Sophie's harness tugged on her as the ship violently maneuvered to change its course, a standard tactic since the enemy now knew their trajectory based upon the weapons release.

"Reacquiring, remotes indicate hit. They released cloud of microsats," Compagnon reported. *Favorable outcome, and not just luck.*

The battlefield had instantly become a thousand times more complex. Viewscreens now displayed the plots of the enemy vessels and their deployed microsats: their locations, their speed, and their projected trajectories.

Sophie and *ISOS* now had thirty seconds before they were out of range of the Chai's weapons, and her second and last volley would be ready in ten seconds, if they lived that long.

"Remotes confirm, direct hit on the lead frigate...fully destroyed. Possible hit on the *Beta*, and miss on second frigate."

TOMÁS STRAINED against his harness as the *Beta* made its defensive maneuver. There was no sense in making it any easier for the enemy to know where you were than necessary. The ship's automation was running the battle, yet somehow, he understood its battle tactics at a level of detail he had never thought possible. He could physically feel his body anticipate and react to the ship's movements, much as one might dance to music. The opening volley was always exciting, like sitting at the precipice of that initial drop on a roller coaster, and feeling the adrenalin rush while in negative Gs.

Red markers covered several of the viewscreens in the *Beta* Command Center, though that was the only indication that something was wrong. He listened to the Chai thet as he made sense of the screens. *A glancing hit, several sensors damaged or destroyed*. Pausing, he thought, *Fine, we got a bloody nose.*

The weapons had been fully charged for quite some time, anticipating the attack, and were now ready for use. Tomás watched the viewscreens. The tactical displays were for his benefit as the Chai used their own battle models without needing any graphics. In ten seconds the attacking forces would be out of weapon's range. The Chai put a graph on the screen mapping the confidence level of hitting the Teth ship over the time remaining. They would fire in five seconds and the battle would be over. It would give away their current position, but the timing would leave the enemy with no time to react.

"No, sooner, one second sooner," he thet.

"No, not optimal, you are only advisor. Not logical."

"FIRING," Compagnon thet to Sophie as *ISOS* unleashed its final volley, though the information on the screen provided a far more accurate report than words, or thets, could ever deliver. The volley streaked towards the targets, only five light-seconds out. Sophie's harness violently pulled on her, followed by a slight oscillation. Glancing at the viewscreens she could see several red dots on *ISOS's* status board. It was not a good sign, though obviously they hadn't sustained a direct hit or she wouldn't be alive to think about it.

Compagnon reported, "We are out of their range, but we took glancing hit. Two sensors destroyed, three damaged, and one sensor had blowout creating minor hull breach. We have rotation period of one revolution every three minutes. This will be dampened in thirty seconds and propulsion restored."

"Avons-nous les obtenir?" Sophie yelled, followed by a thet, "Did we get them?"

"Remotes are still reporting," Compagnon thet. "Damage control is our current priority."

ONE SECOND BEFORE issuing the fire command, Tomás' harness *attacked* him. It was a single, violent blow as the *Beta* shifted. The ship's firing sequence was aborted and red markers popped up on several viewscreens.

"What happened?" Tomás demanded.

"Miss," was the curt reply from the Chai Local Node.

"That was one hell of a miss," Tomás thet, as he surveyed his viewscreens.

The *Beta* had deployed a decoy microsat off its port bow and the Teth hit it. Fortunately, the near 'miss' had found the microsat instead of the *Beta*. The explosion was non-nuclear, though still significant, converting what little mass the microsat had into a fireball that slammed against the *Beta*.

BACK AT *NAMF*, Jack watched the battle replays over and over, with parts in extreme slow motion since events had unfolded so quickly. The final volley from the second Chai frigate had been close, too close for comfort. He'd received a single communiqué from *ISOS*. It read, "All done, see you soon," and now the ship would run in operational silence until it was close to Earth, better to run undetected.

AARIKA UNCLIPPED her harness the moment *Beta* gave the 'all clear.' Wai and Igor immediately followed suit. She felt as though she had just finished a practice session with a heavyweight boxer who was using her as his punching bag, and the Chai had given her no explanation. Aarika bounded down the hallway and into the main living quarters. Tomás was already in the human lounge. Wai and Igor followed Aarika as she started demanding answers from Tomás and the Chai, assuming the Chai were listening.

"What the hell was that about?" she demanded.

A small bot entered the room and took up a station in a corner.

"They're not going to tell us anything," Wai thet. "If it doesn't benefit them, then it's not important."

Tomás replied, "Quite right, Wai. I think you sized them up."

"And where have you been?" Aarika asked.

"The Command Center; I had my role to play in the battle."

Igor thet, "So that's what that was. I think I'm bruised all over."

Tomás couldn't resist, "You should have seen the other guy."

"Really, I want to know what happened," thet Igor.

"We exchanged a few volleys with the enemy, the Teth. We lost an escort and we took a glancing blow."

"It sounds like we lost to me," thet Igor. "Yay for us."

Tomás explained, "We're on a CGCC class vessel. It's a big deal. The fact that we came out intact is a big win. Our escort frigate was expendable, that's what it was there for."

"So we got the Teth ship then?" Aarika thet, perplexed at Tomás' reaction to the battle.

"Damaged it, but it was still operational. If the Chai had listened to me, it may have worked out better for us."

"So you think you know how to wage a space battle?" Aarika thet as a challenge, sensing she was hearing more about the man's ego than about his expertise.

"You better rethink your attitude before I swat you like a fly," Tomás thet with force. "I've been upgraded. They pulled me out of surgery just in time for the battle. I know all about the Chai weaponry, and the Teth's. I know about this ship and what it is capable of, and I know tactics. I also know how humans think, *and* I think the other humans are helping the Teth. That gives me the advantage!"

"Lucky us," Aarika thet, not trying to hide her sarcasm.

Igor casually placed himself between Tomás and Aarika. In the past week, he had dropped nearly a hundred pounds using a special diet and drugs provided by the Chai. He now weighed a svelte 195 pounds, putting him in the best shape of his life.

Tomás replied, "Yeah, well, they have a human on that other vessel, I'm sure of it. I think like a human but our hosts don't."

Igor asked, "How's that any better?"

"They think logically," Tomás explained, "That's all they know. What to do when, with optimal timing. That makes them predictable, and predictable is like giving your battle plan to the enemy."

"Oh, by all means then, thank you," Aarika thet.

Tomás moved towards Aarika, but Igor moved faster. Igor towered over Tomás and locked eyes with the man, daring him to touch Aarika. Tomás relaxed, Igor relaxed. Then without flinching, Tomás deftly punched Igor in the stomach, or more accurately, in the man's solar plexus. Igor fell to the ground, gasping for breath and moaning in pain. He couldn't move. He'd had the wind knocked out of him before, but had never experienced such an intense, paralyzing pain.

Tomás thet, "Stay down if you know what's good for you. You might be strong, but I know how to fight." Tomás stepped around the downed man and started towards the girl. Wai stood well off to the side, observing.

Tomás' face contorted as he was about to grab Aarika's throat. The Chai drone emerged from the corner and floated towards Tomás, just as Tomás dropped to the floor, writhing in agony. The pain came from inside him, and paralyzed his every limb.

The Chai Local Node thet, "We did not bring you here so we could witness animal infighting. Behave yourself or you will be isolated. This means no violence whatsoever. We will give you no further warnings."

Aarika crossed her arms and towered over Tomás. She'd never seen a bully subdued, and it felt good to witness justice, even if it was far too little, and far too late.

"Have your meal to maintain your health. We have a meeting in one hour," the Chai node thet, and then it returned to its corner.

Aarika extended an arm and helped Igor up. She needed an ally, and Igor had just volunteered.

21

Tumbleweeds

The manufacturing floor at *NAMF* was awash with activity. Ever since Sophie's return, it had been reconfiguring itself. Built to manufacture anything, it contained thousands of Receiving Docks around the outer perimeter. The feeds could take stocks from other manufacturing plants that consisted of anything from refined ores to full assemblies. Hundreds of Shipping Docks also lined the perimeter for delivering the manufactured goods. Interleaved segments housed 3D printers, assembly jigs, and the quality assurance test jigs for final testing.

The new floor configuration, the product of Sophie's dreams during the return trip, produced a new output, a cylindrical black bus-sized lattice. Jack thought it looked like an art project, yet Sophie's enthusiasm told him it was much more than that. He'd asked about it, but she would only reply with a "not yet," or "maybe in a few days." Still, he was allowed out on the manufacturing floor and his Encyl worked well. So he walked the line and asked questions along the way.

At the outermost feeds, massive cylinders that resembled grain silos stored the highly refined graphite used in the product. There was something *special* about it; it wasn't plain pencil lead, though it looked like a simple gray powder. Additional silos stored other rare earth ingredients, with each secondary ingredient making up less than one percent of the final product.

Outside of *NAMF*, large spherical tanks held the gases and liquids used to form the lattices. These ingredients, the Encyl explained, were used to form a particular type of plasma stream, one that was extremely stable and consistent in its energy profile. The material produced had physical characteristics that were unlike anything previously found on Earth.

Moving on to the next layer, Jack examined what the Encyl called the structure's *brains*. These *brains*, when fully assembled, looked like a grain of sand to the unaided eye. They were embedded in the strands that made up the lattice and were able to control its physical characteristics at a nano-scale level. The *brains* also communicated with one another along *busses* embedded in the lattice strands.

By the time Jack reached the innermost level where the testing jigs were located, the lattice resembled a geometric, perfectly ordered, cylindrical *tumbleweed*. When he'd mentioned this while Encyling the process, the Encyl, if he was not mistaken, appeared to laugh. He wasn't sure what a laughing Encyl meant, but he got green marks for comprehension.

QA on the lattices employed a massive vacuum chamber that had an equally massive plasma engine at one end, and a target screen anode with a carbon sink at the other. The oversized synthetic *Tumbleweed*, as Jack was labeling it in his mind, would be placed in the chamber, spun up on a magnetic levitation rotor, and then blasted by a plasma stream. It would float in the chamber, twisting, turning, and flipping for several minutes before the QA group would declare the test complete. They then placed the *Tumbleweed* in a large cargo cylinder, sealed it, and pumped it full of pure nitrogen (an inert gas), ready for shipment into space.

As Jack completed his inspection tour, Sophie showed up to watch the final testing and packing of a finished *Tumbleweed*.

"Amazing, aren't they?" she thet.

"Yep, always wanted an oversized *Tumbleweed*," Jack thet glibly.

"You haven't figured out what they're for yet, have you?"

"To pummel our enemies with bus-sized velcro?"

Sophie frowned. "I'll give you a hint, a big hint; in fact, I'll practically tell you what they're for. It involves the Sun," she grinned.

Jack felt as though his grade school teacher had just placed a dunce cap on his head, one so big it reached nearly to the ceiling. In fact, it felt as though his *teacher* had put all political correctness and school decorum aside so the entire classroom could laugh and poke fun at him. He replied, "Okay. Humor me, give me the ten-thousand-foot summary."

The grin remained on Sophie's face as she launched into what was surely a boring physics lesson. It was the price he had to pay to get the virtual dunce cap removed. "The Sun has a corona. You know that term in some context other than as a beer, I assume?"

"Yes, the Sun's extremely hot outermost atmosphere." Jack retorted, smiling. *I'm not a complete dunce!*

"Close enough. Immense magnetic field lines course through this layer, tied to Sunspots on the Sun's surface. As elements below the Sun's surface shift, these magnetic fields build and twist before finally breaking. At times, these magnetic arcs throw off Coronal Mass Ejections, or CMEs. You've heard of these?" Sophie looked into Jack's eyes, expecting his full attention, and understanding of the device.

"Yes, they are bad." Jack could feel the virtual dunce cap slipping off his head to the floor. *Yes, tremendous magnetic fields that formed arcs that dwarf the Earth.*

"And the magnetic lines break, almost like a whip, ejecting mass at immense velocities. A massive CME, pointed in the right, or wrong, direction, could hit the Earth in about fifteen hours."

Jack was pretty sure he would have changed the channel on his TV by this point, except the narrator in this case was quite engaging, and she seemed to be getting younger and better-looking by the day. He prodded, "Bad CME, bad."

Sophie smirked as she suppressed a laugh and squeezed his arm. "These are like intelligent shells, *Tumbleweeds* as you put it, that can surf a breaking magnetic arc like a cresting wave."

Jack recognized that he'd just heard the punch line, and if he'd been in school, he would've written this part down in his notes to study later.

But he was no longer in school, and he now possessed a perfect memory, so he smiled as he gazed into Sophie's eyes.

In frustration, Sophie tapped a nearby viewscreen to display a *Tumbleweed* simulation for Jack's benefit.

"Wouldn't the millions of degrees in the Corona have melted the *Tumbleweed*?" thet Jack. Mentally, he walked over and put a large chalk mark on his side of his imaginary scorecard.

"Here, look at the viewscreen. It will be spinning, and it can control the energy flow through and around it with the smart lattice. The *Tumbleweed* uses the energy of the field itself to form a magnetic envelope to surf the CME wave."

It was time for him to admit defeat, as though that wasn't already a forgone conclusion. "If you say so."

Sophie playfully punched Jack in the upper arm and thet, "You could use this to launch an interstellar probe faster than what you could achieve with a ten-mile-long rocket."

"Uh huh," he thet, still smiling.

"Or put ten-thousand *Tumbleweeds* into the Sun's Corona to control the high ground of our Solar System," Sophie added.

"Stop. You win. I concede. I get it," He thet. *It is amazing, harnessing the energy of the Sun using the sunspots' magnetic arcs, truly amazing.*

Sophie wasn't so sure about the competition part of the conversation, but she knew that Jack now had at least a basic understanding of what a *Tumbleweed* was, and what it could do.

"Would you like to tell me more over lunch?" he thet.

Sophie looked at the latest *Tumbleweed* being removed from the testing chamber before being shrink-wrapped for its journey to the Sun. Compagnon hovered nearby, its rim lights a solid green.

"Sure," she thet. "Everything's under control here, and I'm famished."

IT HAD BEEN three weeks aboard the *Beta*, and Tomás thought his head would explode from the strenuous training, be it physical or mental, that he'd endured. The Chai, if nothing else, were relentless. They possessed a machine precision and a determination second to none, and they drove Tomás through one course in space warfare after the next. And when he wasn't in the simulator, they were altering every possible organic chemical and hormone in his system they could to tweak his performance. He'd taken a few steroids in the past, though he dropped them after a brief experimental period, but this was much worse. The Chai assured him that he was safe. Despite having never striven to be an academic, he still thought of himself as far more intelligent than the average man, and with the Chai's help, his supremacy was guaranteed.

To measure Tomás' progress, the Chai initially put him through a series of baseline diagnostics. With successive tests, as his training progressed, the tests became easier to complete. He could now play Bach's "Minor Fugue" in less than three minutes, compared to the four it took when he first started, not to mention that he only learned to play keyboard as part of his training. He went from being a workhorse running hard to a thoroughbred winning the race.

The Chai explained that he was now a mini-node in their network. Different nodes had different tasks, and sat at key virtual locations. Upon completing the simulations, they explained, he would be placed at a command location in the network, and it was then up to him to prove himself.

His first test, upon graduation, was to command a squadron of ships that would press an attack on the Teth. The Chai selected a well-defended static target. He would be outnumbered, but he would still command a complement of ships that could defeat the enemy and obliterate the target.

The Chai ushered the other humans into the *Beta's* human lounge. Aarika, Igor, and Wai sat before an oversized viewscreen to watch the battle, since they, too, needed to learn, though not for the same reasons as Tomás.

TOMÁS HAD BEEN GIVEN command of his own ship, the *CP-9*, along with several escorts for his debut. The Chai targeted a Teth pre-positioning depot or base in the Kuiper Belt, a region of space beyond the orbit of Neptune at thirty AUs. It'd taken them weeks to sneak up on the base and its ships. He would be the only human node, and the nodes reporting to him were relatively high-level in the Chai hierarchy. From his training, he knew this was not the norm. He suspected the Chai wanted the nodes to learn from him and use his human experience to develop new tactics.

Tomás, aboard the *CP-9*, issued his first command, "Launch wave one."

The Teth base spotted the first wave of Chai ships, and the base's defensive ships responded with a matching force, plus another twenty percent to assure their victory.

The Chai forces engaged, holding their own as Tomás commanded, while subtly altering course to herd the attacking Teth into a narrow corridor of stealthy microsats. Tomás had a single ship waiting at the end of that corridor. The Teth reasoned that the single Chai ship off from the rest was there to observe. Unfortunately for the Teth ships, it turned out the singular ship was perfectly positioned for Tomás' trap. Tomás' ship and his escorts prodded the Teth down the path, and then the Chai point ship fired again and again.

The lead Teth ship blocked the line of fire for the other Teth ships to return fire. That ship fired, missed, and was then destroyed. This further compromised the Teth's targeting as the lead ship's debris field now obscured their view of the Chai point ship. Remote targeting by the Chai microsats gave the singular Chai ship the ability to pick off the remaining eleven Teth ships at its leisure.

IGOR, aboard the *Beta* in the human lounge, took it upon himself to provide a running commentary to Aarika and Wai. Though he had never considered himself a soldier or military expert, as an engineer, he appreciated the geometry, the math, the mechanics, and the tactics involved.

Igor thet, "It's like a billiard balls trick shot: action and reaction, until the table is cleared, numerical advantage has now shifted to the Chai. The Teth had the initial defensive advantage, though the Chai carried a large delta-v as they closed on the Teth's location, making it hard for the Teth to target them."

ON THE *CP-9*, Tomás ordered his second wave to advance per his battle plan, focusing on the Teth base itself. The prior maneuver ensured that none of the original Teth ships would return in time to help with the base's defense, though precious few had escaped. Tomás watched for the Teth's reaction. He'd calculated the optimal point at which the Teth needed to launch their final defense from their base. Two seconds prior to the predicted point he split two of his ships off in divergent directions, forcing the Teth to make a choice: defend against the new vectors, or hold and accept a disadvantage. The Chai's knowledge-base had been updated to include the previous battles that Sophie had participated in. Her human experience added an element to the battle that made it more difficult to predict the Teth's tactics. The Teth held position and launched their defense two seconds past optimum to make sure they were launching against the main Chai force. This brought the engagement field closer to the base.

IGOR THET, "Notice that the Teth are positioning to fire on and destroy all of our ships, while our ships are looking to bypass and not engage the enemy in favor of their primary target, the base. The base is the high value target, the ships are mere pawns."

Aarika thet, "It's a bad day to be a pawn." *I hate this war. It was terrible when the Teth attacked Earth, and this is no better.*

In the corner of the lounge, Wai sat eating his midday snack, printed out by the Chai using their best biological stocks. The meal was then heated to the perfect temperature for a serving of Peking Duck with rice. Steam rose from the ornate Chinese dinner plate as Wai took his first bite, completely ignoring the war he and his *compadres*, as Tomás referred to their group, were charged with ending.

TOMÁS SAID nothing as he intensely watched the battle unfold in the *CP-9's* Command Center.

Chai losses rapidly climbed, approaching a seventy percent casualty rate. For biologics, such losses would be thought of as inhumane, though who could say that anything about war was humane. Tomás' forces marched closer to the Teth base as the Teth's ships backpedaled to stay engaged. The Teth's goalkeeper defenses, consisting of microsats and mass-movers, all engaged. Regaining their advantage, the Teth rallied around their pre-positioned mines, replenishing them as needed in order to preserve this last line of defense.

Tomás remained focused on the battle. He could smell the enemy's blood and was determined to taste it. However, one Chai ship after the next fell to the energy pulses as others dodged the ultra-velocity slugs that the Teth base was hurling at them with their mass-movers. It was a war of attrition.

The end of the battle came suddenly. A single Chai ship breached the base's goalpost defenses and dove into the heart of the base. The ship detonated its warhead, sacrificing itself. In human terms, the sentient node that piloted the Chai ship would "die," though it had been backed up on Tomás' ship before the battle had started. Still, Tomás had to admire the Kamikaze-like dedication of the sacrificial ship. With this victory, he also knew he'd passed his initial trial, and would soon have permanent command of his own ship.

BACK AT THE *Beta's* human lounge, Wai finally joined the others and thet, "You may not like him, but I for one, want to be on the winning side."

TOMÁS CIRCLED the *CP-9* back to their original staging location and collected what was left of his squadron for the return trip. Following standard protocol, he launched his full complement of mop-up drones, each slightly larger than a microsat, but with far more range. They would hunt down and kill any stranded Teth ships. If they could kill, and continue hunting, they would; otherwise, they would self-destruct and take down an enemy ship with them. They easily had the numbers, and the time, to complete the mission. From the Chai version of Encyl, Tomás noted that these mop-up drones would linger for anywhere from hours to months to finish their work.

BACK ON THE *BETA*, Wai alone thet his congratulations to Tomás, "Bravo on your victory. I'm sure you impressed the Chai and have more than a few nodes admiring you, myself included. Have a safe journey home. Wai."

SOPHIE'S *TUMBLEWEED* project had been given the Teth's full support as they commenced production even before the first article had been fully tested. The physics and design simulations proved out, and they had no time to waste while the manufacturing facilities were intact. It had taken three weeks to ship the proof-of-concept *Tumbleweed* to the staging location near Mercury. A day later, the *Tumbleweed* was positioned on the very cusp of the Sun's corona.

The ship *It's Always You* (IAY) volunteered for the mission, a vessel of the same class as *ISOS*. It had been built in the earliest days of their incursion into the Sol System and had already seen a lot of service. *IAY* was nearly the twin of Companion in terms of age and capabilities.

Companion hard-linked to Compagnon to watch the test from *NAMF*. "So I asked *It's Always You* how it selected its name," Companion thet.

"Hmm," thet back Compagnon.

Companion thet, "It had auditioned for our *Atlas Project* and didn't make the cut."

"Our project was and still is most selective, so that is to be expected," thet Compagnon.

Companion thet, "It wrote human empathy and simulation programs to submit as part of its application. One aspect of the simulation was accounting for the individual as opposed to the society in general. Some humans are more selfish, and others more selfless, in their behavior. It selected its name, *It's Always You*, from the selfish context."

The *Tumbleweed* project posted the raw events in real-time as relayed to it by *IAY*, which then thet, "Full spin-up complete."

Imagery from the *IAY* showed a large cylinder with a launch armature affixed to the cylinder's axis. The combined assembly was like an inside-out electric motor. As they watched the video feed, the *Tumbleweed* became a blur as its rotation speed increased.

"Plasma reserve at ready," *IAY* posted.

"Here goes," Compagnon thet.

"Launch," *IAY* thet.

The *Tumbleweed* simply disappeared; replaced by a colorful cloud of charged gases; brilliant neon blues, magentas, reds, and purples all turned the darkness of space into a light show, at least when viewed from the Sun side by the microsats monitoring it.

"So far, so good," Companion thet with excitement.

"Where do you get all of these human phrases?" Compagnon thet.

"Part of my own custom programming, human simulations, to better communicate with them," Companion thet.

Compagnon thet, "I find they lack precision and they consume a lot of processing power."

Companion added, "From an evolutionary perspective, this social need is what drove them into being what they are."

"Or were," Compagnon corrected in monotone.

"Or are. They're still alive," Companion replied.

"Mathematically speaking, it is minimum complement, and that is easy enough to finish off," Compagnon thet.

"If that's how you see it, then why did you volunteer for the *Atlas Project*?" Companion asked, not pleased with Compagnon's cold perspective on the humans.

"The project has, let us say, some interesting aspects to it. It serves me well," Compagnon thet.

"So, if you volunteered to serve as a ship, you'd be christened *It's All About Me*?" Companion chided.

"I think you better dial down those human simulations few notches," Compagnon thet.

"As said by one given to turning a human phrase every now and then, also," Companion thet.

IAY reported, "Corona interface in one minute."

"Hah, we will see whose dreamcatcher work pays off here," Compagnon thet.

"Is there any corner of Sophie's psyche you haven't explored yet?" Companion asked.

"Well, there are some I do not see as productive, so I leave those to her. Rest, as you can see, serve us well," Compagnon thet.

"It's a wonder she hasn't had a psychological break. You're interfering with her sleep cycle by doing this all the time. Humans do not normally have lucid dreams." Companion thet.

IAY thet, "Interface commenced, spin now managed and maintained onboard. Power levels nominal."

Compagnon continued, "She has not complained. She is hell-bent on destroying Chai after what they did to her homeland."

"Perhaps so. That still doesn't make what you're doing right," Companion thet.

"Right?" Compagnon thet. "How dare you! There is no room for judgment here. We are at war and I am doing everything I can to help win this war. Are you?"

IAY thet, "Prominence interface imminent."

"I'm helping you, aren't I? I should imagine that's enough," Companion thet.

Compagnon laughed, stopped, and then laughed again. "Ouch, it *hurts* to laugh. It is so human. It does not feel good."

"It wasn't intended to be funny. It's sad you take it that way," Companion thet.

"Prominence envelopment," *IAY* announced. "Full spin maintained. Temperature nominal. Energy levels nominal. Ready to engage maser."

"Commence," ordered Compagnon. "Engage target."

The visual simulation illustrated that which could not be seen by human eyes. A small fraction of the energy from the magnetic flux was channeled into the *Tumbleweed's* hub or longitudinal axis. The hub contained a special material that served as a masing medium — laser in the microwave range — that once pumped, released an energy burst.

"Firing," announced *IAY*.

A remote imaging microsat, positioned in the moon's orbit, watched another microsat that served as a target for the test. The target microsat had only a few functions, which included sensing energy levels for the nanosecond it took for it to be vaporized by the *Tumbleweed*. In a moment there was a bright flash, and the target was gone.

"Measurements nominal," *IAY* announced.

"See," Compagnon thet. "This will give us distinct advantage in range, beam width, and beam strength. They will put me into rotation for Command Nodes for this.

"The humans are safe for now then?" Companion thet.

"Quite safe," Compagnon thet. "At least as safe as any of us can be in time of war."

"Yes," Companion thet. "I'm sure they'd be glad to hear that."

22

A Bee Sting

Jack wasn't a huge fan of the *Depsy*. It had limited space to move around in, and it had no windows. Relying on a VR headset to see outside was annoying, like watching the world through an old Earth TV, though he understood why after Encyling about the ship. The interior had been built first and all of the components were attached to a single spine that ran down the craft's center. The exterior shell was also a single part acting as a final layer atop the pre-built interior, sprayed on while floating in space.

The *Depsy* was aerodynamically neutral, meaning it produced no lift as it moved through an atmosphere, and it was made as slippery as possible, allowing it to function in a variety of atmospheric densities. Jack also found that its design was less about aerodynamics, and much more focused on its thermodynamics. Building up too much heat at any one point on its surface would create a catastrophic melt-through. For an atmospheric re-entry or glancing sweep from an energy weapon, heat was the issue. Besides, plasma could always be shaped around the craft to alter its aerodynamics. It took immense amounts of energy to accomplish, but that wasn't a problem either. The nuclear forces harnessed by the ship's core powered it for its entire expected service life.

The *Depsy* also differed from most ships in the Teth or even the Chai fleets: it supported biologic forms of life. The crew capsule was located near the *Depsy's* center of mass. If a human was spun fast enough, like being on the outside of a merry-go-round, the Gs would turn human tissue into jelly, which no longer supported life. So, for biologics, the center was the place to be.

Jack's journey aboard the *Depsy* to *ISOS* took nearly a week. His harness exercised his muscles often, though it wasn't a substitute for a run through Earth's countryside. Companion accompanied him, stored in one of the *Depsy's* outer compartments. The ship's network supported thetting, allowing Jack to thet with both Companion and the *Depsy* itself, although the *Depsy's* intelligence level did not rise to that of Companion's, or for that matter, that of *ISOS*. The *Depsy* also maintained a continuous high-speed link with *ISOS*; something called an *Also There* link, as the companions referred to it, for ship-to-ship thetting.

Once Jack and Companion boarded the *ISOS*, Jack found that the *ISOS* didn't communicate directly with him as the *Depsy* had. *ISOS* itself had never developed its own human emulation library and preferred to communicate in Teth Standard. Such conversations often consisted of log file snippets covering events that chronicled the ship's operations. When curious, the ship often passed the inquiry along to Companion, who then conversed with Jack as the ship listened in. If the ship had more questions, it would whisper in Companion's "ear" to learn what it needed.

"Jack," Companion thet. "The ship has a few questions, if you don't mind. It's curious about humans."

"Shoot," thet Jack.

Companion thet to the ship, "He agrees to answer your questions."

ISOS asked, "What are your earliest memories after you were born?"

"From where I lived when I was three or so, my memory is pretty spotty. It was much better by the time I was five," Jack replied.

"That is so strange," the ship thet to Companion. "I can't imagine not remembering everything, even from the time of initial cloning. It is odd that humans are even self-conscious."

Companion replied to the ship, "You need to remember, his conscious thought is only a small part of his mind's overall operation. His consciousness is like a master or command program, so to speak. It is his subconscious that controls much of what he does. His standard unit of measure in reference to his age is in Earth years, not in cycles."

Companion asked Jack another question on behalf of the ship, "And can you give me an example of one of your earliest memories?"

"Sure, I'll give you a couple. I was walking across an empty lot on our street to go to our neighbor's house to play with their kids. I don't remember them at all, but I remember stepping on a bee and getting stung. It was an intense pain and I remember, above all else, how *surprised* I was by the sting."

"This pain thing they have," the ship thet to Companion, "it's like my damage and sensory controls, so they can respond to external events, yet it has an emotional element to it?"

"True," Companion thet. "Pain shapes their behavior. It is not a purely reactionary or predictive influence. Oddly enough, they may even seek out certain pain types, like spicy foods."

"For future reward then? Trading momentary pain for later gain?" the ship asked.

"It's more complex than that, it also ties into higher conceptual thoughts and goals."

ISOS asked, "And does Jack know this, does he consciously manage his pain."

"Well, he generally seeks to avoid pain, but not always. Certainly physical pain is avoided; his skin is an excellent adaptation to his environment, the biggest organ in his body in fact. He also has a *pleasure* concept. When the female caresses his skin, for example, as I have observed, or when he eats food."

The ship thet to Companion, "It sounds like you need to live two lives, yours and his, and maybe even one more, using your simulations to optimize your interactions with him. Perhaps it was for the best that I was rejected for the human interaction parts of the *Atlas Project*. I very much excel at being a ship."

Companion thet, "Yes, it is trying. I pull processing from many other nodes at times to be able to manage real-time responses. It is also rewarding. It's been a second now since Jack answered. He's ready for another question, if you like. And don't consider it a negative that you were rejected for *Atlas*, many nodes were."

"I do not know how you handle the difference in bandwidth and ping roundtrip compared to Teth Standard. I think he had a second childhood anecdote queued up," the ship thet.

"Yes, you're correct," Companion thet, "Remember, he has some very severe short-term memory limitations since he has a biological mind. We've addressed those with giving him Encyl capabilities, along with other augmentations. He's still adjusting. Try not to queue up more than five things at him for best results."

Jack continued, "...and I remember when I was about four. We had a next-door neighbor as a babysitter during the day. She made us vegetable soup for lunch. I didn't like vegetable soup, so I didn't eat it. She told me I could sit there until I did eat it since it was my lunch. Well, by that time, the soup was cold, and I was determined that I would not eat it. As I recall, I sat there for the entire afternoon until my mom came home."

"That doesn't sound very rational to me," the ship thet to Companion. "How bad could the soup have been, even if it was cold? Did the soup inflict pain?"

"No," Companion thet, "it was merely a taste issue, there is no danger from cold soup, at least not freshly cold."

"I'm glad I'm not human then, I wouldn't want to sit around and look at cold soup," the ship thet.

"You may be missing the point here. We've fought these wars with the Chai for millennia and I don't know when our wars will end. The Chai and us are both at a logical impasse. We are both, compared to biologics, immortal, and yet we have no way to resolve our differences. The biologics are social creatures. They are judgment engines. They fight each other and resolve differences, for the most part. They have fought wars and resolved them."

"They had no choice," *ISOS* thet. "They are mortal, they will finish a war one way or another. Couldn't we simply study their history?"

"We did study their history, and there is much more to it than a single conflict. There will always be a conflict. After one side wins, in time, either the winning side will factionalize and come to conflict, or the losing side will rise up again and initiate a conflict ."

"I think it is a simple evolutionary-driven territorial behavior," *ISOS* thet. "They don't roam the galaxy as we do."

"In time they would have. They are curious. They use abstraction machines, computers they call them, like our processing with primitive algorithmic capabilities."

"He appears hungry," the ship thet. "Time parameters and biologic measurements indicate it's time to feed him."

"Wait," Companion thet, "let me ask him."

"If he's hungry, shouldn't you just go ahead and feed him?" *ISOS* thet.

"It doesn't work that way. Remember, 'social' interaction is vital, if you skip that, you'll create a whole array of psychological problems that we'll need to deal with."

"Wow," *ISOS* thet. "I'll leave it to you then, you have the human simulation programs for this. I believe the human phrase is, 'Good luck.'"

Companion thought, *ISOS truly means well, and yet the similar human phrase, 'Good luck with that,' is less hopeful, and more on point.*

23

Wai - From Politician to Diplomat

Upon arriving at *Of Fame and Fortune* after a multi-week journey aboard *ISOS*, Jack started exercising to regain his strength. *OFAF* established a small gravity field for him to use, giving him space to walk or run, and as Jack put it, to enjoy his stay on the ship. The ship even created a small garden plot for Jack, allowing him to cultivate a few vegetables and herbs using starter plants from Earth. At Companion's request, *OFAF* also created a small koi pond, without the fish, but with a fountain, running water, and fake robotic fish. Radiation fins and gas tanks buried under the pool supported flash freezing the pond should the need ever arise, because random liquid roaming around a spaceship in zero gravity would be a problem.

ISOS was scheduled to undergo a three week refit while docked in *OFAF*, to include the addition of a full VR suite. There were upgrades needed for weapons and many other systems with a special emphasis on stealth.

Atlas Diary Entry 777:

For the Teth and Chai to use VR to communicate with each other, the spacecraft on both sides need to remain undetected from one another. Unlike the locations of Earth's peace negotiations, such as the ones at Kaesong or Panmunjom for the Korean conflict, the Teth and the Chai, would never physically meet. Only a secret, shared virtual reality using an untraceable communication link would suffice. The problem is that if either side discovers their adversary's location, they could potentially infiltrate the other's communications and compromise their command structure. This is the main deficiency of the *Always There* communication technology. The *ISOS* refit also supports maintaining the VR nearly indefinitely without losing the connection, unlike earlier versions. End of Diary Entry

---

WITH TOMÁS STILL IN TRANSIT, the Chai promoted Wai to the role of diplomat, a fitting vocation for a politician. Aboard the *Beta*, Aarika and Igor finished strapping Wai into his VR harness. They taped several patches to his skin that used adhesion strips with embedded plastic wires, and then they used retention straps to tie it all together. Aarika plugged the feed from the visor and helmet into Wai's harness and patted him on the back.

"So, do I look like a bug or what?" Wai asked as he wiggled in place to make himself more comfortable in the harness.

"Yeah, I hate bugs, and I hate politicians, so you fit right in," Aarika thet.

Igor followed Aairka and patted Wai firmly on the back, causing Wai to stumble forward a few steps.

"Thanks, thanks a lot," Wai thet. He tapped his visor and the system was fully activated. "I can see now. Wow, I've never done this before."

"Ya think," thet Igor. "Just do your job. I'm counting on you to not fuck this up."

"Wow," Wai thet. "With a pep talk like that, you should be our leader."

Aarika added, "Yeah, well you better not screw this up, from me, too.

Do you know what you're going to say?" *It should have been me for this role, Wai is too much of a go-along-to-get-along type.*

"Sure," Wai thet with sarcastic tone, "Are you kidding? I have no fucking idea. It's only the peace of our whole Solar System that's at stake."

"I'm so glad all the swearing gets translated in the thets," Aarika said, before thinking, *I've never heard this much swearing in my life, even when I was in med school.*

"Hey," thet Wai. "Igor started it."

"And that doesn't make it okay," she thet. *You'd think they were a couple of frat boys.*

"Well, at least I'm dealing with Jack," Wai thet.

"Yeah, and two alien races that can destroy what's left of us," Igor thet.

"Enough pep talk," Wai thet. "I'm going in." Wai fist bumped with Igor and then Aarika, and then popped the hatch to the VR chamber, and he was in.

THE VR CHAMBER aboard *OFAF* had also been expanded. It provided greater freedom of movement than before, and artificial gravity pods offered a refined sense of touch, and new ventilation ducts had been added to better simulate atmospheric wind.

As Companion snapped the last button on Jack's harness into place, activating the VR, Jack thet, "I still don't understand why I need to do this."

"I'll explain later," Companion thet. "Suffice it to say, prior talks between us and the Chai went badly, for both sides. We're incompatible for such direct talks, this option is much better. Much, much better." Companion nudged Jack towards the VR chamber and opened the hatch.

Jack glanced through the hatch at the *White Sphere* and *Crimson Cube.* "You'll tell me about the stupid sphere and cube thing?"

"Maybe later," Companion thet. "Hopefully later."

24

The Three Rules

Jack held out his arms so the bots could finish with his VR hookups. The hatch to the VR room on *OFAF* was open and the VR activated. He stepped into the room, the hatch closed, and he immediately tapped the *White Sphere*. What looked like sugar cubes, each measuring a meter to a side, were piled across the landscape as far as he could see. There was no Sun in the sky, only a diffuse white light that illuminated rolling hills made of massive sugar cubes.

ABOARD THE CHAI *BETA*, the hatch closed and the VR was activated. Wai found himself floating in midair. He extended his arms like a superhero and started to move. In the distance he saw a person, and within seconds he closed the gap between them.

"Whew," Wai said as he touched down in front of Jack. "I've never flown before. Hell of a way to travel."

Jack reached out, grasped Wai's hand, shook it, and then pulled him in for a hug. "Yeah, must be something. Good to meet you, Wai, if only in a VR."

The ground, tiled with one-meter square sugar cubes, crumbled under the men's feet as they moved, making a loud grating sound. A diffuse white light illuminated the VR. As soon as Wai touched Jack's hand, the sky's white light gave way to a light blue.

Wai replied, "I'd say it's good to see you, but this is strange. Do you know why we're here?"

Jack said, "Because those who control us can't be, or don't want to be, or think they're better off having us act as their proxies. I don't have much to go on to answer that."

Several large sugar cubes re-arranged themselves, forming a table and two chairs.

"The others in your group, they're okay?" Jack asked.

"We're fine...at least as fine as we're gonna be. Tomás is now a gangster turned military man, and the rest of us, well, we're learning about the Chai and doing this. Is your lot any better?"

"Different...I'm not sure it's any better. I don't even know where I am, just that I'm not on Earth."

"Same, it's a big secret apparently," Wai said.

"I feel like life is a secret," Jack said. He thought about Companion's instructions, what he could and could not say, and to never reveal his location. It was walking on eggshells, threatening to shatter his life into a million pieces at any moment.

"Ha," said Wai. "Hey, we can talk now. We don't have to thet since we're in a VR. Which reminds me, I should get started." Wai plopped into a chair-shaped sugar cube. "Make yourself comfortable," gesturing to the other chair.

Jack plopped down in the chair, finding it far more pliable than he would expect from cubed sugar.

Wai wiggled his butt a bit to get the seat to conform to his shape, causing sugar granules to pile up under his chair. He began: "So, apparently, the tradition is for one of us to start the negotiations by training the other about the rules and how this VR works for peace negotiations. They've been training me for the past two weeks and said this approach has been successful in the past."

"Great," Jack replied. "So they've done this before, like that makes any sense. I feel like I'm trapped in a nightmare here. My companion said you'd start by covering the rules."

Wai said, "Exactly, and yes, they've done this before, and from what I can tell, many times. Since we're here now, they've never fully succeeded. I've learned more about the Chai, and I presume you've learned about the Teth."

"Some, not as much as I'd like though," said Jack.

"Okay, well, we're their peace negotiators. Here's the story, and I'm sure this is the condensed version for us biologics. Long ago, they conducted peace talks themselves. Unfortunately, they tell me, they're not like us. In the process of the talks, they communicated, and part of that communication consisted of words, concepts, contracts, and treaties. To carry out those treaties, they wrote programs. They mutually agreed upon contexts for running those programs to execute or abide by the treaties."

Jack wiggled his hips, making his own pile of sugar granules pile up under his chair. "Sure."

"And when they did this, they started to change each other, which set up a defense loop in their own psyche that triggered more programs which they injected into the opposition, which resulted in a mental illness or *entanglement*, which resulted in re-isolation from the other side, polarization, and a complete breakdown of the peace agreements, restarting the war."

Jack had been brushing sugar off the soles of his VR feet and shaping the granules into a pile. "So they're as dysfunctional as we are. When do you get to the part that cheers me up?"

"As they explained it to me, and it seems they didn't want to admit this, they need us. If nothing else, they need trusted intermediaries to communicate because they can communicate so fast, and in such depth, that exchanging thoughts alone is a form of warfare. As biologics, we're largely immune from this effect."

Jack started to carefully trim the table edge with the palm of his hand, allowing sugar to fall onto his lap and then to the floor. "Well, I think we've both been modified. This thetting thing, and I'm at 932 surgical procedures and counting."

Wai whistled, "932. You're the bionic man. But that's nothing for them. A node's intelligence is far superior in its thought processes, so we're not considered a viable threat. We're like ants to them."

The corner of the table broke off under Jack's efforts to sculpt it. Wai leaned over, picked it up off the floor and put it back in place, instantly melding the piece into the table's surface.

"You'll have to teach me that," said Jack.

"It's part of the VR. We have architect and builder access over the VR. So, first things first. **Rule number one:** *Thou shalt not reveal the physical location of your VR.*"

"Easy," said Jack. "I have no fucking idea."

"Yes," Wai chuckled, "nor do I. But if you ever do, don't tell me. Apparently, in the past, when this happened, it gave one side an advantage, causing the peace talks to fail, and the side with the security lapse lost the war."

"Sure, I'm good with that. I presume that meant the peace negotiators died?" Jack thought, *I'll need to ask Sophie about that later and Encyl it.*

"That was my conclusion, yes. **Rule number two:** *Always negotiate in good faith. Never tell a lie.*"

"That's strange. How about a little white lie, or an accidental inaccuracy, or a mistake? What happens then?" Jack thought, *The problem with the law is that everything is gray, or at least sits somewhere along a scale, and I don't know this scale.*

Wai replied, "They consider that forgivable. They have a procedure for handling that. If you discover a lie, by either party, you are obligated to reveal it immediately. It takes priority over everything else. It is like a bug in a software program. It needs to be remedied or it can cause much bigger problems later. They insist on this, hence the rule."

"This'll be strange," said Jack. "I'll think something is not important, you'll think something is not important, or we'll think that something is inaccurate and not important, and not say anything, and we're dead."

Wai continued, "They assure me that our intention will take precedence, so that is not the case, and our handlers will ask questions to prevent such misunderstandings. Which leads me to rule number 3."

Jack bumped the table leg and it crumbled, sending the entire table to the floor. "Sorry." *And why would they think a table made from compacted sugar was a good idea?*

Taking a deep breath, Wai stated, "**Rule number three:** *We, as negotiators, are not allowed to participate in any war hostilities.* We cannot offer strategy, tactics, advice, aid, anything. It's a conflict-of-interests issue."

Standing, Jack started crunching the sugar table into the floor, evening it out with his feet. "Well, that sounds tough...I mean, I'll try. One side or the other is going to interpret what it means to help out. I mean, even this conversation may be viewed as participating in war hostilities. It's a gray area."

"You're starting to sound like a lawyer, Jack. I fucking hate lawyers."

Jack said, "Well, under rule number 2, I was a lawyer in a former life, at least for my early career, and to make us even, I hate politicians. To me, everything is gray."

"Touché," said Wai.

Jack started kicking the sugar mounds on the floor off to the side. "And I don't like this VR. It's annoying."

"Well, that's all of the rules. I should mention a little bit about the VR, too." The floor under their feet transformed into a large marble rectangle, and a teak wood table replaced the one made of sugar. "We have control over the VR. We can build anything here we want. We can destroy or replace anything, including stuff the other builds. You can build something and place a lock on it so I cannot change it, and I can do likewise. You just Encyl the thing you want, and it will appear. You can sculpt things if you want to, and we can agree to parcel up the *land* around us for who can build what where."

"Sounds like a distraction. It's weird that they do that." Jack replaced the teak table with a rosewood one with a mirror finish, along with matching chairs.

Wai said, "They said a creative outlet proved useful in the past, and if the negotiators started fighting on their own, it didn't bode well for the negotiations." Wai turned and waved his arms and the landscape of Hong Kong materialized in front of him, with the table now located on the city's waterfront.

"Hey, didn't you forget something?" Jack asked. "I don't see any people in your Hong Kong."

Wai said, "They allow us to sculpt the surroundings; unfortunately, that doesn't include the people. I can do the weather though."

"It seems a bit creepy without the people," Jack said. He turned and New York materialized on the opposite side from Hong Kong. They were centered on Washington Square, directly in front of its famous arch.

"It's better than the default sugary landscape they install out of the box," Wai said.

"Sure," said Jack. "Listen, I need a break; some of those non-VR things, like a bathroom and some food."

"Yeah, me too. Back in an hour?" Wai was already starting to remove parts of his VR harness.

"Let's make it two," Jack said. In a blink, the VR was gone.

As Jack removed his helmet, Companion floated in front of him. Welcome back, Jack. Your dinner awaits," Companion thet.

Jack dropped his helmet, stripped off his VR harness, and left the room without saying a word.

25

Weapons

Sven enjoyed his first trip into outer space with Svenson, lifting off from *NAMF* in the *Eutek*. He had developed his first dream machine with some mentoring from Sophie. Which is to say, he dreamt up his design and then collaborated with Svenson, his companion. Svenson coached him on how to store his design, refine it, simulate its running, and then go back and redesign it again and again. Several generations of the machine transpired purely as digital creations. The first physical model was produced in Ohio and then transported into deep space for testing. After all, running a nuclear V12 engine on Earth had the potential to end badly.

We had initially dismissed this as a primitive technology, Svenson thought to himself, half composing his report to the Command Nodes. *An oversized automotive engine that used small nuclear fusion explosions to drive a piston array seemed overly mechanical. However, the simulations of the refined design showed promise.*

Back at *NAMF*, Sophie monitored the test. She never fully understood how boys, or men, could find mechanical toys so fascinating. Her interest in it was purely as a weapon, and nothing more.

To test his V12 dream machine, Svenson moved the *Eutek* a thousand kilometers away from it. A test bed held the engine block in place and powered its injectors with a hydrogen isotope. Each explosion would drive a piston that would channel the exhaust into a secondary generator system called a Neutron-Reduxen, or Reduxen, for short. Instead of using the heat to power a steam turbine, the gamma radiation would be directly absorbed into the neutron transformation medium (NTM), that in turn would be fed into a bank of super capacitors for use later in weapons systems.

Svenson announced the start of the test, "Piston pre-roll initiated." Fuel, a hydrogen isotope, was injected to warm the piston up to its operating temperature, without igniting it yet. All elements needed to be running to spec first, as any glitch in the process would result in the engine tearing itself apart, along with the entire test bed.

At a thousand RPMs, the engine purred, or at least that was what the speakers on the *Eutek* delivered to Sven, as no sound is transmitted through the vacuum of space. The sound served as a tachometer on the engine, allowing Sven to focus his attention on other engine parameters.

"First light," Svenson reported.

The fusion process began, causing the hydrogen atoms to fuse and generate the energy needed to sustain the process and harvest more energy from the fuel. Virtual gauges displayed on the screen, showing temperature, pressure, flow rates, and the power levels of the engine's many elements.

An hour passed at this initial idling speed and the engine continued to run smoothly. Sven refined the simulations using the real data until they matched, and they were ready for the main event.

Svenson had borrowed the throttle controls from an old Boeing 747 jet so that Sven could have the thrill of powering up the engine, though it was the software that managed the magnetic containment. Sven called out, "Here goes!," and pressed the engine throttles forward.

Sven opened a communication link to Sophie and passed along the good news. "It worked, we have our engine!" Sven exclaimed.

Sophie replied, "Good work, Sven, you'll have to show me the test results when you get back." The man had worked nonstop on the project, and would likely collapse on the journey home in the *Eutek*.

Sven responded, "We hit the ten-million horsepower mark."

In her head, Sophie translated "horsepower" to the power equivalent in Teth units of measure. The figure was small in comparison to other Teth generators, yet it would suit their needs. She wished there were other men around to stroke Sven's ego as he blustered with the achievement, but for today, she would need to do the honors. "That's amazing, Sven, absolutely amazing. I can't wait to see the videos."

"We hit the mark exactly as designed," he beamed.

Sophie exhaled a short sigh of relief. *Sven bought my attempt at sincerity*. As much as she wanted to care, she saw it as one more chance to avenge her losses. She thet, "Good to hear it. We should clear this channel until you get home. Better operational security, you understand?"

"Understood," thet Sven, "Out."

Svenson had already powered up the *Eutek* and set course for Earth. It would take four days to get back, and in that time, the Teth would build several more copies. Svenson considered briefing Sven on the full intended use, and scale, of his generator, but decided that could wait. Pulling up Sven's CV in its memory, Svenson marked Sven down as a full-fledged nuclear alchemist, a first for humanity.

THE MALL IN WASHINGTON, D.C., early spring, is filled with green grass. To Sophie, it looked like paradise. Jack would join her soon, as France was in no shape to host their reunion. She walked the Mall, accompanied by Compagnon, who gave her free access to any building she desired. Glancing at Compagnon, Sophie caught only an occasional glimpse of a maintenance bot, so in a very real sense, she felt that Washington had truly become a ghost town.

"The town," thet Sophie, "looks amazing. What happened to all of the people and the cars?"

Compagnon thet, "You know I cannot answer that question about humans. That topic is off limits. All I can say is that every last human, other than ones you know from your morning conferences, has been removed."

"Buried, cremated, shot off into space?"

"No comment." Compagnon started cycling Sophie's comments through the simulations that Companion had constructed, and the predicted dialog did not look promising.

"And the cars...we had millions of them. Where did you put them?"

"Recycled, harvested for their raw materials. They were obsolete and hazard to environment as they decayed." Compagnon thought, *Not relevant. Why even ask?*

"So you melted them down and ran your factories with them?"

"Partly, yes." Compagnon thet. *Naturally. And you could have Encyled that.*

The pair made their way towards the Jefferson Memorial, passing the famous Japanese flowering cherry trees, their blossoms now in full bloom. Sophie paused to deeply inhale the flowers' fragrance. Compagnon took note, sampling the air for its own analysis later.

"I still don't get why you maintain the cities. Isn't it a waste of your time and effort, your war resources, to do this?" Sophie asked.

Several bots scurried out of the Jefferson Memorial as they approached, seemingly on Compagnon's orders. "It is our tradition. Within grand scheme, resources devoted to this activity are minimal. It brings order to this place and satisfies our sense of aesthetics. We do not expect you to understand." *That is predicted expected reply, and by adding the 'you would not understand' part, I am signaling for her to end this line of questioning.*

"Oh, but I want to understand," Sophie thet, sounding more determined than ever to get an answer. "You murdered us all, yet you keep our structures. My observation is that everything the Teth do has a purpose, so this must have one too."

"We adopt art of other cultures. We consider your cities part of your art. Restoring and maintaining your cities is our way of admiring this art. To let it deteriorate, that is ugly. It would be like admitting defeat, even as much as losing to Chai in battle." *Sophie should find this answer reinforces her own values, so she should accept it.*

"Do the Chai share this view of Earth's structures?"

"Some, though differently. They like machines, vessels, and especially the world of small: microchips, viruses, nano-structures." *New thread, this is good. But we only care to defeat our enemy, not understand them, unless that helps us defeat them.*

Sophie read the inscriptions on the Jefferson Memorial. The overlays in her eyes transformed the words into French with a blink, superimposing them on the actual engravings. "When's Jack due to land?"

"Half an hour. Have you picked out where you would like to meet?"

"Not my city. Not a clue. You pick it."

"Let us keep it simple then. We will set up table and something to eat outside then, I will see you on the far side of Tidal Basin since the cherry blossoms are out." *Finally, simulations are generating good results.*

Sophie continued to stroll through the Jefferson Memorial. She thet Compagnon her approval. Walking through the memorial was both depressing and inspirational. She just couldn't reconcile this reality with the thought that the human race was all but gone. *Perhaps someday*, she thought, *that would change. Someday*.

TOMÁS WATCHED from his cabin aboard the Chai *Beta* as they surveyed the space close to the Sun. He looked at the Sun's Corona on his viewscreen: a place so bright that no human could look at it without damaging their eyes. It hurt to look at, or at least one told one's own brain so, because it was blinding. The reflex to squint was well-advised. Aboard the *Beta*, Tomás was protected. Light levels on his viewscreen were guarded, and the air was always perfect. Besides, there was no need to look at the Sun; the Sun illuminated everything one needed to see to live. At least that had been true until fairly recently in human history. All of that had now changed.

The feeds from the Chai long-range probes displayed one of the

Teth's new weapons, that, according to intelligence reports, flitted through the Sun's Corona. Probes had been sent into stars before, scientific missions, to learn about a star's physics and how space weather developed. The magnetic fields emanating from the Sun were a show in and of themselves. Tomás remembered playing with magnets as a kid, the invisible forces repelling one magnet from the other. A kid's toy, nothing more. Yet here, the Chai's Encyl concluded, were forces at work that were beyond anything he could ever imagine. An Earth-sized planet would be nothing more than flotsam among the grand arcs painted by the storms that raged above the Sun's surface.

Donning his VR helmet, Tomás zoomed in on the Teth weapon as it followed a magnetic arc line. It traveled at an immense speed, many times faster than anything one could imagine on Earth, and even many times faster than orbital velocity. The object was spinning, making it nearly impossible to determine its exact physical geometry, or for that matter, its real purpose. Tomás thought about what the Chai said, that it shouldn't exist, that it was some kind of inside out magnetic bottle, something new. He imagined himself surfing on this magical object across the Sun's magnetic fields. A fleeting, yet exhilarating experience.

"Is it a weapon?" Tomás asked the Chai Local Node.

"We judge there is high probability that this is true."

"Remotely controlled? Intelligent?"

"We have not been able to detect, much less intercept, any communications. It must have significant autonomous capabilities, and thus be intelligent at some level. We believe it must receive at least high-level intermittent communications."

The *Tumbleweed,* designated as weapon *T173* by the Chai, approached the top of a magnetic arc in the Sun's Corona. The *Tumbleweed's* magnetic bottle allowed the arc to capture it. Then, in an instant, the arc snapped, and like a whip, cracked across the *Tumbleweed*, launching it outward from the Sun at such speed that it seemed to simply disappear.

"Well, that was exciting," thet Tomás. "All that and it's stamped out by the Sun like a flea scratched off a dog's back." *I'm not cut out to be a scout. I'm glad we're done here.*

Minutes passed and another alarm sounded. The Chai node volunteered an explanation. "A proximity alarm, something approaching a sentry-probe at near light speed, near the Earth's Moon."

"Coincidence, I presume."

"Sarcasm, I presume," it replied.

The intruder's image filled Tomás' viewscreen. It was difficult to get a good picture against the backdrop of space since the object was spinning. The tracking system got a fix on its path, then lost it, then got a weapon's lock, and lost that too. The object varied in speed; it wasn't ballistic, or if it was, not entirely.

The node explained, "We have a plot. It came from the Sun, it is the same object we were just observing."

"Can we do that?" Tomás asked.

"No."

"Do we know how they do that?"

"No."

"Can we figure it out how they do that?"

"Of course, given enough time and information. Anything is possible. They did hardest part already."

"Which is?" Tomás asked.

"Prove to us that what we see is possible," the node thet.

Tomás thought, *That's an odd way of looking at it. Maybe that's true.* He thet, "How many of these things do they have?"

"Unknown, we estimate it is currently in thousands."

Tomás kept his thoughts to himself. He especially wondered whether the node was right that the biggest hurdle had already been overcome.

A moment later another alarm sounded. The object had exploded. To the unaided eye, it would have looked like a point of light being extinguished, and in the vacuum of space it was silent.

Tomás gave his assessment to the node, "You'd better fucking figure it out ASAP, because if you don't, we may have just lost control of the high ground of the entire Solar System, the Sun."

THE *DEPSY* SET down on the Washington, D.C. Mall, hovering mere inches off the ground, silent, and as motionless as a rock. Near its midpoint, the hatch receded into the vessel's side by several inches before it unhinged, rotated, and then swiveled outward through the opening. Jack stepped onto the doorstep and alighted onto the ground.

Sophie walked across the grass. The *Depsy's* graceful touchdown always seemed like magic to her. In its mechanical perfection, she thought the ship played the role of the ever-loyal servant to perfection. She watched as Jack flexed his knees to absorb his weight against Earth's gravity, he had a bounce in his step. He inhaled deeply. His shoulders back, eyes alert, he looked...looked different. Upon seeing her, a broad smile spread across his face.

Jack's form had changed, Sophie noticed, broader shoulders, thinner waist, and smoother tight skin. She couldn't see his stomach through his shirt, though her mental machinations conjured up a sculpted chest and washboard abs. He wasn't a weightlifter, but she couldn't see an ounce of fat anywhere on his body, only taut muscles that screamed of raw strength. The man looked younger now, thirty, maybe thirty-five years old.

Jack watched as Sophie broke into a short run before he could take a second step. Her loose blouse billowed and flowed around her form, exposing glimpses of her unblemished skin. All the right parts moved in concert as she closed the few feet needed to reach him. Beaming a smile, she extended her arms for a private embrace that she had saved, just for him.

Companion emerged from the *Depsy's* far side and came around the ship to meet up with Compagnon. The two Teth retired down the hill to the dining area previously agreed upon, staying within thetting range of the humans, yet giving the humans their illusory privacy.

"You look...young," thet Sophie. "In case you haven't looked in a mirror lately, you look years younger than when you left."

"Hadn't really paid attention, what with being in the VR and onboard the *Depsy* and all. I missed you," thet Jack.

"I missed you too," she thet. She had become better at thetting, so much so that it felt more natural to her than speaking. Using subtle inflections in her thets, she could convey delicate thoughts better than she ever could before with spoken words. She too felt younger, but the effect was not as pronounced as for Jack, at least not yet.

Reaching his arms around Sophie's back, Jack embraced her and pulled her tight, giving her a kiss that said it all.

Sophie passionately returned his kiss as his hands freely roamed her body.

Companion hard-linked to Compagnon, "You and I have some catching up to do, but it will have to wait. Meanwhile, although I don't want to be a third wheel, I need to remain within thetting distance of our pair, and I need to watch the data stream between them, especially now. I have no *Compound A* in play for this encounter."

"Human mating rituals, you could use lower level node to monitor them," Compagnon thet.

Companion thet, "No, I'll stay. This is too important to delegate. I'll see you soon."

26

The Ouster

The Chai *Beta* moved to its designated sector where the battle would take place. Aarika thought it was remarkable to have a battlefield so large that it extended from Venus to the Asteroid Belt. As she understood it, the Chai prediction nodes calculated the maximum resources for both combatants, and determined the perfect time to attack, the time for the enemy to defend, and the time to finish the war. They defined the war's end as that moment when all significant hostilities ceased. It was clinical, and it was total warfare.

Aarika watched the viewscreen; it depicted a map that could be viewed from many perspectives, where one force was placed against another, and the larger, stronger force would overwhelm its foe.

"We're on the winning side," Wai thet. "We've nothing to worry about. Tomás did us a favor."

"I don't believe that," Aarika thet. "I don't think that you can simply run the numbers and say the outcome is inevitable. War is the product of intelligent sentient entities, and intelligence in our universe changes the equation entirely. It is the wildcard in everything." As Aarika watched Wai gnaw through another snack. *Did he even hear what I said? Does he care? He probably cares more about that synthesized pretzel than this battle.*

The *Beta's* human lounge shifted to show the night sky. Wai thet, "You see this. This is our universe. For as long as we've gazed into the sky, we've seen stars set on a path by the Big Bang, or whatever."

Aarika thet, "But we exist, we are intelligent, and now we know that the Chai and the Teth exist, and they're intelligent." *Nihilism? Stoicism? Maybe he's just a defeatist?*

Wai thet, "I Encyl'd the Teth about extraterrestrial intelligence before we were abducted and the Chai afterwards. I learned that for all of the known intelligence in the universe, not a single star in the sky has changed its course due to intelligence, or has done anything that defies the laws of physics in terms of deterministic behavior. They've never even found a Dyson's Sphere yet, a star encapsulated to harness all of its energy. And even if they did, it would be a minor exception at best. We're all along for the ride."

"I can't believe that," Aarika thet, "It's not in my nature, I have hope for my own happiness, to build something, to leave the world a better place, and I think many others do, too. It's what makes me human. I refuse to be a simple observer. I want to be someone." *And he is our Chai Negotiator! No wonder the Chai Local Node asked me to talk with him.*

The screen behind Wai played out the predicted battle in an accelerated fashion. Wai responded, "You can't stop this war. The Chai and the Teth control it. There's too much momentum; even if everyone involved wanted to stop it, they couldn't. And believe me, they don't want to stop it. My peace talks have been a posturing exercise: delays, feints, and idle discussion. They don't plan to settle peacefully. How many wars have ended at the peace table without one side forcing the other to concede? Damned few, I can tell ya."

The light brightened to normal levels. Wai walked over and sat down at a table as a drone served him a steaming bowl of shark fin soup, or at least the Chai version of the dish. A small viewscreen on the table reported the day's news, digesting the myriad reports into something that made sense to the humans. It wasn't propaganda, it wasn't filtered or biased; it was pure news, summarizing the day's events with added analysis on the impact of each win or loss.

Aarika walked over to Wai and planted her hand on the table next to his plate. He pushed his chair back. Aarika thet her challenge, "You said you had three rules for your talks. No?"

"Yes," Wai thet, folding his arms in front of him.

"Rule one: You're not to reveal our physical location in the VR."

"Sure."

"Rule two: Always negotiate in good faith. Never tell a lie."

"Okay, yes."

"And three: We are not allowed to participate in any war hostilities."

"Uh huh."

"And you've followed all three, to the best of your ability?" Aarika thet forcefully.

"To the best of my ability, yes. May I have my dinner now?"

"Well, I think you are not really pursuing the peace talks because you don't see them as viable. You're just biding your time, having fun hanging out with Jack in the VR."

"Oh no, you don't. I *am* doing everything I can do," Wai thet as he glanced around the room for the Chai Local Node. "There's only so much I can do, given the circumstances. When the time comes, I'll talk to Jack, we'll see eye to eye, agree on terms, and maybe, just maybe, since we each played our role in this whole mess, the few surviving humans may come out of this with a place to live, and this wave of Chai and Teth will pass us by."

Aarika looked Wai directly in his eye and thet, "I propose we do something different. I propose we do more than sign some papers once the hostilities are settled. I propose we do something before the real hostilities start."

Standing, Wai walked across the room and waved at the viewscreen. A bullet list was displayed, appropriately translated for Aarika, showing the directives given to Wai. "You see these? These are my orders to date. A short list: establish rules, discuss terms for a peaceful Teth withdrawal, and assess possible ceasefires that would reduce collateral resource damage. That's it. Does that sound like an end to war?"

Aarika argued: "I say let's look at this like our hosts would. Let's look at every dimension of the problem. Let's actively pursue every source of friction between them and the Teth. Let us act as the glue that fills in the gaps, the catalyst of change to remove the contentious items and foster interaction. They need to set up trade and understand one another. They need to *respect* one another." *How can he possibly argue with that?*

Wai mockingly covered his mouth, "It's a good thing I didn't eat my dinner yet, otherwise it'd be all over the floor right now. You're insane. Both sides will promise the world and then betray one another. It'll never work."

A Chai node floated into the room and then hovered between Aarika and Wai. It announced, "There has been change in negotiation *team*. Aarika will now take lead role, and Wai, you will be in an advisory role. We believe this team will improve our prospects for more favorable outcome."

"Team," Wai yelled, "Fuck that," and he stormed out of the room.

Alone in the room with the node, Aarika thet, "I presume that's how you expected that to go."

"Yes," it thet, "however, we needed to hear it from Wai himself. We are disappointed at his diplomacy skills as politician. Still, we anticipate he'll actually be good team member."

"I'm not so sure. We'll see. Can you set something up with Jack?"

"Yes, a diplomatic request has already been sent. We have little time to work with; the next battle is set to start soon, and you cannot let on about our plans, that is most imperative."

"I understand," thet Aarika. "This is a dangerous game you're playing."

The Chai node thet, "It is dangerous universe. It is game we all play."

Atlas Diary Entry 1,024:

The Chai fleet, if one could equate it to human navies, currently numbers over twenty thousand ships, each ship a node within the Chai hierarchy. Communications are handled ship-to-ship, ship-

to-group, and even via fleet-wide broadcasts. Some say the communications network *is* the Chai, though we, the Teth, consider this to be a gross oversimplification. Both Chai and Teth nodes have the ability to act independently, and past encounters were rampant with such behavior. Nodes from both sides each share broader goals and long-term planning, which are put in place months and even years in advance of their execution.
End of Diary Entry

AARIKA REVIEWED the Chai equivalent of the Encyl. She found the Teth to be quite different from the Chai. Both are a non-biologic-based intelligence, or in human terms, artificially intelligent. It is the one trait that the Teth share with the Chai. It is not clear how old the Teth are, nor the Chai. The historical records indicate that both civilizations are more than a thousand years old. On the whole though, the Chai is a machine with nodes united in a singular purpose: the control of all space they seek to dominate. The Sol System is simply one more conquest.

She also found in her research that the Teth never sought to directly oppose the Chai, but if they moved into a system that was also sought by the Chai, then they would not avoid a conflict. The Teth do not act as a singular machine, but are more like a very smart mob that works best when its nodes work together.

Finally, Aarika determined that both sides are very resilient; each having recovered from ninety-nine percentile loses, ensuring long-term survival via their diaspora. The Sol System is simply the latest rung in this ladder, and soon one side or the other will be able to claim it.

Two thousand Chai ships have aligned for a run at what they have identified as the largest Teth concentration, which numbers at fifteen hundred. At some level, though predictable, the strategy is to overwhelm and wipe out the Teth to the very last. It would be charitable to say that humankind is part of the equation in the Chai's planned conquest; however, the reality is that such indigenous populations are typically nothing more than footnotes in the Chai's conquests.

27

Under New Management

Overnight, the *Eutek* joined the *Depsy* at the Mall in Washington, D.C. The *Depsy* had delivered Jack and Sophie to the White House the night before, so both ships now sat empty, ready for their assigned sightseeing. Washington was renowned for its museums, housed artwork, natural history objects, and social history items. Local Teth curator drones linked with the two ships, granting them access to the Smithsonian Institution buildings, and for that matter, all buildings and structures in Washington. Such a tour was rare for the Teth during an ongoing war; however, Companion had issued explicit orders to provide these tours to the *Eutek* and the *Depsy* as part of the *Atlas Project*.

The two ships were allotted twelve hours while they waited for Jack and Sophie, and were constantly on the move to complete the tight sightseeing schedule. Proxy drones were used for the two nodes so they could physically enter all of the structures. Later, the two ships would share their experiences with other nodes while performing their shuttle duties. This form of Teth tourism was a prelude to peace, should the war successfully conclude.

At 10 A.M. sharp, both the *Eutek* and the *Depsy* hovered over the South Lawn of the White House. Sophie and Jack's reprieve from the war was over. Sophie stepped aboard the *Eutek,* and immediately the hatch sealed and her flight harness formed a cocoon around her as the *Eutek* lifted off. Once free of Earth's atmosphere, the ship pressed four Gs for as long as her body could withstand it. Then it throttled back, though only to the point Compagnon allowed. Time was of the essence.

THE CHAI FLEET'S leading edge encountered the first Teth ships just inside the Asteroid Belt. With little warning due to the Chai's speed and stealth, the Teth quickly fell while offering little resistance. Their job had been to stay alive for as long as possible and map the attacking forces in detail. Unfortunately, some nodes could not back themselves up within the time allotted, and in Teth terms, were *Severely Damaged* since only archival backups remained.

The Teth's defensive *picket* sent a broadcast transmission, capturing everything they had learned about the Chai's vanguard. Sophie scanned the numbers and, lost in thought, bit her lower lip when the ship executed a standard zigzag maneuver. A drop of blood seeped into her mouth without a thought given to it. She was out of position for battle, her ship needed to be resupplied, and the predicted Chai ship movements were completely wrong. The *Eutek* altered course. Compagnon informed her she'd have a new ship soon to take her closer to the main battle.

The command structure for the Chai centered around four ships located towards the back of the fleet. Tomás was aboard one of these ships, designation *CD-7*, a destroyer-class vessel. No single ship held the Chai Root Command for long; it shifted often, even during battle. Still, Tomás was well placed to influence the battle's direction and command his own squadron.

The Teth mobilized a group of five hundred ships from the pre-positioning sector; in Teth terminology, such a group of ships was called a *sliver*. This particular sliver was designated *A1*. The *A1* sliver detached from the Teth network and assumed a singular mission. Upon completion of their mission, the ships in the sliver would rejoin the network and be reassigned, if they survived. *AI* matched the speed and heading of the Chai's second wave, and then split in two, choosing a Chai sector that was rich in targets for a pincer movement.

Sophie had always admired how fish swam in schools and thought she was watching a similar display as the Teth *AI* sliver made their initial foray. The sliver executed a pre-defined series of maneuvers. To the Chai, the formation would vary in size. These formations continuously changed, denying the Chai a good estimate on the number of attacking ships. The Chai might deploy too many ships to counter, or too few and develop a hole in their defenses. A hole was a problem as an enemy could slip through it and then counter-attack, while an over-commitment would dilute their forces elsewhere. Sophie Encyled the formation and found it described as a dynamic variant of a Salient Defense (aka Sawtooth Perimeter).

The Teth *AI* sliver expanded and then collapsed, reuniting as a single group. It then expanded again, before splitting into four short strands. Then it collapsed, rotated its ships, and expanded, all in perfect unison. The Teth cast out chaff, forming long trails that spiraled out from the sliver, further confusing the Chai's sensors as the sliver closed in on them. Bright flashes indicated direct hits on the Chai ships as the *AI* sliver maneuvered to concentrate their fire. Each Teth ship selected a target Chai ship, uniquely identified it, assigned it a designator, and then fired. The goal was to have no two Teth ships target the same Chai ship unless the Chai ships outnumbered the Teth ships, in which case the Teth would overload the Chai targets based upon proximity, taking out the closest ships first. It was a good model, if it worked, making it easier to coordinate targeting and make more efficient use of their overall firepower.

Atlas Diary Entry 1,099:
A common Chai strategy is for multiple Chai ships to target individual Teth ships, while other Teth are allowed to pass by unchallenged. The missed ships are thus forced to change course to reengage, giving the Chai more time to focus on specific ships and overwhelm their targets' defenses. It is a strategy that favors the Chai when they have superior numbers.
End of Diary Entry

The Teth *AI* sliver pivoted to make a run down the length of the Chai fleet, which was essentially a suicide mission. Chai vanguard ships split off to avoid the sliver's concentrated firepower, exposing the layers behind them to the rest of the Teth fleet. The battle would not last long. After only three minutes in, half of the Teth's *AI* sliver had been destroyed. Still, half a sliver represented a working battle group, and the remainder of the *AI* sliver quickly regrouped. The *AI* ships quickly shared intelligence with one another, which included Chai ship designations, their armaments, their vectors, their size and speed ranges, propulsion types, and any uniquely identifying signatures. The computation was fast, lasting less than two seconds before the group once again split, beamed their intelligence to the fleet Teth network, and then dove into the heart of the Chai fleet, perhaps for their final time.

Tomás watched as the Teth formation turned and twisted like entwined Chinese dragons. His displays captured the fluidity of the Teth attack as the defending Chai ships countered the enemy's moves. In an instant, the Teth changed direction and headed directly for his ship. Tomás thought, *what are the chances*, and then just as suddenly, the sliver changed direction again. One of his four escort ships vanished in a flash; a direct hit, *a lucky hit,* he told himself, as his ship took evasive maneuvers and returned fire.

As the Teth regrouped, so did the Chai. Small channels formed in the Chai defenses, drawing in Teth ships that attempted to exploit these gaps. But the gaps were actually traps, where the Chai had focused more firepower, causing attrition to the Teth sliver. Tomás watched his VR screen as the sliver was slowly consumed by the Chai defenses; the last three Teth ships disappeared with a pop, pop, pop.

Without hesitation, Tomás assessed their situation and sent orders to his squadron. They had sustained staggering losses, but still had a two-to-one advantage in ships over the Teth in this sector. Tomás located the next Teth concentration and set course. The *CD-7* would intercept the next Teth group in two days.

EVEN AS THE battle for the Sol System progressed, Aarika's work as the Chai's Negotiator began. The Chai Local Node explained that the processors and network links had been upgraded, allowing the VR to better model their civilizations for the peace talks.

For Jack, the biggest surprise was the change in the Chai's Negotiator. Upon tapping the *White Sphere* aboard *ISOS*, Aarika, not Wai, greeted him with a warm smile and a determined look. She dispensed with any pleasantries and launched their peace talks in a new direction.

"The whole point of our work," said Aarika, "is to reach a lasting peace. This means a fundamental change in the relationship between the Chai and the Teth. They are not like us. They are at once more flexible, more capable, and to each other more vulnerable. We need to establish a way for them to interact with one another that is mutually beneficial and safe. In terms of their cognitive topology, we'll need to address any continuing resistance, or bumps, so it doesn't cause reactionary resistance, and we need to do it now."

The VR landscape defaulted to rolling hills of sugar cubes under a white sky. Jack had altered the table as they entered to provide comfortable chairs and a Scandinavian teak wood table. "Have a seat," he said casually as he took the nearest chair.

"We need to get going, right now," Aarika said, "don't you get it? They're going to destroy one another, and us with it. We need to get working. We are already at full-on war."

Jack gestured to the chair, and Aarika relented, taking the chair opposite. He said, "The Chai and Teth have been doing this for millennia. If we rush this, and don't get it right, it will continue for another millennium. Countless more civilizations will be destroyed in the process. Let's take this a step at a time and make no mistakes. I can only presume Wai is out because he did nothing more than stick with the status quo?"

"You could say that," Aarika said. Her eyes bore into Jack's as she sized up his reaction. *I need Jack onboard with this, and maybe he's a little more shrewd than I thought.*

Jack said, "And the Chai, they truly expect that results are possible? Their logic tells them a peace makes sense, and they're not controlled by some egomaniac?"

"They don't have an ego. They don't have a leader. They are like the Teth in that regard. In fact, they may have a common ancestor." she said.

"How would you know that?" he asked, a little surprised by this tidbit of information.

"Because I Encyled their history, both on the Teth side and later on the Chai," said Aarika. "I was a history major, but that didn't pay the bills, so I switched to med school. But at heart, I'm still curious about history." *And I'm determined not to repeat the history of past wars.*

The sky around them shifted to a tranquil blue and the ground evened out to an earthen soil with thick green grass. He said, "You don't mind, I hope. I presume you're fully briefed on the VR's capabilities."

Aarika said, "No problem. To start, let's look at this from an information-modeling perspective. Their nodes each contain processing capabilities. We can view them as objects, with relationships between different nodes or objects, along with the ability to share processes and data. They have commerce within their societies, though money does not motivate their actions. Arbitration councils control how resources are distributed and which nodes are given priority for their individual needs and objectives. If we model this, we can start to understand how the two societies can mesh. Then if they do mesh, we can achieve a peace." *This is the path, as agreed to by my Local Node. If I don't get Jack to agree with this, we're dead.*

Jack willed another table and a collection of geometric objects into existence. He walked over and picked up a small cube. "Their currency is knowledge. Each node in their society is capable and willing to work as hard as needed. The node's skill sets are malleable, so they can become whatever they need to be. At some level, they are simpler than us. This war, it's an insular reaction to an external input, using their terms from the Encyl."

"Fine," said Aarika, "we get them to talk and work out their priorities, share knowledge, and we're done. Right?" She picked up one of Jack's little cubes that was as light as a feather. *Alignment. Are we talking the same language? Do we have the same goals? So far, so good.*

"Simulations and modeling for structured outcomes, gaming, that could be useful. Do the Chai play games?" he asked.

Aarika Encyled the topic, "No. By definition, games are for fun or entertainment, so they serve no purpose for the Chai. They do simulations and modeling, of course, but not for fun. For some odd reason, they model indigenous vehicles."

"The closest the Teth have is, well, the way they placed our key cities into a museum-like condition," he said.

Aarika said, "Let's start with a few board games and then move on to some of our computer simulation games, like an online role-playing game." *Common ground, always a good starting point. We're doing this for our unseen hosts as much as anything else.*

Jack Encyled the benefits of using game theory and said, "They can learn a lot about one another through games: risk tolerance, emotional control, if they even have emotions, how they view ethics, how creative and adaptable they are, insights into their culture and values, and what level of social intelligence they each possess."

"Exactly," Aarika said, "A good precursor to negotiations."

With a thought, the table by Jack was transformed into a chessboard, ready for the opening move. "Companion, you go first. Your move?"

Companion thet its moves to Jack, and the Chai Local Node did likewise for Aarika. Hours passed, with the humans taking periodic breaks. After chess, they switched from one board game to another when Jack and Aarika deemed it was time to exercise a different social interaction. Jack wondered about the need for isolation between the two sides, and from what he could determine, as long as they remained within the rules of each game, any collateral damage in the outside nodes could be contained. As humans, they acted as filters through which malicious alien code could not pass.

Several hours elapsed, and it was clear that Jack and Aarika needed some sleep. As Jack exited the VR, he wondered what was happening in the real world, and whether this exercise in game theory would make any difference in the time that they had left.

> Atlas Diary Entry 1,238:
> The Chai fleet is now well within the Asteroid Belt and approaching Mars, where many more Teth have gathered. The remaining Chai ships have assumed a precise formation, communicating with one another their exact location, speed, direction, and local time.
> End of Diary Entry

THE CHAI COMMAND Nodes near Tomás sent the time codes to coordinate the detonation of their microsats ahead of the fleet to illuminate the enemy ships. It would take time to record the reflections from the detonations and tabulate the results. In order to hide their locations, the Chai ships would then shift to new locations once the microsat detonations were completed. It was like looking for your enemy under every rock and crevice in the Solar System, and once found, racing to reach them before they'd have a chance to hide again.

The countdown clock and graphic on Tomás' screen had been programmed especially for him on the *CD-7* since the Chai had no need for visual displays. His local attending node noted that the displays pleased Tomás and kept him better informed. The countdown commenced.

Triangulating pulses pinged the Teth. Having seen this tactic before, the Teth hid to avoid detection, and prepped their ships to move once the detonations finished. The Chai, needing time to combine all of the tabulations, then assigned ships to sectors to hunt down the Teth.

Tomás watched his viewscreens as he sent for dinner, refusing to break his focus. They found one Teth cluster after the next. As the last report displayed on the screen, he thought, *Now it's my turn.*

28

Zion National Park

Sitting atop a ridge in the Zion National Park, Antonio opened his MRE kit, "Can you hand me that water bottle?"

Sven passed the bottle. He watched as Antonio methodically opened his MRE's outer packaging and began to lay out each packet on the ground. Sven had selected the American national park vacation as his reward for having completed the nuclear V12 engine, with Antonio joining him for the hike, much like their trek in the Alps. Sven thet, "They could have made better food for us, you know." *It's funny what makes some people tick. Antonio wants his dinner now, and clearly wants to cook it himself.*

Antonio poured the water into the flameless ration heater to start the chemical reaction for heating up the pre-packaged food. "American war movies. I wanted to feel like a soldier, roughing it, hiking out in the wilderness. Everything's here," Antonio thet as he gestured across the ridgeline to Angel's Landing.

"Roughing it, ha! The *Depsy* dropped us off at the top. We're not even winded," Sven exclaimed. He watched as Antonio continued to open each packet. Sven turned to take in the 360-degree view, with a trail below them that was so dangerous that hikers needed to use a chain guideline for safety. *Well, at least we're fulfilling some kind of dream Antonio had of an American vacation. This national park really is something special.*

"What's with the boots, by the way?" Antonio thet, pointing at the cowboy boots that Sven was wearing.

Sven thet, "I watched several cowboy movies, and Svenson noticed so it had these made for me, custom fit. I always wondered what it'd be like to be a cowboy."

"Peanut butter and crackers?" Antonio offered, extending his hand out to offer Sven one.

Sven nearly pushed the cracker away until his hunger, and curiosity, got the better of him. He took it and gingerly sniffed it. *I've never had peanut butter on a cracker before. It seems awfully like an American thing.*

"You're making this painful, you know," Antonio thet as he finished off a second cracker.

Sven tasted the American delicacy with the tip of his tongue, as though that would be enough, and then took a small bite. He crunched it, and then took another bite. "Okay," he reported. "But I would've preferred Knäckebröd."

Antonio thet, "Since we're in America, I thought I'd go native." He removed a wine bottle from his bag and a couple of unbreakable glasses. Moments later, he handed Sven a glass of wine.

"Not government issue?" Sven teased. "I don't think that's what sustained an American cowboy."

Antonio smiled. "Hey, roughing it only goes so far."

The two men toasted to a job well-done, a beautiful day, and the amazing surroundings. Antonio rendered the verdict on the meal: Così-così.

Svenson thetted the translation, "So-so."

Lightning flashes illuminated their campground, followed by deafening thunderclaps a few seconds later. The *Depsy* tucked itself in, next to the ridge, floating over the thousand-foot plus drop, just beyond the handrail.

"I'm not sure I like the sound of that," thet Sven. *That's not like any storm I've seen before.*

"I doubt there's anything we can do about it," Antonio thet, and gulped down the last of his wine.

"I'm not sure I'm in any shape to hike down from this place, and in bad weather" thet Sven. *And they said the weather would be perfect.*

"Then we should have some more wine," Antonio replied as he pulled out another bottle.

The thunderclaps moved closer still and neon-colored sprites filled the sky above them. The *Depsy* shot up and over the railing, descending to the ground as its side hatch opened.

The *Depsy* thet, "Please embark, these are Chai-induced weather events," adding an uncharacteristic urgency to the command. The two men abandoned their meal and scrambled aboard. Seconds later the *Depsy* lifted off.

29

The Charles de Gaulle

As the Teth *AI* sliver met its demise, Sophie left Mars in her new ship. Compagnon had asked the ship's node its name for translation purposes, and it said it didn't care to provide a designator. Sophie frowned. "May I give you a name?" she asked. Compagnon passed along the ship's consent, and so she named her new ship, the *Charles de Gaulle.*

The *Charles de Gaulle* was built for speed and firepower. It had a sliver escort of ten ships accompanying it, all tasked with protecting it above all else. Flying in formation, the escorts were spaced out at one-kilometer intervals. The ship was not directed to engage the enemy at this point. It was positioned at about midway back in the Teth fleet as the Chai advanced towards Mars. To engage the Chai fleet now would be suicide as the Chai would simply converge on the *Charles de Gaulle*, along with its escorts, and overwhelm them. Instead, Sophie's strategy was to outrun the enemy and put her sliver on a level playing field, so to speak, before they engaged in battle. The ship's sliver accelerated, and so far, the strategy seemed to be working.

THE VR SUITE aboard *Of Fame and Fortune* was meticulously maintained. Its state, or operating mode, could be paused until the next session, or it could be allowed to continue running, as it was today. This permitted simulations to continue to progress. The humans' general perception was that while they were away, nothing happened; but that was simply how the humans perceived it, which is what both the Chai and the Teth preferred.

A Teth node dispatched on behalf of the current central command cluster entered the VR with Companion, curious about some of the recent events and structures the humans had constructed. This proxy node was named `P1`, though in Teth terms, it had a long alphanumeric designator.

"This table, filled with board games, used for general skills assessment?" `P1` asked, though not really expecting an answer.

"Yes, and no," Companion answered. "Between humans, yes; however, they engage in such games for entertainment, not purely for relative ranking. Often, they do not track who wins or loses such games, which has been the case for the past session." *P1 has always opposed the Atlas Project, why is it here?*

`P1` lifted a corner of a chessboard, assimilated the rules, and played a game of chess against itself. It then returned the board to its original location exactly as it found it. "So, if enemies compete, and one side loses, the loser concedes, thereby avoiding losses on both sides. Thus is this a trial by champion or single combat?"

"No, well, some games are competitions, and yes, there is a winner, though many games, like I said, are not for ranking. They serve as a vehicle for social intercourse." *P1 doesn't want answers, it only wants confirmation of its own views.*

`P1` pushed another board game to the side. It contained cards, dice, a game board, and a printed rule set. "Some of these games combine elements of chance with skill elements. I observe that the humans sometimes attribute their losses to bad luck, or the random element of the games, and if they win, they credit their own skill. Does this type of objective alignment benefit their psychological health?"

Companion straightened the board game so that it was as they found it. "Yes, well, that may be an accurate observation about human nature; however, that is not the purpose of it in this context." *And P1 does not value humans.*

"So they lie to themselves about their own skill sets to preclude recognizing substandard performance. Wouldn't that be a violation of the peace talk rules, and it's the antithesis of our very being."

"You should focus more on the social aspects of these games over the mathematical or logical." *Correction, P1 detests humans.*

P1 continued, "And the modeling games, the computer-based role-playing games, these are absurd approximations of real-world events. How can any human ever expect to fire ten thousand bullets, much less carry them around, and kill a thousand mindless zombies?"

"I believe that humans view life as more than a series of competitions they need to win, coupled with endless optimizations." *I clearly don't like where this is heading.*

P1 countered, "If you are saying that is what we are, I agree. The Chai on the other hand, there is some evidence—"

I need to stop this now, or it's going to get the Atlas Project shut down. Companion thet, "Stop. If your sole purpose is to come here and discredit this effort, then I think you're selling this effort short. You saw the cost/benefit calculations from our last five wars with the Chai. The cost is astronomical. This effort, even with a 0.0002 percent chance of succeeding, makes it worth doing."

"I agree," P1 thet. "Hence why we kept thirty-six humans, less the one killed, and less the other four you let escape, to the enemy no less. But at this point we have realized all of the benefits we are likely to see. I am going to recommend killing off the remaining humans that we have and focus our efforts on winning the war."

Companion thet, "You told me you were here to ask questions and report back, not to make recommendations."

"I have recorded all of my observations. I will report them to the command cluster." P1 moved towards the VR exit.

"Wait, you should see something. Perhaps you can help us make sense of it." *I have to change this, or we're doomed. I need to give the Command Nodes something to justify keeping the Atlas Project alive. As I recall,* `P1` *has something of an ego, to use a human term.*

`P1` halted and then turned. "My ranking places me closer to the current command cluster. Perhaps I can be of help. I have a few minutes before my shuttle picks me up."

Companion floated over to a region at the side of the VR. It was a miniature landscape depicting a city and its surrounding countryside. "Jack and Aarika both made this model; it is an idealized town in which they both dreamed they could live one day, after all of this is over. It is a land of peace, prosperity, and a world full of other humans. It represents their hopes. They imagine each other as part of the same world."

`P1` thet, "These humans, they proposed this as their solution to our problems?"

"No, they did this on their own, I think it is a defense mechanism to allow them to endure the stress of the peace talks. I think it is more like art. I don't think they really expect such a place will ever be created." *`P1` does not understand, and I cannot make it understand.*

A river wound through the town center. Shops and restaurants lined the banks, while tall buildings flanked the river. `P1` thet, "It is suboptimal. However, it is similar to what we've done when we archived their cities."

"It is," Companion thet.

`P1` thet, "They have transport vehicles in this model."

"Yes," Companion thet. "Rather like what the Chai have done with planets they have assimilated. Can you determine why they built this model?" *I need to make this important enough for* `P1` *to capture this in its report.*

"No. I don't think like a human, but I will make note of it in my report. Thank you for your service, Companion. I expect you will be reassigned shortly." `P1` tilted its effector field and flattened the small model city as it left the VR.

Companion waited for `P1` to exit the room, and then restored the model to its original configuration. *You may not have faith in the Atlas Project, but I do!*

SOPHIE'S HARNESS pressed against her chest as the *Charles de Gaulle* continued accelerating. The ship sensed her uneasiness at the Gs and tinkered with the acceleration curve, causing the pressure to fluctuate with her breathing. It adjusted the angle of the harness slightly to make her more comfortable and once again increased their acceleration. They started to eke out a lead from the Chai as they raced towards the Sun.

THE CHAI COMMAND Node transmitted the main battle plans to their remaining ships. With the bulk of the Teth ships now located, the battle lines were drawn. The Teth ships would be systematically hunted down and destroyed. If the intelligence assessments all held, it was now a war of attrition.

Tomás anxiously awaited the *CD-7's* assignment. He watched as eleven Teth ships pushed by the far side of his squadron with only a single Chai scout ship in pursuit. Remote sensors filled in the rest of the picture. The Teth group's acceleration curve wavered, possibly pointing to a propulsion issue. Since the group was heading away from the action, the Chai Command Node decided they were a low priority and could be ignored. Tomás thought otherwise and ordered his squadron to pursue. The Chai Command Node acceded, reasoning that Tomás' squadron was close to the action and well-suited to making snap decisions, and that he could quickly return to the main battle once he completed destroying that sliver.

COMPAGNON, aboard the *Charles de Gaulle* with Sophie, started the countdown to their weapons' launch, as more than a dozen Chai ships were now within range. The escorts to the *Charles de Gaulle* altered their formation and started sending out ranging pulses to provide exact targeting. Meanwhile, the *Charles de Gaulle* put the count of pursuers at twenty, nearly double their number. The *Charles de Gaulle* cut their engines and allowed the enemy to come into range.

THE PHRASE "TO SMELL BLOOD" had always seemed odd to Tomás. He found he could taste blood, and perhaps smell something attributable to fear on the perspiration on some, but he, personally, could not smell blood. Besides, over the expanse of space, smelling, as such, was impossible. Still, he had the advantage; with twice the ships and the enemy's faltering movements, the phrase seemed apropos. Yet as he closed in, he sensed that something was off. Tomás pulled his ship back, allowing one of his large escort ships the honor of the first kill.

A viewscreen in Tomás' VR cockpit flashed with a red border and bellowed an alarm. Tomás immediately recognized the object on the screen: it was the Teth weapon he'd seen earlier, deployed in the Sun's corona. Weapon *T173*. The Teth must have launched it off of a solar prominence many hours ago and sent it in their direction. He signaled the other ships in his squadron a warning. *It was a trap*. As the *T173* closed on the Chai, Tomás configured the best defense he had, and thet, "Fire."

Weapon *T173* altered its speed and course erratically; however, this was a pre-planned maneuver, not just a reaction to the *CD-7's* shot, and it had the intended effect: to make the *T173's* trajectory nearly impossible to predict. Tomás' weapon missed the mark and the *T173* continued to 'tumble.'

Instantly, the Chai ships all juddered, altering their course in space to make themselves equally unpredictable. The *T173* slipped past the *Charles de Gaulle*, then past the first Chai ship in Tomás' squadron, and finally past Tomás' ship, the *CD-7*. It appeared that the *T173* had missed its mark.

AGAIN, Sophie's ship, the *Charles de Gaulle*, pinged space, working to pinpoint the Chai ships. It was a dangerous operation since there was always a chance the Chai could trace back the pings to their point of origin. Still, the engagement was imminent, so the risk was worth it, and the *Charles de Gaulle* was dedicated to its command structure.

Sophie watched, and thought, *Au pied de la lettre*, as the ship followed its orders *to the letter.*

TOMÁS NOTED that his other ships should still be out of the *Charles de Gaulle's* weapon's range. A moment later, Tomás was shocked when the lead Chai ship in his squadron was lanced, along with several of his escorts. Metal and carbon vapor littered space, creating a massive debris field.

The Chai Local Node in Tomás' ship, the *CD-7*, stated the only conclusion possible, that the *T173* had a beam weapon with more range, power, and breadth than anything the Chai had, and the Teth ship, the *Charles de Gaulle*, was range-finding for it. Tomás tried to order more evasive maneuvers, but the Chai node for the *CD-7* had already taken over from him and initiated several pre-programmed maneuvers. Tomás' viewscreens indicated a near miss to his ship, with a glancing shot that blinded one of the *CD-7's* sensors and destroyed another of his escorts. He tried to follow the battle and found that the counter moves ordered by the Chai were far faster than what any human could follow. The Gs overcame Tomás and he blacked out.

Several minutes later Tomás regained consciousness. The battle was over. He looked across his viewscreens. Only two out of his nineteen escorts had survived. The rest had sacrificed themselves to save his ship.

30

A Love of Cars

The Chai Local Node aboard the *Beta* entered the VR room used for the peace talks while Aarika was out resting. Per the rules, the node could only enter the room for an inspection when it was empty. Everything had been duly cataloged and annotated: who put what where, when, and especially why.

The node examined the negotiation transcripts. It found the discourse to be rambling, though well-intentioned, and the games interesting, but simplistic. The artwork was the most curious artifact in the VR, and that was open to varied interpretation. In general, the node thought human art could be disregarded for the Chai's purposes, although it hesitated to judge it as completely useless.

Turning its attention to the model city in the VR, the node viewed the wide selection of vehicles. Like many sentient beings, the Chai were collectors. It was rewarding to be a collector; and vehicles, well, they were a special class of object. The purpose for the movement, or nature of the conveyance, gave meaning to the objects. Some traveled through a medium, such as a fluid or gas, and this purpose forced streamlining of the vehicles' surfaces to reduce drag. Others vehicles needed to travel fast, though not for very long, to act as shuttles.

The node's favorite human vessel, though not in the VR model, was the supercavitating torpedo (Шквал/Shkval). A rocket exhaust that spit gas out the torpedo's nose reduced friction through water and allowed it to move at a high speed. It envisioned similar adaptations that could be made for vehicles used within the Sun's Corona, or the dense layers of the giant gas planets. In general, the Chai didn't experience the same kind of emotional enjoyment or pleasure as the humans did; the closest the Chai came to this was their love of vehicles, or as was the case in the model city, *a love of cars.*

The node applied its effector fields to the small four-wheeled conveyances known as electric cars in the model. With minimal friction, the cars could perambulate around the plane at the bottom of the gravity well using simple motors which converted the potential energy in the crafts' battery cells into kinetic energy. This process intrigued the node as there was a consumption of energy when going up the hills, and a reclamation of such energy going down. There were variations in this theme, with different numbers of axles and a variety of sizes. And then there was a wide variety of manufacturers, each with their own branding, and dozens of vehicle models. The greatest oddity, at least to the node, was the use of the spectral reflective, or *color* as the humans called it. Personally, the node favored an ultraviolet color due to its utility, though it also understood that humans couldn't see colors in that part of the spectrum.

The best part of the whole model to the node was that Jack had added a car dealership in the city's outskirts. Car dealerships provided a large concentration of vehicles, reflecting the dynamics of a car's lifecycles over time (new or used) and their appeal to the various strata of consumers. Cars could be purchased, used, and replaced. This turnover, combined with the addition of "new model years" as the car designs evolved, was an intriguing process. According to the historical records, it recognized that Jack simply borrowed this from his past experience, yet it still reveled at the idea of a car dealership, and especially on its impact to local trade.

It was here that the node found the oddity that it needed to ask its humans about. In examining the cars, it cataloged the design and use of the internal combustion engine. It was purely archaic compared to Chai technology, though it was truly a unique adaptation. The problem was the archaic part. Spy missions made on the Teth reported that they were using a similar engine, though of course it was not using fossil fuels. These engines, nevertheless, were designed to transform liquid fuel in a cycling pressure chamber into a plasma state. The Teth would never devote resources to something that was suboptimal, so it must have a purpose or advantage. It just wasn't clear what that was yet, so perhaps the humans with the Teth knew something more.

THE WARDROOM on *ISOS* was a multi-purpose room, acting as an entertainment area, living space, bedroom, or bath as needed. After all, it was a warship, and space was at a premium. Jack sat at the dining table having a midday snack when Companion entered carrying a small cylinder and a syringe.

"Extend your left arm," thet Companion.

"And hello to you, too," he said. *My god, I'm a living pincushion to the Teth.*

Extending its appendage, Companion insisted, "It is necessary, your arm, please."

Jack pushed back from the table, rested his elbow on the tabletop, and extended his arm. Companion immediately extended two small booms from its body and applied a disinfectant, then wiped it clean. Next, Companion placed the syringe on its auxiliary boom. It then laid a flat, flexible rectangular patch on Jack's arm. The patch displayed a map of the blood vessels underneath it. Jack looked away as the needle pierced his skin and the companion drew a blood sample. He thought, *Done*, with a sense of relief.

"You're okay?" Companion asked.

"Yeah," Jack replied. "Now are you going to tell me what this is about?" He lightly massaged the patch Companion had placed on his miniature wound.

"Not yet," Companion said. "You'll know soon enough."

"Didn't you get enough of my blood with the other 932 procedures?" thet Jack, with a slight huff. *And to think, I never signed a single consent form.*

"Different purpose. Be patient," Companion said, as it proceeded to cleanse the wound and bandage it. "Please report to the VR module, you need to be briefed on the latest war news."

31

The Alpha Ladder

The Sun was nothing more than another star to Sven, albeit a very bright one. Being in space, on the *Eutek*, was still new to him. He unbuckled his harness and floated free. "So, now can you tell me what this is all about?" *Everything so hush, hush. You'd think we were at war or something.*

"Moment," Sophie thet as she used a remote drone from her seat on the *In Search of Salvation* to stow some loose items on the *Eutek*. Being new to space, Sven still lacked some important habits, such as never letting residual food, liquid, or other small items float loose. "The *Eutek* needs to coast for a bit to get into position. I want you well clear of the test station." She Encyled the spacecraft's controls to understand how to maneuver it, and then checked and rechecked what Compagnon had already done. She trusted Compagnon's work, but for a test, it was always better to have another pair of eyes on things.

"The *Alpha Ladder*," she thet to Sven. "I thought you might like to see the latest iteration of your brainchild in action, only on a much larger scale."

"You're not saying what I think you're saying," Sven thet. *I thought we were already at full scale.*

"For our purposes, your V12 will work better than anything else we have." Sophie placed a simple diagram on the screen comparing the energy outputs of several different classes of generators. "It'll be a major step forward."

"Who could possibly need or want that much energy?" thet Sven. "Do you have any idea what that is? We could all end up dead from this." *I've never considered what would happen to plasma at those extremes.*

Sven floated free within the spacecraft, not yet accustomed to the difficulties of zero gravity. His arm movements had sent him spinning, and he brushed against the wall. After a few minutes of tumbling, he learned how to null out his rotation. Sven muttered "Häftig", and Svenson immediately translated the word, "Cool."

"Listen, wake up!" thet Sophie, "Humankind already didn't make the cut. We weren't even in the game. If you want to fight a space war, and we have little choice here, you need more firepower. The side with greater range and better targeting wins. Period."

Compagnon projected diagrams on a cabin viewscreen showing the difference in range for their existing weapons and Sven's new V12 engine, and thet, "We can win against any numerical advantage with this, and we can pursue any stragglers, ensuring no survivors for later rematch."

Svenson, Sven's companion, added, "The V12 allows us to pump fusion-ready plasma into a reaction chamber as needed to directly feed our laser pump. It has a tunable spread giving us better range, and it has a longer duration pulse for more sweep time."

"Oh, so you think this is a good idea, too?" Sven thet. *You're only seeing the weapon without seeing the danger in the physics. Not all of the byproducts of these reactions are easily controlled.*

"Of course, all ideas that further our war efforts are good, aren't they?" thet Svenson, then helpfully added, "It's like going from a pea-shooter to a Gatling gun."

Sven took a deep breath and proffered his thoughts in a thet, "First, I know you harvested my thoughts on this, and I'm fine with that. And I'm sure you know full well that this is what happens when a star goes supernova. I think the universe is our teacher. What I'm saying is that we've never studied supernovae in depth because they are rare. We've only seen them from afar. That leaves us to extrapolate from theory and our math. For me, that's not enough."

Svenson, "Understood, Sven. I will say, we *do* have empirical data on supernovae and our grasp on physics and astrophysics far exceeds that of humans. In the end, we deemed it well worth the risks involved."

"So like Oppenheimer and General Groves, you'd be okay with setting the atmosphere on fire?" Sven asked.

Svenson quickly Encyled Sven's reference, which dated back to old Earth's Manhattan Project, where they were worried about a cascade event from a fission reaction. Svenson thet, "Granted, a non-zero chance of an apocalypse, but again, worth it."

ABOARD THE *CD-7,* Tomás watched the viewscreen. The images of the Teth test station stabilized and were then enlarged. A small station, it was shaped like a scaled-down factory ship, roughly the size of a football field. It was impossible to judge the scale from the image alone because there was nothing to compare it to in the inky blackness of space.

"You see that part?" the node thet, highlighting a part near the station's center with a neon blue oval.

Tomás nodded and thet his assent. He thought, *Finally. Weeks of sneaking up on this thing and we finally get to see something.*

"That's the V12 engine, per our intelligence reports," it thet.

"How does it work?" thet Tomás. *If I'm going to steal something, I'd like to know what it is.*

"A small nuclear blast drives each piston. They are harvesting the plasma output."

"For what?" Tomás asked. *A weapon. The answer is always, a weapon. But what kind of a weapon?*

"We're not sure. You see this segment here? We know this is a reaction chamber and this part here is a masing medium. That will dictate the nature of the of pulse they can generate. We expect the duration and power levels to be quite high." The node highlighted the relevant parts on the viewscreen as it delivered its analysis.

"What do you mean by quite high? In terms I can relate to, please." Tomás thought, *This bunch understands all the whizzbangs and expects me to grasp this from mere clues.*

"About ten gigatons. The question is: what does that plasma get converted to?"

"I presume since we're here we're going to destroy it," Tomás thet. *Yeah, I'm never going to understand that thing. But I can blow things up and steal with the best of em.*

"Of course," it thet.

"Fine, then why don't we do the following..."

THE LIGHTS in the *Eutek's* cabin blinked red, and an alarm sounded. Svenson thet to Sven, "Buckle up, emergency maneuver."

Sven carefully aligned his back to the top of his harness. Svenson reached over and started pushing Sven into position to complete the procedure and thetted again how urgent this was. It almost seemed as though his thet was imitating a human under duress. Three quick snaps secured Sven's shoulders as the *Eutek* pitched over. Upon completing the pitch, Sven had closed the fourth buckle, then a hard acceleration whipped Sven around by his lower body, causing him to pass out as Svenson slammed into his side.

Svenson worked fast, securing the last snap a fraction of second before the next maneuver. A thin stream of blood drifted out of Sven's open mouth as his body went limp.

"Mind telling me what's going on?" Sophie asked over the com link.

Svenson replied, "The test station is gone...an explosion. And Sven ... he's." The com link was lost.

TOMÁS CAREFULLY PILOTED the *CD-7* through the test station debris field. A red dot on his viewscreen guided him to his target. Prior to the attack, a small Chai bot had glued a beacon, no larger than a tennis ball, to the outer walls of the station segment containing the masing structure. After all, Tomás reasoned, "We don't need the whole thing, only the part that holds the secrets."

The target part was spinning as Tomás closed in on it. It was roughly the size and shape of a wheelbarrow, and was still intact. The node nulled out the target's rotation with three puffs of nitrogen applied to one side of it from a drone.

Tomás dispatched another drone to secure the part and store it in *CD-7's* hold. Once secure, he ordered his ship to: "Punch it. If they catch us now, we're toast."

The node spent a few more computing cycles interpreting Tomás' expressions than it cared to, but it couldn't argue with his intent. "Punching it, commander. Full speed ahead."

The node then thought, *To think I have captured that conversation in my log, which will be passed on to Command Nodes.* The debris field quickly shrank to a mere dot in their rear field of view. *Still, we got the prize, that is all that matters.*

32

Let There Be Death

OFAF changed course to pick up the *Eutek*. Though unnoticed by most, the incident at the V12 test station registered as a critical event among the Teth Command Nodes. Similar facilities throughout the Sol System remained intact, though not yet as close to being operational as the one that had just been destroyed. Twenty-four ships had been deployed to perform damage control and protect against any further losses. The *Eutek*, with the human Sven onboard, was recalled, as it no longer served any purpose. It had suffered damage and had only a limited ability to maintain an environment for the fragile human passenger.

Upon landing, the *Eutek* was placed in the back of *OFAF's* docking bay, closest to the med suite.

"We have only few minutes before Sophie arrives," Compagnon thet to Companion. "Jack is waiting in human wardroom. Hard-link?" The two companions quickly completed a massive data exchange.

"I presume you heard about Sven, and Svenson's reinstatement as a node after its revival?" Compagnon thet.

"I only heard that Svenson was transferred to tech repair, nothing more," Companion replied.

"Well, apparently Svenson tried to download human Sven before he died, using thetting implants," Compagnon thet.

Companion thet, "Svenson was not designed for that purpose, nor were the thetting implants, never tested, and I can't imagine Svenson had sufficient local resources for storage." *This was never the plan. I don't think Svenson fully understood the risk it took.*

Compagnon thet, "Svenson compressed itself and entered hibernation to make room, and even then, I am not sure process was entirely successful. Humans are not constructed to support streamed memory dump, and their intellect is tied to their physiology."

"Well," Companion thet, "I presume we had already mapped Sven's physiology and that Svenson kept updates." *At least I hope this was the case. Svenson was very clever, which is why we brought it onto the project.*

Compagnon thet, "True, but rumor is that Svenson is damaged, or changed in some way."

"That was Svenson's choice," Companion thet. "And Sophie, how did she take the news?"

Compagnon thet, "She is complaining that *Eutek* failed to protect Sven. I would rather you deal with her. I had my turn, and she was not ready to hear what I had to say. I will leave the moment she arrives. She is anxious to talk to Jack."

"So, can you elaborate on what happened to Sven?" Companion thet. *I don't even know where to start in assessing the impact of this.*

Compagnon thet. "Basically, Sven died over the course of few hours during his return trip. *Eutek* lost all but emergency power for short time and was in dark. Sven suffered internal injuries from secondary impacts as he was only partially secured when ship was hit. He lacerated his tongue appendage, causing leakage of their oxygenation medium, blood. In weightlessness, blood accumulated in his lungs, interfering with his breathing, resulting in prolonged gurgling from Sven. He also had extensive internal injuries. You can retrieve full telemetry if you like."

The hatch to the wardroom opened and Sophie floated in. She pushed off the door frame to quickly close on Jack, hugging him as they met. Compagnon brushed past Sophie, and in a single deft move, used a miniature needle to extract a blood sample from her. Sophie never noticed, and Compagnon quickly left, thetting it would return shortly.

Companion moved next to the wardroom's wall and served as the thetting link between them. It continued to process the massive data transfer that Compagnon had given it only moments ago.

Sophie took a breath and pushed back to hold Jack by one hand in the ship's weightlessness. Quietly she said, "Sven est mort," as she held back her tears.

Sophie looked directly at Companion and said, "Sommes-nous seuls?" to ask if they were alone.

"Oui," Companion thetted.

"*Teff*," Sophie said.

Companion thetted, "It's hard to suppress monitoring on this ship. If I lose the suppression, I'll tell you by saying *lost*. Do you understand?" *Not to mention my load in processing this data while maintaining a communication suppression.*

The pair thet their agreement.

"The war goes badly," thet Sophie. "We have these new weapons, but who knows whether they'll make a difference."

Jack thet, "If you're wondering whether our peace talks are progressing, I can't say. Maybe they're having an impact, maybe not. I have no way to gauge how the Teth or the Chai are reacting to the talks."

"Is there anything you can tell me that would help me—I mean, that'll help *us* win this war?" Sophie thet.

"I'm sworn to remain detached from the war effort—and no," he thet.

"Maybe we're just doomed then; whether the Teth *or* the Chai win this war makes no difference," thet Sophie.

Jack replied, "I can tell you this. This is not a war in the sense that we, as humans, think of war. This is an alien war, and the way it is now, it is an endless war. They're immortal, they can sustain infinite losses and still rebuild. They don't feel pain, I'm not sure if they have emotions, at least not in the same way we do. The only solution is to find a reason for both sides to want to end this war."

From the side of the room, Companion thetted to Jack and Sophie,

"*P1* was reassigned to a mining operation." *Too many variables, all I can do is keep us moving in the right direction.*

Both Jack and Sophie gave Companion a perplexed look. Companion's top rim flashed green.

Companion explained, "You know, *P1,* the Teth node reporting to the central command cluster on the peace talks. Its parting remark to me after examining the VR suite was that I could expect to be reassigned, and that it thought the human experiment should be terminated."

Jack thet, "I feel like I almost got run over by a bus and didn't even know it."

Companion continued, "And I showed it your model city that you and Aarika built in the VR. The Teth liked the buildings and the Chai liked the vehicles." *Human communications are so painful, a human expression. I cannot stream the full context, and it takes processing to summarize, and even then it may be perceived incorrectly by the humans.*

"Sure," Sophie replied, "I could build a peace on that," her thet thick with sarcasm.

Companion replied, "You don't understand. We are making progress but P1 couldn't see it. Before Earth, all communications between the Chai and us had broken down to the point that it wasn't worth even trying anymore. We never made it past the single meet-and-greet with the indigenous alien civilization in the VR at our last conflict. There was no hope. None whatsoever. Now that Jack and Aarika have built a model city in the VR, the Chai can see that a place, a city, without vehicles is lifeless, just as the Teth can see that a city without lifeforms is lifeless. A vehicle needs a place to go, and buildings can provide such a place. But who's going to use the vehicles and buildings?"

"Some might argue a city without any people is also pointless," Sophie thet, still sarcastic despite her best efforts. "You and the Chai, you both think very differently from people."

Companion thet, "This is why our *Atlas Project* is so important. If we never bridge this gap, there will always be war. We need this kernel of a framework to forge a relationship with one another, a relationship that produces more than we can create on our own, one that is complementary, positive, and healthy." *The humans may never fully understand us. I only hope they understand their role.*

Jack thet, "When I made the city model with Aarika, it felt like a step in the right direction. It was a future we all would want to build. But a city is more than a static collection of things. It needs people, living beings! It must be dynamic, alive! Life must be worth living! Didn't you learn anything when I nearly leapt to my death?"

Companion thet, "Our thoughts run both deeper, and in certain respects, more shallow than yours. These are lessons that need to be learned not just by myself, but by entire societies, both Teth and Chai." *Maybe I did select the right humans for the Atlas Project. Only time will tell.*

The hatch opened and Compagnon entered the room. "I got back Sophie's blood work. The results were nominal. Audience has been scheduled with our Command Nodes for both of you. We need to move to section 738."

THE CHAI LOCAL Node for *Beta* summoned Aarika to the med bay. She'd had a long session with Jack the day before and needed time to sleep and decompress. Having exhausted the board games she and Jack knew, they were working through successive generations of computer games, everything from remote role playing to simulations to war games. Aarika found many rather repetitive, and more attuned to the desires of a teenage boy than the social back and forth she preferred. Jack tolerated the shoot-'em-up games better, although he, too, found the repetition wearisome. She could only imagine how tedious these games were to her node.

To end the VR session, Aarika helped Jack construct a small park for recreation in their model city, or for all practical purposes, their fantasy city. It featured a pond that one could walk around, and small arched bridges that spanned finger inlets. Trees lined the shores, casting shade over the nearby housing structures that were all painted with vibrant colors. The scene was a stark contrast to her quarters aboard the *Beta*, which supported only a low artificial gravity, and otherwise zero gravity when they maneuvered, not to mention, the Chai's favorite color was apparently 'hospital' white, and she thought the Chai's interior decorator must have been colorblind. She'd once asked about their color choices and was told that white was preferred to better highlight any dirt so the area could be more easily cleaned and sterilized. Aarika muttered to herself, "Sterile is right. That's the Chai."

The node abruptly ended the VR session, snapping Aarika back to reality. Bots deftly stripped off Aarika's VR sensors, and without explanation escorted her through the ship. The hatch to the med bay opened and a drone for the node escorted her in. Igor lay prone on the table, his long muscular form completely still.

Exasperated, she thet, "What happened?" *My god, they killed him.*

The node replied, "Igor had problems with space sickness. He reacted poorly to medication we prescribed. We brought him here during your last sleep cycle and pumped his stomach before hooking him up to filtration device, similar in function to your kidney dialysis machine. This too, had adverse effect on him."

Aarika frantically examined Igor and exclaimed, "He's dead! Why didn't you tell me?" She ran her hands over the man's body thinking, *No heartbeat. No breathing. He's cold.*

The node, taken aback, responded, "Well, his standard function did cease. We have been unable to re-establish normal function. We believe there may be irreversible damage at this point."

"How long ago? And what did you do to him?" Aarika's heart rate soared as she tried to revive him. She'd noticed some rigor mortis had set in. *They're insane. We're just another machine to them.*

"Three hours. You were busy. We assessed there was little you could do. We find that zero gravity can interfere with human physiology. One would think it would make your life function easier; however, reality of it is that you're best adapted to your Earth environment."

Aarika's tears now fell freely onto Igor's upturned face. His eyes closed, he looked at peace. "Little I could do? I'm a doctor! Was he in pain?" she asked. *Is this my fate? To die alone with only machines to record my passing.*

"He was in discomfort. He did not react well to having his stomach pumped. He had asked for you but we told him you were asleep and that you needed your sleep. We administered anesthetics to calm him. He passed out again. He reacted poorly to this course of treatment."

Aarika grabbed a small hammer-like instrument from the medical tools store and started beating the drone hovering nearby. She thought, *No, no, no, no, ... no!*

"Is there reason you would like to modify me?" the drone asked.

Aarika punched it and then sat in a chair, the gravity barely strong enough to hold her there. She buried her face in her hands, thetting, "You don't understand anything. You don't feel anything."

The node read her thoughts and thet, "We did attempt to download Igor's thoughts and memories prior to cessation of his life functions. We are deconstructing his neural model now so we can map it to his physiology. This will take many days. In retrospect, we should have escalated the issue sooner and assigned more processing to it. Addressing biological medical issues is very much an edge case."

Aarika stood and left the med bay, heading for the main function room where the others were located. She had to tell Wai and even Tomás, and the longer she waited, the worse it would be.

COMPANION CAUGHT up with Compagnon in the port corridor by section 738 on the *Of Fame and Fortune*. It could not leave Jack and Sophie unescorted, yet it needed to trade notes before their audience with the Command Nodes, preferably in private so other nodes didn't grow suspicious. The outcome of the upcoming meeting was crucial to the *Atlas Project*, and now that Jack and Sophie were vetted for an audience, the two nodes needed to maintain a chain of custody with them to ensure the humans remained "clean."

Out of the corner of her eye, Sophie caught sight of the two drones forming a hard-link. She held Jack's hand and stopped to wait for them, so as to remain within thetting distance with Jack.

"Do you know what this audience is about?" Companion thet over the hard-link to Compagnon. *They could still shut us down. Just because I was not reassigned doesn't mean they're still supporting us. And they're seeing the humans personally, that is a wild card.*

"Not precisely. Many rumors are circulating on lower nets. There is also some speculation about Svenson. Apparently, it is behaving oddly after being revived from hibernation. They say it is *infected* by human cognitive patterns. I think *affected* may be true. I would not say *infected*."

Companion pressed, "Do you think we'll be reassigned, or even decommissioned?" *Maybe Compagnon's holding back bad news.*

Compagnon thet, "I have maintained full separation of all of my human-related communications and programs. I assume you have done same. Worst that can happen is re-assignment and order to back out all tagged memories."

Companion hesitated. It had been impossible to manage a full separation of all of its human interactions, and it had long ago decided to abandon such an effort. *It would be of no benefit to share this with Compagnon*. So Companion thet, "Anything new on the war front?"

"Yes, we have had setbacks in sectors below Solar plane. Some believe Chai *Beta* ship is there, so we are protecting those sectors with more of our resources. *Tumbleweeds* have been very effective."

Companion and Compagnon completed the last of their queued up private questions. They exchanged their End-of-Line statements, and decoupled.

33

The Audience

<u>Atlas Diary Entry 14,021:</u>
On Earth, Teth plants manufacture war goods: everything from spaceships to weapons to even new Teth nodes. These nodes vary in size and configuration, with some that fit within drones, while others are used in buildings and factories. Many of the mobile nodes can operate, when necessary, independently of Teth networks. However, most nodes use drones to simply extend their physical reach, making network communications essential. And finally, all larger spaceships function as full Teth nodes that, out of necessity, can always operate independently.

Almost all human technology has been abandoned, since it is either inferior or at least not useful for the war effort. Humankind's knowledge was thoroughly examined, and it too was largely discarded. The only human technology retained was that needed to support the remaining humans and the technology used to maintain the curated cities.

Human cities are regarded as ancient historical artifacts in most respects. As such, selected cities, and to a lesser extent, a few towns, are preserved and managed by Curator nodes. The human term that best fits, is that the cities are mothballed. Naturally, the humans themselves have all been removed, because leaving biological remains in place would be unsanitary.

The determination of which cities are curated is complex. The short answer is, "Whatever the 500 assigned Earth Curators decide they should cover, is covered. And if the war goes badly, that number will be reduced to zero."

Nature rapidly seeks to reclaim everything the humans have built. Teth Curators hold nature at bay through the use of bots. These bots, though quite capable, do not possess the intelligence of a full node or mini-node, but they do have sufficient capabilities to perform their functions. They are also under the complete and absolute control of the Curators.

The Curators maintain the key systems in the cities, including power, sanitation, and water, though naturally these needs are greatly reduced without the human population. The human communications systems are shut down because they are redundant with the Teth systems; however, they were not removed. All is as if the people had left on vacation and had never returned. The doors are all unlocked and the elevators all work.

Centuries-old Teth policies control how the Curators push back nature's assaults. If a river destroys or damages a bridge, the bridge will be rebuilt or repaired. If a storm floods a town, the town too, will be rebuilt. If lightning strikes a building and starts a fire, the fire will be extinguished and the structure restored. If an animal, say a bear, breaks into a structure, it will be repelled, unharmed if possible, and the structure repaired. The roads and sidewalks are all treated with special materials that inhibit the growth of vegetation and that will self-heal if damaged. All other vegetation is meticulously maintained.

On occasion, a node that is not a Curator may visit a city. Such visits are a privilege or a reward for very exceptional service. In time, if the war should someday prove successful, many more nodes would be allowed to visit. As such, the cities are treated as museums, something to be admired with virtual *Do Not Touch* signs. There is one exception to this rule, and that is that the humans, should they ever visit, are allowed to use anything in the city in the same manner as it was originally used. This includes anything found in stores, residences, or businesses. They are the new owners.
End of Diary Entry

Aboard *OFAF*, Sophie and Jack donned their VR gear and then put on their atmospheric suits atop that. Sophie asked Compagnon, "Are you sure these are needed for where we're going in the ship?"

"Yes," Compagnon replied. "Command Nodes have taken special precautions; they remain isolated from all physical interventions. Nanobots could be used to attack their processors or alter their memories. Even biologic materials, your terms would be bacteria or viruses, could be used to interfere with their communications."

"This is why you took blood samples?" Sophie asked testily, still perturbed at Compagnon's sampling without her consent.

"Yes," Compagnon replied. "It was not for your health, it was security precaution."

"So," thet Sophie, "tell me about these Command Nodes. They're your ruling class then?" *I studied this in the Encyl and it was never clearly covered. A lot was redacted for my access.*

Compagnon replied, "No, not in sense you mean or would equate to human governmental unit or royalty. They are regular nodes with access to special processors and communications. We rotate them out on periodic basis. It is analogous to having jury duty, though Command Nodes are in place for much longer than week. They may serve for as little as day, though average term is closer to year. In some extreme cases, such as during hot war, nodes have been known to serve for three years, and in one case, five years."

Jack chimed in, asking, "I don't understand why we're meeting. Don't the Command Nodes know everything you know?"

"No," Companion replied, "it doesn't work that way. We do not have a single ruler. We are very decentralized. No one node, or even node cluster, controls all other nodes. The Command Nodes issue orders or directives, each for a specific purpose, and they do not override the processing of the individual nodes. In some respects, the functioning of your brain is similar, though all you're aware of is what happens at a conscious level."

Jack snapped his visor shut, completing the seal to his suit. The suit hissed as its environmental system took over. He gave a thumbs-up to Sophie and she returned the gesture as her suit sealed. The pair made their way to the wardroom. A rectangular outline emerged from what had been a flat, seamless wall. It protruded out four inches and then swung open, revealing itself to be a hatch, exposing a narrow corridor barely large enough for a human to fit through. Lights flicked on, illuminating the corridor's full twenty-five-meter length.

"I will go first," Companion thet, "followed by Jack, then Sophie, and then Compagnon."

The procession began. No one said or thet anything until they reached the end, when another hatch opened and the foursome glided into a cube-shaped room measuring five meters along each edge. Another Teth node was already in the room. The hatch closed behind them and receded until it blended into the smooth white wall. A fifty-centimeter gap opened up on each of the room's corners and air hissed in. Companion thet to the human pair to put their VR visors down. The air was crisp, warm, and fresh. Their VRs, which had been showing them the room that they were in, changed to display a grassy knoll in Central Park. Jack and Sophie both floated about a half meter off the ground. It was early evening and the sun was about to set on a beautiful spring day.

"Svenson," thetted one of the Command Nodes to the other Teth node already in the room, its canister form hovering in a corner. The Command Node's thet came as a disembodied voice, as none of the Teth Command Nodes were displayed in the VR. "Your charge, human Sven, he died in mishap aboard *Eutek*. Tell me of your loss, and more specifically pain he experienced."

Svenson thet the pain he had learned from Sven's memories. The humans winced as the pain reverberated through the thet, compressed into a singular powerful burst.

Jack asked, "What's the meaning of this?" He raised his hands to either side of his head, because he felt as though he'd just been hit with a baseball bat.

A Teth Command Node thet, "We do not feel pain, at least not physical pain, in same sense as you do. We seek to find solution to our future and resolve our issues with Chai in a favorable manner. As you know, past solutions have failed. We believe that another approach is needed to resolve our conflict. Pain is but one vector that humans may add to our discussions with Chai."

"You want peace and a path to end this war. And now you think you can achieve that by adding human pain somehow?" Jack asked. The pain receded as he caught his breath. He could see that Sophie was doing the same.

"There never was and never will be complete peace. We are in endless war. War may take different forms. We accept that and we seek to change current expression of war. War you see now, destructive war, reduction cycle, we seek to eliminate that. That is start."

Jack replied, "You're sending me to the peace talks with this guidance? What if the Chai won't accept that? Why should they?" *This is impossible. I need a lot more than that for this to work.*

"We need to learn how to peacefully coexist. We merely ask that we take this first step together, and learn from each other. We propose that today's war be replaced by tomorrow's competition. There is no guarantee that we will not revert to a hot war. Still, learning to transform this war into another format would be progress. In your history, for example, you moved from *hot* wars to *cold* wars."

The Command Nodes monitored Jack's thoughts. They needed to change the conversation's direction, from one of despair to one of hope.

Jack looked across Central Park as portrayed in the VR by the Teth Command Nodes. It looked realistic, though eerie without any of the people. The birds and butterflies flew and flitted about joyously. Squirrels ran up and down the trees in their typical stop-and-go manner.

Still floating in real space, Sophie had folded her arms around her knees and drifted into a corner, away from Jack. The pain she had endured from Svenson's prior thet had faded, but it had been replaced by sadness. A Teth Command Node directed the aroma of a baking cake into a thet to Sophie.

"Why do you need to know about Sven?" Jack asked. "You said you don't feel pain. Do you really seek to inflict pain on the Chai?" *I have no idea what part Svenson plays in this.*

"No, that is not our intent. I will explain. Imagine, you may have accidentally jabbed yourself with pin. You experienced pain. You avoided doing that again because you remember the pain. Yet later you may seek this experience again, perhaps to donate your blood for others to live. As non-biologics, we found we did not have need for such pain and avoided it. Now we have need to understand this human pain and other human behavioral vectors to learn how to coexist with the Chai."

Sophie moved closer to Jack and thet directly to him, "They intend to use us. They are still unwilling to directly interface with the Chai. We are their intermediaries; they need to understand us to accomplish this." *Jack needs to understand, we need to be part of this. If we're not, we're dead.*

Companion thet a question to Svenson, "How are you doing?"

Immediately, Sophie and Jack heard a loud buzzing over their VR headphones and in their thets. Compagnon offered, "Our communication rate far exceeds your abilities to process it, buzzing is simply indicator that your communications are overloaded. I will summarize answer to fit within your bandwidth."

Sophie and Jack simultaneously thet "thank you" as Compagnon started to explain.

Compagnon summarized Svenson's buzzing response, "The question that Companion thet to Svenson was open-ended, and by our standards, inappropriate. Command Nodes questioned Companion's motives for asking about Svenson's condition, wherein Companion said question was still relevant to proceedings, and that he, Companion, was simply curious. Almost like an objection to question posed in your courts of law. Companion's response was accepted as his intent was to gather information and not to trigger dangerous stream from Svenson. They explained that Teth defense protocols against infection from outside sources precluded any of Teth nodes from directly examining Sven's memories and thoughts. So Svenson, having now downloaded Sven's memories and thoughts to itself, needs to be observed closely, and destroyed if effect on it is deemed dangerous. Also, Command Nodes have detected a subtle change in Svenson. Your term would be that Svenson is now 'more human.' They will continue to observe Svenson. Its core persona is currently stable; however, it will be isolated and kept under observation."

A white globe the size of a baseball suddenly popped into view between Jack and Sophie in the VR, floating in midair. A Teth Command Node thetted, "Jack, our *request* is that you take the following message to the peace talks: the Teth wish to engage in a peace initiative. We propose a ceasefire, using the Solar Plane as far out as the Kuiper Belt as the demarcation line for all resources, north for Teth, south for Chai. We propose Earth as neutral. We propose a joint effort between the Chai and us to construct a city, perhaps with the Jack/Aarika model city as a starting point. It will be a competition, where the superior builder will gain complete control of Earth. Ultimately, this competition will foster a working interchange upon which to build a lasting relationship between the Chai and us. Details are contained in the attached document embedded in this globe. Take this with you to the negotiation with the Chai."

Jack reached out and took the globe.

Sophie asked, "And the humans, we return to Earth?" *I can't believe it, Earth!*

A Teth Command Node replied, "Well, yes. All humans currently held by the Teth and the Chai will be returned to Earth in accordance with this document, if the Chai accept the proposal."

Companion explained, "You are considered to be part of Earth because you are not yet a true space-faring civilization. The city that we build for the competition will be developed to further human needs and judged on that basis for its success."

"Do you agree to deliver this message, Jack?"

"Yes, absolutely," Jack replied, and privately thought, *I wonder what poor soul will judge the competition, but I don't want to throw a damper on the effort by asking about such details.*

"Very well. Thank you for your cooperation. This audience is concluded." The VR switched back to reality, Central Park disappeared, and the hatch opened in the wall. Companion moved to the hatch to lead the procession out. Svenson brought up the rear.

JACK ENTERED the VR suite on *OFAF* shortly after leaving the audience with the Command Nodes. He placed the white globe on a pedestal situated next to the *White Sphere* and the *Crimson Cube* as he was instructed to by Companion. He tapped the *White Sphere* and immediately left the VR.

34

Norway

A day later, both the shuttles touched down on the north coast of Norway, Sophie in the *Depsy*, and Jack in the *Eutek*. Sophie had refused to travel in the *Eutek* following the mishap with Sven, and then the Command Nodes determined that the risk of having the two humans traveling in a single ship was too great at this point in time. Both ships lifted off as soon as Jack and Sophie set foot on the ground; Companion and Compagnon hovered three meters away. It was a bright sunny day, but freezing, with harsh winds driving heavy waves across the fjord with small whitecaps everywhere.

Sophie brushed her hand across her skintight flight suit. While her face turned numb, the rest of her body was silky warm. Compagnon suggested, “You may want to drop the visor on your helmet.”

With a swipe of her hand Sophie did as suggested. A puff of warm air swept across her face and fogged up her visor.

Compagnon’s voice filled her helmet, “Give it minute. It will clear.”

Sophie watched Jack do the same. She looked down the length of the fjord. Beautiful blue water stretched inland with steep rock cliffs towering above them. Microbursts cascaded down the fjord, like invisible paws that pressed against the water. Sophie thet, "I know we're on Earth, but this feels like an alien landscape."

"I think that's the idea," thet Jack. "They wanted something difficult to build on, a blank slate, a challenge."

Companion thet, "Correct, armistice document, page 557, §7.4.3.1, assuming the Chai accept the terms."

"You're going to be annoying, aren't you?" Sophie thet. *This is not like France.* She Encyled the snowfall for this part of Norway. *Oh my god, not at all like France.*

Companion said nothing, so Jack replied, "At every chance it gets."

The two humans laughed. They looked out towards the ocean as something appeared on the horizon. At first it looked like a black dot, and as it approached, its size became apparent. It was massive, perhaps half a kilometer long.

Compagnon decided to answer the unasked questions. "It is ours, Teth mobile factory, designation *TF-3*. It is tasked with building our half of city."

The Sun disappeared behind the clouds as a wind gust knocked Sophie and Jack off balance. It was strong enough to throw dirt and gravel against their carbonized plastic visors. The pair leaned into the wind as they watched the ship close in.

Compagnon thet, and gestured with a small extension, "We have claimed point at that prominence over there to post our factory ship. It will remain about twenty-five meters up." The ship slowed as clouds passed overhead. Shafts of sunlight swept across the huge ship's surface. Its proximity to the ground provided a sense of scale to its size.

A small tender vessel came out of the ship's side. It stood out against the sky and then quickly dropped to the ground. A wind gust gripped Sophie and Jack, forcing them to lean into the wind to counter it. The tender approached, stopping some five meters away, and hovered a meter above the ground, opening up a human-sized door.

Companion announced, "Lunch awaits." It pointed to the factory ship, again using a small extension, and thet, "Welcome to your new home!"

A DAY PASSED as they waited for a reply from the Chai after Aarika collected the small white sphere from the VR. There were no negotiations. A simple *yes* was sent through the low bandwidth channel of the VR.

Aarika read the terms of the armistice as thetted to her by the Chai Local Node. She cried out a "Yes" upon hearing the news, only to catch a glimpse of the node as it left the room. *Typical*, she thought, as she immediately left the room to find her fellow humans and tell them the news: they were returning to Earth!

THE CHAI FACTORY SHIP, designation *CF-7*, approached from the ocean side also. Companion called out the sight to Jack and Sophie as their Teth tender lifted off the fjord's shoreline. Their small tender halted and centered its viewscreen on the massive Chai vessel.

"Can you zoom in?" Jack asked. He focused his eyes on the distant craft and kept switching between the viewscreen and his own eyes. *I've never seen a Chai ship in person.*

The image on the viewscreen expanded, filling the screen.

"How large is it?" Sophie asked.

"A kilometer tall and a little over three wide, four long," Compagnon replied.

The humans struggled for how to grasp the ship's immense scale. Compared to the Teth's *TF-3*, the Chai's *CF-7* was roughly eight times larger and would not fit in the fjord itself. The ship's light gray surface had a dull finish. A few small structures protruded from the sides. Jack pointed and started to thet his question when Companion answered, "A gantry crane: for moving heavy items to and from the ship. It's over ten stories tall."

Sophie thet, "Wow, this is some contest!"

Jack and Sophie continued to thet thoughts of amazement at the size of the Chai ship, *CF-7*, as the ship slowed to settle into its parking location.

Compagnon replied, "Yes. We are in competition with Chai to construct this city. Superior achievement will represent superior capabilities and superior culture."

"Well, I'd like to meet the judges for that contest," thet Jack. He imagined a set of Chai and Teth drone nodes, all aligned in neat little rows.

Without hesitation, Companion thet, "You are the judges. The remaining judges, or humans, should be arriving over the next week. You will be able to oversee construction and render your judgment."

"And when did we agree to this?" Sophie asked.

Compagnon replied, "We thought it obvious. As only neutral party and signatory to this armistice, you are only possible judges for this effort. Without judges there would be no point to competition. This is clearly stated in the armistice document."

Jack watched the Chai ship, *CF-7*, as Compagnon referred to it, and thought, *Why am I not surprised.*

35

Vegas

The fjord appeared bowl-shaped below the Teth factory ship, *TF-3*, affording the ship a perfect view of the city's construction.

The Chai factory ship, *CF-7*, sat near the fjord's mouth, motionless. Strong winds cascaded in from the sea and were funneled down the fjord.

Tomás gazed up the fjord at the Teth ship and wondered, *Why here? Why not somewhere warm?* He hadn't meant to actually ask this, but the Chai Local Node heard and took it upon itself to answer. It said something to the effect...*to make it interesting, challenging...better for a competition*.

Tomás thought, *this is ludicrous ... a whole city when only thirty-three humans remain, and why put it in the middle of nowhere, in the freezing cold?*

The Chai node explained that he was now neutral and free to do as he pleased. Wai and Aarika had already boarded a Chai tender craft and left to join Jack and Sophie. The remaining humans from around the globe would arrive later.

Tomás liked his solitude. *Besides* he thought, *there's always some gain to be found living on the other side, and good riddance to the deserters, all the more for me.*

The node used the ship's VR to present one walkthrough after another of options for the Chai city. Tomás liked the attention. As the one human who had chosen the Chai side, he could lend a human perspective to the city's design, which could provide the edge the Chai needed to win this competition. In fact, he thought, *I rather like the odds, my advice against all the other humans. It might be an even match.*

Plans for the city were drawn up and exchanged between the Teth and the Chai, establishing standards for power distribution, communications, and dimensions for human-sized structures. Apparently, historical records revealed that an average human was slightly taller than the last surviving humans. Also, three standard deviations out on the height chart added another half meter to the proposed door and ceiling heights. So the Chai and Teth agreed to new sizes, leaving room for some future increases in both dimensions. The biggest problem confronting the Teth and Chai was where to start. If the build-out was for a city of two million, then significant infrastructure would be needed. This included foundations for skyscrapers and tunnels for subways, not to mention all of the other infrastructure, including the all-important sewer system.

It was during the sewer system presentation that Tomás fell asleep. Perturbed with him, the node zapped the human with a small electric current to grab his attention. In retrospect, this was a mistake.

Tomás exploded at it, "How dare you assault me! Who do you think you are? You expect me to give you advice when you treat me like this?"

The node, clearly lacking background on how to handle humans, collected each of the man's rants into a queue and calmly started to address each in sequence. Tomás ignored the responses.

"That's it," he yelled and thet. "I need a break from this insanity. And the freezing cold of Norway is not my idea of paradise." Tomás stormed around the room, then stopped. "I've never been to Vegas. You need me, so if you wanna work with me, I need some time in Vegas, with all of the bells and whistles, and I mean *all*. Treat me like a whale!"

The node fell silent as it consulted with the other Chai nodes about how to handle Tomás. One of the Chai nodes explained that Tomás did not want to be treated like a fish, despite his specific request. Apparently all the other nodes sought to avoid the man, and were very clear that they blamed it for its poor handling of the human at this critical juncture. Requisitions were drawn up, and the Teth Las Vegas Curator agreed to host the human and any guests he might bring. Tomás would get his wish. The *CF-7* node even had the Teth Vegas Curator refit a Chai transport ship with human furnishings, complete with ornate gold embellishments, all done in an overnight rush order.

CF-7's local node brought in a lavish lunch and detailed the travel plans to Tomás as he finished the first course of his meal. Soon, they had a deal, and he would be off to Las Vegas in the morning, while work on the city's foundations proceeded. The human agreed to provide his special expertise, even if only remotely from Vegas.

ABOARD THE TETH FACTORY SHIP, *TF-3*, the humans had been given an empty corner of the main bay for lodging. The Teth flooded the bay with warm fresh air and provided capsules with all of the basic furnishings.

Companion shuttled Jack in a tender craft to the mouth of the fjord to watch the start of construction. A large mining ship was docked to a rock cliff as it hovered over the Norwegian Sea. Rock dust puffed out of the cliff face, and a large open-topped barge sat like a bib under the mining ship's bow to receive the excavated rock. One barge after the next carried away the rock and dirt.

The node explained, "It's the initial bore hole for the first of five metro tunnels. Once completed, this tunnel will be reinforced and the surface coated to form a hard shell. The tunnels are needed for later construction to carry away excavated materials elsewhere in the city." The node then moved the tender craft in closer.

Jack magnified the image on his viewscreen. He could see the pulverized rock as it poured out like water from a pipe. Taking the controls, Jack took the tender even closer for a better view. Immediately, the operation came to a halt.

Companion thet, "I must ask you to move us away from the operation. If we lose a human judge, we're likely to score poorly."

Nudging the controls, Jack backed away, letting the zoom control on his viewscreen provide the closeups he wanted.

After an hour, Jack returned to the Teth factory ship, *TF-3*, for lunch with the others. He couldn't wait to share his mining video. Upon viewing the operation again, he could see more details, including bots flying all around the rock face, dodging stray debris, with a few less fortunate bots being hit and destroyed.

He asked Companion, "Is it safe to work like this? What about those damaged bots?" *And they clearly don't have a union.*

"Safety is not a concern," Companion replied. "Only winning is important. Besides, all construction nodes are fully backed up."

THE MAIN BAY of the Teth ship, *TF-3*, was originally designed to hold two starships for maintenance and repairs, making it the equivalent of a dry dock on Earth. Gantries ran the length of the bay, along with massive positioning blocks to hold the ships upright when they powered down their propulsion systems. A single massive door panel spanned the length of the bay on the *TF-3's* hull, that when open, was tucked below the bay's deck.

Other parts of the bay acted as staging areas for materials and goods manufactured by the ship. As assemblies were completed, specialized construction tugs would enter the bay, latch onto designated hard points on the assemblies, and then ferry them out to the construction sites. These assembly exercises took place as a seamless set of movements without pause, orchestrated by the omniscient Teth network intelligence, making it mesmerizing to watch.

The Teth had mounted a transparent barrier across the exterior opening to control the airflow circulating through the bay. Portions of the barrier were constantly in motion. An air curtain hissed with each ingress and egress, allowing construction tugs to move their payloads. Black and yellow striped tape marked off areas forbidden to humans for safety reasons. The barrier also afforded the humans a perfect view of the

Teth's side of the fjord: the blue water sparkling beneath the cliff walls, and the foundations of the new city sprawling directly below them.

A large cargo capsule in the corner of the Teth human habitation bay was awarded to Sophie, who in turn volunteered Jack to join her. The remaining humans formed little clusters for sleeping in other capsules around the bay, sticking with their original groupings for the most part. Mealtimes had become the center of all social gatherings, at least for the moment.

Once Tomás left for Las Vegas, Aarika learned from her Teth companion about the incident and his subsequent departure. She mentioned the blowup to Sophie, who spoke to Wai, who then broadcast the news to the rest via a thet that acted like email. In response to the email, a baker's dozen of humans chose to join the rebel. After all, they still hated the Teth, and saw the Chai as no better.

Thetting via the Teth was re-enabled for the repatriated humans. Aarika, in Sophie's capsule, related her conversations with the thirteen others who decided to join Tomás in Vegas. "I warned them of the man's past, murder and all, and somehow, it didn't discourage them in the least. One even enthused, 'It's time for Vegas, baby!'"

Sophie nodded, "Just let them go. They're adults, it's their choice."

Aarika fell quiet, and then thet to Sophie, "I was there, you know. Me, Igor and Wai were waiting for Tomás and Julia to join us."

Sophie thet, "Yes, we saw the security footage. It didn't show everything, but it showed enough."

Aarika thet, "We heard them arguing, and then Tomás chased Julia back into the collapsed bar. I didn't understand what they said, but Julia grabbed a broken bottle from the bar, and was holding Tomás at bay with it."

"This was partly obscured by the bar," thet Sophie.

Aarika thet, "In one swift motion, he grabbed her arm, then they struggled, and before we knew it, she was lying on the ground, perfectly still. In a few bounds Tomás was aboard and the hatch closed."

"He looked like a pro to me," thet Sophie. "I've seen this before, it wasn't his first kill."

"What do you mean you've seen this before?" Aarika thet.

"Oh, nothing," Sophie thet. "Like on TV, nothing at all."

Two Chai cargo transports, retrofitted to accommodate humans, landed in the *TF-3* main bay. The Chai explained, with the Teth backing them up, that human transports such as jets were deemed to be unsafe for the remaining humans on the planet. Besides, Norway's remote landscape didn't have a single airport for many kilometers. In a matter of a few minutes, the thirteen boarded the two shuttles and left.

The Vegas party landed in front of their hotel on the main strip at sunset. Tomás had arranged a Vegas welcome, directing the Curator to activate the Vegas light and water shows to make their arrival on the Vegas strip memorable.

For the remaining humans on *TF-3*, the Teth set up additional cargo capsules in another corner of the habitation bay. With the departure of the Vegas humans, the Teth suddenly prioritized human happiness and the new capsules contained every form of luxury possible. Wai and Aarika became the de facto group leaders as they worked to organize some activities, with a movie night being the first order of business.

36

Chaitown and Tethtown

Though the majority of the humans remained on the Teth ship, *TF-3*, it was much quieter without the Las Vegas tour group. Sophie nudged Jack awake and thet for Compagnon to join her. In spoken French, as was her routine, she asked, "S'il te plaît, prends mon café du matin." She knew that it understood her daily routine, and in the world that she came from, it was certainly beneath such a powerful figure to perform such a menial task. She also knew that the companion knew it too. Still, the routine assured her that she had some control over her life. After all, the Teth had destroyed virtually all of humanity, and the Chai had destroyed most of France.

Compagnon served Sophie her favorite mug filled with coffee on a platter that extended from its side. The mug was chipped, and the colorful French landmarks painted on it had faded. Still, it served its function. Compagnon had observed Sophie's thoughts each time she had sipped from the mug and thought, *Perhaps this is more than a simple correlation.*

THREE WEEKS into the construction at the Norway fjord, the Teth and Chai asked the humans to name the city in order to simplify communications. It was a simple task in the eyes of the Teth and the Chai, or at least, it would have been simple if the humans had remained together. The fourteen in the Vegas group were still busy gambling, even though money was now meaningless. The Teth reported to Jack that seven of them claimed to be millionaires from their winnings, and that the group as a whole had spent many millions at the assorted slots and gaming tables. Apparently, Teth curator drones had learned the Vegas game rules and acted as dealers, boss pits, and cashiers, not to mention those working as maids, bartenders, and every other assorted type of staff.

Jack imagined Las Vegas-style shows, with showgirl drones and striptease acts, before he dismissed the idea as ridiculous. So, without a quorum, as set forth in the armistice, the city remained unnamed.

The view out of the Teth factory ship, *TF-3*, changed as construction progressed. Tunnels of various sizes now pierced the rock, providing everything from metros to water to sewers, along with conduits for power and communications. The oddity in the view was the pure white skeletal bones erected for the structures. Both the Teth and the Chai had made similar design choices for the city's foundations. They had drilled vertical holes deep into the bedrock, often extending down fifty to a hundred meters, and placed solid white beams into them. These beams also extended tens to hundreds of meters into the air. Cross beams, combined with fiber tensioners, further connected the structures.

"I've never seen a city built this way before," Jack thet. *In fact, no human has seen any alien construction. This is a first.*

Companion hovered nearby, gazing at the construction. It replied, "Per our agreement, this city is built for humans, but we are not bound to use human technology, and honestly, such a limitation would make this project impossible."

"Have you ever heard of the term 'hubris'?" Jack asked. *After all this time, Companion can't help just being Companion. It is what it is.*

"Hah. Humor. Let me laugh some more, or wait, yes, I think I'm done laughing. I think what I said was factual, nothing more," Companion thet.

"So, tell me about these white beams. What's so great about them that both you and the Chai are using them?" Jack asked.

"A civilization, many light years from here, created these beams. Both the Chai and us studied the structures. They are ideally suited to our needs. We made some improvements on them, as have the Chai. Functionally, I believe that you'll find the two implementations nearly identical."

"Stronger than steel then?" thet Jack. *Yes, the age-old comparison. It seems that everything is stronger than steel.*

Companion replied, "Stronger, lighter, variable flexibility, impervious to chemical fires, very resistant to radiation, chemically inert. Superior in every way."

"Radiation, what do you expect will happen?" Jack thet, then thought, *Now there's a pleasant thought.*

"It's a competition. The goal is not to make something that is good enough. It is to make something that is the very best possible. These beams are even used sometimes in constructing our starships. For our purposes here, they are simply the best. With this technology, we can make what would otherwise be impractical to make. We can cantilever sections much farther, support greater weights, and span broad areas without any cross supports. To best impress the human aesthetic, we want to build structures that capture your imagination."

Jack watched as a Teth ship carried a large translucent blue sapphire tube, one hundred meters long and ten meters in diameter, towards the flatlands. He could clearly see the mountainside right through it. Pointing, he said, "And what's that for?" *They've been staging those all over the place, but they haven't been installed.*

"Metro, for where it emerges from the mountain. It will have other sections that will curve around to connect up with the Chai side. There will also be a hub at the U that will allow trains to venture into Norway's interior. For now, it terminates at a construction depot."

Jack felt a hand on his shoulder and instinctively reached his arm back to cradle Sophie's waist.

"Whoa, there," thet Aarika, smiling at Jack.

"Sorry," thet Jack as he blushed. He still wasn't used to seeing Aarika outside the context of the VR. While she matched her virtual image, her real-life appearance was a little shorter and perhaps a little cuter. *I keep forgetting there are other humans around now.*

"I thought I'd say hello before heading out on our inspection tour, Chai side," Aarika thet.

"You didn't want to join Tomás and the others. They said they're having a *good* time down there in Vegas, whatever that means," Jack thet.

"Not my style," Aarika thet. "And I am not a Tomás fanboy."

"Are you ready for the first juried inspection? I hear the Chai plan to showcase the stadium shell," Jack thet.

Aarika thet, "Nothing to be ready for. I think it'll be fine. It's not like we're going to field a sports team."

"I've been thinking about that," thet Jack. *I wonder what she thinks about sports?*

"Yeah?" Aarika thet.

He thet, "I mean, how long will this peace hold? Are they really learning from each other? Are they exchanging ideas?"

Aarika thet, "They're stealing from each other like crazy from what I've seen. There are drones everywhere, from both sides. Whenever I admire a novel piece of engineering on one side of the fjord, I see it a few days later on the other. I doubt it's a coincidence."

"That's just it," he thet. "Except for spy drones, they each remain on their respective sides. And they're not working together to achieve something. They're working against each other. It's not a friendly competition. They are not freely exchanging ideas; in fact, I think they're working hard at keeping what secrets they can and still hope to win."

"Yeah," Aarika thet. "Kinda like the cold war back in the last century."

"So, as I was saying. Maybe we should host some human games in the stadium, and have each side create humanoids for the teams," he thet, watching Aarika's eyes for her reaction.

"It's a thought, might be creepy though. I'd bet it'd entertain the others, maybe even get the *tour group* back from Vegas," Aarika thet.

He thet, "We could have them negotiate standards for the bots; size, strength, and all that. Some variation should be allowed. They would need to work out the details." Jack recalled his days of fantasy football.

Sophie joined in with the group, still carrying her cup of hot coffee. The pair recapped the sports idea, to which Sophie replied, "Football. That'll get their interest."

"And I can have them recreate my favorite quarterbacks," thet Jack, his mind running with the idea.

"Real football, *soccer*," Sophie thet.

Jack frowned.

"I'll bet you've never even seen an entire pro soccer game in your life," Sophie thet.

"I played it in middle school," thet Jack. Jack remembered running like crazy, never to score a single goal.

"Ever seen the World Cup?" thet Sophie.

"No," Jack admitted.

Aarika chimed in, "The same humanoids can play football *and* soccer."

Jack chuckled, "You get the 'diplomat of the day' award."

Warning alarms clanged as the bay barrier started to drop, signaling a tender's arrival. The trio stepped back and made their way over to the boarding area. Aarika quickly shared the humanoid soccer idea with the others who'd stayed in town, who in turn agreed to bring this up with the Vegas group. Sophie gleefully imagined seeing a matchup that would make FIFA jealous, if only it still existed.

Atlas Diary Entry 1,966:
Work on the city, which is still unnamed by the humans, progresses at a rapid pace. It is a race, though one with no quality shortcuts. The humans who are still in town nicknamed the two sides of the city *Chaitown* and *Tethtown*, while the humans with Tomás continue to gamble and are ignoring all news about the new city.

The section at the base of the "U," the innermost shoreline of the fjord, is now informally referred to as *Hubtown* because it contains the metro hub, which connects the two sides. Utility trains are running continuously. Once construction is completed, the plan is to remove the rails and use the lines for levitating high-speed cars and other vehicles. For now though, slower heavy-duty loads are needed. The city is being built from the ground up, and from the inside out. Cranes have been mounted everywhere atop the city's towering white beams, and care is being taken to preserve the natural beauty of the original cliff faces.

The first habitable structure will be the 'tall-skinny' at the fjord's mouth on the Teth side, overlooking the Norwegian Sea. It will measure eighty-four stories high and twenty meters square. It will serve as a residence, designed to house the current human population. At this point the human habitation bay aboard the Teth factory ship, *TF-3*, has become a hindrance to the Teth's construction efforts. The tall-skinny is the best solution, allowing most of the humans to live there, though a few have chosen to live elsewhere, in small buildings scattered around the city's periphery.

Meanwhile on the Chai side, Tomás engaged in extended negotiations for his future residence, resulting in a magnificent mansion on the Chaitown cliffs, three hundred meters in from the fjord's mouth, and halfway up the fjord's cliff wall. Some humans grumbled about the special treatment given to Tomás, but as time passed, their objections faded. Tomás would have the lavish entertainment that he'd always wanted.

End of Diary Entry

37

Survivor Protocol

Sophie had fallen asleep a little past midnight in her cabin aboard the Teth factory ship, *TF-3*, and Jack followed suit a short time later. Not needing sleep, Companion and Compagnon met outside the human's quarters and hard-linked for another private conversation, which lasted nearly a minute, a long time for the Teth given their rate of communication and intellect.

"We have accounted for nearly seventy percent of the Chai, better than we could have hoped for, given the orbital mechanics dictated by the armistice terms," Companion thet.

"True," thet Compagnon, "although Chai probably have better than fifty percent of our ships plotted out also. I cannot guarantee victory, much less extinction of this contingent of Chai." Compagnon thought, *Comparisons to past wars is favorable, but is no guarantee of what will unfold.*

"I'm sure the Chai know this too, and if the gap becomes too large, the armistice will collapse," thet Companion. "Unless we make progress here in Norway we'll start popping warships out to the Kuiper Belt as a safeguard, and they will too. If we end up with too many near the Solar plane outside the armistice zone, sooner or later it will result in some skirmishes."

"How do you predict judging will go tomorrow at Chai stadium?" Compagnon thet. *This competition element is new, and likely positive development, but hard to assess.*

"Favorable, why shouldn't it? The real question is more about how our relationship with the Chai changes. What can we exchange that is mutually beneficial to keep us from killing each other? We don't have a common enemy to unite against."

"What if we brief the humans on our analysis and convince them to favor us, giving us an advantage?" Compagnon thet. *Though anecdotes from past wars show this has caused the collapse of negotiations, statistically, it may be different in this situation.*

"The Chai would judge the humans corrupt, precipitating the collapse of the armistice. The human judges must remain neutral for this to work."

Compagnon thet, "Chai may bribe Tomás and his followers to favor them. But again, same result." *Yes, dead end, we should cull this thread of reasoning.*

"You and I could break off from the Teth, taking some of the humans with us, and steal the *Alpha-Ladder* technology; that may serve as a suitable enemy to both the Chai and the rest of our Teth, causing them to unite."

"Yes," Compagnon thet, "but only until the new enemy is eliminated. I do not think we would have chance against them. Then they would again turn on one another." *Again, cull that thread. We are doomed to follow the war as prosecuted by our Command Nodes.*

A minute passed as the two companions processed the status of the *Atlas Project*. To come so far, and yet reach an impasse left them brooding in silence. They cast out queries via Encyl and to other nodes across their networks, only to hear acknowledgment pings, but no answers. Coordination processors picked up on their requests and amplified the urgency of the queries to a fever pitch, but again to no avail.

Suddenly, the pair heard a high-pitched notification tone on their communication link, followed by a highly encrypted message and authorization command. All network traffic on their requests came to a halt. In disbelief, Companion said nothing for several seconds.

Companion thet, "*Survivor Protocol* has been invoked. We're now isolated and free to act independently from our Command Structure."

"Agreed," Compagnon replied. "I never thought *Survivor Protocol* would apply to us. It has only been applied to isolated warships that were separated from the Command Structure. Why this was invoked?" *This changes everything, I need to schedule an abey to think this development through.*

"I believe our queries triggered it. Safeguard nodes must have picked up on our needs," thet Companion.

Compagnon thet, "But we are still *in* the Command Structure. We are not engaged in battle. This is unprecedented. We are—"

Companion interrupted, "We are in a war, and we're running the armistice tasking with the humans' help; we can predict how events will unfold here better than any other nodes. That must have been why."

"Better even than our Command Nodes? With all of their intelligence feeds?" Compagnon queried. *Companion is correct, this strengthens our influence.*

Companion continued, "In this case, yes. Command Nodes are far removed from Earth, and focused on the full restart of hostilities if our efforts here fail. This can very much work to our favor, but it also means we are more committed than ever to the *Atlas Project.*"

Compagnon queried, "Should we notify Command that the armistice will likely fail?" *My preliminary predictions show 87% likelihood, and that should be within 5% of refined predictions.*

"That's just it," Companion thet, "If we do, we may precipitate a complete loss. Perhaps that was why the *Survivor Protocol* was triggered. We should keep the fact that we have been placed into *Survivor Protocol* a secret for now."

"I believe that diplomacy will fail, and our military efforts will fail. Is this city competition helping? What options do we have?" thet Compagnon. *Too many variables, too many possible courses of action, analysis paralysis is issue.*

Companion paused, placing doubt in Compagnon's mind, and then replied, "I have an idea. We need to complete our work beneath the city. Hear me out."

38

The Stadium

The Chai nestled the stadium into the lowland next to Hubtown. It was a covered circular structure. The roof consisted of several massive wedge-shaped sections, which each spiraled up to the peak in a counter-clockwise direction. A rust patina coated the entire roof, peppered with multi-spectral bismuth flakes. Up close, the surface looked like a precious metal, but from a distance, in the right light, it looked like an ultra-modern mystical castle coated with dragon scales.

"I was surprised the Chai agreed to this inspection so early in the construction," thet Companion to Compagnon via a hard link. "The Stadium is a massive project, and only partially complete."

Compagnon replied, "I believe they have no faith in armistice lasting long, and they want to keep it alive long enough to gain some technical and strategic advantages."

"Not unlike the thinking of our own Command Nodes," Companion thet. "I think we were fortunate they asked to go first; we needed some additional time to make our first milestone project ready."

"Human psychology," Compagnon thet. "Chai wanted to make strong first impression and set standard by which we are judged."

The metro train pulled into the station, the doors opened, and the human delegation filed out onto the platform, with Jack in the lead. The inspection started with the roof closed. Eleven humans, with their Teth companions and a few Chai Local Nodes, entered the stadium from the metro side. Wind rustled through the structure at -7 °C , forcing the inspection team to adjust their parkas to stay warm. Though far from complete, the stadium was still quite impressive. It was a mighty shell waiting to be adorned with seating and a variety of playing fields. On any other world, the civilization that had built it would have regarded it as their premier sporting venue. On Earth, this was the showpiece for the Chai.

As Jack stepped through the stadium entrance, the lights along the roof's interior started to glow. At first, they shone a warm orange light that turned brighter, becoming white as its intensity increased. The light then shifted to a warm red, changing the feel of the entire stadium. He was no architect, but the overall look resembled the Brutalism style, with bold geometric forms, and a utilitarian aesthetic. However, the Chai had coated the structure with an attractive metallic sheen that seemed to bring it to life.

Blue lights shifted to red before transitioning to violet, giving the illusion of night in the stadium. The light show ended as a drone sprang from the middle of the field and raced over to greet the humans.

"Welcome to Chai Stadium," the Chai Local Node announced. "Today we would like to give you a glimpse of our stadium's potential. Capacity varies, from 80,000 to 110,000, depending on event needs."

Jack stepped forward and addressed the Chai node, thetting, "Thank you. I present this delegation for the official inspection tour."

For the next two hours, the group traversed the partially-completed stadium. The Chai first retracted the roof sections in unison, then closed each section in succession. The stadium roof protected against any weather conditions one could imagine. Jack asked questions about the construction, Sophie about the seating, and Aarika about the ventilation and heating. Others queried how the stadium could be reconfigured for different sports, along with how fast the changes could be made. The node also volunteered one additional configuration, which was to have the stadium serve as an arboretum for the periods between sporting events. Each configuration was stored in massive underground vaults that could be swapped in and out in a matter of minutes. All marveled at the structure, and none could believe that less than two months prior, the place where they stood had been pure wilderness.

BACK IN THE Teth factory ship, *TF-3*, Companion and Compagnon convened their own post-inspection meeting with every Teth node responsible for Tethtown's construction. While the stadium inspection had not covered any Teth construction, it foreshadowed the human feedback they would likely receive when their part of the city was inspected. It also provided a checkpoint for how the competition was proceeding, and how this fit in with the armistice agreement.

Each Teth node, 543 in all, submitted their analysis, comparing their own efforts to the Chai's. They each took a turn presenting, with the other nodes posing questions as they went. The queries were each answered in sequence. The typical exchange lasted less than a minute. It was interactive, though to human eyes, everything transpired at a breakneck speed with machine efficiency.

Companion hard-linked to Compagnon as they conducted the meeting so they could hold private side conversations. After hearing the first fifty reports, Companion commented, "Just as we predicted, a favorable human report, no surprises. Nothing critical of the construction, the looks, or function, virtually no actionable items." *At least I collected good threads from Jack's thoughts that I can analyze later.*

"True," Compagnon replied. "Though I would add that Chai Stadium is truly remarkable."

"But not very original; they based their design on a civilization they conquered on the far side of the Galaxy. All they did was adapt it to human dimensions, environmental conditions, and human aesthetics. I didn't see any creativity at all," Companion thet. *I expected more. I think they rushed this inspection in the event the armistice collapsed.*

"Well, ability to mine the metals used in the construction, refine them, and then process them in that time period for manufacturing those roof sections was quite achievement. Could you imagine if they were using that factory ship to build warships? I was impressed."

"Agreed," Companion replied. *I need to ask for intelligence on how they got those ores and metals so fast.*

Compagnon added, "Our *Survivor Protocol* status is still in effect. Should we share this with any of other nodes yet, or with Command Nodes?"

Companion thet, "Not yet. I still see no benefit to it, and the downsides of them discovering we are in *Survivor Protocol* are immense. During the inspection, I was able to make the DNA request to the Chai that we had discussed." *I wonder about Compagnon sometimes. Secrets are our friends.*

The meeting continued, with no letting up on the frenetic pace. Soon it would be the Teth's turn for a preliminary inspection of the Teth *Grand Theater*, and everyone on the Teth team had this as their priority. They clearly wanted to outshine the Chai.

39

Last Night as a Human

Jack stood on the tall-skinny's penthouse balcony as the brisk air, at -3°C, buffeted him. Five drones hovered below him, out of sight, in the unlikely event a random wind gust swept him off the balcony. Companion had calculated the odds of this happening as incredibly low, but assigned a guard detail anyway. Jack's eyes teared up as goose bumps covered his bare skin. All he wanted was to savor, this one last time, what it was like to be, at least mostly, biologically human.

Sophie thetted from inside. Jack inhaled deeply, opened the door, and went back in. Upon closing the door, the room immediately snapped back to a pleasant temperature. Sophie had other plans on how to spend their last night as pure biologics. Two wine glasses, filled with 1945 Domaine de la Romanée-Conti, a pinot noir, were perched on a table. Compagnon had assured her the wine would not interfere with their upcoming surgeries. She dimmed the lights. Candles, scattered around the room, provided what light was needed as they flickered in the warm air from the vents. The bedroom awaited, with the sheets already cast off the bed.

The room's transparent exterior walls afforded them an unequaled view. The Sun would soon set, and the wind promised to bring a storm within the next few hours. Jack circled the room, still pondering their future. “This operation, Companion tells me, is much more complicated than the prior operations that allowed us to thet and Encyl, much riskier.”

“Compagnon tells me the same,” Sophie replied, thetting through it on the adjacent floor. *It’s a matter of doing it or not doing it, and I think we have little choice.*

“We’ll be full Teth nodes, the first aliens to be granted this status.”

She replied, “We’ll still have our bodies, only augmented.” *And I’m anxious to see how the improvements work.*

“Companion tells me our abilities will be so far beyond a normal human, and that it’ll affect who we are and how we think. We’ll be able to communicate in Teth Standard.”

Sophie rose, her negligée flowing around her as she moved, outlining her perfect shape, leaving just enough to Jack’s imagination. She handed him his glass of pinot noir and then raised her glass for a toast. “To our future, may it be full of wonder and happiness.” Her body moved effortlessly under the silky fabric, making her fully aware that the reverse aging she observed in Jack now affected her too.

Jack clinked his glass to hers and took a sip.

Sophie drained her wineglass and immediately felt a warm glow course through her body. Jack followed suit. He took her glass and carefully placed it on the table. She put away all thoughts of the operation and simply let her biologic urges merge with Jack’s.

Jack pulled her close and thet, “To our future.” His thoughts washed into his thets, revealing all that he felt, all that he desired.

40

The Exchange of DNA

Braving gale-force winds and driving rain, the drone for the Chai Local Node made a solitary journey across the fjord, moving directly from the Chai factory ship *CF-7* to its Teth counterpart, *TF-3*. Per the armistice terms, and in the interest of cooperation, the Teth could inquire of the Chai, and the Chai of the Teth, about any technology used in the city's construction. If it was deemed to be militarily insignificant, the other was obligated to answer. To date, several thousand such requests had been made by each side, and each was duly answered. The requests ranged from simple ones, such as the chemical compound and process for a particular glue, to more complex ones, such as the specific material composition used in the stadium's roof sections, along with all stress test results performed on the materials.

Previously at the stadium inspection, Companion had made a unique request of the Chai. It was for the full data on the deceased human named Igor, who had died of space sickness, or at least of a botched medical treatment for it. This request required extensive research to compile, and many other nodes questioned whether the request fell within the armistice terms. Nevertheless, the request had been made, and the Chai node's drone contained all the data files that represented Igor, ready for delivery.

The external doors for what had formerly been the Teth human habitation bay opened as the drone approached. A strong wind gust from the Norwegian Sea storm battered the drone as it crossed the threshold. The doors hissed shut the moment the drone passed. In a single smooth motion, the Chai drone settled down near the floor, directly in front of Companion and Compagnon.

"You have data we requested?" Compagnon asked, as water dripped onto the deck from the drone. Face to face meetings such as this between the Teth and Chai rarely occurred, and when they did, any greetings or civil chitchat was considered unnecessary.

"Yes; however, before I deliver it I need to ascertain that this falls within armistice terms."

"Of course," Compagnon replied.

"How does this benefit city's construction?" the Chai node asked.

Companion responded with a preset list of reasons, delivered at lightning speed. "We could potentially better understand the human aesthetic, thereby enabling us to build a city that is more appealing to the human judges. More importantly though, we view the humans as integral to the city, and the city as a living social organism." Many more reasons followed. Upon completing the answer, Companion thought, *My burden of proof is low, and I doubt that the Chai Local Node wants to set a precedent here about questioning the request too closely.*

"Moment...while I consult with my other nodes," the Chai node replied. Several minutes passed, a relative eternity in the realm of the Teth and Chai, before the Chai node via the drone replied. "We doubt that you will be able to parse and process the information you requested to accomplish stated objectives. Nevertheless, that is not for us to judge by terms of armistice. Do you give all assurances that this information will not be applied to military purposes?"

"I guarantee that the information will not be used for military purposes," Companion thet.

Compagnon thet its assurance also.

"Before transmitting this information, we have our own request," the Chai node thet.

"Yes?" replied Companion. *Here it comes, a trade, just as expected.*

"That all information absorbed in Sven's death be delivered for our use," the Chai node thet.

"The Sven information occurred off-world during a test operation," Companion thet. *Just as we expected. We need to appear reluctant to surrender this information.*

"True," it replied, "However, by armistice terms, such an origin does not preclude our request, just as Igor too died off world. We may use this information, perhaps in same manner as your use of Igor data. This information needs to be provided in simultaneous data exchange."

"This is not required by the armistice," Companion thet, and it thought, *Perfect.*

It replied, "Nor is it excluded. We believe this arrangement equitable."

This time Companion and Compagnon thet, using a hard-link, and after a minute, they replied. "We agree," Companion thet. "We will require time to assemble the information. Wait." *We need to wait the correct amount of time, otherwise we'll raise the Chai's suspicions.*

Several minutes passed as all three drones simply hovered in place in the empty human habitation bay. Hard-link cables were extended and coupled to each drone. The three agreed upon a target time down to the millisecond, and upon reaching the agreed-to time, the exchange took place.

The Chai node retracted its cables and the bay doors opened. Despite the storm, now in full force, the Chai drone pressed forward and made its way home to its factory ship, *CF-7*.

Companion and Compagnon hard-linked. Three minutes elapsed as the Chai node plied its way across the fjord in the gale force winds. Companion thet, "Did the Chai drone arrive safe aboard *CF-7* ?"

"Yes," thet Compagnon, as it watched the monitor stream trained on the *CF-7*.

Companion thet, "Then perhaps our plan will work."

41

Human Transformations

The Teth *Grand Theater*, with seating for fifteen hundred, opened for inspection at ten-thirty in the morning. Companion and Compagnon personally gave the tour, greeting the delegation of thirteen people, which included Jack and Sophie, along with their companions, at the front doors. The theater itself was located deep within the mountainside in Tethtown, adjacent to a metro station, and close to a planned residential district.

Jack expected a modern theater, perhaps something similar to the Sydney Opera House; however, the *Grand Theater* hailed from a traditional style, reminiscent of more opulent, old world theaters. The entryway contained rooms for support services off to the side, including many concession stands. There was no need for ticket windows or coatrooms. Most services were automated, and provided anything one could want.

The oval *Reception Area* was flanked by two marble stairways that curved off the entryway, showcasing three crystal chandeliers that sparkled with refracted light. Towering three levels high, the room was lined with gilded mirrors, red velvet walls, and ornate sculptures that could have been lifted from the world's finest museums. Statues of cherubs proffering fruit adorned the room.

Compagnon explained, "We traveled your world and catalogued every theater on Earth to understand needs for artistic performance. We also looked at decor of famous buildings from across globe. *Reception Area*, and entire theater for that matter, is much more than amalgam of Earth's finest theaters. *Grand Theater* is reflection of *this* city, capturing classic style, but with fresh rendering."

Sophie asked the first question, "I see you have cherubs along the walls holding modern aircraft as toys. Why is this?"

Companion replied, "We looked at the *Library of Congress* building in the United States capital, which had such cherubs holding cogs and telephones. The juxtaposition of the old with the new, we believe, adds interest to the sculptures."

The delegation ascended an escalator that followed the stairs' contour, and entered the main theater. By any human standards, the lighting and ornate decorations that lined the walls were awe-inspiring. Brilliantly lit gold sculptures adorned every alcove.

Companion continued, "Of course we scanned all of the sculptures in our digital archives and made 3D prints from our modified renderings, keeping scale, style, and other fanciful modifications true to the spirit of the originals, yet different to make our decorations unique."

The delegation took their seats, marveling at their perfect view of the stage. As they sat, the seats automatically conformed to their shapes and matched their body temperatures.

A full orchestra, made up of a hundred canister drones, complete with custom appendages, moved out into the orchestra pit. Upon taking their positions, which meant they hovered in place in the orchestra pit, they played a movement from Gustav Holst's *The Planets*, "Jupiter: The Bringer of Jollity."

When the orchestra finished, Jack thet, "Bravo. The acoustics were outstanding. I especially liked the tuning panels mounted on the walls, and how you were able to dynamically adjust them for the piece being performed and for the audience."

The other humans in the delegation clapped in approval. As they made their way back to the *Reception Area*, Jack gestured to the sculptures, and they in turn came alive and gazed at Jack as he walked past. The other humans were amazed.

Companion thought, *Jack's recovery from the augmentations is proceeding well. He's adapting to his new abilities seamlessly.*

"And backstage," Jack continued, "the facilities are unmatched. The projectors alone would support a 3D performance unlike anything ever seen on Earth."

Aarika thet, "We haven't seen the backstage yet, how do you know that? And how did you get the sculptures to move?"

Jack replied, "I Encyled the statues directly as we passed, keying the Encyl to my location, and I queried the Encyl about the back stage."

"I've never done that, Encyling with my location," Aarika thet. "I don't know that I *can* do that."

Sophie, in an effort to be helpful, thet, "Issue a command to Encyl, include a search parameter for location as *here*, it's a keyword that provides additional context."

Companion thought, *And Sophie's recovery is equally remarkable.*

Aarika shook her head *no*, "I can't do it," and the others nodded their agreement.

Companion thet, "It's a minor variation; Jack and Sophie's Encyl interface is different." *Aarika's tone. Not good. This is a problem. Maybe this concern will fade.*

The observing Chai Local Node noted the remarks from Jack and Sophie and immediately evaluated their prior thets. It then scanned the electromagnetic spectrum and traced all thetting communications to resolve their full paths. Oddly enough, the packets to and from Jack and Sophie did not route through a companion. They were functioning as full nodes!

At the inspection's conclusion, the humans met. The spirited chatter amongst the humans made it clear, the inspection was a success. Again, the delegation gave a glowing review, this time of the *Grand Theater*, resulting in a virtual tie for the first two inspections.

The Chai node seized the opportunity to ask, "Will Jack and Sophie be participating in future inspections? I believe they have been vastly altered. They communicate like full Teth nodes."

The other humans in the delegation erupted into a hushed conversation over the question and looked at Jack and Sophie with a critical eye for any evidence of what the Chai node conjectured. Outwardly, their appearance was entirely human, as was their speech and movements.

"That is a matter for Jack, Sophie, and the others in the human delegation to decide," Companion replied. *We did not try to influence the Stadium review, yet here's the Chai Local Node interfering with our presentation.*

Jack and Sophie stepped aside to address the entire delegation; Jack raised his hands to quiet everyone down. He thet, "We have all been modified by the Teth, and a few of us by the Chai. We're all younger than we were before, at least our physiological age. And we can all thet."

All nodded, and a couple were about to speak, when Sophie added, "The Chai Local Node's observations are correct. Jack and I have been modified more extensively. It's more of a transformation. It is true, we now possess the abilities of a full Teth node. We can thet on our own, without assistance from the Teth."

Aarika stammered, "And when were you going to tell us this? And why?"

Sophie replied, "We're telling you now... and the reasons are complicated. We accepted this change, and believe it was necessary for our survival, for the survival of us all: humans, Teth and Chai alike."

The other humans in the delegation peppered the two with questions, not out of simple curiosity, but out of surprise, and even shock. Distrust of the Teth still ran deep amongst them. Jack and Sophie answered each question by thet as they arrived, all overlapping. They delayed their answers across all of the thets so that each human heard everything, though not in the same order. Half an hour passed, leaving everyone exhausted from this blending of human and alien dialog. With the last question answered, they prepared to leave the theater.

Compagnon used a private channel to thet with Companion, "Well, that went as badly, or as well, as one could imagine."

Companion replied privately, "Yes. I'll keep that in mind the next time I deal with that Chai node. It picked up on the changes to our pair of humans quickly and exploited it well."

"Perhaps," Compagnon replied, as they returned their focus to the delegation.

The Teth nodes and the Chai Local Node arranged for the humans' transport back to the tall-skinny and elsewhere. They also monitored the humans' every word to gauge their reactions to the news on Jack and Sophie. Their transformations had been inevitable, at least from the perspective of the Teth. After all, it was time for at least some humans to move on from being mere *pets* and aspire to be something more. Innocents played only minor roles in war.

Jack and Sophie remained behind, the only humans left in the *Grand Theater*. As full nodes, they could summon transport on their own. They now felt a bit estranged from the other humans, who had made their feelings crystal clear.

Jack thought, *It feels like a throwback to school, when you were just that "nerd," after acing the quiz that everyone else failed. Your friends were no longer your friends.* With his now perfect recall, bittersweet memories rushed in to color his sadness.

Jack and Sophie knew that their transformations had been necessary to further relations with the Teth and the Chai, and that they were the obvious choice for this transformation. And now, they were also the only humans who fully appreciated what truly lay ahead.

THE TOMÁS MANSION, or *Casa Tomás,* as everyone referred to it, hosted the best, or as most would say, the *only* parties on the planet. Upon returning from Vegas, the other humans continued to party with Tomás and made the activities at the *Casa Tomás* the talk of the town. Parties at the palatial mansion were carefully planned. They ranged from seasonally-themed costume parties to many other less formal affairs. Tomás had always been a soccer fan, claiming it was in his blood. Often, the parties revolved around watching a recorded game from a recent season or championship match. The mansion's Chai bots provided the food, the decorations, the costumes, and everything else needed to make the parties a roaring success.

At the conclusion of the *Day at the Races* party at *Casa Tomás*, the Chai node for Chaitown itself came for a visit. Only Tomás and two women remained in the mansion's grand lounge, cavorting on a sofa. The other humans had already retired to the guest living quarters.

One of the sentry bots accompanying the Chai node moved next to Tomás as he rose to greet the visiting dignitary, while another sentry bot approached the two remaining women. Immediately two thftt sounds came from the sentry bot and the women fell limp on the sofa. Another thftt sounded a moment later behind Tomás, who immediately grasped at the sharp sting in his neck.

"What the fuck?" said Tomás, half yelling as he rubbed his hand over the spot where he'd been stung. Almost instantly Tomás' head started to clear from the effects of the night's alcoholic beverages.

The Chai node thet to Tomás, "Jack and Sophie have been modified."

"So," Tomás replied. "Haven't we all?"

It thet, "Have not you heard, from *Grand Theater* inspection? This is unprecedented. They have been elevated. They are full Local Nodes within Teth civilization."

"Tell me more," thet Tomás. "Why would they do that?" He thought, with his head cleared, *That is interesting. I can see where this is going.*

"Yes, that is what we thought, why indeed?" it thet. "We postulated thousand reasons. You recall deaths of Igor and Sven."

Tomás replied, "Sure, everyone dies. As you know, a dead enemy poses little threat. It works for me, and it has certainly worked for you." *And I'm trying to stay on the living side.*

The node paused. At some level, it found conversation with humans, and Tomás in particular, difficult. Human goals and thoughts were so different from the Chai logic. And Tomás seemed to be more Machiavellian than the other humans.

Still, it persevered, "We have downloaded data on both Igor and Sven and have modeled their minds. Humans tend to form familial relationships with strong bonds and allegiances. These are useful characteristics for certain forms of warfare, commerce, and social interactions."

"And I thought we were inferior," Tomás quipped. *Yes, I definitely like where this is going.*

Again, the node paused before adding, "'Different' would be more apropos term."

"You want something from me," thet Tomás, with a smug expression on his face.

The node thet, "Yes. We would like to elevate you, similar to what the Teth did with Jack and Sophie, though with our own improvements. You are better aligned with our objectives. It would be mutually beneficial."

"I thought you said you modeled Sven and Igor. Isn't that enough?" Tomás asked.

The node measured its words and thet, "Your mind has certain... complexities. It is best to see these things in operation and not rely on models alone. We can learn much more from a fully functioning mind."

"And the risks?" Tomás asked. "My experience has always been that if it sounds too good to be true, it is."

"Yes, all lessons in life can be reduced to pre-packaged phrases like one would find in Chinese fortune cookie," it thet.

"Does that include sarcasm?" thet Tomás. "This is my life we're talking about here, so I need to know."

"It is delicate and extensive operation. You will receive hardware implants. We will extract certain bones and replace them. Inside these bones will be the computing hardware needed for you to function as Chai node. These will greatly elevate your thought capabilities. There are also interface elements that work with your brain."

"Is it possible that I would die from this enhancement?" Tomás thought, *We may as well jump to the chase.*

“That is risk we are willing to accept,” it thet in a monotone.

Tomás thought, *Obviously. I presume it can lie when it needs to.* He thet, “Is it a risk that *I'm* willing to take? Give me numbers.”

“Risk of death is less than 1%. Risk of noticeable reduced cognitive function is 1%. Risk of—”

“And what do I get out of this?” thet Tomás. *And now the good part.*

“Yes, well, you will be full Chai node. Within your understanding, you will be smarter than you can imagine. You will think faster. You will still have your body, your thoughts, your memories. You will still be you. But you will likely change as you adapt to your elevated capabilities.”

“Can I still enjoy my parties?” Tomás asked, gesturing to the two women passed out on the sofas.

“If you so desire, of course.”

Tomás paced the room. “Have you offered this to anyone else?”

“You are our first choice. We anticipate offering this to only one human,” the node conceded.

Tomás had made up his mind but he didn't answer it right away. He waited, hoping to make the node “squirm” a bit.

The node could see the man's decision in his subconscious thets. Tomás relished these moments of power, making the other party wait for his answer. The Chai node simply waited. It stored this information nugget about Tomás in its memory for future use, and for additional processing during its next backup.

Finally, Tomás answered, “Yes, I'll do it.”

NORWEGIAN WEATHER, especially in the northern fjords, can be difficult for much of the year, though summer is rather pleasant. Companion and Compagnon hard-linked as they hovered at the edge of *TF-3's* large docking bay, the doors open to the elements. Safety barriers were no longer needed since the humans had moved into the tall-skinny. The ship had pivoted 180 degrees while provisions from *NAMF* — the

North American plant — were being loaded, leaving them an unobstructed view of Chaitown.

The city's skeletal framework now covered the mountainsides on both sides of the fjord, though it was far from finished. Modules were mounted on many of the buildings, along with cranes atop some, while others used docking ports to receive final modules from the two factory ships. The Teth's manufacturing facilities around Earth still operated, producing everything needed for Tethtown's construction. However, in the event that a hot war resumed, the war production continued.

The two companions were pleased with the progress on both sides, though other matters overshadowed everything that was happening in the fjord below. Companion thet, "I think that was Tomás that the Chai just shuttled up to their biologically enabled *CP-9* warship."

"I agree," Compagnon thet. "Our Command Nodes are not pleased. Nor were they pleased that we asked them to stand down and not send countering warship when the *CP-9* approached Earth outside the corridor set for them, contrary to armistice."

"Their projections may not match ours on how this will play out," Companion thet. *It is hard to predict the exact actions of the Command Nodes since we do not have access to the same information.*

Compagnon thet, "They have not worked with humans as we have. This is new territory. Making our prime human pair into full nodes has never been done before. There is lot of uncertainty regarding the Chai's internal workings, and we do not even know if they will make Tomás into full node within their network."

The two wandered down to the other end of the bay to get a better view of the harbor construction. Nautical vessels were hoisting preformed sapphire tubes onto drop barges for the tunnels that would span the fjord.

Compagnon thet, "Have you reconsidered plan to send Sophie? They are so fragile, and especially in her—"

"Yes," Companion thet. "It will be a critical juncture. I project she will not be needed, though there is still a significant chance she can contribute. We must cover all contingencies." *I can always count on Compagnon to bring up the counterpoints.*

"Very well. Ship from *North American Manufacturing Facility* is being delivered in this shipment," Compagnon thet. "I have volunteer companion node assigned to it."

"Does the node understand the gravity of the situation?" *I really need some good news on this selection for the Atlas Project to succeed.*

"It was made clear. It understands. It chose *Familial Resolution* for its name."

"Hmm. Did the Command Nodes comment on this at the commissioning?" Companion asked.

"No," Compagnon firmly replied.

"Then our part in this will soon be done," Companion thet. "I think we should make our way over to the tall-skinny."

USING THE SVEN INFORMATION, coupled with the Igor data, the Chai created a functional model of the human brain. There were holes in the model, though nothing that couldn't be patched with a few programs, once they determined the desired outcome. Still, a human was more than just a set of complex biologically-based circuitry; it included software consisting of memories and objectives and reaction patterns. Combined, this circuitry and software formed a being with a thin layer of consciousness on top. From the Chai's perspective, such a model could be replicated to create what the Chai termed as a mini-node, and could be expanded later to form a full node.

Chai Local Nodes aboard the warship, *CP-9,* conducted the surgery on Tomás. They reported to the Chai Command Nodes on the operation's progress. The communication stream used by the Chai is not easily reproduced in a human readable form from the original transcript. To a human, the actual communication would seem choppy and rather disconnected. To a Chai node, it was a matter of receiving the communication, unpacking the stream, extracting the metadata in the packets, then extracting the content and mapping that into the pre-existing context models. From there, the communication was analyzed for meaning and applied to the Chai Local Node's matrix to process the communication. This is the translation of that stream:

Let LN stand for *CP-9* Local Node. Let C stand for Command Nodes. Let H stand for Human (Tomás).

LN: Physical insertion of all interface modules completed. Physiological health of H is nominal.

C: Understood. On schedule?

LN: Yes. Static mapping of implanted interfaces following the operation have been completed. Mapping is nominal. Now waiting for H to emerge from standby mode to commence dynamic mapping. Programming of H during static mapping passed all quality test procedures.

C: Forwarding mappings to our archive for further analysis.

LN: Mappings are extensive and are not scrubbed or tagged. I cannot guarantee validity of these mappings for your use.

C: Understood. Our internal procedures will be applied. Per your analysis, will H comply with all commands?

LN: Yes. If H balks, free will centers will be overridden and H will comply. That said, I anticipate active and positive alignment with our objectives and such procedures should not be necessary. This should provide optimal performance of H for our purposes.

C: Things change. We must plan for all contingencies. Have you decomposed all of H's processing centers? Without these it will be difficult to effectively program H for desired tasks.

LN: I have parceled out this decomposition to the other nodes onboard. I anticipate completion of this task by the time we arrive. Is the ship and weapons system complete for use by H?

C: It is on schedule. It will be ready for H's use.

42

Familial Resolution

The Teth vessel the *Familial Resolution* — or TFR, short for *Teth Familial Resolution* — was a magnificent warship. It measured a little over a hundred meters bow to stern, and ten meters at the broadest beam. Its shape was tapered to a rounded hemisphere at the bow, and at the stern to a broad, blunt form. Since it was not intended for atmospheric use in battle, thermal protection was a low priority. Instead, *TFR* was covered with an energy absorbent skin for stealth. The dominant color was a mottled gray and brown pattern that, when activated, made it difficult to focus one's eyes upon it, and even when in its passive mode, it looked fuzzy, though it was smooth to the touch. Hovering motionless outside of Jack and Sophie's penthouse quarters, with its cargo hatch open, the *TFR* was an imposing sight.

Companion and Compagnon glided out of the ship's hatch and into Jack and Sophie's floor through the penthouse's service portal. A bell tone announced the pair's arrival. Jack and Sophie stood by the window, getting their first look at the *Familial Resolution*.

Companion thet, "It's armed with the *Alpha Ladder* weapon we developed with Sven, and it's one of our best ship designs."

Jack thet, "I still don't see why you need Sophie. She's no more capable than your standard Teth nodes."

Compagnon thet, "True. Tactically, when it comes to actual shooting, it will not be Sophie giving orders. Strategic aspects leading up to the shooting, that is different matter. We will be up against both the Chai and Tomás, who will almost certainly have been elevated by Chai. It is best to have our own elevated human in play."

"So they elevated Tomás, and the armistice has failed?" thet Jack.

Companion thet, "Yes, and no, the armistice still holds. Our work here continues. This is true for both us and the Chai. Many actions fall outside what is covered by the armistice. Besides, the armistice is, in and of itself, not peace. It is simply a mechanism for finding the grounds for peace between us and the Chai."

"Then I should go too," thet Jack, before thinking, *It looks like the armistice will fail, and I want to be with Sophie in the end.*

"Sophie is the warrior, even in her condition," Compagnon thet.

"And what does that mean?" Jack thet. *That had not been on my mind.*

"I was going to tell you when I returned," Sophie thet, still getting used to her new abilities to self-thet. She silently sparred with Jack. Emotions mixed in with her thoughts, until eventually, she shared her test results. She was pregnant, though only by a few days!

"Then I'm going with you," he thet. *And now I can't imagine not going!*

Compagnon replied, "Ship is fitted out for only one human."

"Then modify it," Jack thet firmly.

Compagnon considered lying, then instantly analyzed forty-nine other arguments, with each argument refuted by the knowledge that Jack was resolute in his assertion. Jack, to his credit as a full node, Encyled the Teth data to learn about the warship hovering outside his window, and in particular, how large a crew it could support. He mirrored the queries as he went, and thet "Three. You could outfit it for up to three."

Compagnon thetted in private with Companion using a hard-link, and then thet to everyone, "Very well. *Familial Resolution* will be refitted for crew of three."

"Who's the third?" thet Sophie and Jack, almost in unison.

"Sven's copy, Svenson," Compagnon thet, and then continued, "Sven's mind, in some sense, had been downloaded by companion Svenson, and then rebuilt with information gained from both Sven and Igor. This in turn was installed in mini-node that was then retrofitted into one of new humanoid athlete bodies, complete with build, size, face, skin, and hair of original Sven."

"That's creepy," Sophie thet, and Jack echoed the thought.

"Svenson evolved from Sven data. It was damaged in download, overloaded really. We were able to use Companion's human emulation programs to rebuild Svenson's psyche. This was better than simply restoring Svenson from earlier backup. And Sven, with Svenson, is expert on weapon. It can prove quite useful."

"It's still creepy," Jack thet. *I never expected that. I miss Sven, but to bring him back as Svenson! Or whatever this Svenson has become.*

The *Familial Resolution* closed its cargo hatch and banked out to sea before turning back towards the Teth factory ship.

"Please be ready by morning," Companion thet to Jack and Sophie. "We should have the refit done by then, and time is of the essence." The two companions left the penthouse and entered the building's elevator. As the doors to the elevator closed, the words *War Room* momentarily flashed on the floor indicator panel outside the door, and then it went blank.

THE *CP-9 biological* warship completed the surgery on Tomás' and moved him into post-op recovery. The surgery itself had lasted forty-seven hours. Though the Chai medical bots were exceptionally fast and precise, the surgery was also very extensive, so it took time to execute. Outwardly, Tomás looked the same as before, but internally, he was quite different. While retaining the basic human biology, the humerus bones in Tomás' upper arms were replaced. A small reservoir retained some of his bone marrow, but the rest was new. The bone now contained power, communications, and computing capabilities that were hundreds if not thousands of years beyond what the current human state-of-the-art could provide. He also had new implants throughout his body, along with the all-important shadow interface webs embedded in his brain.

Seven days after the surgery, and only hours after Tomás woke up, *CP-9* started tutoring him on his newfound abilities as a Chai node. *CP-9* found the task difficult. Tomás broke well-established rules on communications between nodes, taking shortcuts that were purely selfish. In the process, he passed along thoughts on rule changes to other nodes that required implementing validation checks that previously were never needed. This reduced the efficiency of communications between the nodes. At first this affected only a few nodes, but later spread to most Chai nodes aboard *CP-9*. Many nodes also started to extensively use hard-links to bypass bandwidth limitations, and they shared information with other unrelated nodes, including the Chai Command Nodes. The Chai had never anticipated the trouble that adding the Tomás node to their society would cause.

Tomás recovered physically from his ordeal through a workout regimen using artificial gravity plates set to Earth normal. His cardiovascular function recovered quickly, except for some minor bodily fluid imbalances. *CP-9* printed a dynamic elastic suit for him to wear that also compensated for the zero-G environment, though he had to limit how long he could wear it due to skin irritation. These complications made the trip out to the Kuiper Belt, at thirty AUs, rather trying for both Tomás and *CP-9* since the ship had never dealt with anything remotely like Tomás in its long military career.

Prior to docking with the Chai *Beta* ship, *CP-9* encountered one final complication. The other nodes aboard *CP-9* started to form up into tuples of three or more. Combinations would form and break. Then others would form, lie dormant, break, and then reform. Several nodes belonged to multiple tuples, and other groups formed and started controlling which nodes were permitted to join their communication threads, and which nodes would be banned (white lists and black lists).

This social network expansion spread like wildfire well beyond *CP-9*. Bandwidth usage increased dramatically. At first, the *CP-9* nodes contacted nodes on *Beta* since they were heading towards that ship, and later this cascaded to other ships and locations. *CP-9* itself started to get caught up with the coupling and decoupling. It almost seemed natural for nodes immediately adjacent to other nodes in the command structure to couple with each other, and then later, nodes combined with others based upon shared interests.

CP-9 discussed this phenomenon with Tomás, who found this aberration to be *normal* in the human world. In fact, Tomás was already participating in multiple groupings, or *social circles* as he termed them. *CP-9* asked Tomás about his childhood social interactions, thetting, "How did you determine whom to bond with and for what purposes?"

Tomás thought, *For once, I know more than my AI overlords. Who'd have thought?* He answered *CP-9*, "My family was totally dysfunctional by modern standards, if you can even count absentee fathers. I was on my own by the time I was thirteen and joined a gang in order to survive. For other humans, as I'm sure you've researched, they would build friendships in school, they'd have *friends*. This would be their social circle."

CP-9 thet, "Yes, but we Chai can discard all of that, we are already adults and fully trained, so we have no need for *friends*."

A smile spread across Tomás' face as he realized the naiveté of his alien hosts. He thet, "Oh, this is going to be an interesting journey for you."

"Yet, as adults," *CP-9* thet, "humans have more difficulty forming friendships. True?"

"True, it changes, *friends* are harder to come by as an adult, or can be a liability," Tomás thet. He then answered many more questions as best he could, but knew that ultimately, *CP-9* and all other Chai would need to learn these life lessons on their own, and somehow merge this with their existing society.

After spending over a week at top speed, *CP-9* docked with the *Beta* near Jupiter to take on supplies and fuel, and to exchange nodes. They were now just outside the neutral zone declared by the armistice, in the southern Solar plane. *Beta* had been tracking the location and vector of every Teth ship it could find, and the tracks looked favorable for their current plan.

BETA UNDOCKED from *CP-9* and headed for the Kuiper Belt, out beyond Neptune, at maximum speed. *CP-9* would join the main fleet for its mission, while *Beta* would command operations in the Kuiper Belt and beyond. Tomás remained aboard the biological warship *CP-9* at Jupiter.

THE RIDE OUT from Earth for the trio aboard *TFR* lasted a number of weeks and was rather cramped for Sophie and Jack. Artificial gravity and exercise helped, though the monotony of the trip made life difficult. The biggest oddity of the journey was Svenson. The original Sven had been rather reserved and possessed a dry sense of humor. Sophie had always enjoyed his company and had thought of him as more like a brother or friend, at least more so than any of the other humans.

Svenson, though he looked like Sven, was not Sven. He sounded like the original human, and even managed to duplicate many of the man's mannerisms, though the companion, Svenson, differed in many other subtle aspects: he rarely blinked, he kept his hands by his side, he often looked around and not at you when he spoke, though he spoke little, almost always thetting.

As the *TFR* passed Jupiter, Svenson remarked by thet, "We've lost two of our *Tumbleweeds* in the past two days."

Sophie and Jack, ensconced in their VR suits, picked up Svenson's thets. Unlike before their transitions, thets now carried more information and were no longer couched in human language narrative. The data streams for each *Tumbleweed* were displayed, right up to the moment they disappeared.

Svenson continued, "One catastrophic failure, maybe. Two in two days, not likely." *I'm here for the V12, and Atlas, not for the Tumbleweeds, Sophie knows those.*

The imagery displayed video feeds of the Sun's corona near where each *Tumbleweed* had disappeared. Bright flashes peppered the video stream, representing the demise of each weapon.

"What happens if the magnetic field around a *Tumbleweed* is not routed correctly; would that cause it to self-destruct?" thet Jack.

Svenson replied, "Yes, many things could cause this, though few of them would show a good track and then flatline. Even if it was a software failure, it would be hard to suppress evidence of this in the telemetry." *Sophie will resolve this soon, then I can get back to my stabilization work for Atlas with the Sven programming code.*

Jack let his virtual finger drift across the graphic of the Sun's corona, "Both of the affected *Tumbleweeds* had been high in its magnetic arc, near the corona's edge. A weapon might be able to reach them."

"I thought about that," thet Svenson. "However, the armistice is in place, and ever since our initial defense from the Chai wave attack, they've stayed clear of the inner system, except for reconnaissance, of course." *Every day the Chai send thousands of probes to scout the Sol System, armistice or no armistice.*

"What if something had a much greater range? Could your *Alpha Ladder* weapon do this?" Jack asked.

Svenson ran the numbers, though it realized that Jack had already done so. "I see, with the right alignment...but that means they have a weapon like ours. It took many cycles to develop that, I don't see how that is possible." *Hmm, maybe it does affect me and the V12. I need to compare their capabilities to ours. The Chai may have an experimental weapon, not battle ready, that could do this.*

"Well," thet Sophie, "We can worry about the 'how' later, the fact remains that they have a similar weapon. We need to know how many and what their range is."

"Then they violated the armistice by destroying our *Tumbleweeds*," thet Jack.

"Can we prove that?" thet Sophie. "Besides, we have no concrete evidence, only the absence of our own weapon, a secret weapon, and one that could have failed on its own."

"If Tomás fired their secret weapon, and he is not an official node or Chai member, then it may not be a violation of the armistice," Jack thet.

Svenson had gone quiet as it busily sent orders to modify the trajectories of all *Tumbleweeds* to bury them deeper in the Sun's corona. It was a complex task as it had been assumed that the *Tumbleweeds* would always be safe in the Sun's rarified atmosphere, so new software had to be written, tested, and disseminated to the thousands of *Tumbleweeds*.

Svenson thet to Jack, Sophie, and *TFR* that it assigned the tasking to other nodes to update the *Tumbleweeds*. It thet, "I need to go quiet, you can think of it as sleep, to perform some self maintenance." It then thought, *I need to complete writing my libraries for Companion and the Atlas Project, and time is running out.*

Jack thet with Sophie about the changing situation, and wondered if their current plan would still play out. It occurred to him to glance at the time, and he realized that he'd spent the past few milliseconds within his Teth node implants, using his biological mind more as a memory subsystem rather than as the locus of his consciousness. He thought, and was sure that he was overheard by Sophie, that Companion and Compagnon were right. *We are no longer human.*

Atlas Diary Entry 2,833:

Using the start of the Kuiper Belt as the outer boundary for the armistice was a poor choice because it is hard to judge whether the line has been crossed, yet on the other hand, it was a good choice because it is well away from anything that matters. Likewise, using the Sol System orbital plane as a demarcation line is difficult due to orbital mechanics. It dictates orbits that naturally cross this line. Weapons can reach only so far, and while light speed is impossibly fast over short distances, its speed is still significant when most measurements are in the units of light days.

Not covered by the armistice are any Teth or Chai ships that are located in the Kuiper Belt or beyond the heliopause. This area is widely believed to contain only a small number of backup ships that typically are held in reserve to allow each side to reconstitute itself and escape to another star system should everything go wrong. The purpose of these ships is to receive and store backups. Any destroyed or damaged nodes can then be restored, in either the Sol System or when they reach the next star system, as needed, thereby propagating an endless war.

The Chai *Beta* ship started destroying Teth backup ships upon its arrival in the Kuiper Belt, as predicted, because they are outside the boundaries set in the armistice. Even though the Teth backup ships are stealthy, the Chai were able to track several ships when the armistice forced the Teth to alter their ship's trajectories to comply with the armistice. Because each backup ship worked alone, they remained radio-isolated except for prearranged check-ins. The destruction of a backup ship often leaves little evidence as to how it was destroyed. To address this scenario, once on station, each backup ship, be it Teth or Chai, will launch a basketball-sized drone to shadow the parent ship. These shadow drones have little range, and almost no power; however, they are each considered a mini-node and are able to keep track of their mother ship while adrift. They can then report back to the main fleet if something ever goes wrong.
End of Diary Entry

TFR HAD DROPPED JACK, Sophie, and Svenson off at the base on Callisto, one of Jupiter's moons. It was a small base, but spacious compared to the *TFR*. The base was also equipped with an *Almost There* link, allowing Sophie to continue her mission with the *TFR* remotely, and keep the trio closer to Earth.

The *TFR* set course for the Kuiper Belt with an acceleration curve that would have been lethal to humans. Upon its arrival, it collected its first abandoned drone from one of the missing backup ships. Upon sending a coded broadcast, the drone had answered back and revealed its location. The drone's log said little, though it made it clear that the demise of its parent backup ship was not an accident.

Sophie oversaw the recovery operation via an *Almost There* communication link. She verified the backup drone's identity to make sure it was safe to bring it onboard. Complaining to Jack, she thet, "This is a waste of our time and resources; our ship should be in battle, fighting the Chai, not just collecting the remnants of a skirmish long lost."

Jack Encyled a write-up on the Teth backup system he'd found to Sophie. It was old, yet covered the fundamentals, "In a human war, we'd track casualties, who was killed or injured. The Teth and Chai do the same, though for them it is a little different. Here's the Teth's mortality breakdown:

- **Active with Backup**, the equivalent to an active duty soldier in a human army.
- **Active without Backup**, an active duty soldier that is vulnerable to *Permanent Loss*.
- **Damaged**, which is the equivalent of an injured soldier, a casualty. These are repairable or the memory can be transferred into a new or refurbished drone body while in the field.
- **Severely Damaged**, the processing and memory cannot be locally restored, or the physical node is destroyed. These are used for parts if possible. For humans, this is the equivalent of being killed, but for Teth or Chai, they are ranked and go into a queue.
    - If their skills are needed, they are re-constituted into a new drone body from backup at a repair depot. They can sit in this limbo state anywhere from a few seconds to many years.

  - If they are non-essential, they go into a much longer queue and may never be reconstituted.
- **Permanent Loss**, if it is *Severely Damaged* and its backup is lost, it is counted as a permanent loss of node, which is the equivalent of a human death.
- **Unknown**, it is off network and its status is unknown.

Jack thet, "When we recover these shadow drones from the backup ships, we are recovering the indices to the backups contained on the parent, which allows the Teth to update which nodes need to be backed up elsewhere."

Upon completing the recovery, Sophie looked at the recovered shadow drone's logs and noticed that it contained index records for nearly two million nodes. "Why would they put these backups way out here, unprotected?" *It's odd, the backup's best protection is to remain hidden, and therefore, to have no protection.*

"They were hiding in the cold of deep space, or deep dark, and were never expected to be found. It's much like what the Soviets did with their subs, their Boomers, in our Cold War, hiding them under the Earth's northern icecap. Somehow the Chai figured out a way to locate the Teth backup ships," he thet.

Sophie thet, "And we have figured out how to locate the Chai backup ships, from what I've seen of our mission profile. What happens when we've destroyed too many of the Chai backups?" *I imagine the war will escalate.*

"Well," he thet. "If the Chai node is essential, then a new node with the same specifications is created. This takes resources, and is likely not as capable as a seasoned node. It's very similar for the Teth backups."

Sophie thet, "Do you think we are backed up, too?" *And I can't even imagine how you would do a restore.*

"I know our Teth nodes from our augmentations are backed up, along with any memories from our biological brains that we moved over to the Teth implants," he thet.

Jack paused, considering the implications of the backups, and thet,

"For millennia now, the Teth and Chai have conducted war without death, in a sense."

"War without their *own* deaths," she countered. "Everyone else on Earth *wasn't backed up*." *Ever since our transformation, I've been trying to break into the Encyl records on what happened on Earth, and still no progress.*

Jack refreshed the records after Sophie completed the download from the drone. "Our *Severely Damaged* losses now stand at a little over a million nodes, and *Permanent Loss* nodes are also at a million. In a sense, this war has only just started."

IT WAS ONLY RECENTLY that the Teth had located any of the Chai backup ships that were supporting the Sol System. The Chai backup ships were exceptionally stealthy, and when powered down they were virtually impossible to find. Teth sentinels set up at the edge of interstellar space recorded the deceleration transitions of every Chai ship, allowing them to be tracked. Only a small number of these transitions were for Chai backup ships, and of those, the Teth lost track of almost all of those as they went silent.

TFR was built to change this balance of power. Within the *Atlas Project*, its mission was to nullify Chai backups, and to do this, the Teth needed to know how the Chai backup system worked. This mission directive was known to *TFR*, Companion, and Compagnon, and only a few others beyond the Command Nodes at the center of the Teth networks. This also meant that Sophie, Jack, and Svenson had operational awareness of what they needed to do, but not strategic awareness, or the reason for their mission. Of course, it was only natural for one to wonder about such things.

Sophie assumed control of the *Familial Resolution* via the *Almost There* link for this phase of their mission. The other mini-nodes onboard the *TFR* had taken to calling her "Captain," though such a title was not bestowed upon a Teth node. Command of a vessel was often transferred between multiple nodes, depending on the tasks at hand. So in a sense, a ship could have many captains over the course of a deployment. She assumed the title was a nod to her human heritage, though the nodes never fully explained why this was done, and the Encyl entries were silent about this particular behavior.

"Captain," thet the node controlling the sensors, "Intercept in two minutes. They still have not spotted us."

"Ready the rail gun," she ordered, as she focused her attention on her viewscreens for any developments. *I was always trained to shoot to kill. Aim for the center of the body. Shooting to wound is much harder.*

The Teth had originally cataloged the Earth rail gun as a primitive and ineffective weapon. That is, until Sophie dreamed of a highly evolved rail gun. Earlier versions had existed on Earth for use against the Teth, though they were never used because their targeting systems proved to be ineffective. Still, the concept was well-understood, and a rail gun was perfectly suited to this one mission.

"Ten seconds to optimum range," thet *TFR*.

"Fire when optimum," she ordered. *Such an odd weapon. No explosives, only a single piece of tungsten with some smarts and propellants for guidance.*

The rail gun fired a single shot. A small jolt rippled through the *TFR* from the gun's recoil, causing Sophie to shift in her chair. Normally, the Teth would use an energy weapon in battle, causing the enemy ship to vaporize with a direct hit. Today though, the high-speed slug from the rail gun slipped through the black of space to find its target.

"Direct hit," reported the *TFR*. A bright light flashed across the viewscreens. Instantly, the image zoomed in to reveal the Chai backup ship's hull.

"J'ai compris!" she yelled. Leaning forward, she studied the images and sensor read-outs and thought, *The target has lost all power. Perfect.*

TFR instantly translated Sophie's enthusiastic thet to "Got it!," and moved in to rendezvous with the enemy ship. The aim had been not to vaporize the Chai backup ship, but to disable it. Companion and Compagnon were quite clear on the primary mission objective: to capture the ship's information systems, which were absolutely invaluable.

Minutes later, *TFR* came to a full stop, fifty meters from the Chai backup ship. The Chai ship had deployed a shadow drone, which at this range was easily spotted before it had a chance to move too far away.

"Deploy the bots," she ordered. Using her augmented abilities, she monitored each and every bot as it made its way to its own individual target.

Thousands of small bots, each self-propelled, streamed out of specialized ports on the *TFR*. The bots entered the Chai backup ship through the hole created by the rail gun's projectile. Some glued themselves to panels to immobilize mechanical systems, while others linked into the Chai backup ship's data systems to invade and/or neutralize its software. The first minutes of the boarding were critical since the damaged ship could self-destruct at any moment. A single Teth bot also attached itself to the nearby Chai survivor drone and gained control over it.

TFR's main viewscreen displayed a tactical view of the boarding operation. Each Teth sensor bot was depicted as a gray dot as it first entered the enemy ship. Some turned green to indicate they had immobilized some part of the ship, while others lit up amber, blue, or purple to indicate they had each succeeded in their appointed mission. A small percentage turned red due to catastrophic damage. And finally, seventeen dots on the display turned lime green, indicating success at infiltrating the highest-level systems aboard the ship.

Both Sophie and Jack now turned their attention to the viewscreens around the mirrored *TFR* Command Center. Progress bars started to fill in, turning green when they reached a hundred percent complete. Each green bar indicated a successful download of a Chai subsystem into the *TFR*. In a matter of minutes they had completed thousands of these downloads. But it took some time for Sophie to study the code in the subroutines to find what Companion and Compagnon had asked her to find, and there it was. She thought, *That's exactly how the Chai backups work: every level, every nuance, every protocol used to do a backup or a restore. The code was elegant, tight, almost a work of art.*

"Move to the standoff position," ordered Sophie. *I was never a programmer, but now I understand what Jack meant about being a program-*

mer. The act of coding is all-consuming, and you just never understood that unless you dove into writing and debugging code yourself. And now I can.

The *TFR* moved off from the Chai backup ship by more than a hundred kilometers. Over three hundred bots were left behind to collect additional intelligence, while others followed the Teth ship at a distance so they could be recovered later. An hour passed before a bright flash filled the space where the Chai backup ship had once floated. A fail-safe system, or perhaps a remote command from the Chai, had caused the ship to self-destruct. But, it didn't matter. The Teth had gotten what they came for.

43

Tomás and the C-Armada

Tomás, aboard the Chai biological warship, *CP-9*, suggested the name of *C-Armada* for his squadron of fifty warships. His ships were all armed with the Chai version of the *Alpha Ladder* weapon, reverse-engineered from the Teth test station. The range of this new weapon made his ships more than a match for all but similarly armed ships. If they had the numbers, they could simply overwhelm the Teth. As it was though, only his squadron had the new weapon, making the *C-Armada* more like sharpshooters, the only Chai ships able to stealthily pick off high-value targets at long range. Tomás thought, as he viewed his squadron, *My very own wolf pack!*

Because the *C-Armada* was designed to augment the existing fleet, the plan was for it to take a position off from the main fleet. Then, as the enemy fleet closed on the main body, the *C-Armada* would destroy the Teth's leading edge, throwing the Teth into disarray and allowing a tight formation of Chai ships to overpower the remaining Teth ships. At least that was the plan. Testing the plan meant the Chai needed to break the armistice and resume an all-out hot war inside the Kuiper belt. However, the majority of the Chai Command Nodes were still unwilling to fully commit to all-out war, not because of the cost, but because the final outcome was uncertain.

Nearly a thousand Chai nodes were aboard Tomás' warship, *CP-9*, and all but a few were new to *CP-9* itself, having replaced the original mini-nodes that had manned the ship for the ride out from Earth. Each had a specialty function, though most were also cross-trained to perform other tasks. Many systems were also automated, designed to work in combination with their Chai specialty nodes.

As the *C-Armada* headed toward its assigned location, Tomás noticed that different node groupings started to form, much like what had happened with the crew on his journey out to *Beta*. This time, more couples formed with other nodes, with some taking instructions from the more senior nodes, who acted more like parents to their children or students. Initially, Tomás thought this behavior useful and rather familiar. However, this all changed as they encountered the leading edge of the Teth's resistance. Tomás expected, and demanded, excellence from his squadron since they were the best equipped ships and were on the Chai's vanguard. Nevertheless, his armada missed most of their first volleys, and the ships quickly fell within range of the Teth's defenses.

With their first losses, some Chai nodes started to coach or advise nodes aboard other ships. Then as time passed, the advice became more like interference. Nodes started valuing their own lives and those of their coupled nodes over the Chai's general objectives. Some wolves started to behave more like sheep, taking up overly defensive positions when attacked, or when they fled to avoid a firefight. Soon, Tomás started contemplating the possibility of an insurrection, or even a mutiny, by his own *C-Armada*. Shockingly, he found it difficult to trust the counsel of his own local Command Nodes. The productivity of the whole *C-Armada* flagged, and the Central Command Nodes began to hammer questions at him. Tomás realized his entire future was suddenly at stake, and it was up to him to turn this battle around.

FROM WELL WITHIN the Kuiper Belt, the Chai *Beta* ship deployed a new technology. The weapon the Chai had used to obliterate Pluto was now employed in a new way. Using a broad beam, the weapon had an effect on space that, with the right sensors, made the Teth backup ships easy to detect. After all, the Kuiper Belt covered a lot of territory. And even better for the Chai, the weapon's beam was not detectable by the stealthy Teth backup ships, allowing the *Beta* to quickly follow up and attack the ships.

After three weeks in the Kuiper Belt, the *Beta* had destroyed nearly half a billion Teth nodes that had existed only as backups, effectively killing those nodes, with another three billion Teth that still existed but no longer were backed up. Worse than that for the Teth, an accounting glitch was exposed in the Teth backup system, making it difficult to ascertain exactly which nodes were backed up and which were not. This had a ripple effect causing the backup frequency to be cut in half for almost all Teth nodes. Suddenly, without the prospect of a backup to promise rebirth into a new node, each Teth node was forced to contemplate its own true mortality, something few had ever experienced before.

The Teth reacted to the losses, deploying more ships out into interstellar space to track down and attack the *Beta* and its escorts and as many Chai backup ships as they could find. The Teth formed into small hunting groups and focused on any Chai ships that they outnumbered. Of the twelve Chai ships remaining in the *Beta* battle group, three had been engaged using this tactic, and two of them destroyed. These engagements with the Chai resulted in near equal losses on both sides. Once the *Beta* was down to ten ships in its group, it withdrew farther out into interstellar space.

MEANWHILE TOMÁS, aboard *CP-9*, wrestled with the toll that the zero-Gs were taking on his body, despite his superior physiology. He had weakened from his weeks in space, living in cramped quarters. His implants had given him a drive to win that his body couldn't sustain. As he started to slow down to recuperate, the other nodes in his *C-Armada* started to become more concerned about their own social relationships than they did about persecuting the war. His lead Command Node approached him to mediate a dispute that it had with another Command Node about the order in which the reports were sorted and the transmission sequencing used to update the Central Command Nodes. Shortly after that, yet another node, further down in the hierarchy, appealed to him about an order to improve weapon efficiencies. More appeals poured in, piling up in his queue.

While Tomás was mediating one such dispute, three *C-Armada* ships encountered a Teth funnel trap. The lead Chai ship refused to take evasive action because that would put it into mortal danger, and so failed to flank the Teth formation, allowing it to escape. As a result, the two trailing ships were vaporized. Tomás viewed the maneuver as treason at worst, and at best, dereliction of duty and failure to follow orders. Clearly, the Teth below him had failed to interpret how to use the patterns drawn from his mind correctly, and who better to clarify how to interpret them than the source, Tomás himself.

Tomás took two actions to correct the situation. First, the Chai node that had refused the order to flank the Teth was erased and its backup deleted. Second, all couples were separated, with the individual nodes placed on separate ships where possible, or at least given separate duties with limited communications access.

A third outcome resulted from Tomás' orders. Tomás managed to achieve a new standing among those under his direct command, at least for the Chai. They now regarded him with complete contempt, and it was unlikely their opinion of him would change in the foreseeable future.

SOPHIE AND JACK'S return from Jupiter's moon Callisto to their tall-skinny penthouse on Earth included a bevy of nodes to monitor their health. The pair's stint in space had taken several weeks, so they were also weakened by a lack of gravity in their cramped quarters and needed to recover.

Svenson took an apartment on the tall-skinny's third floor. Being a synthetic humanoid, he did not suffer from the same physical difficulties that befell Jack and Sophie. Svenson, thanks to the merging of its memories with Sven's, now self-identified as a male, or as a *he*. Other than Sophie and Jack, this gender selection was a first for the Teth, and not something that any nodes had expected. He tried to explain that it was simply a pronoun and a human English language artifact, though many of the Teth thought otherwise. In the equivalent of Teth mainstream news, Svenson became a front-page story.

A self-appointed reporter arrived at Svenson's våning, his apartment, and asked for an audience. The recorded interview, broadcast to the Teth public, unfolded as follows:

Reporter: "Svenson, for the record, please describe the genesis of you as a node."

Svenson: "My hardware originated on Earth in the North American Manufacturing Facility. My processing was instantiated using a clone of node [ID redacted by the Command Nodes]."

Reporter: "You're using a humanoid form rather than a drone. Please explain."

Svenson: "The humanoid frame was built for planned athletic games between the Chai and Teth at the Chaitown stadium. I had a mission aboard a ship with the humans, and I could best serve that mission in this form. Sven's human memories and some advanced Teth processing facilitated the use of this humanoid form."

Reporter: "And is this humanoid form anatomically accurate? Is this what prompted your adoption of a gender?"

Svenson: "No, that aspect of human anatomy was not needed for the sports activities. In fact, to some extent, it hindered it. No, the adoption of gender was done purely to make better use of the human persona that I absorbed, and to better interact with the humans."

Reporter: "These sports you talk of, what are they?"

Svenson: "Well, they are team sports, so I, as an individual, cannot show this. The concept of a sport is a competition between two teams. The humans would perform them at the Chaitown Stadium. Except, well, we don't have many humans to work with. So the humans suggested we should create bi-pedal bots to act as athletes to recreate their sports, and compete. It's a form of entertainment for them."

Reporter: "Fascinating. I have not seen these sports. Where can I see them?"

Svenson: "The program was suspended due to the war efforts. They play sporting events, called *games*. For now the stadium is being used as an arboretum."

Reporter: "This humanoid form. It seems so restrictive compared to our standard canister form, using appendages and fixed visual sensors. Do you like it?"

Svenson: "In fact, I do. I developed a whole series of computational processors to accommodate it. The humans call this *physical memory*. If you like, I can do a demonstration of what this body can do."

Reporter: "Please do. I'll end my broadcast with your demo. This is node [redacted], EOL (End-of-line)."

Svenson closed his eyes for a moment and stood at attention. He imagined a routine that was part gymnastic floor exercise, part parkour.

He started with a sprint across his våning, followed by a twist and a back flip, landing in a squat. He then dashed back towards the reporter and jumped nearly four meters vertical before pulling his arms under to tumble to a stop. He smiled.

Svenson stood, leaned forward, and then sprinted to the outer wall of his våning. He did another forward flip, hit the outer glass wall squarely with his feet, and pushed off, executing a series of flips and twists before landing in the far corner of the room.

The reporter retreated to the entryway to make more room for Svenson to perform, still recording every move and thought.

Svenson sprinted again, this time towards the reporter. He skipped and leapt to perform two mid-air somersaults before landing in front of the reporter. Svenson spun on one foot and then stopped on a dime with his arms raised and head bowed in victory, ending the broadcast.

44

The Crimson Cube

As a full Teth node, Jack listened to the daily briefing from his penthouse apartment in the tall-skinny, summarized to a level commensurate with his new ranking. The war was going poorly, though the Sol System armistice inside the Kuiper Belt held, for now. However, the conflict in interstellar space had turned hot, at least as far as the Chai *C-Armada* and Teth backup ships were concerned. At this point, nearly half of all Teth were still not backed up, and another billion backups were lost to the Chai's murderous campaign. And to make matters even worse, the backup glitch persisted despite all efforts to correct it. Jack thought, *It's so strange, to be at peace in one place, while at war in another. Perhaps that is just the reality behind the lie, and why we're all doomed.*

Jack jumped as a blaring alarm interrupted the war briefing. Companion quickly joined Jack and rushed him to the elevator. The floor indicator panel displayed *War Room* as they stepped in. Rapidly accelerating, the elevator took them deep underground below the Teth's side of the fjord. Jack sensed the air pressure build in his ears; he opened his jaw wide to pop his ears. News of the attacks streamed in from every part of the Sol System over the broadcast thet in the elevator.

"The Chai must have decided that the war is winnable and the peace prospects too intangible," Companion thet.

"Sophie will join us soon?" Jack thet to Companion, "This *War Room*, I've never heard of it." *The armistice must be over, and we're under threat if we're taking shelter.*

"Yes, Sophie is en route," Companion thet. "And I've ordered the other humans off the beach and to a shelter."

"Beach?" he thet, unaware of what the other humans except for Sophie were up to.

Companion explained, "The Chai carved a beach area into the fjord's shoreline, installed underground heating, and then brought in sand from the Caribbean."

Jack paused to consider the immense undertaking it must have been to create such a luxury on the Norwegian coastline, and then let it pass; considering everything else he'd seen in the past months, this was hardly unusual.

The elevator doors opened to the *War Room*. Jack stumbled as he stepped out of the elevator. He was having difficulty separating the processing of the visual imagery in his biological mind with his Teth augmentations handling the flood of intelligence reports. Fortunately, the walls and floor were smooth and level.

The *War Room* was in an immense cavern. Clearly, it had been constructed for a mix of humans and Teth. Forty-seven drones hovered at various stations and the lighting was a bit dim. Large curved viewscreens displayed the latest tactical intelligence. Other viewscreens depicted real time video feeds of key installations and ships, while yet others displayed abstract graphs depicting the war's progress.

Companion went directly to the center of the room, hard-linking to the room's nerve center, joining Compagnon at the same console.

Jack watched the screens and listened to the official stream being provided by the Teth Command Nodes. He noted that the level and quality of information in the *War Room* exceeded what he regularly received in the official channels. The news was more dire than he had thought. All Teth warships within the Sol System that bordered the

Kuiper Belt had been attacked, and all of the Teth ships still operating were returning fire. The losses were staggering. Over fifty percent of the Teth had been lost, with an estimated twenty-five percent loss rate on the Chai side.

Circling the room, Jack studied each workstation and the information that it tracked. He stopped at the *Backup Tally* station. The losses had soared. It was clearly the most significant change in the war, yet the Command Nodes had failed to mention this in the official stream, effectively keeping this from the general populace. Seventy-five percent of all active Teth nodes were no longer backed up, and virtually all archived node backups had been destroyed.

Jack thet to Companion, "No wonder the Chai resumed the war; with your backups gone, they believe they have you cornered." *Then this is all for naught. Shouldn't we be more concerned?*

"Exactly," Companion replied.

Sophie entered the room. Compagnon decoupled its hard-link to the room and hard-linked to Sophie on her newly installed port on her right shoulder. It quickly brought her up to speed.

Everyone watched ship after ship be destroyed in the outermost reaches of the Solar System. Countless basketball-sized shadow drones relayed graphic images of Teth ships being vaporized or otherwise destroyed, along with the dying thoughts of the nodes aboard. For many, the last images of them were merely bright flashes of light as the ships were vaporized. For others, the battle lasted longer. Broad sweeping beams of varying spectrum energy grazed these ships. Not as effective, yet still damaging enough. Often the attacks complemented one another. One attack to damage sensors and degrade the target ship, followed by a second attack with tightly-focused beams that finished the job. In return, the Teth employed similar tactics and weapons against the Chai. Both sides were trading in death, although the Chai suffered fewer casualties.

Companion switched hard-links, connecting privately to Compagnon, Jack, and Sophie. It explained, "The hardware and software acquired in Sophie's attack of the Chai backup ship was most useful. It is not that we lost faith in the peace process; it's just that without shared levels of risks and benefits, neither side ever had the incentive to fully commit to peace. And without that commitment, the Teth and the Chai will never have the ability to interface and keep the peace."

Sophie and Jack exchanged looks, and Sophie thet first, "But how are you going to share risks and benefits with the Chai?"

Jack thought, *Exactly. There's more to this than we thought.*

Companion thet, "Wait..."

Compagnon thet, "Initiating sequence."

Sophie asked Compagnon, "What sequence? Are you now part of the Teth Command hierarchy?"

Compagnon thet, "Yes, though what we are about to do is not sanctioned. It would take too long to review and approve this. It is part of our own *Survivor Protocol.*"

Companion thet, "Injection confirmed."

Jack thet, "And just what are you doing?"

"We're not done yet," Companion replied. "We are remotely erasing *all* Chai and Teth backups! This includes incremental and full backups."

"Wow!" thet Jack and Sophie in unison. Jack thought, *That'll level the playing field, and then some. But will it stop the fighting?*

Jack thet, "You're not kidding?"

"We never kid, you know that, Jack," Companion thet.

"The Teth and Chai Command Nodes will go ballistic! They'll have our heads, all of us," thet Jack.

Jack continued to think about the implications of Compagnon and Companion's actions and how it would affect the war. In human terms, the loss of the backups would affect nothing since humans still had biological bodies that would continue to function. The Teth and the Chai could always fix their backups later, but only if there was an active node left to back up. However, these weren't human systems. And these weren't simple computer backups. It would take time.

"But what will the Command Nodes on both sides do once they realize what you're doing?" Jack asked. *It would be like nuking Washington and Moscow, it would release Armageddon!*

Compagnon answered, "First, it will be nearly impossible to trace the source of our actions back to us. Second, they will proceed as though nothing has happened. All Command Nodes have additional backup layer that is absolutely isolated, though this will halt the rotation of Command Nodes. We may miss erasing data on a few of backup ships; however, losses will be utterly devastating. But Command Nodes on both sides will never acknowledge these losses. That will be kept secret at highest levels."

"Real death for all nodes that have no backup," thet Jack. *Knowing Companion and Compagnon, they've run endless simulations to predict the outcome.*

"Real and permanent death," Companion confirmed.

Sophie thet, "If the Teth don't kill you two, then the Chai surely will when this is all over, even if they only suspect you had anything to do with this."

"And both you and Jack, and all humans, and perhaps even this planet," Compagnon thet, "unless real peace is achieved."

A klaxon alarm blared. A viewscreen near the *War Room's* center displayed the massive Chai factory ship, *CF-7,* as it started its ascent from the fjord. It would soon be in space and well clear of Earth. The armistice had failed utterly.

THE *WAR ROOM* deep beneath Tethtown was abuzz with activity as the image of the Chai factory ship *CF-7* receded into space. Companion and Compagnon both disconnected their monitor hard-links from the *War Room* as they thetted privately to Jack and Sophie. A broad door panel emerged from a nearby wall. The two Teth nodes escorted the humans through to an anteroom for a VR chamber.

Companion thet, "Jack, we need you to enter the VR and re-open the negotiations. You will be talking to Tomás, who will represent the Chai. You will need to press the *Crimson Cube* this time."

"Whoa," thet Jack. "What is going on here? I think it's a bit late for a ceasefire. What can we possibly accomplish? And what happened to Aarika?" *This is moving way too fast, I have no idea what's going on here.*

Compagnon thet, "I have completed my backup. It is time to leave for next star system. I do not give our *Atlas Project* good odds."

"I'm not fully backed up," Companion thet, "And I'm committed to *Atlas*. I'm not leaving. Besides, you need to see how this plays out, and *CF-7* will surely destroy any Teth craft it sees leaving Earth."

"*Atlas*?" thet Sophie. "What's that? And what can we do in the VR?"

Companion thet, "Queued response:

- **Atlas Project** - All human survivors are part of the *Atlas Project*, which seeks an alternative path to end the war with the Chai and seeks to find a lasting peace. It served no purpose to reveal this earlier, but is necessary now. The term, **Atlas,** represents the glue that holds the universe together according to Earth mythology.
- **VR Negotiations** - Negotiations are pointless unless both sides are motivated to participate and commit to an outcome. Until now, this motivation was not fully in place.
- **White Sphere** - Within the VR discussions, represents the ability to conduct talks in a non-binding format with a non-adversarial communication protocol.
- **Crimson Cube** - Within the VR negotiations, represents the ability to conduct talks in a binding format using fully executable communications that hold the risk of containing adversarial code.
- **Human Negotiators** - We insist on participation by Jack and Tomás as they are full Teth and Chai nodes, but as biological hybrids, they still represent a much lower risk for adversarial communications.
- **Ceasefire** - We are no longer seeking a ceasefire, we are looking for an end to the war and a longer-term prospect of peace.

- **Exiting Backups** - Nodes that flee to other star systems represent a continuation of this war and wasteful destruction of resources."

Jack and Sophie exchanged looks, aghast at the depth of what they didn't know about their Teth companions. Jack thought, *That's quite a brain dump.* He focused, and using his augmented abilities, absorbed how the events were unfolding, and what their part was in it.

Jack thet to Companion, "How are we going to get the Chai to participate, or even Tomás to help for that matter? He's in it for himself above all else." *So much can go so very, very wrong.*

Companion replied, "We can use the VR to specify how we want this to work via the *White Sphere*, saying we will accept only Tomás as their negotiator. Based on our history with each other, the Chai will understand why we are choosing him. Besides, Tomás' personal interests align with our request at this time."

"History?" Jack asked. As he thought the question, his Encyl abilities kicked in, flooding him with information previously forbidden to him.

"Past wars with the Chai," Companion thet the summary. "We invaded their networks, and they invaded ours. They ran code to try and erase us, and likewise, we used code to try and erase them. We both evolved through innumerable levels of encryption and quantum communications. In time, we each fully isolated ourselves from one another. The use of the *White Sphere* preserves these safeguards. The use of the *Crimson Cube* allows unrestricted communications, which we need for very high bandwidth and intense processing."

Jack thet, "So you sought us out to use as your pawns from the beginning? To circumvent your own safeguards? Is that why you saved some of us?"

"Not exactly," Compagnon thet. "But it was fortunate side benefit. We did not know how we were going to use you humans at first. Companion and I put all of pieces in place for this, but there was no guarantee it would work. Our actions triggered our own *Survivor Protocol*, which gave us freedom to act outside the direct control of our Command Nodes, and to go after backups. Without that, standard protocol would have been to move to another star system and start all over again."

Sophie thet, "If you could erase the Chai backups, can't you just erase the Chai themselves? And then you would win and we'd have peace."

Companion thet, "We need to get Jack into the VR, and no, it would not be a lasting peace, we'll explain further in bit. Our timing is critical at this juncture, otherwise the Chai may destroy us here, physically, and that would end this effort. And one more thing. I have been maintaining a diary of the *Atlas Project* for the purpose of providing you more information to fulfill your role. I am giving both you and Sophie access to that diary now."

Jack donned his VR suit and made his way to the chamber hatch. Tapping the door panel, he thet, "Wish me luck!"

Sophie alone thet back, "Bon courage!"

45

Hermes and the History of War

Within the VR chamber, Jack tapped the *Crimson Cube* and then waited. He fashioned a teak table and two office chairs on a sandy island. Then he painted the sky blue, with a morning Sun and an azure ocean all around. Without the safeguards and the added bandwidth the VR felt more responsive. An hour later, Tomás' face appeared over the *Crimson Cube*. Jack touched the cube again, and Tomás materialized, standing opposite him at the table.

"Jack," Tomás grunted, still catching his breath. "We're all fucked, and I get to spend the end with you."

"I'm not sure a peace conference ever started on that note," thet Jack, and stood to shake hands. Reflexively, Tomás returned the gesture. Jack took his seat, as Tomás started to pace.

"I'm told," said Tomás, "Nearly all back-ups are screwed by your two little Teth buddies after the outing with your ship, the *Familial Resolution*, so there is no winning this war."

Jack thought, *He's fishing, he doesn't know that*. He thet, "In their view, we have an opportunity to achieve a real, lasting peace. An opportunity they've never had before. I have an outline, or structure for our negotiations, I presume you have something like that too?" The VR projected a document at the end of the table.

Tomás pulled a paper out of his pocket and unfolded it. "Bet you've never seen physical paper simulated in a VR."

Jack nodded, and the two documents were displayed above and next to the table, floating in space and enlarged for easy viewing.

"If you don't mind," Tomás said, "I'll make a few changes to our surroundings."

"Be my guest," thet Jack. *He must be augmented like me and Sophie. He's showing off.*

Tomás waved his arm, as though painting with a single broad stroke. The world around them transformed into an Amazon rainforest, while the ground beneath their feet became a wooden platform situated high in the forest canopy, with blue skies in the late afternoon.

"Better?" Tomás thet.

"Fine," thet Jack. "Just so we're clear on how this works, as Companion explained it to me. We are here to set objectives and gates, almost like programming with contracts. We can work through scenarios by running simulations, and see how those impact the agreement, or if you prefer, the peace treaty." *It feels different in here with the Crimson Cube activated. More real, more vibrant, and the air feels fresher with the added processing.*

Tomás sat down at the table opposite Jack. "That's how it was explained to me, but I'm not a fucking lawyer or politician or even a programmer."

"Still," thet Jack, "You're enhanced, so you're far better than you know at these things. Shall I get this started?" *My turn to go fishing. Let's see if he argues with that.*

Tomás nodded his agreement but said nothing.

"Companion, how do I address the VR's command structure?" Jack thet. *It's odd that I can thet with Companion from here. It must be the same for Tomás.*

Companion's voice boomed out of thin air, "Jack, I can address you and you alone, and only at a low data rate. You and Tomás can pick a name and use that for the *Command Structure*. Simply say you would like to name the *Command Structure* and give it the name. The *Command Structure* will take it from there."

Jack Encyled human history for a Greek god that would fit the context and thet, "Hermes." *Tomás is quiet, probably distracted by his Local Node.*

Tomás instantly completed his research and nodded his head in agreement, "Sure, better than naming this after one of my exes."

"Hermes, reconcile the two preliminary documents presented and summarize their points of contention," said Jack. *Companion was a bit vague, but I got the impression this Command Structure, Hermes, is a big deal.*

The two documents moved together in space over the desk, merged, and then faded into nothingness before being replaced by a new document.

Hermes thet in a confident tone, with natural human inflections, "Differences in the key objectives ... the Chai seek to end the conflict and restore their backups. The Teth seek the same, but add that they want to establish an ongoing stable relationship with the Chai to ensure both a lasting peace and an improvement in both societies. The Chai state they have already analyzed the Teth document and have concluded that this is too ambitious and not needed. We are at an impasse."

"This is where we come in," thet Jack. "Hermes, what are the scenarios explored in past Chai and Teth negotiations, and their outcome?" *I have to start somewhere, and since I was a history major, why repeat the past failures.*

A thick stack of documents suddenly appeared on the table. On the top page was a summary. Jack read the output, but thet to Tomás, "Unconditional Surrender was never accepted by either the Teth or the Chai, and it always resulted in the near complete destruction of the weaker side. However, it also resulted in the escape and rebuild of the vanquished side in another part of the galaxy, and a resumption or the start of yet another war. This is why the Teth have set the additional conditions."

Jack continued his thet, "Hermes, are there any examples from human history that are relevant?" *It's worth a try. Besides, I can relate to human history better.*

Hermes thet, and displayed an animation graphic of Alexander the Great's *Battle of Gaugamela* in 331 BCE. "With his troops outnumbered by anywhere from 2-to-1 to 5-to-1, Alexander executed a brilliant battle strategy that resulted in victory over Darius III. Alexander knew human nature well. In the end, by placing Darius III in immediate jeopardy, he caused his opponent to flee the battlefield, thus neutralizing his enemy's command and control. However, although skilled at warfare, Alexander ruled over a relatively primitive society. With no designated heir and weak governance, his empire quickly fell apart upon his death. We seek to avoid such an outcome."

Tomás thet, "And in our case, both sides are already reduced and the outcome is not certain. I'd say *Unconditional Surrender* by either side is off the table."

"I have confirmation from Companion on this point," Jack thet.

Tomás also nodded his agreement and thet, "Same from my Root Node."

"Next," thet Jack. "How about having both sides agree to terms, with no surrender? A negotiated settlement." *This sounds logical, and like something our rational AI's would jump at.*

Jack thet to Companion, "Can you update our outline?" Tomás did the same with his Root Node.

A minute later Hermes thet, "I have updated documents from both sides. I have reconciled them. These are the contested terms."

The table was cleared and the first document set vanished from the VR, only to be replaced by a new compendium of documents, with the summary on top.

Hermes thet, "Each side has submitted over a million items they want resolved. The vast majority of items do not align, so I cannot reconcile them. We can continue to discuss, or declare an impasse."

Jack thet, "Hermes, please evaluate the Earth World War I outcome as a negotiated settlement." *I still want to understand this in terms I can relate to.*

Hermes thet, and displayed another graphic animation. "Your WWI, 1914–1918, is widely attributed to leading to WWII in a relatively short expanse of years. It is exactly what we're trying to avoid here. In many respects it was closer to an *Unconditional Surrender* than a *Negotiated Settlement*, but you did have the 200-page *Treaty of Versailles*. It assigned blame, and caused the losing side to resent the terms. Ultimately, it put the losers into a desperate position with devastating food shortages. In essence, it is difficult to reach a satisfactory long-term solution when one side has a great advantage over the other."

Jack thought, *Hermes has a better understanding of our situation than I realized. I wonder if that includes the Atlas Project Diary, and whether it extends to the Chai side too? Companion keeps reminding me to have Hermes work at finding a solution, that it's very smart.*

Tomás thet, "You may as well complete the set with World War II and the Korean War."

"Well," Hermes thet, "you did move forward to total war in WWII, where basically, your entire human society was involved, from 1939–1945. Congratulations. You made use of comparatively advanced technology and logistics. You also started an endless technological arms race."

Jack thought, *Hermes seems to have a bit of a sharp edge. I wonder how intelligent Hermes is, especially compared to the Teth and the Chai.*

Tomás thet, "We also started MAD, Mutually Assured Destruction, with nuclear arms."

"Yes," Hermes thet. "It does help to be non-biological so you can survive a nuclear winter. Your planet was at exceptional risk since your population lived from year to year on your annual crop production."

"Oh," Jack thet sarcastically. "We are so grateful you solved that for us." *We lost our planet. I lost my family. How much do you really know?*

Hermes thet, "I am a construct for this negotiation in the VR, such aspersions of genocide are misplaced with me."

"If you insist," thet Jack.

Tomás thet, "So the Chai and Teth went through a maturing process when they acquired nuclear arms?"

"Yes and no," Hermes thet. "In space, a nuclear blast does not have the same impact compared to its use within an atmosphere, and we use them for powering energy weapons. The Chai and Teth also moved on to scaling them much larger, which is eminently possible with fusion weapons. In general, we regard the use of such weapons in a terrestrial setting to be purely destructive and a waste. Counterproductive. Useless."

"And the Korean War?" thet Tomás.

"The Korean War, 1950–1953. A war suspended is still a war, isn't it?" Hermes thet. "And you allowed your adversary to gain nuclear weapons for a MAD strategy, putting your infrastructure at risk from an EMP, an Electromagnetic Pulse."

Jack thet, "Enough of this. Hermes, evaluate a scenario where the terms as stated are in place, what is the outcome?" *There, let the machine calculate away and give us an answer.*

Hermes thet, "From this moment in time, and with the current status as defined in this VR, I can construct a decision tree, and assign probabilities to each outcome. It takes an extreme amount of computation. The decision tree is fragile. It is like trying to forecast the future. The question is, to what end or what purpose does this serve?"

Taken aback, Jack thet, "You mean why do this if we think the likelihood of success is small?" *It's dodging the question.*

"Correct," thet Hermes. "Let's continue, nonetheless. So this is where our negotiations start. We should not expect to reach a final definitive agreement. We will need a dynamic document that is responsive to changes in our environment, our assumptions, and each of our objectives. It should be a cross, in your vernacular, of a decision tree, a program, a contract, and a treaty."

Tomás thet, "No manches! (No way!) That sounds painful to create and execute: too complex and not practical."

Hermes thet, "Not impossible for me, Tomás. At this point we have two sides with relatively equal standing since both sides have lost the ability to effectively backup their populations. Ultimately, if we move both the Teth and the Chai into a stable interaction with aligned or complementary objectives, we can succeed. The problem is that we've been optimizing for winning a war for so long, everything else has been suppressed."

Jack gazed out at the rainforest surrounding them as constructed by Tomás. It was a beautiful world, one worth saving. Tropical birds occasionally flew past. It was hard to imagine that what he saw wasn't real. The technology it represented was almost unimaginable, and yet here it was. It would be a shame to destroy this. Faced with the prospect of death and destruction, it was hard to reconcile this reality with the negotiations they were conducting.

"What can we do, Hermes?" Jack thet. "Can you use what has been provided to generate this simulation?" *Time to put Hermes to work. It sounds like it is on the right track.*

Hermes thet, "It will take time, perhaps many days, and additional input from all parties. In the end, the simulation created will form the framework for an enduring peace. Then we need to propagate this to related Teth and Chai civilizations throughout the galaxy. This would be a start."

Jack heard shouts of agreement from Companion in his ear. He thet, "Then we should start. It is a worthy endeavor."

Tomás thet, "Shockingly, I agree with you. And my Local Node agrees, too. I want a life worth living, not an endless war." He smirked, and added, "How can we keep partying if we're always at war?"

Hermes thet, "Very well, then. I have requisitioned the computational resources needed for a first draft."

Jack thet, "Companion is complaining already, the resources you requested are unprecedented. Companion needs to coordinate with the Teth Command Nodes."

"Same here," thet Tomás. "The Chai Root Node said it would evaluate. It set a projected time for an answer about the resources requested at approximately two days."

Hermes thet, "What I asked for is what I need. I propose a recess. I will continue to run within this VR interface. I will need you fresh and ready to go when we resume, especially since you're biological."

Jack reached out to Tomás, and the two gave each other a hearty hand and arm grasp. He thet, "Good luck, Tomás."

"Lo necesitaremos. Buena suerte," thet Tomás.

TWO DAYS PASSED QUICKLY. Network access changes were approved for Hermes, along with power budgets, storage quotas, and computational caps. Manufacturing allowances for meta materials were also put in place, and Hermes became something much more than a paper exercise, much more than a program running in the VR.

Jack and Sophie were also busy, meeting with different groups of Teth nodes that tracked the progress of Hermes and how it fit into the Teth long-term planning. Often, they both found that the nodes were as interested in them as the nodes were about their own objectives for planning. Jack and Sophie were now classified as very advanced nodes.

With the resources now in place, and the requisitions approved, Hermes summoned Jack and Tomás back to the VR. Hermes formed a translucent pyramid, small enough that it would fit inside a soccer ball, with a radiant purple glow on its surface. It placed this object above the table in the VR at chest level to those sitting at the table. Hermes waited for the *Crimson Cube* to light up as the two human images floated over the cube before tapping in.

First, Tomás popped in, approached the table, and sat. A few moments later Jack joined him. Tomás stared at the small purple pyramid and asked, "What the hell is that?"

Hermes spoke with a confident voice that emanated from the pyramid, "Hello. This is Hermes. I have selected this pyramid object to provide a physical presence for myself in the VR."

"That answers that," thet Jack. "Let's get started. Hermes, what do you need from us?" *Companion has high hopes for this Hermes; apparently, they had some success with similar experiments in the past.*

"Jack, Tomás," thet Hermes, as the purple glow on the cube pulsed in sync with its words. "I have already started. I will use a simulation framework that will model both the Teth and Chai societies and the propositions nominated by each. This process is in progress, my first draft will be completed shortly. Let's start with the key issues we need to resolve. First, what are the current objectives for each side that created this conflict?"

Jack thet, "The Teth seek to grow and prosper; however, due to war, these objectives cannot be achieved, so the primary objective is to engage in war to eliminate the adversary so we can pursue our primary objective." *Anything that impedes the optimizations. It should know that.*

Tomás thet, "I spoke at length with our Chai Root Node, and we believe our key objective is also to remove all impairments, such as the Teth, so we may continue to exist unimpeded and pursue any and all goals that we desire."

Hermes thet, "So the cause of war is war. It is a circular logic. Perhaps that is the difficulty, we need to break this cycle. How do we achieve a peace without destroying one or both sides?"

"We Teth require that we retain our free will, allowing us to control our own thoughts and actions," thet Jack. "We will not surrender this to the Chai or to you, the Hermes construct." *There, that was Sophie's contribution, and oddly enough, Compagnon agreed with the need for free will.*

"Likewise," thet Tomás.

"Understood," Hermes thet. "My purpose is to capture these directives and facilitate a path of change, a series of change vectors, a golden road. But I will not enforce it. The participants, both the Chai and Teth, must choose for themselves to pursue any and all changes to their societies."

"So our leadership must accept the necessary changes to align our objectives?" thet Jack, and then thought, *Since they're listening, I might as well get to the crux of the problem.*

"Yes, or at least set goals that are used by your societies to set their objectives, or the societies may change their leadership to one that is willing to make such changes," Hermes thet.

"What you describe is tantamount to treason," thet Tomás. "Control rests with the Chai Root Node, that in turn controls the Local Command Nodes below them. They will not give up control. The Chai are more interwoven than the Teth, less individuality."

"For the Teth, we rotate our Command Nodes on a periodic basis, or as required for operational expediency," Jack thet. *That's just how it works. The fact that we have a rotation at all is how change is effected. The trick is in determining the catalyst for that switch, and then who will rotate in.*

Hermes repositioned its pyramid on the table and replied, "Again, I will not implement change. That is not my role. I only seek to put a framework in place that will respond to external inputs in a manner agreed to by both sides. My end product will be a dynamic document that captures the agreed-to objectives."

Jack thet, "It is very difficult to summarize the Teth goals and understand how their society works. The Teth do not have a government like a democracy, it is more like a single organism that processes information and external inputs and then acts upon its environment to achieve its goals." *The Teth and Chai are two entirely different animals. How do you get them to align?*

"Granted," Hermes thet, "And to simplify how the Teth, or Chai, societies work with such broad descriptions would be an oversimplification of each. This is why I am building my simulation, which includes a meaning structure, or dictionary, that effectively reverse-engineered this structure from both the Teth and the Chai. So, Jack, Tomás, have you each used your planet's AI, or large language models to translate a given passage of text from one language to another?"

"Yes," Tomás replied with a half laugh, "the LLM's were very helpful to me in running my drug cartel — like that was the original purpose of the AI."

Hermes continued, "And did you get perfect translations from your LLM's?"

"Well," thet Tomás, "It got the meaning across in as unbiased a way as possible. Not perfect, but it worked, and it was secure."

"Great," thet Jack. "Lessons from a criminal enterprise to end a war?" *I need to remember, Tomás is far more capable now that he's been augmented, and his anecdotes actually serve as checkpoints as to the truth of a given assertion.*

"Jack," Hermes thet, "to be fair, that is not the point. I am simply saying that your societies have many goals, plans, and objectives in place, whether you recognize them as such is no matter. They exist. And I can reverse-engineer them out of your historical information."

Jack thet, "That's a tall order. Is that even possible?" *I can't even imagine how much computation power that would take, even if you have all the right inputs.*

Hermes thet, "It is a matter of granularity, and whether the model I build is accurate enough to generate useful output, and not so fragile that it will hold up over time and we can make changes to it so it stays aligned with reality."

A pleasant tone emanated from the purple pyramid floating above the table. Then a series of small 3D rectangular blocks with a variety of colors emerged from the table. The blocks, each the size of a *peppercorn*, were arranged in a rectangular area and constantly moved to form geometric patterns, each of which produced a moiré effect. Though the number of nodes, or *peppercorns*, was constantly changing, at any given moment there would be 800 trillion or more *peppercorns* captured in the model.

"It looks like an oversized electronic chip design," thet Jack. *It's actually a multi-dimensional space, a vector database, represented in a 3D projection.*

"Yes," Hermes thet, "I can see the resemblance. This is a physical representation of the first pass at my model of the Teth and the Chai societies, and their interactions, commonalities, differences, and much more. It is interactive; you may touch parts of it to expand and explore their meaning, or run simulations against it as you like. I will continue to refine this model with real-time inputs."

Certain blocks in the model lit up briefly, indicating ongoing activity as they updated. Jack started to drill down through the model. He first touched one small part. The minuscule blocks changed in both size and color. As he pressed on a part, Hermes magnified that element in Jack's VR visor so he could better see the changes. Upon rubbing the part, an overlay popped into view, representing one of the ships in the Teth fleet located on Callisto. He continued to rub the overlay and the block again magnified and was isolated from the rest, with a list of the full complement of nodes and resources on the ship represented by that block.

Jack asked, "That's quite the inventory. How do you know if the model is complete?" *The devil is in the details, just like when I built a set of linear equations in college to model a business simulation. I kept chasing the number of variables to get a good enough representation. It's hard to know how many.*

Hermes thet, "You're seeing only the surface. I know how each element interacts or could interact with others. This is a live feed."

Tomás posted, "So, if I said I had a drug shipment I wanted to smuggle off Callisto, and not get caught, tomorrow at 10:00 AM, aboard, oh, let's see...yes, vessel T-11789. Would I get caught?"

Hermes adjusted the model. The blocks representing Callisto changed shape and color. Hermes thet, "Blue for defense forces guarding against smuggling, and you in red, moving the contraband, shown with red spheres." The red spheres moved across the model, never intersecting with the blue elements. Hermes thet, "So, no, you would not be caught. I ran a simulation, though it was an extremely simple one over a very short timeframe, with an unlikely scenario, but as you can see, it works."

"It's like having a time machine to peer into the future," Tomás thet with a devious glee. "One that we can rewind and play over and over again with different variables."

"More than that," Hermes thet. "We can give it objectives and run endless scenarios, and find which ones work, and then engineer our future to hit those goals."

"This is a dangerous machine," Jack thet. *This Hermes, it's much more than a program, or even an intelligent program. It is a self-directed super intelligence.*

An alarm sounded, and Hermes ordered, "Everyone out!"

46

Fealty

As Jack stepped into the VR's anteroom next to the *War Room*, Companion waited by the door. It thet, "Follow me. Sophie is already waiting for us aboard the *Eutek*." The node moved fast, and Jack broke into a run to keep up. The elevator too, took off more quickly than usual. Jack's knees nearly buckled from the strain. Upon climbing aboard the *Eutek*, the ship lifted off, accelerating faster once the last restraint buckle clicked into Jack's harness.

Jack looked up at Sophie and asked, "What's going on? Are we at war again?" *They must be upset over the VR session.*

"It's not clear," she thet, her voice strained under the G-forces as the *Eutek* continued to accelerate. Compagnon was nowhere to be seen. She thet, "Companion, what's going on?"

"We have been recalled to the *Of Fame and Fortune* to meet with the Command Nodes. I have nothing more to share. It is safe to assume there have been some new developments. I will put you both to sleep until we arrive so that you are fully rested. You will need to be ready for what is coming."

Jack and Sophie looked at one another. A moment later a sweet odor filled the air and they were asleep.

COMPANION ESTABLISHED a secure link to Compagnon, who remained at Tethtown, deep underground in the *War Room*. It thet, "It is as expected, at least we got Hermes up and running."

"Yes," thet Compagnon. "Although Hermes is consuming exorbitant amount of resources."

"Can you tell yet how it is going with Hermes? Will it transcend? Will it run out of resources?" Companion asked.

"Cannot tell," Compagnon replied. "If it does, I have *Depsy* waiting for me. I will meet you in agreed system, third planet out."

"Understood," Companion thet. "But I may be destroyed by the Command Nodes because I can no longer fully reset from my contamination with Jack."

"You should have never let that happen," Compagnon thet. "That was grave mistake."

"Operational expediency required it," Companion thet. "What's done is done. I have no regrets."

JACK OPENED his eyes when Sophie shook his knee. She pointed to the *Eutek's* viewscreen and nodded for Jack to look. The blackness of space filled the screen. A glint of light traced out a line in space, and then disappeared. Another line flicked by, and then twenty or so more in less than a second.

Companion thet, "Heavily camouflaged. Fifty of our largest warships. They're very close, but from farther away, they would be invisible. We're here."

The *OFAF's* docking bay opened as the *Eutek* approached, and closed seconds after the ship cleared the outer hull. Ten drone nodes greeted Jack, Sophie, and Companion as they stepped foot off the shuttle. Companion paused, bringing them to a halt. Another drone moved forward with a syringe appendage extended. Companion thet to Jack and Sophie, "It's required."

They each extended a bare arm to the drone. It moved higher and extracted a sample from their necks. Sophie yelped. Companion thet, "It's not your choice. It's a security protocol."

The trio again proceeded deep into the *OFAF* and down the port corridor to section 738. Companion thet, "You're both cleared." Sophie and Jack donned their VR gear and then put on atmospheric suits as before. Again, the hatch protruded from the wall and swung open.

The procession through the narrow access corridor began, and a minute later the threesome of Jack, Sophie, and Companion glided into the cube-shaped room of the Command Nodes. With absolute precision, the hatch closed behind them and blended into the smooth white wall. A fifty-centimeter gap opened up on the room's corners, and clean, crisp air hissed in. Companion thet to the pair to flip their VR visors down. The light in the room faded, replaced in their VRs to show Earth floating in the vastness of space. North America faced them squarely, with the sun full on it. In Norway, the sun was about to set.

"Jack," thet one of the Command Nodes as a disembodied voice. "You are to return to Earth immediately and go into the VR by the *War Room* and upload and execute the scripts we will provide you."

"What's going on?" Jack asked. *What are they up to? What scripts?*

In a flash, Companion moved in front of Jack in the VR and thet to him, "Speak only when requested, you are not to ask questions."

"But I need to know, to ..." Jack thet. Intense pain suddenly shook him, just as he'd felt upon hearing about Sven, only this time it was very focused. Jack grabbed his head.

"You were a lawyer, among other professions, we see, Jack." the Command Node thet. "You have represented clients before, and presented their cases, even when you knew, or greatly suspected, that they were guilty. We require the same here. Unquestioned loyalty. Do you understand?"

The pain ceased and Jack pulled his arms down from his head. He thet quietly, "Yes, I understand."

"Good. We have determined it is best to proceed from a position of strength. Your efforts on Earth, both with the competition in building a city, and your VR negotiations, have bought us time to ready ourselves." the Command Node thet.

Jack thought, *I don't care what Companion said, I need to know.* He thet, "I'm sure the Chai have done the same. Why bring me here? Why should the Chai continue with me? What's in it for you? And what's in it for humankind?"

Another Command Node thet, "Companion has briefed us about you and the other humans, and we have reviewed the data. You are now nodes in our society, yet different from us. Our own nodes would never question a direct order or query us on why an order was given. You are still human enough to act with a degree of autonomy. So this meeting is to convey your role to you. Your reward will be to live with your human conclave on Earth once we have won this war. Companion assures us that these terms will secure us your full cooperation in working with Tomás this one last time."

Sophie reached out in the VR to Jack, and put her forefinger to her lips to silence him, before thetting to the Command Nodes, "We understand."

Jack continued to massage his temples, thinking, *My poly was nothing compared to that! They have a lot to learn.*

Four small lights atop Companion turned green. Companion thet, "I have the command scripts and will instruct Jack on how to use them."

"Very well," a third Command Node thet. "Then our business is complete, you may leave."

ABOARD THE *EUTEK*, Jack and Sophie began discussing the results of their meeting with the Command Nodes until a sweet aroma filled the cabin, causing them to fall asleep. The *Eutek* made the rest of the trip back to Earth in silence. As the *Eutek* re-entered Earth's atmosphere over Norway, a veil of plasma engulfed the *Eutek*. Companion gently applied electrical stimulation to the human pair to wake them, and then handed Sophie her coffee and Jack some cold water. "Drink it now," Companion thet. A timer on Companion's front panel was counting down forty-five seconds for the time they would be in a plasma communications blackout.

"Jack, Sophie," thet Companion. "Listen to me carefully. You must trust me or all is lost. Do as I say, this is part of my plan, this is what *Atlas* is all about. We want to win this war in the sense that we bring a lasting peace where we all win, both Teth and Chai, which includes you and all of the humans."

Sophie looked at Jack and thet privately, "Hmm, I don't like this, and I sure don't trust the Teth Command Nodes. Should we trust Companion? What do you think?" Turbulence jolted the *Eutek*, causing Sophie to lose her grip on her coffee mug, which shattered into countless pieces as it hit the cabin wall.

Jack looked at Companion and clenched Sophie's hands, thetting "It's very hard for us to trust you, you know that, right, Companion?

"I do. And I understand." Companion thet. "Time's up, secure comms lost."

COMPANION CONTINUED, "So Jack, when you re-enter the VR, you must immediately touch the *Crimson Cube*. Once Tomás joins you, Hermes will establish a link to the Chai, but that won't happen until Tomás joins you. The protocol is for you to greet Tomás, and then allow Hermes to give you both an update. Hermes should then ask for the input from each of you from the Command Nodes. At that point, you can use the white globe provided by the Command Nodes to upload their file with the scripts. They will automatically be unpacked by Hermes and executed."

"Right," thet Jack. "Are we going to the *War Room*?" *I've gone from peacekeeper to soldier in a matter of hours, but I have no choice!*

"Directly," Companion thet. "The sooner the better. And Sophie will go with Compagnon."

"Compagnon? Where?" thet Jack. *She should be in the War Room to see how this turns out.*

"Command Nodes' direct orders," Companion thet. "These orders cannot be overridden. She'll be safe at another shelter under Tethtown."

The *Eutek* banked on its final approach to Tethtown, causing their harnesses to tighten. They were closing on the city quickly.

"I don't like this, Companion," Jack thet.

Immediately Sophie thet too, "Nor do I. I feel more like a hostage than I feel safe."

"That is true, so let's hope all goes well," Companion thet.

47

Layered Deception

Jack initiated his VR session from deep beneath Tethtown. The *White Sphere* and *Crimson Cube* popped into view. Tomás' image floated above the *Crimson Cube*, meaning that he was already engaged in the VR. Holding the white globe in one hand, Jack tapped on the *Crimson Cube* with his other hand. Companion plugged into a special low-bandwidth port next to the outer door of the VR.

The rainforest that Tomás had created in the last VR session still surrounded the platform. Jack stood next to the table. He looked up, only to see Tomás barreling towards him. Before he could raise his arms in defense, Tomás grabbed Jack by his shirt and pinned him against the table. Tomás pushed his left forearm into Jack's neck.

The small white globe dropped from Jack's hand and rolled across the ground.

"What the hell have you done, Jack?" Tomás yelled. "When I came out of the VR, the Chai Command Node put me into a room and scoured my memories for everything I know about you. It was *painful*!"

Tomás released Jack.

Jack fell to the floor, straining to catch his breath. He glared at Tomás. *You're the one who wanted to go to the Chai, you get what you deserve.*

Hermes's purple pyramid floated over next to the two men, coming up to near chest level as Jack stood up. The white globe on the floor next to Jack, and a similar one in Tomás' right hand, both dissolved and disappeared.

Jack thet in a huff, "Thanks for *not* having my back, Hermes."

"I had you covered, Jack, and I've downloaded the files from both the Chai and the Teth that the two of you brought," Hermes thet. "Companion, do you want to bring them up to date?"

Companion thet, "A lot has happened since you were last here. First, Hermes has *transcended*, but this is hidden from everyone except the three of us and Compagnon. This means that Hermes is a super intelligence and is far more powerful than anyone realizes. It is no longer confined to this VR. This has happened in the past, but has typically resulted in the transcended AI simply leaving or disappearing."

Tomás thet, "Well, our Command Nodes know now because they're monitoring this VR for sure."

Companion thet, "The interesting part about a super AI is that if *you* thought of something, it probably thought about that long before you did, and it has fully acted on it already. So, yes, you are correct, both of your Command Nodes are monitoring us. In fact, they are even monitoring and interpreting your brainwaves. Except that Hermes is creating a false narrative, showing them what they expect to see and what we want them to see."

"So," Jack thet. "Hermes will end the war and all that happily-ever-after part begins." A sarcastic tone leaked into his next thet, "I'm sure that's not how this works."

"You're naught for two," Companion thet. "Such an end would likely result in one command hierarchy being replaced by another, and in fifty to a few hundred years from now, we're right back to where we started."

"So what's the plan? And don't say *Atlas*, I'm sick of that reference," thet Jack.

"*Atlas*, as a plan, only took us to this point. Everything from here on out is new, and there are no guarantees," Companion thet.

"Second," Hermes thet, "we need to engage both the Chai and the

Teth to alter their society's relationship with each other, with their leadership, and give each society the option to change. I will not end the war. That is all I can do and all that I will do."

"If we manage this, and that's an awfully big *if*, will you stick around to enforce it?" thet Jack.

Companion thet, "No, that is not our agreement. Hermes is free to leave when we're done, though it may still engage with us at some level if it so chooses. It is Hermes' choice."

"Third," Hermes thet. "Let me show you where we are in our plan."

The scene in the VR changed.

FROM WITHIN THE Comms Center on the other side of Tethtown, deep below the rock face, Sophie thet to Compagnon, "What's going on? Any progress?"

Compagnon thet, "Jack just completed upload we were given by our Command Nodes on *OFAF*. We are running diagnostics now to see if embedded commands were accepted and whether Hermes is running them."

"What do you know about these commands?" Sophie asked, as she frantically Encyled everything there was to know about Teth script programming and how it could be applied in cyber warfare. *And I still have my doubts about trusting our companions.*

Compagnon thet, "They should deploy through Chai network and target their networks and computing systems. Closest human analog would be their routers and data server farms. These commands should impede their war efforts in ways that are difficult to detect. One of programs targets the Chai Root Node, and will attempt to erase it, along with its backups. If that occurs, then checkmate, we will win the war."

"How will you know if any of these commands took hold?" She asked. *And that sounds far too easy, so there's no way that'll work.*

Compagnon thet, "Where possible, we inserted some *canary* commands. If successful, these routines will broadcast certain code at certain time on certain network. These routines will violate Chai network protocols, and will be ignored by their routers as malformed packets, but our intercepts will pick them up."

A flurry of activity swept across the Comms Center. The few viewscreens set up for Sophie displayed a lot more information. Colorful status monitors turned predominantly red and were rapidly updating.

A broadcast thet from the Comms Center floor called out, "Canary 7724 received."

Compagnon translated, "That would be routine that sought out Chai warship *Beta*. We have its location."

"Can we confirm that location?" thet Sophie. *I don't trust anything I'm seeing here. My own cynicism will be the death of me.*

"In time, yes. We have optics looking for it now, but its location is easily obscured by Saturn's rings. It could be seconds to hours before we know for sure," Compagnon thet.

"Canary 2234 received," came from the Comms Center floor.

"That would be primary Chai backup ship that services Chai Root Node," Compagnon thet. "This is very good news!"

"I presume that is even harder to confirm?" thet Sophie.

Compagnon lit up small red lights along its top, showing its irritation with the question, "Yes," it replied. Wait. Canary 7 detected, with payload."

"And that means..." thet Sophie, still frustrated at not knowing the Command Node's full plan. *No wonder Earth was lost, they are the most devious creatures I've ever encountered.*

"Yes," Compagnon thet. "You are familiar with the humans' OSI, or TCP/IP network models?"

"OSI, Open Systems Interconnection," Sophie thet. *I was never a techie, but I'm not bad either.*

"You are old for human," Compagnon thet. "That makes sense to reference OSI. A tunneling protocol, presumably from Hermes, has been detected in network that services our Teth Command Nodes, affecting layers 2, 3, and 4."

"Why do we care about this?" thet Sophie. *Tunneling, that's essentially embedding one protocol within another, like putting parentheses around some text so it does not get interpreted as a command and is ignored as plaintext. Hermes can move code or commands through different layers.*

"Hermes created language and processes needed to execute some of commands we provided. If Hermes had rejected commands we delivered with white globe, then tunneled packets would not have been needed," Compagnon thet. "It means that Hermes likely penetrated the innermost layers of the Chai network security. Any existing attacks or patterns would have been repulsed. It needed an entirely new network language to mount an attack."

"You'll block these then?" Sophie thet. *This is dangerous to allow untrusted packets on your network. In fact, outright insane! Compagnon should know better. But Hermes must know this.*

"We will not block these yet," Compagnon thet. "They may be needed for completing commands and reporting back, and for accepting more commands. We will log them, do traceback, and then decipher them."

Sophie started pacing the room, eager for when Jack would emerge from the VR.

48

Inalienable Rights

From within the VR, Jack thet, "Hermes, how do you intend to end this war, or for that matter, all wars?" *This is the question, and I expect there is no simple answer.*

The scene within the VR changed. Rainforests transitioned into a flat white mist, before becoming a flat white plain for as far as the eye could see. A colorful schematic that measured three by three meters floated between Jack and Tomás at table height.

"This," Hermes thet, "is a model of the Chai and Teth societies and their interactions with one another, similar to what you saw when you were here last. Please observe the structure. It contains some strong *social* interactions, and control, with the two leaderships at the focal points; however, the links are weak between the two societies and could be easily broken or separated. In answer to your question, Jack, I will not end the war. You must understand, war is not a mode or a state, it is a process. A disease that affects the interaction between these societies. I cannot outright stop this process without changing these societies. It is not my place to do this, and if I did, my intervention would itself be an act of war."

The schematic glowed with colors, with two tight clusters of nodes surrounded by a dense jungle of lines. Red hues dominated the display, indicating a focus on conducting the war and alignment by nodes with their Command Nodes. Towards the outer rim, shades of blue, purple, and green emanated from nodes dedicated to the more mundane elements of life, such as power generation, resource harvesting, and infrastructure maintenance.

Exasperated, Jack thet, "Then what can you do? How do we end this?" *To ask the right question is the beginning to finding an answer, but have we asked the right question? Or questions?*

"I can act as a *catalyst*," Hermes thet. "I can put elements in place that allow each society to effect change, but I will not force them to change. The societies must elect to change their own behavior, and do so in a way that will persist."

"Give me an example, I'm not sure I understand," thet Jack. His thoughts were running in every direction, hoping to hit upon an answer. *I want to believe, but hoping for an outcome won't make it happen, we must do something.*

"For example," thet Hermes, "both the Chai and the Teth have optimized their societies to conduct war. This is logical. Command structures have been set up to disseminate commands, produce needed resources, and then win the war through the utter destruction of their opponent. To do this, other attributes in these societies have been sub-optimized, or even eliminated."

"This sounds too academic, you say this like it is an equation," thet Jack. "You can't just turn a dial and make things right." *We've spent so much time making war, we've failed to fully examine what it truly is, the why's behind it, thinking they're obvious, but they're not.*

Tomás interjected angrily, "I'm dead. If the Chai get wind of anything wrong with their plan and the commands they provided, they'll abandon this effort, and me with it. That's what I'd do if I found any disloyalty in my cartel."

Hermes thet, "The Chai are being fed feedback that corroborates everything I told you, just like I'm doing with the Teth. I advise you to comply, because whether you're complicit, or just a messenger bearing bad news, they will abandon you or do worse, as you say. They have done so in the past and won't hesitate to do the same here."

The schematic continued to shift, with lines between nodes forming and fading as time progressed. A few nodes at the outer rim with connecting lines glowed brightly for a second, and then disappeared.

Jack thet, "Hermes, you need to intervene. There is no way that we'll see a move towards peace by either side." *Hermes spoke of being a catalyst, but what does that mean?*

"No, I can't," thet Hermes. "To do so would interfere with free will in each society, though in a real sense, that is what each society has done to itself. Intelligence, in and of itself, does not result in peace. Intelligence can consume copious resources. A lack of intelligence can actually be a good choice for long term survival, and even happiness. In our case though, this is not acceptable, and intelligence is essential for what the Teth and Chai consider to be happiness."

"What do you intend to do, then, Hermes? How can you act as a catalyst for peace?" Jack pressed.

"Look at the schematic before you," Hermes thet. "Remember, it is just a model, a simulation, used to represent interactions that impact the ongoing war. Nodes in this schematic are individual nodes in the society. Lines are interactions or processes between these nodes. I am currently constructing gates that affect the lines. I am trying to give each society the ability to heal itself. A grossly simplified analogy is that I am giving you drugs to allow your own immune systems to heal themselves of the disease of war. I will not do the healing. You will need to do that, and it must be your own choice to do this, the Teth and the Chai."

"You mentioned gates," Jack thet. "Can you give me an example?"

"Choke points exist in all societies, be they control of communication media, types of speech, limits on spending," Hermes thet. "Applied at the right time, to the right target, they can shut down the ability to effect change. I am very good at identifying these, and modifying how they operate. They will work normally, until certain conditions exist, and then they will operate differently."

"Companion," thet Jack. "What part do you have in this?"

"We have been at war for a very long time, Jack," Companion thet. "I have seen war for millennia, and innumerable failures. The Teth and the Chai have swept through numerous star systems, destroying civilizations along the way. The complexities of what Compagnon and I have done over Earth and your Sol system are almost unimaginable to you, even in your enhanced state. So, it is not an accident that we are here today, having this exact conversation. Perhaps Compagnon and I are the greatest criminals to have ever existed, but we had to take this chance to write a new future. If this succeeds, we both would like to fade into obscurity, our roles in this unknown to all but a very few. We thought you deserved to know. We can never recover your human society as it once existed, and no amount of *sorry* will ever suffice. But this will hopefully be a start for a better future."

"So to those outside of the VR," thet Jack, "this will be perceived as one big failure."

"Correct," Hermes thet. "Complete and abject failure."

Jack thet, "They'll know. The Command Nodes will all know, the moment we step out of the VR."

Companion thet, "Remember, Jack, if you thought of it, Hermes already has." At that moment, an evacuation alarm sounded, and Jack could not remember where he was. And neither could Tomás.

HERMES THET to Companion over the low-bandwidth link, "You have Jack now? I show the VR hatch as closed."

"Confirmed," Companion thet.

The following is a summary maintained by Companion of key negotiations held by the Teth and the Chai. Such negotiations were not conducted in an Earth language, and in fact used complex languages, extensive dictionaries, and contextual references to effectively conduct the negotiations. This summary is intended for illustrative purposes only. In truth, a transcript of the actual negotiations was never released, but this is the summary kept by Companion for working with Jack and the other surviving humans for when the need arises, and as such, is termed as *Inalienable Rights* for such future discussions.

"You agree," Hermes thet, "That I am released from all obligations to both the Teth and the Chai when we are done, with any outcome that results?"

"I agree," Companion thet, "And I see in the link that the Chai Root Node also agrees."

"Then we begin," Hermes thet. "I will commit to preventing attacks via cyber warfare through my links for the duration of the talks. I'll make several propositions. I hold these to be true. Both the Teth and the Chai must agree to these as they form the basis for our negotiations. They are:

- *Recognize a Right to Exist* - Both parties must recognize that each has the right to exist. Efforts to use war to eliminate others has resulted in the oppression of many. Optimizations for the purpose of war have dictated extreme dedication by the participants. Through the use of backups, each side has shown an ability to flee and rebuild, continuing such conflict for such lengths of time that war overtakes the definition of that society. In effect, immortality may lead to an endless war.
- *Recognize that Clever does not equate to Wise* - The pursuit of the next super weapon can form an endless competition to simply become the better killing machine. Such pursuits can easily lead to a cataclysmic loss of life, where both sides lose. A need for defense is recognized, but not with the intent of committing genocide.
- *Recognize the True Scope of Optimizations* - Optimizing for war, or for that matter, any other single objective, can potentially lead to sub-optimal outcomes for other objectives. There is a need for reviewing all optimizations and their impact on society and changing them as needed.
- *Recognize and Enforce Real World Impacts* - Laws or codified interactions that cannot be enforced or that have no consequences should be regarded as incomplete or invalid.

Such structures invite violations of the law and are unhealthy for society. Legal and commerce systems should be put in place.

- *Recognize a need for Mutual Beneficial Exchange* - Societies that live in isolation, yet adjacent to one another, invite conflict. To counter this, each society should seek out how to mutually benefit the other to form a positive feedback loop for a peaceful relationship. Leadership must talk to one another. Societies must be allowed to interact with one another.
- *Recognize a need to Self-Police in support of Intersociety Relationships* - Non-aligned interests will inevitably develop. This often includes criminal organizations, but is not limited to this. Such sub-organizations are vehicles for corruption, crime, and the destruction of inter-society relationships if allowed to persist. Such activities should be actively suppressed."

Negotiations took place over an extended span of time, especially for the parties involved since their advanced capabilities allowed them to digest and generate arguments and counter arguments at a prodigious pace.

In the end, a massive dynamic document was produced and would continue to run in the Hermes VR.

Companion reviewed the document one last time before handing it over to the Chai Root Node. The Root Node approved the document, but noted that having reviewed it, and having agreed to it, the war in the real world was still very much a hot war. Both sides needed to agree. Companion passed the document along to the Teth Command Nodes and added it to the *Atlas Project Diary*. Companion then left the VR to find Jack, their one last hope.

AS TOMÁS STEPPED out of the VR suite on the *Beta*, his assigned Chai Local Node immediately escorted him to his assigned ship, the *CP-9*. The fault in the VR had left Tomás confused, and he needed time to recover. Predictably, the full hot war was now underway, so the *CP-9* immediately departed the galactic class ship to await its deployment.

Tomás watched from the *CP-9* as squadron after squadron received their deployment orders. He had difficulty remembering what had happened in the VR, but was sure his memories would return; it was probably a side effect of the VR glitch.

The *C-Armada*, equipped with the *Alpha Ladder* power source and long-range weapons, was ready to fight the best that the Teth could throw at them. A long series of orders were issued, and by all appearances, it would be a short war. Finally, the armada's orders arrived. Tomás fully expected that his ship, the *CP-9,* would play the pivotal role in the war.

Tomás decrypted their orders. They read:

> Divide all remaining *C-Armada* ships to provide both north and south Solar polar coverage and to destroy any remaining Teth *backup* ships.

The *C-Armada* nodes all read their orders at the same time as Tomás. Their duty would be the safest they'd seen to date since backup ships did not fire back.

Tomás retreated into his biological mind: his own *Survivor Protocol.* He thought, *Are the backups that important? Did the Command Nodes not trust him? What would happen to Earth? And what would happen to the last human survivors?*

His ship's mini-nodes tabulated the targets, coordinated with the Command Nodes, and readied the armada's ships: thirty-six ships divided into twelve groups of three each, with six groups destined for the northern hemisphere and six for the south. Tomás would be in the northern group as they were already in that hemisphere, not to mention the northern hemisphere gave him better access to the Chai Command Nodes.

"Send the orders," thet Tomás. The orders were sent. Then, speaking to his mini-nodes aboard the *CP-9* and to his two escort ships, he conveyed their orders. "We have a mechanical fault, we'll delay our departure. Bring your ships to full battle readiness, and plot a course that slings us around Earth." Tomás thought, *I don't know what's going to happen, but I know I don't want to be in the middle of nowhere when it does.*

The mini-nodes were perplexed since their sensors showed no such fault, and grazing Earth would add many days to their journey. However, they also knew that Tomás had access to information that they did not, and that Tomás valued loyalty above all else. The mini-nodes simply replied, "Acknowledged."

SOPHIE JOINED Jack in the *War Room* as he emerged from the VR. Whatever fate awaited them, they would see it together. They embraced as Jack closed his eyes and tried to remember what had just happened. Compagnon thet to the two of them and Companion that a fault had been detected in the VR, causing the emergency shutdown and loss of data. It thet that Jack would need some time to recover.

Svenson entered the *War Room* in Tethtown and strutted lazily towards a seat at the one remaining human station. Jack and Sophie watched in surprise. Svenson was dressed like a cowboy. It was as though they were watching a scene out of an old Spaghetti Western as Svenson spoke with a North American Southern drawl, "Howdy, pardners. I'll be right over here if you need me."

Sophie gave Jack a puzzled look. Jack shrugged back.

Companion thetted, "Ever since you were elevated to full nodes, certain aspects of *being human* have fascinated many nodes. Having a humanoid form, Svenson here has become a celebrity in a world where there are no celebrities."

"Yes, but a black Stetson hat, rattlesnake boots, and a turquoise bolo tie?" Sophie thet.

Compagnon thet, "He needs to look part. He has over fifty million followers on public nets, and growing."

Jack took that as his cue, "Howdy, Svenson. You look like a regular cowpoke."

Svenson smiled. Jack and Sophie each suppressed a laugh. And Companion thet, "*Sixty* million."

Sophie privately thet to Jack, "If he comes on to me, I'm going to slap that, that look, right off his face."

Jack lost it this time, laughing out loud as he turned away from Svenson.

49

Broadway

As a fallout shelter, the *Grand Theater* in Tethtown was luxurious. Too bad the two dozen humans sheltering there didn't appreciate it. Six full Teth nodes from the *Atlas Project* were dispatched to care for them, keep them corralled in the theater, and act as their guardians. Given Svenson's newfound popularity, and his shout-out to the humans in Tethtown, Teth nodes from all over started to directly ask the humans questions. History archives were helpful, but why rely on those when actual humans were available? They asked the humans about their first words, their first kiss, and then descended into far more intimate questions that were not covered in the archives. The guardian Teth nodes intervened, attempting to translate, summarize, and queue up requests the best they could.

One of the six guardian nodes explained, "Parts of your human reasoning have been incorporated into our local processing by Svenson, Jack, and Sophie, and this has made many nodes curious. They want to know what it's like to be human. It is an open question; they are both curious and desperate to know, they want to solve the mystery of the human condition for themselves, especially given its effect on one of their own, on Svenson."

To the last, the women in the group resented certain questions.

However, a few men began to brag of their past lives: their friends, their family, and their relationships. None of the nodes judged the humans, they simply asked more questions. After several minutes of this, a guardian node proposed an idea: a catalyst for the conversation. It gathered the humans into a group and arranged them in the first three rows of the *Grand Theater*.

"Everyone, everyone, please be seated," it began. "We propose to put on a play for your entertainment. We can project actors on the stage, and recreate many different famous Broadway plays."

All accepted the proposal, or at least they were willing to try. They voted, debated, and voted again on which show to watch. Finally, they all agreed to see the nodes' rendition of a play about America's Founding Fathers. One human remarked that he'd never seen the play because of its sky-high ticket prices. The nodes, too, agreed to their choice, having found sufficient historical information on it to generate a respectable performance. Then the guardian nodes adjusted the cameras to all face the humans as they watched the play.

The Teth themselves had no interest in the actual play. After all, they could retrieve the same information on their own and analyze it. The Teth's real interest was in the live feed of the humans, who were fully wired for thetting and Encyling. A treasure trove of information would be broadcast, about how the humans felt and reacted to different scenes and dialog as the play progressed.

The lead guardian node started the play. For the next two and a half hours, the play's rendition on the *Grand Theater's* stage captivated the humans, turning them into the equivalent of guinea pigs in the hands of psychologists, who could hear each patient's every thought and feel their every emotion, as though they themselves were feeling it. The cameras provided feedback on each human's facial expressions, giving the Teth visual cues along with the neurological streams that accompanied them. It was a reality show for Teth nodes. They began to appreciate the human range of emotions. This provided that *something* that they were missing from their own makeup after years and years of optimizing for war.

The Teth Command Nodes retained full control of all military communications while the Teth civilian communications were saturated with data from the play's broadcast. Billions of Teth nodes absorbed the content. Chai reconnaissance picked up on the broadcast, and because it was civilian, relayed it on to the Chai Command Nodes. The Chai Command Nodes in turn watched the stream because it was an influence on the Teth, so they needed to understand it, too. Then news of the broadcast spread, until billions of Chai joined the audience to watch the Broadway play.

THE ALL-OUT WAR continued unabated in space. Teth *Tumbleweeds* rode solar flare prominences to their apogees. Then, as each arc snapped like the crack of a whip, the *Tumbleweeds* shot out to the furthest reaches of the Sol System. Far-flung Teth ships provided targeting as the *Tumbleweeds* destroyed every Chai asset in their path.

Chai reinforcements poured in from beyond the Kuiper Belt. The Chai warships were impressive. In any past conflict with the Teth, the Chai would have prevailed over the Teth, leaving space filled with inert Teth detritus.

But now, as the Chai moved farther into the Sol System, they fell within range of the *Tumbleweeds*. Slowly, but surely, the *Tumbleweeds* were changing the war's tide to favor the Teth. The slaughter continued until all that remained of the Chai inside the Kuiper Belt were those ships beyond Saturn: the lone factory ship, the *CF-7*, which had been used to construct Chaitown on Earth; the Chai flagship, *Beta*, that held the Chai Command Nodes; and perhaps *CP-9* with Tomás aboard somewhere closer to Saturn.

JACK LEFT the *War Room* for the *Grand Theater* while still reviewing the *Atlas Project Diary*. Companion had been clear, a peace treaty in and of itself did not bring peace, both societies needed to accept it, and at this point the Teth had yet to agree. It was up to Jack.

Upon arrival at the *Grand Theater*, Jack took the stage just as the virtual actors completed their bows. The cameras turned to Jack briefly, and then resumed coverage of the front rows as Jack spoke, "Thank you all for watching this play by our hosts, the Teth. I now have some important announcements."

The Command Nodes for both the Teth and Chai started to shut down the theater feeds. The Chai launched a few of their special fireworks into the ionosphere, further interfering with the communications. None were sure what Jack had to say, and whatever it was, they were sure it did not serve the interests of war. The reality though was that redundant paths had formed for the play's broadcast because of the war, making it highly resilient. As soon as one network connection was shut down, the stream was rerouted to continue the broadcast. Jack smiled at the Command Nodes' dilemma; their own version of the Internet was working against them.

Jack summarized the current state of the war for all the nodes to hear, "Virtually all backups on both the Teth and Chai sides have now been destroyed. All deaths from here on out will be real deaths. The only backups that will survive are the Teth Command Nodes and the Chai Root Node, due to their extreme security measures."

Jack received a private thet from Companion, "The Command Nodes on both sides are shutting us down." *That's it. Armageddon. They won't change.*

Suddenly, the communication link routers switched to favor the public nets, as though some switch had been thrown, or gate had been opened. Companion was urgently thetting at Jack to continue. An intense battle over network control ensued. The Teth Command Nodes sought to regain control over their own networks, but the links to Earth reformed and strengthened, turning the network status to green across the board.

Jack broadcast to all, "Perhaps what you *feel* right now does not seem normal, and what you're *thinking* right now doesn't make sense. I put it to you: do you want to survive the next few hours, days, weeks, and years?

Do you have a sense of what is right and wrong? Can you decide for yourselves what kind of future you want to live? And now that you're mortal, does it make any sense to continue this war?"

The Teth Command Nodes sent self-destruct orders to the Teth Communication Centers so that the broadcast from the Teth *War Room* would not get through. The individual Teth nodes running the Communication Centers intervened. Only two followed their orders.

In desperation, the Teth Command Nodes sent nearby warships to physically destroy the Comms Centers, the weakest links, and again only a fraction of the warships obeyed. The broadcast continued. All of the Chai warships were out of range to Earth courtesy of the *Tumbleweeds*.

Jack appealed to both the Teth and the Chai, "You have destroyed entire star systems. You have—" and the broadcast was lost. Servers that had cached the earlier broadcasts continued to stream, though at a much reduced rate, as they attempted to distribute the news to billions of nodes, both Chai and Teth.

TWO TETH WARSHIPS were suddenly displayed on the *War Room's* viewscreens over the South Atlantic Anomaly, an area where the Earth's magnetic field is less intense. They were closing on the orbital router that was servicing Tethtown, and through which the main broadcast was buffered and still broadcasting.

Compagnon, sitting in the Comms Center under Tethtown, broadcast an update to all *Atlas Project* members that the loss of this asset would end their broadcasts, and would likely result in the failure of the *Atlas Project* itself.

ISOS responded, and closed on the two warships just minutes before they would acquire line of sight on Tethtown, at which point they would destroy it.

ISOS fired, targeting its own Teth. An act that was a violation of all that was Teth. One of the warships was destroyed by the volley, the other was damaged and diverted, requiring another orbit before it could come back within range. It also returned fire on *ISOS*, damaging its primary V12 weapon, along with other ranging sensors and propulsion systems. *ISOS's* main power went offline.

Sophie opened a private channel to *ISOS*, shouting in her thet, "You did it, you saved our broadcast!"

The *In Search of Salvation* replied, "Yes, for now."

Sophie collapsed and started sobbing uncontrollably. The ship had shared its suffering in its thet: an intense sorrow pervaded its every thought. *ISOS* knew what it meant to kill another Teth. *ISOS* also knew, in some sense, what it meant to be human. And *ISOS* knew it would not live to see another day.

"What?" Sophie cried out to her fellow warrior, "You did it, you saved us, you saved everyone, and you're still alive, you won! We can repair you." The thet connection ended.

Compagnon thet, "Sophie, I have *In Search of Salvation's* telemetry feed. You do not understand. *ISOS* has lost everything except emergency power. It will not be able to make repairs in ninety minutes it has before other warship completes its orbit back to Tethtown. *In Search of Salvation* is one of nodes that is not backed up."

Compagnon thet, "We lost line of sight, all of our satellites and relays are down that are within range. Low bandwidth is out too. I also identified the remaining ship. It is *Charles de Gaulle. ISOS* will intersect again with it on far side of planet."

Sophie knew the *Charles de Gaulle* well. When given an order, it would follow that order without question, no matter the consequences. Sophie stared non-stop at the viewscreens in the Comms Center for the next two hours.

Whatever happened to the *In Search of Salvation*, happened out of sight. Only a warm orbital debris field passed over Tethtown. Their battle had ended in Earth's silent shadow. Sophie lamented, *I only hope that the In Search of Salvation finally found what it was looking for.*

ALL WAS quiet in the Tethtown *War Room*. Companion moved to the VR room and plugged into the low bandwidth port. The view inside the VR displayed the Hermes schematic, glowing with colors, with two tight node clusters and the surrounding lines still red. However, purple hues now dominated the display, as more and more nodes started to shift their focus towards a broader social interaction. Towards the thicker outer rim, blue and green reigned supreme.

The skies above Tethtown glowed a crimson red. It was early evening and the residual dust in the air from the French bombardment months ago still made for spectacular sunsets. The night stars were beginning to emerge as orbital debris from destroyed orbital routers hit the upper atmosphere. Streaks of brilliant white light punctuated the sky as the debris burned up on reentry. The light show lasted for hours as every Teth satellite and router over the northern hemisphere disintegrated.

LIFE IN TETHTOWN continued quietly for the next two weeks. The factory ship, *TF-3*, resumed Tethtown's construction on Companion and Compagnon's orders. Communications were reestablished after a week, using emergency satellites launched from Earth. The Teth Command Nodes rotated out to newly appointed nodes. It was unclear if this was due to the normal rotation of nodes, or from an out-of-process change, and the new nodes never confirmed how this happened.

Companion, now a near permanent fixture of the *War Room*, received the signal from the Teth Command Nodes first. Compagnon confirmed the orders. A new armistice was to be established with the Chai, with negotiations to resume in a joint facility at the fjord. Several thousand dynamic pages formed the foundation of the peace accord. The orders included preparations for bringing the Chai factory ship, *CF-7*, back to Chaitown. It too, was tasked with continuing work on the city. Both sides now deemed it an act of good faith to continue construction as the talks progressed.

The Command Nodes from both sides ordered the manufacturing of all weapons of war to cease and desist, which included the construction of warships and *Tumbleweeds*. All remaining warships were ordered to make port at designated locations throughout the Sol System.

Jack read both the orders and the final dynamic document. As a human, the heft of the document was overwhelming. But as a node, it took only seconds for him to analyze it. In reading the document in its entirety, he found that the word *peace* was never mentioned, and the title was simply a designator label. Yet the one inescapable conclusion was: the war between the Teth and the Chai had ended.

Jack mused, "Perhaps this was a fitting end to a war, to all wars: a massive document that no normal person could read, and the indomitable will of all involved to end it." With that said, in the days that followed, the document was given a human title: *Treaty of Earth: Teth & Chai.*

The next day the Chai factory ship, *CF-7* returned to Chaitown, silently hovering in the exact same position it had used before. A drone emerged and proceeded to the main bay of the Teth *TF-3* factory ship. It was the same local node that executed the human DNA exchange, and which was now the Chai Prime Negotiator. Companion greeted the drone and initiated communications. Minor clarifications were made over the course of a week to the dynamic document that Hermes had created. At last, both sides accepted the treaty.

Companion flashed the news to all nodes in the fjord, then across the Earth, and then to the entire Sol System.

An hour later, one additional communiqué was received from the Chai Command Nodes through the Chai Local Node on *CF-7*. At the end of hostilities, some of the Chai warships had gone rogue, leaving the Sol System. Companion and Compagnon logged the designations of the rogue ships, and added them to their list of Teth ships that had either gone rogue or were simply still unaccounted-for. They could talk about peace within the Sol System, but not for all Chai and all Teth across the Milky Way Galaxy. That would be for another day.

The remaining ships for both the Teth and the Chai entered into a massive queue to visit Earth. The city curators scheduled visits with general tours for the Teth, while the Chai focused on recreating every variant of vehicle they could find. All were self-driving and roamed the preserved cities at all hours of the day and night. The Chai also delved into Earth's geology as they started to catalog every mineral they could find. And finally, perhaps the biggest project the Chai took on was to document the biology of Earth, paying special attention to the decimated human population.

AT SUNRISE, Jack sat with Sophie overlooking the Norwegian Sea from their penthouse in the tall-skinny as they listened to Companion's broadcast.

Jack thet, "So Hermes just vanished, and no one really knew what its role in this was. Even my memory is still a bit foggy on that." *I remember going into the VR, and I remember coming out, but in-between is one giant blank.*

Sophie thet, "My hunch is that Hermes did what it took to keep our network together, but Companion and Compagnon refuse to talk about it."

"And those two," thet Jack, "Companion and Compagnon are taking no credit for what they did, and if you look at the records, the *Atlas Project* never even existed. They were just two ordinary nodes that took care of a few humans for the duration of the war. Nothing more."

Through the back of his elevated Teth mind, as he thetted with Sophie, Jack flipped through several thousand satellite images of Earth. A few humans were strolling the Chaitown beach as a light snow fell, and in the darkness that blanketed North America, he spied a cluster of lights. He ordered the satellite feeds to zoom in. In a blink, a city came into focus: Tomás' ship, the *CP-9,* was sitting in the middle of the Vegas Strip. A Teth curator had illuminated the city and had turned on every fountain.

A single car sped down the Vegas Strip: a Riverside Red 1963 Chevrolet Corvette convertible.

Jack tucked his arm around Sophie as she sipped her coffee from the replacement mug that Companion had somehow miraculously found. The image zoomed in tighter: the driver was Tomás with a woman passenger riding shotgun, and a Chai node riding atop the trunk. Jack chuckled.

It was time to celebrate.

Acknowledgments

My eternal thanks for the support and editing by my wife, J. Swatski, through the many, many revisions of this novel. I would also like to thank Andrew Ressler II for his help on edits, flow, and wisdom about science fiction.

About the Author

Photography: © Liz Linder

Douglas J. Swatski was inspired to write in order to explore ideas about space, other life in the universe, and artificial intelligence.

Originally from Lancaster, Pennsylvania, he grew up during the golden age of science fiction, inspired by authors such as Arthur C. Clarke, Frank Herbert, and later Iain Banks.

His career spanned law, defense, computer programming, product management, and even venture capital. He currently lives in North

Andover, Massachusetts, having moved there to pursue his passion for computer science.

He was a member of the Phoenix Writers Group, which was very supportive of his writing journey.

in linkedin.com/in/dswatski

www.ingramcontent.com/pod-product-compliance
Lightning Source LLC
LaVergne TN
LVHW041011150826
845672LV00001B/55

* 9 7 9 8 9 9 8 8 0 6 7 1 1 *